A *LESS THAN ZERO* ROCKSTAR ROMANCE

LIMITLESS

KAYLENE WINTER

ENDLESS: A Less Than Zero Rock Star Romance
Copyright © 2020-21 by Kaylene Winter

Cover photography and design: Regina Wamba
Cover Models"
Jace: Garret McCall
Alex: Carson Hunstead
Formatting Cat at TRC Designs

A *LESS THAN ZERO* ROCKSTAR ROMANCE

LIMITLESS

KAYLENE WINTER

CHAPTER 1
PRESENT DAY

Under any other circumstances, spending Christmas in my hometown with my band, Less than Zero, would have been something to look forward to. Over the past few years, we'd been on the road. In the early years, dinner would have been take-out food in a shared hotel room from whatever restaurant was open. After our success, the past few years had been spectacularly catered events.

Today, I had planned to immerse myself in the chaos at my Deveraux family home with the woman whom I hoped would represent my future. That's not how it panned out. Instead, I was at our lead singer Tyson Rainier's house watching him propose to Zoey Pearson, the girl who had stolen his heart almost a decade ago.

Ty and Zoey's romance had permeated the fabric of LTZ since the day they met at our epic Mission show all those years ago, and I'd played a big role over the years in facilitating their star-crossed lovers myth. Gossip sites and social media couldn't get enough of them. Fan fiction about their love story had taken on a life of its own, ranging from bubble-gum, heart-eyed, teeny-bopper swooning to the dirtiest erotica. Which translated to tremendous profits in both record and merch sales for all of us.

Our crazy rock star success story meant that we were all now rich enough to retire. We were too young for that, but every single one of us was looking forward to having at least a year off to chill, reconnect with family, and have some personal time to relax for the first time in a decade. Personally, I had been looking forward to settling down as well.

So, my feelings about being here tonight were bittersweet. After so many years apart and the ups and downs of reuniting, they were finally together and getting married. I should only have positive, happy thoughts today.

Except, my world had crashed down around me, and no one in my band knew it. Happiness for my friends was far from what I was feeling. More like tired.

Terrified. Pissed. Confused. Heartbroken. Petrified. Scared. Panicked. Alone.

But, also loyal. Always loyal.

So yeah, I needed to be here today. Ty and Zoey were also my family. Despite my own problems, I loved them both.

I couldn't focus, though, with all that was on my mind. Sure, I kept a slight smile fixed in place and my gaze deliberately aimed at the happy couple to appear normal. Inside, my stomach churned, and my brain was all over the place. My entire future was up in the air, a fact that I'd kept secret from everyone but my dad and one other person.

Like a beacon, my eyes were drawn to her.

Alexandria LeRoux, Zoey's best friend, was the ethereally beautiful woman of my dreams. Her honey-blonde hair bounced like sunbeams off her tanned, defined shoulders. She clapped her hands gleefully when Zoey kissed Ty and accepted his proposal. Tall, lithe, with legs for days and the most perfect, perky breasts, Alex wore a fitted, white, off-the-shoulder sweater, skin-tight Levi's, and red jingle-bell earrings.

And, her ever-present black Frye boots. Boots that had traveled the world. Sometimes, even with me.

God, she was marvelous. I watched intently as her perfect pink lips pressed against Zoey's cheek and her long, slender fingers caressed Ty's shoulder. Alex's smile always lit up the entire room. Her deep-blue eyes crinkled up with joy for her best friend.

Goddammit. I'd fucked things up so royally.

This time, there was no going back.

After so many years of cat and mouse, Alex and I had finally, *finally* been on the same page. We were actually together. Planning a future. Tonight we should be announcing our own engagement, except for the fact that a few weeks ago I'd received news that destroyed any chance we'd ever have to be a real couple.

There was no way I could ask her to compromise the phenomenal life she had created for herself. Not when I couldn't wrap my own head around what had happened.

So, like an asshole, I'd avoided her. Evaded her calls. Ignored her texts. In effect, ghosted the most perfect girl in the world. Maybe not to the extent Zoey had ghosted Ty all those years ago, but still.

Tonight, because of Ty and Zoey's big announcement, our interaction was unavoidable. And, God, sheer torture. Covering my eyes with my hands, I breathed deeply into my palms to control the anxiety threatening to take over. I could not lose my shit. No one would understand. I was always the rock of this band. The steady hand. The voice of reason. The cool head. The Fonzie.

"Finally," Connor McLoughlin, our big, ginger bass player interrupted my thoughts, thankfully unaware of my inner turmoil.

"Word." I glanced over at him and we shared a smile.

"It's about fucking time." Zane, our virtuoso lead guitarist bounced over, his dark curls wild around his face. "Although, Ty's going to have to find new inspiration to write killer songs now that he's got the girl."

"He'll be fine." Connor rolled his eyes, crossing his bulging biceps across his chest.

"God, I'm hungry. It smells amazing in here. Ty has cooked up a feast!" Zane, not known for his attention span, raised his nose in the air and sniffed.

"Yeah, well, I can't stay for dinner, my dudes." I shrugged. "I've gotta go to my folks' house. I've missed too many Christmases, and everyone is home this year."

"But it's the last time we'll all be together for a long time." Zane looked stricken.

"I'm heading home too, my dad's not doing so great right now." Connor had seemed very distracted lately, it was the first I'd heard about his father's health issues coming back. "I want to be with my family."

"You're leaving too?" Zane crossed his muscular arms.

"Relax, Zane. Your dad is here. If you come over tomorrow, *my* dad would love to see you," Connor placated our high-energy guitarist.

"Okay. Yeah. I'll text you." Zane's attention was already redirected across the room where his father, the famous Limelight guitar player Carter Pope, was motioning him over.

"Jen told me she'll stop by later tonight." My sister Jennifer had dated Connor for years before she realized her true love was her friend Becca.

"Cool." Connor was a man of few words. I respected the hell out of him. Already strong, our friendship had been sealed forever when, despite his heartbreak and confusion at their breakup, he'd treated my sister with compassion and honor after she came out.

With the big engagement event witnessed, though, I had to get out of this house. I couldn't fake any more happiness today. "I'll go congratulate Ty and Zoey and then I'll catch you later."

As I made my way over to the happy couple, my phone pinged, causing my heartbeat to go into overdrive once again. Pulling my reading glasses out of my back pocket, I sighed at the incoming text.

Jessica: Ru coming by?

Jace: no

Jessica: Ur going to miss Xmas with her then?

Jessica: I promised.

Jessica: Jace!

Jace: Stop contacting me there is a court order.

Jessica: Fine, but it won't change anything Jace.

Yeah, whatever. The insanity was real.

"Are you okay?" Alex's long, slender fingers gently touched my elbow, her intoxicating ocean-breeze, tropical scent tantalized my senses. She was like a ninja. I hadn't seen or heard her approach.

"Yep," I moved my arm away abruptly.

She winced but pasted on her usual sunny smile in record time before attempting to slip away from me. "All-righty then."

I guess we were both faking it today.

"Wait, Poppy. I'm sorry. I don't mean to be a dick." I gave her a half-smile, and I lightly grasped her slim wrist, stroking the top of her bronzed hand with my thumb. "It's supposed to be a happy day for Ty and Zoey."

Alex sighed and looked down at my thumb rubbing her, undoubtedly feeling the electricity pulsing between us. It had always been this way, even when we fought it. Her eyebrows knit together, and she sighed again, turning her baby blues up to gaze at me questioningly. She was breathtaking, and I couldn't believe how stupid I'd been for so long. If I'd been less stupid, I wouldn't be in this mess.

"It's going to work out, Jace." Alex tucked a strand of hair that had escaped from my LTZ skull cap back in place. "It will."

"Well, I already know *how* it's going to work out." I tightened my grip on her wrist. "I just have to go through with all of the steps."

Alex didn't speak at first, almost as if she was choosing her words carefully. "So you've told me. And as I told you, this should be an opportunity for us to be closer as a couple. I know you're scared, and I've tried to be understanding. But you keep pushing me away."

"Alex—" I pleaded.

"No, Jace." She focused her eyes on mine. "You're playing games with my heart. It hurts. It's not acceptable to treat me this way."

"I'm protecting you." I fixed my gaze on hers, daring her to argue with me.

"Nope, try again," Alex yelled in a whisper voice. "You're the one who finally convinced me to be all in. You're a hypocrite if you're not all in too. Gahd! There's no point to this."

"I understand." I swallowed the lump in my throat and glanced around to see if anyone was paying attention to us.

They weren't.

Everyone was gathered around the happy couple across the room patting Ty on the back and trying to get a glimpse of Zoey's ring. I couldn't speak for fear of breaking down, and I couldn't look at my beautiful nymph for fear of giving in.

"And there you have it." Alex pulled her wrist from my grasp and folded her arms across her perfect, perky breasts.

"Not everyone has a love story like Ty and Zoey." I folded my arms across my chest too, keeping my eyes directed at the happy couple.

"Everyone has their own path, Jace. I'm truly happy for them." Alex's expression softened when Ty planted a scorching kiss on Zoey's lips. "They belong together."

"They have been a pain in *my* ass for nearly a decade. They have been their own worst enemies," I grumbled bitterly before stealing a glance back at her.

Alex's eyes narrowed at my crass comment, but she tried to hide it by looking down. Kicking the toe of her worn black Frye boot into the ground, she muttered, "Pot calling kettle—"

"Shit. I'm on fire today. Alex, I'm sorry."

"Quit apologizing." Alex stopped me, breathing in deeply to tamp her emotions down. "*We* are supposed to have the same happy ending."

"Dammit, Alex. I won't force you into a life you don't want." Secrecy be damned, I gripped her shoulders and drew her to me, breathing her in. "I can't do that to you. You deserve someone who can give you—"

"Excuses." Alex cut me off. "Just. Stop. Enough with the martyr bullshit. I've got the message loud and clear. After all we've overcome, it sucks to realize how little you really know me. How little you know what I want."

Her words pierced my soul. I wanted to protest and to reassure her that I did know her, that she was everything to me. I couldn't form the words. Clasping her close to me, my dream of having what Ty found with Zoey slipped out of my grasp with each passing second of silence. My heart ached. Alex was not only my best friend but the funniest, goofiest, sexiest, and most beautiful, dedicated, loving woman I knew.

And now, because of a shit hand that I'd been dealt, instead of revealing our long- time secret relationship to our friends and family, Alex and I were over. For real this time.

"This isn't cool, Jace. I've really gotta go." Alex broke free from our embrace to find the entire room looking at us strangely. After composing herself, she abruptly turned away from me and walked out toward the powder room.

"Jace, what did you say to her?" Zoey flew at me from across the room and grabbed my arm, her wild, blonde hair flowing around her. Ty followed close behind, his eyes constricted and curious.

Refusing to answer her, I kept my gaze on the two of them steady. "Congratulations, I'm really happy for you both, you know."

"Thanks, man." Ty clapped me on my shoulder. "Are you okay?"

"Yeah, it's just that my family is holding dinner for me, I've gotta head out." I hoped my family obligations would keep the questions at bay.

"I'm going to go find Alex." Zoey threw me a pointed look before searching for her best friend.

"Dude." Ty watched his fiancée walk away. "You need to have a little more faith in her."

"What do you mean?"

"You're together now." Ty looked me in the eye. "Right?"

"Umm . . ." I closed my eyes and sighed heavily.

"You love her." Ty cocked his head. "She loves you."

"It's not enough, Ty," I breathed. "There are things going on."

"Look, if that girl is your daughter, Alex will love her because she loves you." Ty spoke softly, confidentially. "Wouldn't you feel the same way if the situation were reversed?"

"How—" I was shocked that Ty knew my secret. Which meant only one thing. Alex had clearly told Zoey who had, of course, told Ty. I hated unnecessary drama; Alex *knew* that. My wishes had been made *very* clear. No one, not the band, my family, and especially not *Zoey* was supposed to know anything until I knew for sure. Even though I'd been avoiding her, I still couldn't believe Alex had betrayed my trust.

A minute ago, it felt like my heart was breaking. Now, steam was coming out of my ears and my head felt like a pressure cooker ready to explode.

"Jace, relax. Let us help. You've been there for us all these years. We—I want to be there for you." Ty looked at me earnestly.

"You can't help me, Ty," I said through clenched teeth. "Leave it alone, you're not supposed to even *know* about this."

"Dude, relax. Alex only told Zoey, she had no one to talk to and she broke down completely. Zoey told me because, after everything we went through, we just don't keep secrets from each other. Ever." Ty gripped my shoulder firmly. "We are the only ones who know. It's going to be okay. You don't always have to be the strong one, I'm here for you."

"I'm so fucking sick of this." I shrugged off his hand. "Just leave me alone."

"Jace," Ty pleaded.

"No! Mind your own business. You finally have your girl. Focus on her and let me live my own life. You know *nothing* about me and Alex and you know nothing about my situation. Why? Because I keep

13

my fucking problems to my fucking self," I hissed, not quite yelling but not exactly being quiet. "God, having a long break from all of you couldn't come at a better time."

"Jace!" Alex was horror-stricken. She had apparently returned to the scene of the crime with Zoey in tow to hear me berate poor Ty.

By then, the entire room of the people closest to me were staring at the spectacle I had created with similarly shocked expressions. Somehow, this unleashed a rage inside me, unlike anything I'd ever felt.

I was exhausted. Exhausted from always being the voice of reason. Exhausted from always looking after the well-being of grown men. Exhausted by my secret relationship with Alex and trying to make it into something it wasn't. Most of all, I was exhausted and terrified about the prospect of raising a baby. On my own.

I couldn't help lashing out at that moment because I was done. D.O.N.E. Ty could fuck himself. Alex could fuck herself. Everyone else could fuck themselves too. The only thing that mattered was finding out if Helena was really my daughter. If she was, then her well-being would become my sole focus going forward.

The universe was telling me that it was time for me to move the fuck on from all of them. That's why I didn't give anyone in the room a second glance before storming out of Ty's house and slamming the door behind me.

CHAPTER 2

NEARLY NINE YEARS AGO

"C'mon!" I pleaded with my best friend Zoey. "We're going to be late."

"I can't help it if I need extra time, you look amazing in a paper sack," she whined.

She drove me crazy sometimes with her going-out-on-the-town prep-time, but I kind of understood. She rarely ventured out with me, which made the nights we went to see music a bigger deal. She was adorable, and her dry sense of humor matched my own. Not to mention, she was the best friend a girl could ever have.

"You look gorgeous, you always do." I gave her the thumbs-up on her outfit and glanced at myself in the mirror.

Clothes didn't matter that much to me. I preferred not to think too hard about what I wore. It was easier to have a general uniform of V-neck fitted T-shirts, jeans and, as of my birthday last month, killer black Frye motorcycle boots. My blonde hair was lighter and not nearly as long as Zoey's, but I'd just had it cut in a cool shaggy style that made it easy to just mess it up with my fingers and go.

"Well, this is as good as it's going to get." Zoey shook out her long, thick blonde hair as I checked my phone.

"Thank God, the Uber is here." I gestured for her to wrap it up.

I had been following Less Than Zero for months on social media, but never saw them in person because they mostly played bar shows. Finally, they had a show at the Mission, Seattle's largest venue that happened to be all-ages. Seattle had caught on to the throw-back guitar-driven rock band, so the show would be packed due to their serious buzz. I was so excited; my adrenaline was on overdrive.

"Are you staying over tonight, Alex?" Zoey's dad called out as we bounded down the steps to catch our Uber.

"No, Mr. Pearson. Mom and I have plans early tomorrow morning," I replied.

My mom and dad, Andrea and Allen, had finalized their divorce in my junior year, and I lived with my mom. My brother and sister, Ariana and Aaron, were a few years older than me and were off in college in other states. Mom and I had become close these past few months, especially when the mail-order pie business she started on a whim last year became a huge success. We were going to look at a couple of commercial kitchens in the morning to accommodate the demand for her pies.

Tonight, however, was all about the rawk. After we made it past security, I dragged Zoey to the front of the stage so we could drool over the gorgeous guys of LTZ up close and personal. Sweet Jesus, they were even more delectable in person than in their YouTube videos. Losing myself in the music, I bumped hips with Zoey and she gleefully

16

bumped me back. Gahd. There was nothing like hanging with my best friend watching a cool band.

As Zoey and I held hands and gyrated to the beat, Tyson Rainier, the brooding, dark-haired lead singer stared at and sang directly to my petite friend. Internally squealing, after all this was a dream come true for both of us, I couldn't believe that she wouldn't even look at him. She could be such a shy, loner dork, but she was my BFF and I loved her.

Luckily, I was not quite as reserved. My social skills were going to come in handy for our plans to lose our virginity to hot guys this summer. I couldn't help but smile, my job had just gotten easier. It seemed like the lead singer of LTZ was a prime candidate for my bestie, which meant surely one of the other rockers would be perfect for me.

Surveying the rock bounty onstage, it was time for me to pick from the remaining hotties. Lead guitarist, Zane Rocks, was a sexy option. His bouncy dark curls, handsome, boyish face and boundless energy made him seem like a hell of a lot of fun. Oh, and holy shit. Soooo talented. I became mesmerized by the blur of his fingers as he effortlessly worked the frets of his vintage Les Paul.

Bass player, Connor McLoughlin, was as broody as the singer. I wasn't a moody-boy fan, but his Herculean, muscled body was unbelievable, and his reddish-brown hair was gorgeous. Perhaps a ride on the ginger-train could be fun this summer.

Turning my attention to the back of the stage, my eyes popped out Bugs-Bunny style when I focused on LTZ's shirtless drummer Jace Deveraux. Of all the guys, he was the least-featured band member in their social media feeds, and by God, it was a damn shame. His dirty-blond Viking hair was swinging around his phenomenally muscled tattooed arms and shoulders. He meticulously punctuated each song with amazing percussive beats. His eyes clenched shut and his mouth opened almost orgasmically while his hands blurred through a pounding rhythm to end the song. He was the one. I was overcome by instantaneous lust.

Shaking his hair out after the song finished, Jace clasped his drumsticks in one hand and took a long sip of his beer. Gazing out at the audience through his kit, I could see him peering in my general direction.

Look at me. I stared at him, willing him to notice. Just for a second, as he scanned the room, I could have sworn he caught my gaze. Then he became aware that his lead singer was focused on my friend. He smirked at Ty and nodded to Connor. Undeterred at his lack of eye contact, for the rest of the show I danced and swayed to the music, watching him intently while he was lost thrashing on his skins.

After the show, I basically forced Zoey to be the star of my Instagram story about how badass LTZ was. Based on the success I'd mustered up for mom's pie business on social media, my plan after I graduated was to fund a gap year of travel by boosting up my own Instagram following and getting paid for posts. College held no interest to me, much to the chagrin of my dad who wouldn't STFU about it. My goals weren't overly ambitious, I just wanted to earn enough money to be self-sufficient and do what I wanted, when I wanted, for at least a year.

Tapping into LTZ's impressive following with a fun post and a few strategic hashtags would hopefully get me a few more followers. Plus, maybe one or two of the guys in the band would think we were hot.

"I think he looked right at you," I shouted at Zoey, hoping to convince her we should go back toward the stage and find Tyson.

Knowing she was smitten with Mr. Broody singer, I wanted to start planting the seeds to lay the groundwork for my master plan to talk to Jace.

But to my surprise, McBroodypants himself shocked us both when he approached Zoey and hit on her. Badly. Not wanting to be a third wheel, I stepped away and covertly tried to listen in as they talked, hoping she wouldn't blow it. Strike that, hoping *he* wouldn't blow it. My sweet little bookworm certainly wasn't the most confident talking to hot guys. Ty had laughably little game as evidenced by him forgetting to even get her number before he stalked off back to his band.

Not wanting to crush her spirit and hoping to reinstate my plan to go meet the fine- as-fuck drummer, I encouraged her, "OMG are you *serious*! He is the most gorgeous man I've ever seen in real life. Although—No. The drummer is a delicious piece of eye candy, more my type."

"Alex, I just royally fucked that up," Zoey interrupted glumly, oblivious to my comment. "I'm such a tool, I basically put the hottest guy that ever talked to me on blast. I missed my chance."

"Shut the fuck up. Did you see the way he looked at you?" I reassured my little dove. "He'll be back, trust me. Let's just chill and hang out for a bit more. Just look nonchalant, cool. As your dad would say, 'Be Fonzie.'"

I managed to talk her into staying for about ten minutes as we both scoped out the loading area from our vantage point. My attention was laser-focused on hottie McSticks who was breaking down his drum kit methodically while the bass player unstacked and loaded the amps next to him. Zane the guitar god sat on the edge of the stage animatedly talking to half a dozen women of various sizes and shapes as they were enraptured by every word. There was no sign of Ty, and as Zoey's curfew loomed, I could tell her heart wasn't into being at the grungy club for one more second.

Just as Zoey ducked out to catch her Uber, the scrumptious but sullen singer emerged from the makeshift dressing room and barreled through the club in my direction.

"Hey, do you know where Zoey went?" He frantically looked around; his blue eyes wide as saucers.

"Um—" I was confused and a little starstruck.

"Aren't you her friend?" He stuck out his hand. "Ty."

"Alex." I took his hand. "Yes, Zoey's my best friend."

"Do you know where she is?" He continued to look around wildly.

"Um . . ." I gestured toward the side door. "She grabbed an Uber; she has a curfew."

"*Fuck*," he yelled and then immediately looked at me with horror. "God, I'm sorry. I

didn't mean to yell at you."

"No worries, dude. She literally just left, maybe you can catch her." I pointed again to the side door.

"Thanks!" He didn't give me a second glance before dashing outside.

"Rainier! Wait!" a gravelly, sexy voice called out from behind me.

My head whipped around just as Jace, the super-sexy shirtless wonder drummer, skidded to a halt next to me.

"Fuck!" He sighed crossing his arms across his cut torso.

Knowing this was my opportunity, I opened my mouth to confidently captivate the object of my affection. Unfortunately, instead, I stood mute, staring at him, slack-jawed. I really couldn't be blamed, though, considering that his cargo shorts hung dangerously low on the "v" of his hips, revealing a happy trail. His bulging biceps sported the most amazingly intricate and colorful tattoos, and his eyes. Lord, his eyes. This man's eyes were the most striking, hypnotizing light-green orbs rimmed with dark lashes. And they were trained right on me.

"Hey, did you happen to see where the singer of my band went?" He looked around the room but directed the question to me.

"Um . . ." Mute times two. So much for being Fonzie.

"Never mind." Jace sighed and turned away. "Sorry to bother you."

"Wait! I think he went to talk to my friend, Zoey." My voice came out in a weird, breathy tone as I pointed with my thumb to the door.

"Huh." Jace smiled at me. "Really? You have no idea how weird that is."

"Crap. Is he a serial killer?" I mimicked a shocked face.

His otherworldly green eyes crinkled as he laughed deeply. "Jesus, no. About the furthest you could get from a serial killer, more like a serially clumsy puppy."

I giggled at his surprising sense of humor. "That's funny. He just followed her out the side door, but she had called an Uber, so I don't know if he caught her."

"Only one way to find out." He started toward the door. "I'm Jason by the way, but everyone calls me Jace."

"Alexandria." I followed him to the door. "Everyone calls me Alex."

"Nice to meet you, did you like the show?" His deadly, killer smile was complete with two dimples on each side of his full lips.

"It was amazing, it's the first time we saw you guys live." I gushed in full fan-girl groupie mode. "But I watch your YouTube channel all the time, and your Instagram feed is off the chain!"

"Cool. That's awesome to hear." Jace opened the side door and I peeked over his shoulder. There was no sign of either Ty or Zoey.

"I guess she went home. She still has a curfew." I mentally thwacked myself at revealing how young we were. Again, I was so not cool.

"How old is she?" Jace turned back to me.

"Um . . . why?" I wrinkled my nose.

"How old are you?" He cocked his head.

"Eighteen," I answered honestly, even though it had only been two months since my birthday.

"Huh. Okay. Goddamn it. That *fucker*." Jace scrubbed his strong hands through his long hair. "Where the hell did he go?"

"Should I text her?" I tried to look out from under my bangs in the flirty way I practiced in the mirror.

"Hmmm." He considered for a minute. "Nah, odds are he just went home if he didn't find your friend. He's a slippery mofo. He *knew* that I was going to film him for our Instagram."

"Do you do LTZ's social media?" I was surprised.

"Guilty." Jace rubbed his decorated arms absently.

"Jay-ceeeee." A curvy redhead with smudged, smoky eyeshadow and glossy pink lips teetered over in a zebra-striped tank dress and black stiletto booties. "When are we leaving?"

"Jesus, Cassie." Jace looked pained. "I thought I told you to go home."

"I was waiting for you," Smudgy pouted.

"All right, fine. We'll drop you off at home." Jace walked away before turning around. "Well, thanks for coming to the show, Alex. I've gotta head out."

"Sure," I called out, but he already had forgotten about me as he

22

walked away toward the rest of the band by the stage.

Holy shit. I just missed my shot and let him walk off with some skank. I stood staring, frozen in place while the band gathered and loaded the final items of their gear out the back exit. I raised my hand to wave goodbye but none of them, including Jace, looked back before the steel door shut behind them with a loud *bang*.

A few hours later when I was snuggled under the covers in bed obsessively playing and replaying some of the videos of the show that were uploaded to LTZ's YouTube channel, my phone buzzed.

Zoey: *Ru up?*

Alex: *Y WTF happened?*

Zoey: *Squee!!!!*

Alex: *Did u hook up?*

Zoey: *He jumped into my Uber, came all the way home w/me and met the rents.*

Alex: *Shut up!*

Zoey: *We made out omg so good . . . dying*

Alex: *So cool, will u see him again?*

Zoey: *yes def*

Alex: *The drummer was looking for him.*

Zoey: *Ooooooohhhhhhh realllllyyy?*

Alex: *He's not interested, but lord he's killer sexy.*

Zoey: *I don't believe he's not interested.*

Alex: *believe – gotta go gotta be up in a few hours for mom*

Zoey: *Ok, ping me tomorrow.*

Alex: *(emoji hearts)*

Zoey: *(emoji hearts)*

Damn! I felt super happy for my bestie, but also a little blue for myself. Oh well, the summer wasn't even here yet and there were plenty of dudes to hook up with. Plus, if Zoey's hookup with broodypants became a thing, I'd have plenty of opportunities to be around the band. Jace-the-drummer wasn't going to know what hit him.

CHAPTER 3

"You owe me big time, pretty boy," Connor growled from the back seat of our beat-up green van where we were sitting.

"I know, I know." Ty smiled back at our grumpy bassist from the passenger seat. It was nice to see our singer happy, he hadn't been able to keep a shit-eating grin off his face for weeks. We all knew that his home life was terrible, but Ty never wanted anyone to know about it and he certainly never, ever discussed it.

"Do we have to stay long?" I rolled my eyes. "My family dinner is at seven."

"No, we'll just play a few songs, and then we can go." Zane smirked at me through the rear-view mirror from the driver's seat as he socked Ty in the arm.

"I really, really appreciate it, you guys." Ty slugged Zane back.

"Zoey makes me so happy, she's incredible."

The four of us had loaded up a few guitars, a snare drum, and a practice amp and were on our way to Ty's new girlfriend's house to play a fucking high school graduation party. Leave it to Ty to complicate his life with a serious relationship right before we were going into the studio and leaving on a six-month tour. With jailbait, nonetheless.

"Dude, I still don't know why you're hooking up with a high school chick. She's too young for you." Connor must have been reading my mind.

"She's the one for me, I don't care how old she is." Ty crossed his arms and stared out the window.

We pulled up to a big craftsman house in Wallingford, parked and each grabbed our acoustic gear and instruments. I led the way as we walked down the paved walkway toward the bright-blue front door. Before I could ring the doorbell, the door swung open and a gorgeous blonde MILF wearing tan capris and a white T-shirt ran down the walkway toward us.

"Hi guys, I'm Olivia, Zoey's mom." She held out her hand to me before pulling Ty into a hug.

"Jace." I smiled. "Drummer."

Zane and Connor introduced themselves and we stood on the stoop awkwardly, grinning at Zoey's mom for a minute, unsure of what to do.

"Right." Olivia took charge, pointing to the side of the house. "Let's go through here, Zoey and Alex don't know about this and they're upstairs getting ready."

We didn't have much to set up, so after about ten minutes Zoey's mother ushered us into a room on the first floor where a large TV with an Xbox was set up next to a desk. On a side table, a platter of sandwiches and a cooler of beers were set up for us.

"Hopefully, you guys can hide out here for an hour or so. When the guests have all arrived, I'll come get you." Zoey's mom gestured around the room. "Is this okay?"

"It's fine, Olivia." Ty gave her another side hug. "Thank you so much."

After we devoured the food and drank a few beers, Connor and I played old-school Halo while Zane watched, and Ty was busy with his phone.

"Zoey is freaking out that I'm not here yet." Ty chuckled. "She's going to be so surprised."

"Dude, I know you like this chick," Connor said. "But it's such shitty timing."

"Connor! Give it a rest." Zane scowled. "You're going on and on about it."

"What?" Connor held up his hands. "We're supposed to be focused on the band right now, not chicks."

"Says the guy who is practically married." Ty deadpanned.

"Well, I don't understand it either, Ty." I chimed in supporting Connor. It tended to go this way in our band, Ty and Zane usually backed each other while Connor and I had each other's backs.

"I can't explain it." Ty shrugged. "I keep telling you guys, she makes me happy. I like being happy."

"For fuck's sake, Ty. You're twenty-one years old. She just turned eighteen." I couldn't wrap my head around it.

"I'm not going to justify it to you, Jace," Ty said definitively.

Although our band was tight, Ty had always been hard for me to get to know. Except for the songs he wrote, he didn't speak up that often. When he did, it was usually because he had a really strong opinion. Then his stubbornness was legendary. I had to come to terms with the fact that Zoey was not going anywhere anytime soon.

Zane's guitar skills were what had initially convinced Connor and me to join LTZ two years prior, but Ty's front-man presence is what had sealed the deal for us to stay. Me, Connor, and Zane all still lived with our families and basically spent all our time together to work on the band and socialize. Ty spent as much time as he could, but he had to work a lot of hours as a line cook to support himself.

Dividing up what little time we had with a girl pissed both me and Connor off.

Carter, Zane's famous rock star father, was pulling in so many connections that LTZ was primed to make it big. As long as we focused and took our careers seriously. We all did. Ty did too. I mean, he was such a good-looking dude who ordinarily was utterly and completely shy and awkward around women. Maybe having the beautiful Zoey by his side would build his confidence. On the other hand, I didn't understand why he, of all people, would potentially muck up his bright future for a woman. Well, not really a woman. A girl.

"Are you guys ready?" Zoey's mom knocked softly and then quietly opened the door.

"Yes, let me text Zoey so she thinks I'm running late." Ty smiled.

"Great idea." Olivia gushed. "Ty, you're so wonderful. Guys, you all are. Thank you for doing this for our daughter and Alex."

We moved through the house, out the sliding glass door to the back yard and across the lawn to where we had set up our gear. Connor removed the tarp that was covering it up and I glanced out into the yard to see it filled with a bunch of friends and family of the graduates.

A petite, curvy girl with a crazy mane of streaked blond hair wearing a simple black tank dress was clutching the hand of a tall, honey-blonde, willowy beauty wearing low- slung white pants with a fringy turquoise halter that exposed her tan, flat stomach. My eyes zeroed in on the sparkly white jewel pierced through her bellybutton. Both were wearing blindfolds and giggling.

The tall girl looked really familiar, and man she was smokin'. On second thought, maybe Ty was onto something with the high school graduates. I chuckled to myself as I sat behind my bass and snare. The rest of the guys sat on stools and picked up their guitars, adjusted their mikes, and gave the thumbs-up to Zoey's mom. Two older guys, who looked like the girls' fathers, gently removed the blindfolds from their daughter's eyes just as we began to play.

Instantly, I recognized the tall beauty as the girl who I chatted with at The Mission when I was trying to round up Ty. She and Zoey were clinging to each other, jumping up and down with utter delight at the fact that we were playing their graduation party. Zoey and Alex ran up to where we were playing and danced. The rest of their friends surrounded them.

Ty was a lovestruck puppy, emoting each song for his girlfriend, causing the rest of us to give each other side looks and secret gag-me grins. Still, I couldn't help but notice that Alex was pointedly trying to get my attention and it was working. Watching her gyrate with her hands thrown high in the air revealed her taut, sexy stomach. And a jeweled belly-ring. The sight caused my traitorous dick to swell despite my attempts to avoid looking directly at her.

Jokes aside, nothing would convince me that getting involved with a barely-out-of- high-school girl was the right thing to do for a nearly twenty-three-year-old man.

The girls kept whispering and giggling as they watched us, and although I had grumbled about doing this favor for Ty, playing the party was actually kind of fun. I laughed to myself when Zoey kept making kissy faces at Ty, causing him to blush. After seeing the two of them together, I changed my mind. How could any of us be pissed when Ty was finally so frickin' happy?

After we played all the songs we knew, we continued for over an hour by jamming through a few old-school covers from the eighties and nineties. By this point, all of us— even Connor—were having a blast. Everyone at the party was dancing and celebrating.

When we finally wrapped things up, Ty introduced Zoey and Alex to all of us and a few of their friends. A couple of older dudes walked up.

"Gentlemen, thank you so much for putting on an amazing show. We really appreciate it." Zoey's dad, Mike approached us and handed Zane a thick envelope.

"Oh, no, Mr. Pearson, we can't accept anything. We were glad to play." Zane tried to hand it back.

"We insist." A tall, gray-haired, suave guy wearing a navy sweater and gray slacks stepped up and put out his hand. "I'm Allen LeRoux, Alexandria's father."

"Nice to meet you, Mr. LeRoux." I shook his hand and introduced myself. Connor and Zane followed my lead.

"You guys will be on tour and every little bit will help." Mike Pearson smiled.

"Wow, thank you so much. We had a great time." Connor spoke up, surprising both Zane and me.

After the dads left, the three of us looked around aimlessly, wondering whether we should stay, when I felt a tap on my shoulder.

"Hey." Alex smiled shyly and clasped her hands behind her.

"Oh, hey." I gave her a small wave. "I remember you from the club."

"You do?" She looked surprised.

"Of course. What's up?" I was genuinely curious.

"Well, Zoey thought—Um. Here's the thing. I was wondering if I could talk to you about the social media stuff you're working on for the band. I have an idea for a project I want to start, but I'm not sure how to get going." Alex wrinkled her nose. "But, if you need to go."

"I have dinner at my parents' house, but I could chat for a few. No problem." I pointed to the catering spread. "I'm parched and really could use something to drink."

"Dude, I gotta get home." Connor interrupted, tapping an imaginary watch.

"Can you grab an Uber?" I asked. "Zane and I can take the stuff with us later."

"No can do. I'm going to The Mission, remember?" Zane backed away from the conversation, so he didn't get stuck loading out with me. "Maybe Ty can help you if you want to stay longer."

"Fine, you guys take the van and the gear, and I'll take an Uber." I planned to outsmart my band brothers, I always had to load out.

"Fine. We'll load, you unload. Make Ty help you. It's only right. Happy graduation, Alex." Zane gave her a huge hug, and Alex's expression was wide-eyed.

"Happy graduation." Connor saluted and my bandmates headed toward the side gate with the remaining gear.

"Thanks, guys!" She waved enthusiastically; her smile was radiant. Pure light. "Please tell me there are beers here." Without thinking, I ripped off my sweaty T-

shirt and grabbed a replacement LTZ shirt out of my bag.

"Um, yeah. Over there." Alex's eyes were transfixed at my bare torso as she pointed toward the deck.

"Great. Well, let's go." I gestured, flexing my biceps. She quickly looked away, embarrassed at being caught ogling me.

Externally, I kept a neutral face but internally I was secretly pleased that she liked what she saw. Having a hot, young woman like Alex find you attractive wasn't the worst thing in the world. Even if I'd never do anything about it.

We headed toward the makeshift bar on the deck. I grabbed a Manny's and she grabbed a Coke.

"Sucks that me and Zoey can't drink in front of all of the parents." Alex pouted. "God, I can't wait to be twenty-one. Or to be somewhere it doesn't matter."

"Ah, it's not all that different." I laughed. "How old are you?" Alex asked.

"Twenty-three." I smiled. "Too old for you."

God, her eyes were the most amazing combination of blue with dark flecks. Her skin a smooth, caramel-colored tan with the slightest pink tinge on her cheeks. With only a hint of mascara and lip gloss, she was quite possibly the most naturally gorgeous woman I'd ever seen. Girl. Not that I'd ever, ever, ever do anything about it.

"True, you're an old man." Alex's eyes crinkled when she laughed. "You're practically retirement age."

"Ha ha." I grinned.

"So, Zoey and Ty have really hit it off." Alex gestured over to where our friends were tangled together, giving each other googly eyes. "They're a little over the top."

"Ty's never had a girlfriend before, so she must be pretty cool." I knew how girls worked, especially best friends. I wasn't going to give up any intel to Alex on my man Ty.

"Was that redhaired girl at the club your girlfriend?" Alex cocked her hip and pulled a long drink on her soda. I couldn't help but watch her lips as she took a swallow of her Coke, thinking that she was more beautiful than the models who usually advertised the beverage. Again, not that I'd ever do anything about it.

"Um, no." I raised an eyebrow at her.

"Hmmm." She raised her eyebrow back at me.

"We're leaving on tour for six months." I sputtered. "Uh-huh." She held my gaze.

"She's not my girlfriend." I huffed. "Now is not the time for a girlfriend."

"I said the same thing to Zoey." Alex looked at me directly. "She's going to college in the fall, it seems a little irrational to get *serious* about a dude this summer."

"Well, I like to tend my own garden. Ty can tend his." I glanced around, not super interested in the way the conversation was heading.

"Fair enough." Alex took the hint good-naturedly, absentmindedly playing with a few of the bangle bracelets on her wrist. "I'm not going to college; I want to travel the world. It's pissing my dad off to no end."

"Really? Where will you go?" I was genuinely surprised, figuring Zoey and Alex were attached at the hip.

"Everywhere! That's actually what I wanted to talk to you about. I figure if I can get a good following on Instagram, maybe I could even start funding my travel that way." She gestured excitedly. "I know it will take a few months, but maybe you know some shortcuts or ways to get there faster."

"Hmmm, well, I have a marketing degree, but in real life, I'm not an expert at all. It's been a bit of trial and error with the LTZ account. Basically, it's all about watching your analytics and seeing what is working and what isn't and just doing more of what resonates." I explained.

"Well, it will be a piece of cake then," Alex said sarcastically.

"Look, I can help you get started, I've discovered a few shortcuts." I took another pull of my beer.

"Oh, for the love of God. Get a room," Alex muttered when her attention was diverted to the show our friends were putting on.

Ty and Zoey were full-on making out in the middle of the backyard and everyone was trying to avert their eyes, which was nearly impossible. I started laughing. Clearly, they didn't care at all who saw. Why should I?

"Well, Alex the Adventuress?" I nudged her with my shoulder. "Are you gonna stare all night or should we figure out a way to make you famous?"

"Yes, please. I'll need a project because I'm pretty sure that I won't be seeing much of Zoey for the rest of the summer." Alex laughed.

I couldn't help but flash her a smile, hoping my dimples were on full display. Chicks dug my dimples.

"So, um, Jace, just so you know I don't want to be another annoying Instagram model. No cheesy, posey, pouty stuff. I mean, I'll do what I need to do, but I want to find a clever way to travel and also raise awareness about animal rights." Alex said as we walked over to an open bench seat.

"Piece of cake." I followed her. "No fish lips, only fish."

As we sat on a bench over our phones and went over a few plans, I was impressed. Alex already had a great vision of what her brand should be, and her sincerity and passion for animals was really cool. With or without my help, it wouldn't take long for this beautiful, funny girl to take over the Internet.

CHAPTER 4

It had been a few weeks since our graduation party and, just as I suspected, I was a best- friend widow. Zoey spent all her free time with Ty. They were, officially, in love. We texted every day, so I was privy to my BFF's romance unfolding. I had to admit, as happy as I was for my somewhat introverted friend, I was really disappointed and kind of melancholy for myself. This summer was supposed to be ours. Our last one together before we started adulting. Stupid emo-Ty had gone and hijacked it from me. LOL. Although, I wasn't really laughing.

Not that I could blame Zoey. If I had a bae as gorgeous and sweet as Ty—say a green-eyed drummer—I'd probably be ghosting her ass too. I was just envious. Stupid Ty. Stupid hot-as-fuck Jace. Gahd. My summer was turning out to be so boring.

I'd hoped so bad that Jace would be into me even half the way that Ty was into Zoey. I'd pictured the four of us hanging out, having coffee, going on double dates, and doing all sorts of cool girlfriend-boyfriend things around Seattle. Zoey and I would both be in love for the first time with our hot, rocker boyfriends. We'd be able to confide in each other about our relationships and console each other when they left on tour.

No such luck. At our graduation party, Jace had been really nice and helpful when we discussed my social media strategy. We even exchanged phone numbers and then— nothing. Every day I'd try to come up with some clever excuse to text him, but I wouldn't allow myself to be "that" girl. The bottom line was the delicious, six-pack-abed, long, blond-haired, emerald-eyed hottie-hot drummer had been nice to me for a few hours at a party.

I hadn't realized *Mr.* Deveraux had a degree in marketing or that he was slightly older than Ty. He had been really helpful, encouraging even, and gave me some great ideas to validate my concept. Avoiding the pretentious, sexy posed location shots that could put me firmly in the "basic bitch" category, I still wanted to stand out. My best plan would focus on clever travel hacks for single girls in each city that I visited.

With so much time on my hands, in between helping my mom out with pie stuff, I decided to be proactive by researching and planning out my itinerary for the first leg of my trip. Most of my graduation money was in, and I had enough to pay for an open- ended flight to Europe and funds to last for six months if I stayed in hostels and used wi- fi. Plus, my mom gave me a first-class Eurorail pass for graduation. I was literally counting down the days until my flight departed for Paris, which was the day before Zoey headed up to Bellingham for school.

Once I was satisfied with my travel plans, I downloaded and experimented with a few apps to create more professional-looking social media posts. With so many choices of graphics, photo filters, and analytics tracking, I tested a ton, picked out some favorites, and deleted the rest. I also immersed myself in the world of social media success stories to figure out the best ways to gain a loyal audience without buying a bunch of fake followers.

Unfortunately, my planning activities only took me so far, and by mid-summer, I was bored and itching to get out of the fucking house. While watching yet another YouTube travel video about France, my phone beeped.

Zoey: U there? Alex: "Yo!"

Zoey: "Yo!"

Alex: When r we hanging out, dude, texting is lame. Zoey: Now??

Alex: U wanna come over????

Zoey: No. Can u come over to Carter Popes to watch LTZ jam?

Zoey: ???

Alex: WTF?

Zoey: serious . . . Ty told me to ask u

Alex: Holy shit . . . text me directions, asap.

Zoey: (sends map)

Alex: what do I wear?

Zoey: Casual, don't try too hard. They are all really normal.

Alex: ummm

Zoey: Well better looking than normal but . . .

Alex: Lol ok, I'll ping you when I get there.

Zoey: yeet!!!!!

Alex: yeet!!!!

My nerves were frazzled as I pulled up to Carter-fucking-Pope's Lake Washington mansion in my lime-green VW Beetle. After taking a few deep, cleansing breaths, I texted Zoey to let her know I'd arrived. Smoothing my white V-neck T-shirt that I'd paired with a mid-thigh, blue-floral flippy skirt and my Frye boots, I shook off my nerves and headed for the front door.

"Hi, Alex!" Ty and Zoey opened the front door within seconds of me ringing the doorbell, his arm ever-possessively wrapped around her.

"Hi, Ty!" My voice came out a little like a kid going through puberty. Coughing, I added, in a more normal tone, "Thanks for inviting me over."

Zoey grabbed my hand as Ty led us through the huge, carved wood front door and into the stunningly beautiful house. We walked past a vast wall of windows overlooking Lake Washington in the living room and then down a hallway lined with a ton of photos of Carter's band Limelight and pictures of young Ty and Zane. My mouth was open like a slack-jawed lunatic, which seemed to be my go-to expression around these LTZ boys. Plus, I'd never been to a famous person's house before.

"Alex, wait. Look at this one." Zoey gestured excitedly, stopping us at a picture of Ty and Zane as sullen teenagers holding guitars. "Aren't they adorable?"

"Jesus, butterfly." Ty's cheeks reddened as he covered his face with his hand. "It's so embarrassing."

"Butterfly?" I mouthed to Zoey when Ty turned around.

Zoey's face reddened. She was so over the moon for her man, her always-manicured hand still clutching Ty's big paw. We arrived at the last door in the hallway. Ty opened it and we entered a room filled with instruments and three gorgeous band members, who all turned to stare at us when we walked in.

"Um. Hi," I said somewhat aimlessly.

"Hey." Zane acknowledged as he switched guitars and looked me up and down.

Connor-the-gruff nodded at me almost imperceptibly from his bass. Jace looked at me from behind his drums quizzically and gave me a small two-finger salute. Ty led us both to sit on one of the amps and enveloped Zoey's small frame briefly before kissing her on the forehead and taking his place at the mic. I nudged Zoey as I sat next to her on the amp, stretching my long, bare legs out in front of me.

"Hey," I whispered.

"Hey." She gave me a pointed look and waggled her eyebrows when she glanced over at Jace.

"Not gonna happen." I shook my head.

"We'll see." Zoey got a defiant gleam in her eye. "Stop." I shot her the "look."

"You're here. We'll see." Zoey resumed watching the band. "He's older than Ty." I gave her a side-eye.

"How do you know that?" She smirked. "Stop." I shushed her.

"An hour ago Ty and I nearly got the job done right here on this amp," Zoey whispered in my ear. "Connor caught us. It was so embarrassing. I didn't have a shirt on. Ty had to shield my bare boobs."

"Oh my god. What?" I yell-whispered and Zoey clamped her hand over my mouth. We giggled uncontrollably. Super mature.

"Everything okay, butterfly?" Ty stopped the song, his blue eyes filled with concern.

We burst out into another fit of giggles. Still not really helping our case.

"It's fine, babe. We're just being girls catching up, we haven't seen each other in a couple of weeks." Zoey managed to stop laughing to assure him.

"Oh my god," I mouthed once the band turned their attention back to playing. "His dick is huge." She leaned toward me and spoke softly in my ear, "Massive!" We looked at each other and giggled some more. *Jesus.*

"You *saw* it?" I knew my eyes were like saucers.

"No, but I felt it." Zoey gulped. "Zane told a story about it at the firepit earlier."

"I miss everything." I sighed.

"No more, I'm sorry that I've been so caught up in him. But I promise, you're gonna be part of this from now on." Zoey reassured me.

"I've missed you." I leaned my head on her shoulder.

"I've missed you too." She leaned back against me. "But Alex?"

"Yeah?"

"He's the one." She regarded me seriously.

"Um, Zoey. You're barely eighteen!" I looked at her quizzically.

"We both know it." She sighed. "I don't know how to explain. It's like he's my other half."

"Huh." I didn't want to burst her bubble that it wouldn't likely last. Plus, I thought I was her other half.

"I know, it sounds nuts." She looked at me earnestly, almost for approval. "It does." I wanted to be supportive. "But hell, he's a very pretty man."

"Even better, he's strong, loyal, and kind." She sighed again dreamily. "And yes.

Soooo easy on the eyes."

"He treats you well." I put my arm around her.

42

"Yes. So respectful. So loving." Zoey was watching Ty now, and he beamed at her with the same moony expression.

"And he has a big dick." I nudged her.

"Yep. I can't wait." She stuck out her tongue.

The band played a new song *Rise* and worked through a bunch of iterations, which was fascinating to watch. Connor would play with different rhythms, eyes locked with Jace in silent communication. Zane effortlessly experimented with different licks to complement Ty's earth-shattering vocals. I'd never witnessed the process of making music or working through a new song, and before long an hour had gone by. When the guys took a break, Jace left the room and returned with a black-haired girl named Fiona and a few other dudes who sat around with us on various amps watching them practice.

During breaks, Ty made no secret about his affection for Zoey. Holding her tight, stroking her hair, gazing at her like she was a queen and giving her soulful kisses. They were both so head-over-heels for each other my heart couldn't help but melt. Zoey was in love and deserved to be. Despite how I had hoped the summer would turn out, I realized that I couldn't and wouldn't begrudge her experience.

Plus, now I was in LTZ's inner circle and hopefully, Zoey would keep me here.

When things wrapped up, Connor, Zane, Fiona, and the other guys disappeared into the house. Ty and Zoey followed close behind. It had been a long day and I was ready to drive myself home.

"Alex, hold up." A shirtless Jace stepped from behind his kit, mopping his shoulders and six-pack with a towel.

"Um, okay." I had no problem stopping to admire, um, his tattoos.

"I've gotta go." Zoey scrunched her nose. "I still have a curfew."

"It's cool, Z. Go ahead. I'll walk Alex out." Jace shooed them on.

Zoey cocked an eyebrow and smirked at me over her shoulder as she turned and walked out with her hand once again fused together with Ty's.

"What's up?" I turned to Jace and tried to act nonchalant.

"How's project Instagram?" He shook out his damp hair and wrapped it up into a knot at the back of his head.

"I'm going to launch it when I'm on the plane, only six more weeks!" I smoothed my skirt and rocked on my heels, trying not to stare into the depths of his eyes, which were actually a mix of green, gold, and a bit of aqua, truth be told. Not that I noticed or anything.

Jace pulled on a vintage Nirvana T-shirt, picked up some of the beer bottles, and put them in the empty boxes. Silently, I helped him. Within minutes the room was cleared up.

"Thanks, you didn't have to do that." Jace stacked up the boxes by the door. "The guys are fucking heathens; I'm going to lose my mind on a bus with them."

"Why, are you a neat freak?" I placed the last box on top of his pile.

"A bit." He stopped to look at me, his expression was hard to read. "I'm still looking forward to it."

"Well . . ." Despite the small talk, I was no clearer as to why Jace kept me behind. Was he into me? Unfortunately, my women's intuition wasn't developed enough to trust the signs. If these were actually signs. Maybe they weren't. Gawd.

"Did you have fun?" His husky voice was so sexy, his eyes so twinkly. He embodied effortless confidence and cool. I could barely respond.

"Yeah. Of course. You guys are great," I finally answered, hoping my voice didn't sound weird.

"You can come by anytime, you know." He took a step toward me, looking directly into my eyes and grinning. This man had all of the game that Ty lacked, that was for sure.

"To Zane's house?" I babbled while trying to maintain eye contact.

"Well sure, but to LTZ band stuff." The dimples in his smile were crazy. The cleft in his chin dreamy. No man should have both dimples and a cleft, it was unfair to all the other men. "I mean, it looks like Zoey is here to stay so you're welcome to keep her company."

"Oh. Okay, thanks." Inadvertently, I crossed my arms and then quickly dropped them to my side—like a spaz—as he stopped right in front of me.

"So, Alex." Jace tucked my hair behind my ear.

Zing. Fucking. Zing. It felt like two batteries were sparking against each other. My heart started beating superfast. He leaned in closer until we were nearly nose to nose. Holy shit, was he actually going to kiss me?

"Dude!" Connor burst through the door, causing Jace to blink and step away from me quickly. "Oops. Sorry—Hey, Alex, I thought you left with Zoey and Ty. Jesus. This room is really getting a workout today."

"No, dude, not the case. I was just walking her out." Poof. The moment was gone in an instant. Jace turned and beckoned me to follow.

"Yeah, I was just heading out." I murmured, following his lead.

"Right. Sure." Connor growled, giving Jace a pointed look and dismissing me. "J, we're out by the firepit. Jen, Jess, and Cassie are here waiting for you. Catch ya later, Alex."

"Yeah, okay." Jace actually winked at me as Connor departed. Fucking winked. "Well, I should really get going." I recognized the name Cassie and abruptly I

turned my back to him and followed after the big ginger bassist.

Jace's strong drummer hand grazed my lower back just slightly, sending another *zing* up my spine. Silently we walked back through the house out the door to my car, stopping only once I was at the driver's side door. I turned to face him and Jace gripped both my shoulders. Before I knew it, his pillowy soft lips placed a platonic smooch on my forehead. I sighed and looked up. Our eyes locked. As we stood looking at each other for a second, I wondered if I should seize the moment and kiss him for real.

"Good night, Beanie." Jace released my shoulders and he took a step away so I could get into the car.

"G'night." I slurred dreamily, wishing I could stay. "Wait, Beanie?"

"It's just a nickname." Jace laughed. "For a sexy girl who is as skinny as a string bean."

"It's not sexy, it's a nickname for a dog." I hated it. My face must have shown as much.

Jace belly laughed and took a step back toward the house. "You don't like it?" Without answering, I got into my car, started it, and rolled down the window before I waved and drove off.

"Later!" I heard him call out as I drove away, wondering what the hell just happened.

All the way home I replayed the scene in my mind over and over again and couldn't figure out what Jace's story was. Or, if there was a story. Did I only imagine that he was going to kiss me? He said that girl Cassie wasn't his girlfriend, but she was waiting for him. And WTF on the nickname? Beanie?

My thoughts were all over the place, and I couldn't get a wink of sleep. After I tossed and turned for most of the night, the sun eventually rose, and light filled my room. Exhausted, I pulled the black-out shades down and crawled back into bed, determined to find out whether my crush was even somewhat reciprocated. By the time sleep finally came, I'd decided that if there was a next time with Jace, I was taking matters into my own hands.

After all, why let a dude—even a snack like Jace—control *my* destiny? I was the one who planned on bagging a rock star this summer. Sure, Zoey beat me to the punch and had her guy. Now, it was time to get mine. Jace Devereaux wasn't going to know what hit him.

JACE

CHAPTER 5

After Alex drove off, I mentally berated myself. What was I thinking? She was so fucking stunning, but what was I doing flirting with her? Eighteen. She was a baby. I was on Ty's case 24/7 about Zoey, and yet, just now I was about one second away from following him over the jail-bait edge. Jesus, if Connor hadn't walked into the practice room when he did, I would have kissed the hell out of her.

With the crisis averted, I was determined to put Alex in the friend zone—no, the little sister zone. Giving her a dumb nickname would remind me of how it needed to be with her. Alex's horrified look when I called her "Beanie" meant that I hit the mark.

Shaking off the near-disastrous turn of events, I rejoined the guys at the firepit along with my sister, Jennifer, her high school best friend, and my former friend-with-benefits, Cassie, and Cassie's sister, Jessica.

Grabbing a cold beer, I deliberately took a seat in between Jen and Zane away from Cassie, who pouted when I didn't sit in the open seat next to her.

Aesthetically, Cass was a beautiful girl with long, glossy red hair, full lips, wide, China-blue eyes, and a tight, toned body. The problem was, she relied upon her looks to get what she wanted, and her personality seemed to get more superficial with each passing year. Everything was always a show for Cassie. Even tonight when we were casually lounging around a firepit, she was dressed for a club in a low-cut, black tank dress and high-heel, black, cut-out booties.

We'd been hooking up on and off for years. For me, non-exclusively, and I'm pretty sure it was that way for her too. Not that she didn't try to persuade me to take things to the next level. It just wasn't what I wanted. Over the years I'd broken off contact with her hundreds of times. It never worked for long. Cassie pursued me relentlessly. She scared me sometimes with her persistence.

She made no secret of how much she loved being with a guy in a successful band. I mean, LTZ wasn't there yet, but she'd taken it back up a notch as our social media following increased. Luckily, after hearing so many of Carter's cautionary tales, I had always been religious about using condoms. My gut told me that if I wasn't careful with Cassie, she'd find herself "accidentally" pregnant.

This didn't mean I wasn't a weak man. Fuck. Cassie oozed sex appeal and knew how to get me going. I was a twenty-something dude, ruled by my cock. She was an absolute animal in the sack. I gave in. Often. Who could blame me?

Well, Jen could. She thought her little brother was a misogynist pig by continuing to hit it with Cassie. When the tour dates had firmed up a couple of months ago, she sat me down and gave me a stern lecture about how I needed to treat the women in my life. Which, according to her, was the way that I would want my own sisters to be treated. It hit home; it was time for me to grow up.

A couple of weeks later when Cassie offered to blow me in the men's room at the Mission show, I'd turned her down and held firm—pardon the pun—when she suggested half-a-dozen alternate locations. She had been furious but finally left me alone. I knew that it wouldn't be the end. It never was. I guess it shouldn't have been a surprise that Cassie and her sister had found their way into another band function via my sister.

As I stared into the fire, watching the orange and yellow flames dance, Jen got up and sat on Connor's lap and nestled into his big frame. He wrapped his muscled arms around her and kissed her temple. I loved Connor and Jen together. They made a perfect couple.

Now twenty-four, Connor was the oldest of four brothers. His mother worked numerous jobs to support the family after his dad became disabled in a car accident when he was seventeen. He took construction work all through high school and during the entire time I was in college to help support his family. Quiet, pensive, fiercely loyal and protective of his younger brothers, Connor became a master carpenter so they could focus on academics and get into good colleges. It also freed his mom to tend to his dad's health needs.

Naturally pretty, strong, outdoorsy, and extraordinarily handy, Jen broke gender barriers as one of Seattle's only female contractors. She met Connor at a jobsite for a multi-million-dollar mansion on Lake Washington. Within weeks, she had brought him home to meet my parents, and he and I bonded over our shared love of hard rock. We played music together and he became my best friend and honorary brother.

Despite how young they were, Connor and Jen's devotion to each other mirrored my parents' strong marriage. Jen knew that Connor built homes only out of financial necessity and that he really wanted to be a professional musician. She was the one who helped convince him to pursue his bass wizardry and devote his spare time to join LTZ with me.

As much as we wanted the big ginger to be a permanent member of the band, his family obligations had always been something we had to work around. So, we were thrilled last year when his dad's recovery enabled him to return to work and Connor was free to commit to the band—and all that it entailed—fully.

Meanwhile, Jen actually loved her work as a contractor, and she was going places in her chosen field. I'd never known anyone more secure with themselves than my sister. As one of the only women on the labor side of construction, she didn't allow anyone to fuck with her. Her talent and professionalism allowed her to rise through the ranks, and she had just been promoted to foreman at one of the largest construction companies in Seattle. Driven, focused, and confident, my sister was the complete opposite of Cassie, who didn't seem to have any ambition beyond bartending at the latest hot spot.

I honestly wasn't sure why Jen and Cassie were even still friends.

The second Jen vacated her seat to cuddle with Connor, Cassie launched herself into it and scooted into the chair closer to me.

"Hey, handsome." Her red curls shone against the fire, reminding me of the fire- woman from *Game of Thrones*. "You look good enough to eat."

"I'm not in the mood, Cass." I barely glanced over at her.

"Oh, I can get you there." She purred.

"No thank you." I hated to be a dick, but . . .

"J-bird, we only have a few weeks until you're gone for six *looong* months. Can you blame a girl for wanting your thick cock inside her as much as possible before you leave?" Cassie lowered her eyelids and looked up from under her eyelashes, licking her lips in a supposed-to-be seductive sort of way.

"Jesus," I muttered to myself, knowing that the standard Seattle passive-aggressive route wasn't going to cut it with her.

As I contemplated how to handle things, my mind inexplicably wandered to the natural, blonde beauty who had just left in her green Beetle. The differences between the women were vast, age difference aside. Alex was, quite possibly, the sexiest woman I'd ever encountered. She was clearly inexperienced. Pure, even. Her sensuousness was innate, she didn't try at all. I knew she couldn't be mine, but it opened my mind to new possibilities.

Cassie's aggressive sexuality simply didn't do it for me anymore. I felt nothing for her but annoyance. At this point, we had nothing in common but the fucking. It made me feel gross. Plus, it wasn't fair to her. Jen's lecture had an impact on me. In a family of amazing sisters, I wasn't going to disrespect her or any woman again.

So, yeah. It was time to man up. Own my shit. Time to end the dysfunctional "relationship" with Cassie for good.

"Cass, let's go have a talk." I got up and held my hand out to her, which she gleefully grasped, mistaking what was about to happen.

Without speaking, I led her back into the house to catcalls from the peanut gallery teasing us with a million euphemisms of "having a talk." All I could do was roll my eyes. Once inside, I sat on Carter's plush, corduroy couch and patted the seat next to me. Cassie sat and without a beat pressed her body against mine as she leaned in and kissed my neck.

"Let's go back to Zane's room, baby." She put her hand on my thigh, her long, pink, acrylic nails stroking suggestively up toward my package.

Gripping her hand to prevent her from reaching the intended destination, I gritted my teeth and began. "Cassie, you need to know that it's completely over between us. I don't want this anymore."

"What do you mean?" Her eyebrows knit in confusion. "You're breaking up with me?"

"Stop. We aren't together, Cassie. I'm not your boyfriend. You know that." I leaned back, pinching the bridge of my nose.

"Oh, Jace. You're so funny. Let me fuck all of this tension out of you." Cassie tucked a long strand of her shiny red hair behind her ear and leaned in again, stroking my nape and brushing her breast against my arm in the process.

Standing up abruptly, I moved to the big stone fireplace and turned to face her.

"Please, Cass. Don't do that. I don't want this, and I sound like such a dick, but

there is no 'we.' It isn't going to happen with us again. It can't." I kept eye contact and tried to make my voice seem firm and decisive.

"Who was the jailbait girl?" Cassie deftly changed the topic.

"Zoey?" I decided to play dumb. "She's Ty's girlfriend?"

"I know who Zoey is. The other blonde, Jace. The one who just left. Are you fucking her too?" Cassie spat.

"Do you mean Zoey's friend Alex?" I mentally thwacked myself for saying her name out loud.

"Is that her name?" She crossed her arms over her ample cleavage, sulking in the cushions.

"Um, she's only eighteen. So, no." I squinted at her as a warning.

"She's pretty." She ignored my denial, determined to play it cool. "You want to smash her? It's okay. Get her out of your system. You'll realize I'm the one for you eventually."

"Cass, shit! Stop. We've been friends for a long time. I can't do the FWB anymore. Okay?" I pleaded, feeling sick that she'd have so little self-esteem and any part I'd played in making her feel that way. "We aren't a couple. We aren't going to be a couple. Please let's not make this weird."

Cassie buried her face in her hands and started wailing hysterically. Considering that I'd spent my life as an only boy amongst sisters, I had to physically resist the Pavlovian impulse to comfort her. The thing is, I'd been suckered by Cassie's histrionics before. There were always a lot of sobs but never actual tears. She knew what she was doing. So did I. Without another glance, I wasted no time heading for the sliding door.

"Cass, it's over." I tried to sound empathetic on my way out, knowing that I was failing. "I'm leaving on tour in a few weeks. Please don't call, don't text, don't come to band functions. I'm sorry to be harsh but it's best if we don't see each other again. I'll send Jessica in and you guys should leave."

Once outside, I closed the sliding door and breathed a sigh of relief. I was so ready to be on the road with my dudes. There was no need for me to be involved with anyone right now. Satisfied that I'd headed things off with Alex and cut things off with Cassie, I went back to my bandmates feeling a bit lighter.

"Cassie needs you." I motioned to Jessica with my thumb as I approached the firepit.

"You're such a fucking asshole," she spat before jumping up and running toward the house.

"Yeah, so I've been told." I grabbed another beer.

"I'm assuming you ended it?" Jen came up behind me.

"Yeah, because she wasn't my girlfriend and she kept trying to claim me. You're not mad?" Fear of disappointing my sister was one of the reasons I'd let the situation with her friend drag on for so long.

"Of course not, little J." Jen grasped my hand and pulled me into a hug away from the others. "It's actually a relief. She's not the right girl for you, but she doesn't deserve to be led on either."

"Yeah, I know."

"Just go out on the road and have fun, you're too young for such a big commitment." She clinked my bottle with hers.

"Pot calling kettle?" I teased.

A cloud crossed her face and she regained her composure. "No, I'm too young too.

 I'm a hypocrite."

Shocked, I stared at her. "Jen—" I started.

"Oh, stop. It's nothing." She shooed me.

At this point, the entire night had been such a psychological mindfuck, I knew I just needed to call it. As I rode home in my Uber, my thoughts drifted to the lovely gypsy Alex. There was a twinge in my heart when I saw her. My mind filled with happiness when I spoke to her. Tonight I learned there was a palpable zap of energy when we touched even just a little. Was that what Ty and Zoey felt? Connor and Jen?

It didn't matter though. I was resolved. Even though my dick got hard just thinking about how close I had come to kissing her tonight, I wasn't going to act on it. Zane and I could be the carefree single guys on the tour and sow our wild oats, as my dad liked to say. It was time to stop thinking with my little head and use my big one. Alex would remain firmly in the little-sister territory.

Of course, those were best-laid plans. Suddenly Alex was always with Zoey at rehearsals. She also showed up nearly every day at the studio while we recorded. It was like she was taunting me, even though we barely spoke. She seemed to have a uniform of either a black or white tank top with cutoffs, faded, ripped overalls or some sort of short, fluttery skirt. Always with those Frye boots. She was so fucking sexy.

As far as I could tell, she either didn't wear a bra or perhaps just a wisp of a bra. In the cold studio, her nipples were always just barely visible through her tanks. Goddamn, those perky, firm tits of hers. They did it for me, big time. I had to deliberately avert my eyes, which meant I deliberately avoided Alex. Board shorts were out. Whenever she was near in one of those tank tops, my body reacted. Cutoffs or jeans provided the only coverage that would allow me to discreetly shift my junk around, so I didn't come off as some sort of creeper. The crisis was real.

I couldn't help but notice everything about her. Sometimes she'd wear a fisherman's cap backward over her honey-blonde hair, it made her look so badass. Often, she'd be buried in her tablet while we ran through yet another take, of whatever song we were working on, her long limbs tucked up under her on the black-leather studio couch. When she and Zoey got in one of their giggle moods, her joyous, gleeful face was a sight to behold.

On lunch breaks, when I amused myself by posting social media videos of Ty and Zoey in full slurpy-durpy PDA mode, Alex would joke around with all of us while we ate. Every day, she'd bring in a different flavored pie from her mom's online bakery business, which endeared her to everyone, including all of the studio techs.

So yeah, I found myself drawn to her like a fly to honey. Which meant I retreated into my shell more and more. Self-preservation. My plan was to ignore her as much as possible and get myself on the road, and then I could forget all about her. It wasn't that hard to avoid her, I was either able to hide behind my drum kit or my phone to post new videos of our studio time. Alex often tried to engage me when I was in the middle of our social media stuff, but I'd taken to giving her one-word answers and acting disinterested, when I was anything but.

After our last night in the studio, we loaded everything out and everyone had left but I still had to pack up the last few pieces of my drum kit. When I brought the bass drum to the band's new green Ford passenger van, Alex was leaning against the side of the brick building where it was parked.

"Dude, are you mad at me?" Alex inquired, sucking on an orange lollipop. Today wearing a white tank with cutoff shorts and those boots. I swear, I could see her nipples through the fabric of her top.

"Nope." I pushed my hands into my jeans and slouched next to her against the side of the building, avoiding her gaze. And looking at her chest.

"Oh-kay." She leveled her gaze at me.

"I'm just focused on my band right now." I shrugged. "We have a lot riding on this."

She didn't break eye contact. "Yeah, I'm aware."

"We leave in just over a week."

She bit off the orange candy and crunched it. "Yeah, I know."

"Carter has really set things up for us. We have a real chance to make this work, so I have to focus."

"What did he say to Zoey?" Alex squinted at me. "She was crying earlier."

"Maybe he was comforting her because she's upset about us

leaving." I really had no idea what she was talking about.

"I don't think so." She was unimpressed. "She was upset by something he said to

   her."

"I don't know, Alex. I mean, don't you think Zoey and Ty are a little too serious for having just met a couple of months ago?" I usually kept my feelings to myself, but it was something that Connor, Zane, and I had talked about with Carter.

Unlike Connor, who had been with my sister for years, Zane who would fuck anyone for the sheer pleasure of it, and me who was slightly more discerning but not in the market for a serious relationship, Ty was a sensitive soul. He was our lead singer. We needed him to give 100 percent to the band right now. We all loved Zoey, but the odds of them working out were next to zero. Less than zero, pardon the pun.

"Yeah, I think they are too serious." Alex surprised me. "She's going to get her heart broken, and I can't stop it."

"What do you mean?" I was similarly worried about Ty's heart.

"You guys are going on the road. You'll have your pick of beautiful women in every city you visit. Zoey thinks Ty is the one for her. I know that Ty will not be able to resist temptation." She raised her eyebrow.

Despite my feelings on the matter, her comment made me angry. "Wow. You don't give him much credit."

"He's a dude." She shrugged as if it was a foregone conclusion.

"You know nothing about him, do you?" My voice raised even further. "He's not wired that way. If anything, Zoey will meet someone at college and forget all about her fling with a rock star."

"Hmm." Alex walked over to the trash and threw away her lollipop stick.

"Hmm, what?" I followed her, wanting to complete this conversation and stick up for my man Ty.

"You just seem very defensive." She smirked defiantly. "But, I'm glad to hear you say that about Ty, it makes me feel better."

"Why?"

"Because tomorrow she's going to lose her virginity to him, and he better goddamn know what a gift it is." Alex crossed her arms across her perky tits, drawing my eyes to them. Christ.

"Jesus." I was shocked. "The way they carry on, I could have sworn they have been going at it all summer."

"Nope." Alex smiled. "They're making it special. Seems unnecessarily dramatic."

"Well, it's none of my business." I walked back over to the van we'd dubbed "The Green Dragon," unlocked it and loaded in my bass drum.

"Can I tell you something?" Alex walked up behind me, her hands clasped behind her, causing her breasts to jut out slightly.

"Um, sure." I couldn't help but lick my lips.

"I was hoping that you'd do that for me." Her cheeks reddened just a little, but she kept her composure.

My heart stopped. What? "Do what, Beanie?" I gulped.

"God! Stop calling me that. I hate it." She cocked her hip and narrowed her eyes.

"Okay." My heart was pounding.

"All summer I've been hoping you'd notice me because I wanted *my* first time to be with you," Alex said boldly before looking down at her boots.

I couldn't speak, my dick filled at the thought of her naked and writhing under me.

All I could do was stare at her like a nutjob.

Alex looked up at me innocently, yet there was lust and passion behind her big blue eyes. She was impossible for me to resist. I reached out and stroked her lips with my finger and all bets were off when she opened her mouth and sucked in the tip, still staring directly into my eyes.

"Fuck. Alex. That's such a bad idea." I stroked her hair with my free hand as she drew my finger farther into her mouth and then released it.

"Probably." She grinned.

"You really thought I didn't notice you?" I stared into her eyes, questioning. "Sure hasn't seemed like it." She playfully pouted.

"I'm too old for you." I shook my head but couldn't help but smile. "You need to be with someone your own age."

"Do you want my first time to be with some un-showered hipster in a hostel somewhere in Europe?" She cocked her brow. "Or a sexy drummer that smells like, God, whatever that awesome cologne you wear is."

"Sandalwood essential oil," I murmured into her hair.

"It's so yummy." She leaned into me, pressing her tits against my chest just slightly.

I swallowed. I couldn't speak but resumed eye contact, still threading my fingers through her soft, blonde tresses.

"I want it to be you, Jace." She reached up with both hands and placed them on my shoulders.

Her words stunned me. My voice came out rough, shredded. "Why?"

"Because we're friends. And you'll also let me go do my thing without trying to make this into a Ty-Zoey situation." Alex's hands had intertwined behind my neck and she leaned up toward me, her lips parted.

"Where?" I closed my eyes for a minute, willing myself to say no.

"My mom had to go out of town for a couple of days. No one is home at my house until late tomorrow." Alex pressed herself even closer to me, willing me to say yes.

Alex won. Cupping her face with both hands I lowered my lips to hers, holding her gaze. Her grip tightened on my hair at the base of my neck. My lips brushed against hers slowly, gently. Barely even a touch. I could feel the energy between us buzzing all the way to my toes. Drawing in a tight breath, my lips moved more firmly against hers. I parted them gently with my tongue. Savoring the orange flavor of the remnants of her lollipop, I began a warm, languid exploration of her mouth. Alex's body stiffened and then melted into me. She tilted her head and kissed me back. Softly. Nothing wild. Our tongues slid against each other, lips melding as we found our own rhythm.

Everything inside me ignited when I yanked Alex tightly against me, gripping her ass to grind my swollen cock against her. The hard points of her nipples pressed against my chest, causing me to moan against her mouth. She shivered in my arms. Her fingertips explored my neck, my cheek, and then moved back to grip my hair as we nuzzled and sucked on each other's tongues. Exploring deeper, grinding against each other until the loud clang of the studio door startled both of us apart.

"You gonna finish loading out or what, man?" The tech stood glaring at us with his arms crossed. "We need to turn the studio."

Red-faced and laughing, Alex helped me load out the rest of my drums into the Green Dragon and jumped into the passenger seat after we were done.

"My house?" She slipped her aviator sunglasses on.

"Are you really sure?" I felt like I was going to go to hell but would enjoy the ride.

"I'm positive." She smiled saucily. "If I had any doubts, after those kisses I don't now."

CHAPTER 6

My heart couldn't have been beating harder unless I was having a heart attack. I couldn't believe my boldness. I'd put on a confident persona and had gone through with it. For weeks after that first night at Carter's, I took advantage of every opportunity to hang out with Zoey and the band. Hoping for a repeat of the near-kiss. Instead, Jace went out of his way to avoid me or treat me like a kid.

Time was running out. The band was done in the studio and were heading on tour. Zoey was off to college and my plane left the same day. Mom had made plans for us, but then got called out of town unexpectedly to help my aunt, who broke her ankle. With her return looming to send me off, desperate times called for desperate measures. I put on my big-girl cutoffs this morning, determined to get my man.

"Alex, this really isn't a good idea." Jace looked at me from the driver's seat.

"Don't think so hard." I rolled my eyes at him.

"Look, I just got out of a friends-with-benefits situation, it doesn't end up good for anyone." He shook his head sadly. "I don't want you to be hurt."

"Dude, I'm not going to get hurt." I laughed. "I'm going to Europe to explore and soak up the culture and have a great time. I have no idea when I'll be back or if I'll ever come back."

"You're a beautiful girl, you need to be very careful." Jace narrowed his eyes at me.

"Awww. You do care." I teased.

"Of course I do," Jace muttered.

"Can you just enjoy a moment in time with me?" My voice came out almost begging. "We won't have any strings, if that's what you're worried about. I won't be like that girl Cassie who kept showing up at the studio."

"You couldn't ever be like that." Jace winced like I'd punched him.

"Exactly. Turn here, my house is over there on the corner." I pointed and Jace followed my direction.

Silently, we got out of the van and strode up the walkway to my front door. Jace put his hand on my nape, his palm expanding to cup the back of my head. After unlocking the door, he followed me through the entryway into the adjacent living room. Kicking off my boots, I sat on the overstuffed, floral-patterned sofa and tucked my feet underneath me. He followed, sitting on the edge of the seat, his elbows bent on his knees. His hair fell across his shoulders like a curtain.

"Are you excited to get on the road?" I wanted to draw him out.

"Yeah, I'm so ready to go." He glanced sideways at me.

"Yeah, me too." I leaned toward him, hoping to ignite the spark again.

"Alex." His clear, green eyes caught mine, the cleft in his chin quivering.

"Come here," I whispered. "I want another kiss."

Jace groaned and leaned back against the couch, dragging me to him. I couldn't help but nuzzle his neck, breathing in his manly scent before tilting my face up to meet his lips. His strong biceps stretched across my shoulder, his hand caressed the side of my face and I snuggled up flush against his muscled chest. Our tongues danced again. Sometimes a tango. Sometimes a waltz. Sometimes crunking. My Gawd, this man could kiss. So unlike the high school boys that I was used to.

"Alex, I've never been with a virgin." Jace kissed my temple. "My mind is going nuts. I don't know if this is the right thing to do."

"You're very cerebral." I raked my fingers through his hair.

"I have three sisters; I don't want to be a jerk." He smiled down at me and ran his fingers lightly through my hair too.

"Give me some credit, I see you." I gestured with two fingers pointed at my eyes and then at his.

"I know you do." He gave me a slow, drawn-out kiss before abruptly standing.

"Don't leave me hanging." I reached out my hand to him, the silver bracelets jangling as I shook it, willing him to take it.

"If we're doing this, let's do it right." Jace grasped my hand and pulled me up. "We need to set the mood."

Together we moved through the house, collecting some tea candles, a couple of wine glasses, and the half-opened chardonnay in the fridge. Jace spotted my mom's prize roses blooming out the back and dashed through the back door, returning with a couple of giant, pink blooms. After we gathered up all the stuff, my heart pounded out of my chest again.

"Let's go up to my room." I gestured and walked up the stairs, not wanting to lose my nerve.

"Lead the way." Jace's arms were full, but he followed close behind.

I'd never had a guy in my room before, and suddenly I was a bit shy about how my full-sized canopy bed draped in a denim duvet cover and crazy mash-up of Kings of Leon, Lady Gaga, Bruno Mars, and the Black Keys posters looked to this sexy rocker. He didn't say a word, just poured two glasses of wine and set them on my dresser. Next, he turned the lights off, leaving only the glow of my desk lamp and proceeded to rip all the petals off the roses and spread them out all over my bed.

"I'm such a weak man." Jace strode over to me and captured my mouth with his, gripping my ass and lifting me off the ground to straddle his waist.

I wrapped my legs around him. His strong arms held me tight, even as he devoured my lips hungrily. Things were getting real. I was ready. Clinging to his neck, I got lost in his messy, passionate kisses. Without skipping a beat, Jace walked me over to the bed and gently placed me in the middle of the petals on the duvet. His fingers were fumbling and desperate, his mouth never leaving mine. He pulled up my tank top, exposing my bare breasts.

"Fuck me. I knew you didn't wear a bra."

Jace groaned and placed a brief, suckling kiss on my distended nipple and then went back for seconds on the other one.

My entire body shook with desire. He moved his calloused

hands down my body, caressing my sides, sliding over my hips, never releasing the suction from my nipple.

Slowly, his fingers trailed up the side of my thigh to the button on my cutoffs, which he deftly unclasped. Working them slowly down my hips, when he reached my knees I wriggled and kicked them to the floor, leaving me wearing only my black G-string.

Being here like this with Jace was all I had dreamed about this summer. I was so scared, but I also knew that I didn't want to stop. My breath hitched and a moaning sound emanating deep inside me caught his attention. Releasing my puckered nipple from his lips with a distinct pop, his eyes pierced my soul when he looked up at me. The look told me everything, my mind knew I was where I was supposed to be.

My body knew it too. Jace pulled off my panties, which were absolutely soaked. His nostrils flared because he could smell how much I wanted him. His erection throbbed through his jeans against my thigh, and I rubbed against the bulge like a cat. Jace groaned at the contact while his fingers inched down my body to the junction between my thighs. Gently, he eased my legs apart, his fingers hovering over my swollen pussy. I could feel my clit pulsating in anticipation of his touch.

"We can stop anytime," Jace whispered against my ear. "Just say the word."

"I don't want to stop, ever," I moaned. "Please, touch me, Jace."

His gaze dropped to my slit. He pressed his thumb between my wet lips, the rough pads of his calloused fingers following suit, never directly touching my clit or entering my body. Jace took his time, stroking and slipping through my slick juices, varying pressure and speed, his eyebrows knitted as though he was studying my reaction to each touch. My hips moved on their own volition, bucking, circling, clenching, sometimes seeking more pressure, sometimes avoiding more contact when the stimulation was too intense. Through it all he breathed in, inhaling my arousal, making guttural sounds when I gushed around his fingers. It felt like I would explode if he didn't touch me where I needed it most. As though he had ESP, he bent down and his tongue lapped through my folds like he was starving, sucking my clit in between his lips.

The keening yowl filling the room was me, I realized. My eyes squeezed shut, fireworks popped beneath my eyelids, pleasure so intense it was nearly painful. I didn't know if I could take any more. My hips bucked against his mouth while I clutched his long hair at the scalp, pulling him toward me and pushing him away, not knowing how to process the extraordinary sensations down below. Finally, I gave in while his lips continued to suckle and feast on my clit. I spiraled into a dark vortex of pleasure. Every single muscle in my body tensed before I experienced a release so staggering it brought tears to my eyes.

When I became coherent again, Jace was up next to me, cradling me in his arms, one finger teasing my nipple into a tight little bud. Smiling at me, he leaned forward, and his lips closed over the dark tip as he suckled and stroked my stomach and hipbones.

"Wow." It was all I could say as I lay there like a noodle.

"You're absolutely gorgeous, Alex." Jace smiled up at me. "Thank you for letting me do that."

"You're gorgeous too, Jace." I tickled his side. "But why am I naked and you're still dressed?"

"Because I need to ask you again. Are you sure you want to go further?"

"Yes." Definitive. I was sure. After experiencing his magnificent

KAYLENE WINTER

oral skills, I knew it would never be better than this. I was certain.

"Do you want some wine?" Jace held up the glass and chuckled nervously.

"No, I mean I appreciate the romance, but I'm not that into wine." I laughed and gestured to myself. "Plus, underage. To drink. Not for the sex."

"Ah, shit. You had to remind me." Jace's face became heated. His gaze roamed across my naked body; my already-hard nipples became painfully tight with anticipation.

"Your body is insane; you could be a supermodel." Jace stroked my ribcage and once again teased each of my tight buds with his thumbs.

"Methinks you have a boob fetish." I swatted his hand away playfully.

"You have no idea what you've done to me all summer going braless in those tank tops." He swallowed, covering my entire breast in his hand.

"I'm a good girl, I don't know what you are talking about." I winked at him.

"I *knew* it!" Jace swatted at me. "You're a vixen."

"Well, lucky for you I took matters into my own hands or where would we be?" I sat up and grasped his T-shirt, tugging it up over his head.

"I was trying so hard to be good, and you've corrupted me." Jace grabbed the shirt from me and tossed it on the ground.

"Right. Flashing your tattooed pecs and flexing your biceps at me." I swatted at his arm. "I noticed."

Jace caught my wrist and pulled me to him, my breasts pressed against his naked chest. I wrapped my arms around his waist, running

71

my hands over the definition of his muscled back. He suckled at my earlobe and lightly gripped each side of my face to move me where he wanted. Which, apparently, was to nibble at my neck.

"I loved watching you come," he whispered into my ear, causing an instant jolt and another gush of wetness between my legs.

"Maybe I want to see you come too." I licked his ear naughtily.

"Thank God." Jace kissed my nose before standing up to kick off his sneakers.

Slowly, my sexy drummer undid his jeans and pulled them down together with his boxer briefs in one fell swoop. Although I'd seen him shirtless countless times by this point, I'd never seen him or any man fully naked before. Which was probably why I couldn't keep myself from staring at his thick, impressive cock, which jutted up flush against his stomach. I swallowed when he wrapped his fingers around his wide base and stroked himself root to tip, his green eyes never leaving mine.

Unable to resist, I reached out to touch him, and he caught my hand to bring it to his girth and show me how to mirror his strokes.

"Fuck." Jace's eyes rolled back in his head when he let me take fully over.

"Can I suck on it?" I looked up at him.

"Jesus, Alex." Jace's eyes bugged out as I moved toward him. "No! I'm too close."

"Fine, then get down here." I motioned to the bed, still stroking him.

He nearly dove on top of me and suddenly everything became a blur of messy kisses and groping at each other, rolling all over the bed and crushing each and every rose petal into mush. Jace climbed on top of me and his hot, smooth, skin covered my writhing body. I continued to caress his hard muscles while his hair tickled my neck. Everywhere our bodies touched felt like an inferno of desire.

We couldn't stop kissing, there was literally no way for us to stop. After all these weeks of him denying his attraction to me, he was unleashed. For me, being with him like this was all I'd dreamed of all summer. It was everything I ever wanted and more. Gawd. I could taste myself on his tongue.

Still lost in our kisses, Jace covered my body with his and settled in between my legs. His sandalwood scent permeated my senses as I breathed him in. I could feel his thick cock rubbing against my folds and instinctively I tilted my hips to give him better access. There was nothing I wanted more than for him to be inside me. Immediately.

Instead, Jace slowed way down, suckling my lower lip while bracketing me with his arms. As he looked into my eyes, his fingers smoothed my hair from my face. Touching his forehead to mine, he canted his hips against my core. I could feel his shaft throbbing between us.

"Alex, please tell me you have a condom." He gritted out in a strangled voice.

Fucking hell. Of course I didn't.

"I'm on the pill." I blurted. I'd been on the pill to regulate my period since I was fourteen.

"Jesus, Alex." He sighed and rolled off me.

"I trust you." I leaned toward him, my head on my elbow.

"You shouldn't." Jace sat back on his knees and flopped on his back beside me, his cock bobbing against his stomach, weeping at the tip.

"You're clean, right?" I rotated so I was sitting on top of him and gripped his girth, loving the heft, the velvety heated texture of his iron-hard length. "Carter's always preaching to all of you, so you've probably always used one."

"Of course I have." He gripped my ass to pull us tighter together. "And for fuck's sake, don't talk about Carter when we're naked like this."

"Fine. I won't talk about him; I won't talk about anyone." I captured his mouth again. Now that I had him here, there was no way that I wasn't going to kiss him as much as humanly possible.

"Fuck. I don't know. If we do this will you promise me that you'll always carry condoms with you when you travel, Alex?" Jace scolded.

I playfully bit his lower lip. "So now you're talking about me being with other guys while you're about one millimeter away from popping my cherry?"

"Ow! Just promise me." He growled.

"Fine, I promise. Now will you please, pretty please just fuck me?" Still gripping him, I rubbed him through my folds, enjoying how the tip of his cock felt against my clit.

"Alex." He gripped my hips and moved me against him.

"Do you trust that I'm on the pill?" I knew I had to ask. "Yes." He said definitively.

"Please, I've never wanted anything more than this." I pressed just the tip of his cock inside me.

"Oh fuuuck. Are you sure?" He winced with pleasure but grabbed my hand to stop me.

"Unless you don't want to?" I swallowed hard; I couldn't hold it against him if he wasn't comfortable without a condom.

"God, I want you so bad, more than I've ever wanted anything." Jace's breath whooshed out.

Without saying another word, he rolled me onto my back and propped himself on his side, his entire body touching mine and his granite-hard erection resting on my thigh. Jace reached down between us and worked a finger deep inside me, adding a second as he bent his head to suck on my nipple in perfect cadence. The combination of his rough, thick digits created friction inside me, and his warm lips on my breast made me literally cream into his hand.

"Holy fucking hell, Alex." Jace's eyelids were at half-mast when he added a third finger and used his thumb to tap on my completely distended and sensitive nub, which had popped out from between my folds. His other arm cradled my head as he watched my face intently.

"So good, oh God." I flung my arm over my head and writhed against his hand.

"I don't want it to hurt, but I do think you're ready." He kissed the side of my head and changed the angle of his fingers, stroking what must have been my G-spot.

"Yes. Yessss. Ohmyfuckinggod!" My back arched at the exquisite torture, thrusting my breasts upward, and Jace's eyes were dilated to nearly black, obliterating the green.

After nuzzling my neck, Jace's tongue traced a sensitive spot behind my ear. His fingers rubbed the spot deep inside me over and over again until a tremor built deep within my body to the most delightful rolling gratification I'd ever felt. My hips couldn't stop moving and my entire body spasmed with another intense orgasm. In that exact moment, in one motion, Jace withdrew his fingers, rolled on top of me and thrust his cock deep inside.

Apparently, I had been so primed that he slipped right in with no resistance. His thick invasion filled me up completely and made me gasp as my pussy clenched around him tightly. Jace had timed his penetration perfectly, I didn't feel any pressure, pain, or discomfort. Just an amazing fullness. And, oh my gawd. That feeling was everything I'd ever hoped for.

Then it really hit me. Ohmygawd. Jace Deveraux was inside me. I clung to him, reaching around and grabbing his ass to push him in deeper.

"Alex, oh Christ. It's never felt this good. I'm losing my mind. Are you okay? Did I hurt you? Please say I didn't hurt you." Jace babbled a bit when, on raised elbows, he checked in with me, caressing my hair while his hips continued to slowly surge against me.

"No, this is perfect." I sighed, circling my hips to meet his, wanting him deeper. As deep as he could fit.

He rolled his hips slightly faster through my slickness, his eyes squeezed shut with what looked like utter gratification. Trying to remember every detail, I gripped his thick wrists at the side of my head and breathed his sandalwood scent. The silky strands of his hair brushed back and forth against my neck each time he pushed in and pulled out of my swollen pussy. His groans took on a helpless cadence, which made me feel powerful and sexy.

Reaching down between our writhing bodies, Jace tapped on my clit before rubbing it in light circles in time with his increased pace. All while deliciously licking and suckling behind my ear. The slight shift in his position meant his cock rubbed against the deep spot his fingers had just been with each flex of his hips. Tremors coursed through my body with the intensity of the stimulation and another slow, swelling wave of pleasure built from deep inside. Gasping for air, I flung my arms limply above my head.

"Oh, God. Alex. Yes. Let go, baby," Jace encouraged as he cupped my cheek. At the sound of his voice, I pressed my hips up against him, another release unleashed through my entire body.

"Jace, oh gawd this is amazing!" I moaned, grasping fistfuls of the sheets above my head, never wanting this to end. "Why haven't we been doing this all summer?"

Jace laughed.

"Alex, open your eyes." I heard him say through my moans, though I could barely comprehend him. "You wanted to watch me come."

Immediately, I fastened my eyes on his.

Reaching up with the same hand he'd been rubbing my clit with, he gently unclutched one of my limp hands and brought both of our fingers to his lips. My eyes popped when he suckled my release from our fingers while grinding his hips against my pubic bone. It was like he couldn't get close enough or deep enough. Our eyes locked and Jace's entire body shuddered when he pounded into me so hard the sounds of his flesh slapping against mine filled my bedroom.

"You are fucking perfect, Alex," he gasped. "So fucking perfect."

Unleashed, Jace swiveled his hips faster and faster before he arched up almost violently, his biceps quivering, and he let go with a deep, guttural, raw roar. I felt his hot release fill me up completely and trickle out onto the duvet.

For a moment we lay there stunned, his cock still inside me quivering. We were both panting from the exertion of it all. Eventually, Jace pulled out and curled his muscled body around me, his cheek against mine. Somehow, I managed to turn my head to nuzzle his neck. Eventually, our breathing slowed, and our bodies stopped heaving. He'd closed his eyes, and I thought he might have dozed off. When he felt me looking at him his eyelids fluttered open and he pulled me in for a deep kiss, stroking my back tenderly. Sighing, I nestled my head into the crook of his neck, my face resting on his hard pecs.

"Are you okay?" He pressed kisses to the side of my head.

"I'm pretty sure that was the best first time in the history of the universe." I traced the pattern of the tattoo on his shoulder.

"Might be the best time, period." His gravelly voice was so sexy.

"Aw, you don't have to say that." I grinned against his chest. "It's the truth."

"Well, that's a bummer for me." I tickled his six-pack lightly.

"Well, we might need to try again," Jace murmured.

We lay there on top of the duvet for a little while before he gently rolled me on my side and lifted back the covers so we could crawl into bed. Once underneath where it was warm and cozy, we couldn't stop touching, caressing, and kissing each other. Jace's arm snaked under my neck and wrapped around my shoulders, gathering me tight against him. Our arms were wound around each other, and our long legs threaded together.

At some point, Jace untangled himself from me and padded gloriously naked out of my room. Wondering where he was going, I enjoyed the view of his muscular butt when he disappeared into the hall, shortly returning with a warm washcloth. Sitting on the edge of the bed he stroked my hair and smiled at me.

"What's that for?" I was basically eating him up with my eyes because it was physically impossible to stop admiring his hot, fit body.

"I need to wash you up." He gripped the edge of the duvet and flung it back.

Mortified, I realized that I might have bled on him and my eyes immediately focused in on his now-flaccid penis.

"It's okay, I'm cleaned up," he said tenderly.

"Ohmygawd. I . . . I . . ." I was mortified and couldn't meet his eyes.

Gently, he tipped his finger on my chin, so I had no choice but to look at him.

"You gave me a wonderful present, Alex. It's the least I can do. Let me take care of you." He rubbed my lips with his thumb.

Touched and nearly in tears, I let him pull back the covers and softly wipe my inner thighs and open my legs to get to my private parts. Grinning because my nipples hardened into points at his touch, he touched one of the tips with his finger.

"You're so tempting, but I have to get home." He cupped my breast more fully, the dimples on his face like craters.

"Oh. Um, okay." I wasn't sure what I was expecting, but part of me had been hoping for him to stay the night. When I moved to sit up, he gently pressed me back down on my back.

"No, rest. Do you feel sore?" His tenderness was killing me.

"Not right now, but I probably will feel it," I answered honestly.

"I'm not sure what the right thing to do is, Alex." Jace shifted to rest on his side facing me, propping up his head on his bent arm. "I'm not a stay overnight kind of guy."

"Do you want to go home? Or do you have to go home?" I looked up at him, genuinely curious.

"What do you mean?" He watched as I traced the beautiful, intricate design that covered his left arm completely with my finger.

"What is this tattoo? It's really cool." I didn't want things to be weird, so I switched subjects.

"Viking dragons intertwined with a traditional navigation compass." He watched as I continued to trace the art.

"It almost looks Celtic."

"It incorporates a lot of traditional Viking art styles. I'm Norwegian and French."

"It's so sexy." I caressed his taut biceps.

79

Jace swallowed and looked back over at me, unable to keep his eyes averted from my breasts and nipples.

"I don't want to go home." His finger reached out and traced my erect bud.

Before my eyes, his cock had begun to harden and now stood more than half-mast against his thigh. I put my hand around his neck and pulled him down to me. We devoured each other again. Jace scooted me over and crawled back into bed, then pulled me on top of him.

"Straddle me." His gaze pierced my soul. He stroked my sides with his thumbs and held my hips in place with his strong hands.

With me kneeling astride his body, he managed to position me so that his now-erect shaft jutted between my pussy lips and lay against his stomach.

"You're, seriously, a goddess." He was looking down at where our bodies were nearly joined.

"Um, only because you're a sex god." I couldn't help but watch him watching us.

"Oh yeah?" Jace chuckled as he caught my eye. "You say that, but you don't have anyone to compare me with."

I tilted my head and gestured to his cut torso and muscled arms and said with a scoff. "Look at yourself."

"I'd rather look at you playing with your clit," Jace purred, taking my hand and bringing it to my pussy.

I'd never heard dirty talk at all, let alone in person, and my body reacted. I watched him move my finger to the juncture of where I was straddling him, his thick cock millimeters from being inside me. My pussy contracted and wetness seeped out of me onto him.

"Mmm. You like a little nasty talk." Jace smiled wolfishly when my moisture coated the base of his cock.

He held my index finger gently in his fist and rubbed it up and down my distended clit. I was so aroused I was beginning to believe that it was actually visibly pulsing.

"I've never done this in front of anyone." My voice was a shy whisper.

"I'll help you." His husky voice caught.

Jace controlled my movements by moving my finger back and forth across my sensitive nub slowly and then more rapidly in circles. My nipples were puckered almost painfully tight again, my hips circled against his base, trying to get more pressure against my opening. Jace's dick was twitching as it grew even harder against his stomach.

"Jesus, you're so fucking hot, Alex." Jace couldn't take his eyes off his hand and my finger.

With my other hand, I swiped from the flood of wetness leaking out of me and used it to stroke his cock. Jace bent his knees, allowing me to rest back against his thighs and he thrust up and ground against me while we stimulated each other at the same time. I yearned to have him inside me again. Impulsively I lifted my hips and angled his penis back toward me and impaled myself on his hard length.

"Christ!" Jace gripped my hips to still my movement. "That was too fast, I don't want you to hurt yourself."

Admittedly, I'd gone a little quick and his cock filled me completely, but my body adjusted quickly and was on board with the invasion. Looking down, watching where we were joined, I had another moment of thinking *Holy fucking hell, Jace Devereaux is inside me.* Jace's gaze was also completely transfixed on our now-merged bodies.

"Should I move?" I asked sweetly.

"You're going to be the death of me." Jace shook his head, still focused on our fusion, his hair splayed out across the pillow.

His hands bridged nearly the entirety of my hips, so he was able to firmly yet gently move me back and forth against him. He lowered his knees, and one of his hands spanned my lower back. He slowly pressed me down on top of him and held me there, which allowed my clit to rub against his pubic bone, giving me the most amazing stimulation. Controlling my movements, Jace ground me against him in an almost maddingly consistent but slow pace.

"Brace yourself on my chest." He growled.

I obeyed the expert in this situation. My hands splayed out against his ripped pecs; my thumbs traced his flat nipples. My breasts jiggled just inches away from his lips. Never stopping the pace, Jace sucked my nipples into his mouth, one after the other, over and over. Deep inside me, pressure rumbled and built. I was getting the hang of this sex- thing, my hips gyrated faster of their own volition, chasing what I knew would be a mind- blowing pleasure.

Jace kept me firmly rooted against him as he bucked up inside me. This time, it was more of a building pressure that started deep inside me and spread down through my entire pelvis and electrified my feet through my toes to my legs, up my torso, and across my arms into my fingertips. He panted and groaned and thrust up into me harder and harder like a jackhammer against my G-spot until it hit me all at once and my keening guttural wail was thunderous and uncontrollable. Jace's throaty moan escaped him as he emptied inside me for the second time.

Exhausted, I slumped over him, my face buried in his neck. His arms clasped in fists around my lower back tightly, keeping himself from slipping out. Our bodies were slick with sweat and sex, our combined scents permeated the air in my room. Panting, we couldn't move as we came down from what, for me, was the highest high I'd ever experienced.

Maybe ten minutes later, or it could have been an hour, Jace rolled me off him and once again padded out of the room and returned with a warm washcloth to clean us up. Without another word, he climbed into bed with me and cradled me into the crook of his arm. Sighing, I relaxed my head against his chest. He placed even more soft kisses on my forehead.

"Let's sleep for a while," he said softly. "Okay."

"I'm going to remember this forever," he whispered into my hair.

"Me too." I kissed his neck. "You made it wonderful, Jace. Thank you."

But he was already asleep, his breathing regular. My mind was on overdrive, the magnitude of what had just happened—twice—washed over me. Never in a million years when I'd set out to seduce this delicious drummer had I known what a considerate, caring lover he would be. Or, how talented. My expectations had been mediocre at best, I just wanted to get it over with and have a great story about my first time. In reality, I knew that I'd just won the lottery.

At some point, I must have fallen asleep because when I woke up around noon the next day, Jace was gone. On the pillow next to me, he'd left me a single pink rose with a note:

Alex,
Last night was special. You're special. It's not usually like that.
At least, it's never been that way for me.
Part of me wishes we were both in different places in our lives,
who knows where this could lead. If we weren't both leaving, I'd
want to hang out more and get to know you better. I'd really like

to make love to you a million more times.

We both know the deal. You're going to have the time of your life, and I'll try not to think about you breaking the hearts of all of the men who fall in love with you. Please enjoy your adventures, live life to the fullest, don't deny yourself any experience. This is your time, and you're going to be amazing at whatever you do. Know that you will always have a piece of my heart, and I hope that I have a piece of yours. Who knows, maybe someday our timing will be right.

More than anything, Alex, we are friends. I care what happens to you, and I want to keep in touch and share our adventures from afar. It will give us something to look forward to, don't you agree?

So, I'll be sliding into your DMs until you get sick of me. Count on it.

xoxo Jace

My heart swooned. What a note. Every minute I'd spent hoping he'd notice me and being disappointed that he didn't had been worth it. My girly bits tingled at the memory of all that we had done the night before. He wanted to stay in touch. All I could do was hope that he meant what he said.

Realizing that my mom would be home soon and that I needed to clean my sheets, I got to work and put everything into the laundry. There was a ton to do before I left so I got to work, but I was on cloud nine. Lugging my travel backpack out of the hall closet, I packed my clothes. I organized my electronics and double-checked my sim cards and made sure I had passwords backed up in a few locations. I ran to the bank and once back home, I was waiting for the sheets to dry when my phone pinged.

Zoey: RU packed?

Alex: mostly

Zoey: I'll miss u. Have a great time.

Alex: You too, I'll ping you when I get settled. Zoey: Ty's here, we're leaving.

Zoey: love u Alex: love u 2

Alex: Oh gawd! Tonight's the night. Have fun!!!!!

Alex: Z?

CHAPTER 7
TEN MONTHS LATER

y head was pounding by the time the bus rolled into the load-in area at the Sonar festival in Barcelona. After a whirlwind year, LTZ had hit the jackpot. Our first single *Rise* was holding strong at the number-one spot on charts all over the world. The band's meteoric ascension was mind-blowing. We'd toured the US to sold-out crowds in increasingly bigger and bigger venues and moved on to our first stop in Europe with no sign of slowing down. Our manager, Katherine, had let us know that we'd likely be heading to Japan, Singapore, Australia, and New Zealand when we finished the European festival circuit after Oktoberfest in Germany.

Pulling double duty as the drummer and social media director, I never had a break. I loved every minute of it. Sure, until we'd been on the road, my idea of touring had been so naïve. I thought we'd be hanging out together all the time writing songs, shooting the shit, exploring the cities, and then going onstage and rocking our asses off.

But the day-to-day reality was much different than I had imagined. We had a tightly packed schedule and because we were rising stars, there was very little time off. Each day of a show, we'd roll into the venue, get cleaned up, rehearse, do a sound-check, have hours of press, radio and appearances, and I'd have to also make sure to keep all our social channels populated. On days off, we were packed tightly in the bus struggling to catch up on sleep. Luckily, we had a road crew now, so we at least didn't have to hump our gear anymore.

Zane and Ty were hotly in demand, but because Ty was still heartbroken from Zoey ghosting him, Zane had pretty much taken over as the band's spokesperson. He reveled in the attention and was great at it. Funny, zany, and full of energy, he made my job easy to document LTZ's antics as we lived life on the road.

Ty was the consummate professional, his stage presence was otherworldly. His reputation as a performer was already leaning toward legendary. Playing live seemed to be his salvation, he'd release every bit of anguish, sadness, anger, and bitterness into his performances. When he wasn't onstage, however, he'd withdraw into his own world. Retreating into his shy, hermit tendencies, he rarely left the bus or his hotel room. Lucky for us, he was writing. His notebooks were filled with dozens, if not hundreds, of new songs or ideas for new song lyrics. This was great for LTZ, but all of us were worried about his state of mind.

He'd stopped trying to contact Zoey after months of obsessively trying to get her to talk to him. Until, for him, hope at reconciling was in the toilet. Bearing witness to his utter heartbreak was awful so we did our best to protect him. Nothing about Ty was suicidal, thankfully, we just needed to keep him going until he could ignite his own pilot light again.

His looks combined with his reclusiveness made him irresistible to women. Under the theory that the way to get over a girl was to get one under you, all of us in LTZ took turns trying to get him to partake in the bounty of beautiful ladies at our disposal. He had no interest whatsoever and was back to the chaste existence he lived before Zoey.

My wistful thoughts of Alex and the night we shared had been pushed into the back of my mind. I certainly hadn't disclosed it to Ty or anyone else for that matter. Furious at Zoey for eviscerating Ty's feelings, I hadn't kept my promise to stay in touch and ignored all her messages until she stopped texting me. A little time and space made me realize that she'd been as blindsided as the rest of us, but I never reached back out.

Zane and I most definitely became each other's wingman. We'd partied and fucked our way across the US with women of every size and shape and ethnicity, which for a while was my teenage fantasy come true. My sisters would give me shit, but they didn't really need to. Reality was setting in for me. The more well-known we became, the more I was starting to get grossed out at getting with random, naked women. Monotonous blowjobs and hurried fucks in strange and often public locations were sordid and dirty and utilitarian. It reminded me that no sex came close to the night with Alex.

I was pretty sure that no night ever would.

Things took a weird turn when Alex reached back out to me a few months later and asked, on behalf of Zoey, to remove all traces of her from LTZ's social. It meant that I had to let Ty know I was in contact with his ex's best friend and tell him that Zoey had indirectly reached out to me but still wouldn't speak to Ty. I was furious because it put me in a horrible position. I refused to take any action without Ty's approval, and he was visibly crushed but acquiesced immediately. Even after she hurt him deeply, he still wanted to take care of her.

Alex tried to defend Zoey, which I found somewhat endearing because she was a loyal friend. I was loyal too—to Ty. He was my priority. It took six solid weeks to chase down all of the links and posts and get them removed. Ty's utter devastation at knowing the love of his life would be erased from LTZ's history was gut-wrenching. Those memories were what he clung to and kept him going. Now they were dust. The aftermath was agonizing. He retreated even further into his shell. His confidence was completely shot.

After that incident, I was ready to erase Alex out of my life for good in solidarity with our lead singer. I unfollowed her social, which had grown to epic proportions over the past few months. When I lost my phone, I took the opportunity to get a new number. Consequently, we lost touch.

A few months later, I received word that I was to be included in a photo shoot for *Vanity Fair* with other social media influencers. Glancing through the list, I was surprised to see that Alex was also invited. Apparently, she was in the throes of her own meteoric success and her reach had grown. She now had over five million followers. With those numbers, I couldn't help but be proud of her exceeding her modest goals. People were probably paying her phenomenal money to endorse their products and her travel expenses were likely now covered in full.

Knowing we'd see each other in New York in the fall for the photo shoot, I refollowed her and sent a DM apologizing for being a shithead, together with my new phone number. Graciously, she replied, and we occasionally texted back and forth. Not before setting some ground rules, agreeing to keep our own friendship a friendship only and completely separate from the romantic drama of our BFFs (her words, not mine).

I hadn't realized how much I needed to have a connection with a friend who had known me before I became famous. Sure, I had my family and friends at home, and my sister Jen was my rock. But, Alex was sorta famous too in her own right, so it was like having the best of both worlds. We could relate to this strange new life where people recognized us. We also knew each other for the people we were before the fame.

She and I had similar feelings about our new normal. Even though I was the least photographed member of the band, it was shocking to me at how many fan sites were dedicated to me. I was used to Ty and Zane being recognized, but now I couldn't be out in public for too long without people figuring out who I was. To my utter humiliation, Alex had gleefully shared links to a few social accounts that were dedicated to me. "VikingJace" had over a million followers where fans tagged pictures of my hair. "OFaceJace" was newer but had close to three million followers and was filled with pictures of expressions I made when I played.

Although she didn't have any embarrassing fan sites, Alex found it crazy that she was actually a "brand." As a coveted "influencer," companies paid her stupid money to pose with their products or visit their stores. Resorts begged her to stay in their finest rooms fully comped. Tourist boards of cities all over Europe invited her as a VIP. Billionaires wanted to pay her crazy money to join them on their yachts for a weekend, which so far, she had declined. But she taunted me mercilessly one night about changing her mind for the money.

We both loved what we were doing, though she was winning in the seeing-the- world department. None of us in the band were able to enjoy the cities we were playing in; our schedule was just too hectic. Living vicariously through her adventures, which were increasingly exotic, I was a bit envious that she had so much flexibility with her schedule. She was following her heart by volunteering at a horse rescue on Ibiza where she planned to stay the entire summer during the European tourist season.

My heart was strangely happy that we were back on good terms. My memories of our night together triggered something hopeful about seeing her again. When we got our tour dates, I realized Ibiza was only to be a hopper plane trip away from our show in Barcelona. I nearly invited her but had second thoughts thinking about how awkward it would be. No one but us knew we'd slept together. No one but us knew about our burgeoning friendship. Explaining her sudden presence to the guys, especially Ty, would be too weird.

I was still looking forward to Barcelona, the European tour gave us a lot more time in between shows. After the festival, we had three days off before the next gig. I had plans to take at least one day off to play tourist. Perhaps with a cute local girl to show me the sights.

Strolling the grounds of the festival on the day before the show, I filmed a lot of the set-up process for our social. Taking in the production from the stage rigging, to signage to catering, I was fascinated by the frenzy of activities all around me. Watching dozens of staff running around with their walkie talkies made me feel so appreciative. So much went into the event. Soaking in the buzzing atmosphere gratefully, it felt surreal to have come so far. A year ago, we were preparing for the Mission show. Now, we were near the top of the bill on the main stage of one of the largest festivals in Europe.

Insanity.

The next day, despite the unbearably hot late-July temperature, the show was easily one of our best. Ty was in a rare good mood, probably because there were close to 100,000 screaming fans singing the words to our songs. So powerful. The energy at an event this size was unlike anything we'd experienced so far, our biggest show in the States had been half the size. It was impossible for our singer to brood when the fans loved us so much. His insane performance spurred all of us to new heights, and it was the most incredible experience of our career.

Playing this high on the bill to crowds of this size meant that we had achieved yet another new milestone. With the success, we had additional responsibilities. Unlike when we were openers, LTZ wasn't done when we played our last encore. Generally, there were two levels of meet-and-greets with fans who paid top dollar to get their picture taken with us and LTZ swag signed. These after-show interactions were crucial to developing a strong fan base, so our management made it mandatory for us all to participate.

Once the Barcelona show was over, we quickly showered and changed in our dressing room and were ushered by a publicist through a makeshift corridor into an outdoor VIP area for the top-tier meet-and-greet event. Exclusive because it was so expensive, there weren't a lot of people who were allowed in. That was part of the draw, these fans were willing to pay to get one on one time with each of us.

As usual, Zane and I did the heavy lifting with the fans, we both enjoyed interacting with them and knew how to keep the VIPs happy. Zane could and would happily chat all night long with anyone and everyone. My talent was enabling him to ease out of conversations gracefully in order to keep things moving. Connor had no patience, but he pasted on a smile and bumbled through. Ty did the bare minimum, rarely spoke, and disappeared as soon as it was humanly possible. Oddly, it made the fans rabid for our elusive singer.

The Barcelona VIP area was a sight to behold, full of lush greenery and twinkly lights. An amazing spread of both hot and cold tapas lined the walls, Cava was flowing. Immediately, my eye was drawn to a tall girl with a hot-pink, shaggy bob, wearing aviator sunglasses. She was leaning against a willowy tree sipping a martini and checking her phone wearing a scant, black, silky slip dress that barely reached mid-thigh and draped gorgeously on her thin but muscled frame. My eyes traveled down to her incredibly long legs accentuated by spiky knee-high boots, which were held together by about thirty dainty buckles, exposing skin all the way down to her pastel-blue-painted toes.

Hallelujah! I've found my tourist girl.

She hadn't only caught my attention, Zane was staring at her too. Luck was on my side because he was sidetracked by some Spanish royalty dude who wanted guitar lessons. I was about to make my move when Pinkie noticed I was staring at her. Smiling wide, she held the cocktail up in a toast from across the room. Still technically on the clock, I wasn't drinking, but I nodded and toasted from across the room with my water bottle. Her smile lit up and she beckoned me over.

"Hi, I'm Jace." Slipping into my band VIP persona, I stuck my hand out to her.

Silently, she held her hand out to me with nails that were painted in the same shade of blue as her toes, her lips curved in a bemused smirk.

"And you are?" I encouraged, hoping she spoke English. I gallantly clasped her hand in both of mine.

The gorgeous girl just smiled and shrugged. Shit, I thought. She doesn't speak English.

"Are you here with someone?" I gestured around the area.

She just smiled at me saying nothing, her eyes hidden by the mirrored lenses of her glasses.

Zane shouted out my name to take a picture with the royalty guy and the rest of the band, so I held my finger up to her, hopefully indicating in some rudimentary sign language that she should stay put. Quickly, I fulfilled the last of my obligations for the night, never letting her out of my peripheral vision. By the time we were finished, Pinkie had moved over to a seating area and was watching me from one of the overstuffed chairs. Her long, tan legs encased in the sexy boots were crossed in front of her.

By then, Ty and Connor had left, and Zane's attention luckily shifted to finalizing plans with a young heiress and her friends to go clubbing. Finally, I made my way to the couch to join the scrumptious mystery girl.

"Hi, again," I said sitting next to her.

"Ello," she said with a weird accent, still smiling.

"What's your name?" I raised my eyebrows.

"Poppy," she said in the odd dialect, though it also sounded strangely familiar.

I squinted, looking at her closely, and recognition dawned on me, and I reached up and pulled her sunglasses off.

"Alex! Holy hell! What are you doing here!" My eyes must have been wide as saucers.

"Shhhh! I'm in disguise!" She nodded over at Zane, then laughed until she had tears in her eyes and continued in her terrible accent. "Tonight, my name is Poppy."

"Nice to meet you, Poppy." I joined in her laughter. "It fits because you're crazy!"

"I couldn't let you know it was me until Ty left." She looked around. "I did see him leave, right?"

"Yeah, he's not a fan of the social aspects of the job." I glanced around.

"How is he?" She asked sincerely.

"Devastated. Still." I said sadly. "He's getting better at hiding it, but I don't think he'll ever get over Zoey."

"I need to talk to you about all of that, but not here." She said quietly. "We agreed not to—" I started.

"This is important. But not here."

"Okay, well I'm done, let's go do something. Wait here and I'll be right back." I motioned for her to stay put while I grabbed my things.

Moving like lightning, I ran back to the dressing room for my backpack, took a second to post pics of the VIP party to social, and then I chatted with Bodie, my drum tech. Within ten minutes I was back to retrieve Alex from the party and bring her through the labyrinth of pathways to where the tour buses were parked.

"How long are you in Barcelona?" I asked as we ducked into my waiting car.

"Only until the day after tomorrow. I wasn't planning to be here but got offered ten thousand euros to post myself attending the festival today." She shrugged good- naturedly. "I couldn't say no."

"Seriously? You're making more per day than I do!" I laughed. "We've gone double platinum but haven't seen a decent royalty check yet."

"Yeah, it's pretty sweet. They put me up in a hotel, it's nice. Wait! Do you want to come back there with me?" She wrinkled her nose as if she didn't mean to blurt out the offer.

"Do you think I'm going to say no to that?" I put my arm around her, and she showed the driver the address of her hotel.

"Well, I'm not your typical skank groupie." She gently slugged me in the shoulder.

"Thank God." I leaned closer and breathed her in, she still smelled like a tropical

summer breeze on an ocean.

"Are you *smelling* me?" She looked at me incredulously.

"You smell amazing." I pulled her leg up over mine and stroked her muscled calf.

"*You* smell amazing." She lay her head down on my shoulder, sniffed my neck, and

then her blue eyes blinked up at me.

"You look gorgeous." I touched my lips to hers.

We looked into each other's eyes as we softly kissed. With the tip of my tongue, I traced the seam of where her lips met, probing gently until she opened for me. Nestling her closer against me, I wrapped my arm around her shoulders, so she was nearly on top of me. Satisfied, I stroked her inner thigh under the skimpy dress she wore. Her nipples were beaded into tight nubs, clearly visible through the thin fabric of her black dress. My dick was hard as a rock against her hip.

"Jace—" She gripped my hand when I inched closer to her pussy.

"Oh, God. Alex." I immediately stopped what I was doing. "I'm sorry, I just thought . . ."

"Oh, you thought right. It's happening. I just want to get this thing I need to tell you off my chest first." She squirmed off my lap into the seat next to me and smoothed her dress back down.

"Fine." I was so goddamn horny, and now a little annoyed. "What is it?"

"I found out what happened with Zoey." She clasped her hands together in her lap and looked down. "It's not good."

"We agreed it wasn't our business, *Poppy*." I crossed my arms and slumped back into my seat.

"Well, it also wasn't *Carter's* business." She fixed her stare at me. "Do you know what he did?"

She didn't have many details, but she explained that Carter had told Zoey to break up with Ty so that he could have a chance at living his rock star dream without being tied down. Apparently, he told her that it was for her own good since Ty would likely cheat on her after being on the road for so long. I couldn't comprehend how or why he'd do that to our singer, who had been struggling with severe depression since Zoey left.

"Fuck me. I've got to tell Ty." My face was buried in my hands, he was going to feel so betrayed.

"I know." Alex stroked my forearm.

"This could break up the band," I mumbled through my fingers. "Fuckity fuck."

"Zoey moved to Texas, you know. Just to get away from everything. She's not the same person, she's buried in schoolwork. I barely talk to her anymore." Alex looked a bit devastated by this.

"Why would Carter do this?" I looked at her, knowing that she probably didn't have the answers.

"All she would say is that Carter was convinced that Ty would give up the band to be with her." Alex nestled back under my arm. "He told her that all of you guys thought so."

"That's so manipulative." I was appalled. "I'll admit, Zane and I talked to him about it casually. Neither of us could understand why Ty wanted to get so serious at his age, but it's his life."

"Well, she was really conflicted until the night they—um." Alex scrunched her nose.

"Actually did the deed," I said helpfully.

"Um, yeah. He confessed that he didn't want to go on tour, that he would rather move with her up to Bellingham. After that, she didn't feel like she had a choice." Alex paused as if thinking about whether she wanted to say more. "That's why she's disappeared, she wanted Ty and you guys to have this chance without her holding any of you back."

"This is all so dramatic. And fucked up." I shook my head in disgust.

"Yeah. I felt the same way, but she loved him." Alex sighed. "She thought it was the only way."

"Well, maybe talking to him would have been a better idea." I opened and closed my fist. "I don't understand this at all."

"Me either. All I know is that my best friend is so heartbroken that she's a shell of her former self. She's lost twenty pounds, easily. And, in case you were wondering, I've never told her about what happened with us."

"Ah. Well, I've never told anyone either." I gripped her slender hand in mine. "As you can plainly see, Ty's still a wreck too. He's doing his best for us, but he's not all the way there."

"Do you think Zane knew?"

"No. No way." I vehemently shook my head.

"Maybe we can help them get back together." Alex searched my eyes. "Alex, I think people have fucked with them enough."

"You're probably right. Anyway, I don't mean for this to take over our night." Alex clasped our fingers together more tightly.

"Yeah. Me either. I'm not looking forward to telling him, though." I stroked her slim wrist with my thumb.

Watching the busy streets of the Gothic Quarter speed by, we sat silently snuggled together for the rest of the car ride. When the car stopped at the end of what looked a secret, private street, Alex led me through the sophisticated lobby to the elevator, where we rode up to the top floor. Lined with red, cream, and black plaid wallpaper, the hallway to Alex's room was dark but luxurious. A lot more luxurious than the hotels we stayed at. Alex swiped her card key. Smiling when the lock clicked open, she lifted her lips and kissed me hungrily. My blood pumped when she yanked me by the shirt into her room.

ALEX

CHAPTER 8

When the door shut behind us, Jace carefully turned the deadbolt and pulled me flush against his muscled body. I could hardly believe he was here with me. When I came up with my disguise caper, initially I just planned to spy on the sexy drummer boy and see if I could figure out a way to pass on the information about Carter to Zane. Immediately, Zane was giving me vibes, which was weird. Luckily, all of that went out the window when Jace walked into the VIP area. So did my plans, the minute I saw him in his tan, linen shirt with the sleeves rolled up and a pair of worn jeans. I wanted him in the worst way. So, I stared him down.

He noticed me immediately. When he approached, I panicked, and the next thing I knew I was talking in a bizarre accent. Luckily, he let me get away with it. Now, our hands were roaming everywhere on each other's bodies, rubbing, gripping, clinging, trying to touch every part.

We were kissing like we'd never kiss again. Backing me up against the cream, wainscoted wall, Jace hitched my leg high up under his strong arm and ground his pelvis against my core.

"Do you feel what you do to me, Poppy?" Jace nipped at my earlobe and gyrated his hard, throbbing shaft against me.

"Condom." I gripped the sides of his face in my hands and leaned into him.

Jace arched his eyebrow, but without missing a beat released my leg and pulled out his wallet from the back pocket of his jeans. Unable to wait, I unbuckled his belt, unzipped and pulled off his pants. His heavy, thick cock was velvet and steel in my hand, his tip dripping with moisture. Eagerly I knelt down, determined to make another first happen for me with Jace.

Suckling his bulbous tip into my mouth, I swirled my tongue along his slit, tasting his saltiness. Jace's fingers threaded into the synthetic hairs of my pink wig to hold me gently in place. I looked up at him, his ever-piercing green eyes locked with mine. He sighed heavily, watching my lips suckle his cock. Gripping the base with one hand, I kept eye contact while swiping my tongue along the length of his shaft to the root and back again.

"Alex, I'm too far gone. I'll come in your mouth if you do that again." Jace rasped before lifting me to standing position.

Using his thumbs to hook the spaghetti straps of my slip dress, Jace slid them gently off my shoulders and down my arms. The black dress floated to the ground in a puddle, leaving me naked aside from my sexy peek-a-boo boots. Gazing at my nipples, Jace suckled them both in succession while he inserted two fingers inside me, finding me dripping wet. Retrieving the condom from his wallet, he rolled it on his thick length, once again hitching my leg over his arm and backing me against the wall.

"I want to fuck you standing up." Jace guided himself against my opening and then thrust into my pussy with a groan.

"God, yes!" I cried out.

Bracing one hand against the wall, Jace's other strong arm held my leg up and to the side and drove into me over and over again with abandon. Feeling him pounding so deep inside me made me crazy with desire, and I threw my arms around his neck to hang on for the ride. When the leg I was still standing on shook after a while, Jace's strong arm lifted it up under his other arm, leaving me impaled on him, but floating and weightless.

Grinning in full dimple mode, Jace tightened his grip under my thighs and carried me across the room to the bed, bouncing me up and down on his cock. He gently laid me on the clean, white linens. My legs hung off the edge of the bed. In the kerfuffle, he slipped out of me and I felt empty, but only for a second. Gripping both of my ankles, he bent my knees almost up to my armpits, stood between my legs, and then slowly pushed himself inside me again.

Looking down, I watched him rock in and out of me, his cut stomach muscles contracting with each pass. He seemed to be just as fascinated by the view of our bodies merging, and from his vantage point, I was pretty sure that nothing was left to his imagination. When he released his grip on my ankles, I held my legs in the same position with my own hands. Jace reached down and spread my pussy lips with his thumbs to expose and rub my clit while he circled his hips to drive deeper and deeper.

"You're seriously the sexiest woman in the world," Jace growled as he picked up the pace.

The endearment made me feel shy, and I threw my arm over my

eyes. Undeterred, Jace placed a thumb, now coated with my juices, against my lips.

"Suck," Jace whispered.

So, I did.

"Ah, Fuck. Alex, I can't get deep enough." Jace fully covered my body with his, both of our legs still hanging off the bed. Gnashing teeth, colliding limbs, we ground our bodies together desperately. He took both of my hands in his and raised them above my head and he suckled my neck and lips as we sought our release.

"I'm so close." His hoarse voice was in my ear.

My body remained in motion, but I stiffened because although I felt like I was on the edge of an explosive orgasm, I needed something more and I wasn't sure what to ask for. I didn't want to disappoint him.

"Hey, hey . . ." Sensing my discomfort, Jace slowed way down and cupped my cheek. "Relax, we aren't in a hurry."

"I . . . I . . . I don't know what I need." My bottom lip quivered. Jesus. I had to stuff down my sudden urge to cry.

"Shh. Baby. Shh. It's okay." Jace pulled out of me and guided me to my feet, threw back the linens, and gestured for me to sit on the bed.

"Jace, I don't want to stop," I said, feeling like a wreck sitting naked with the ridiculous boots still buckled all the way up my legs, my skewed pink wig, and makeup melting down my face.

"Oh, we're not stopping. We're taking a little break to get you more comfortable." Jace said kindly before taking off the condom and tossing it in the trash. He knelt at my feet and got to work on the buckles.

When he removed the torture boots, he rubbed both my feet and kissed each of my toes. He then sat next to me and smoothed my fake pink hair down, reached under and took out the pins holding it to my own hair, and tossed the wig to the ground.

"Better?" This was the most gorgeous, sweet, sexy man in the history of the world.

Hands down.

"Better," I whispered.

"Scoot over." Jace motioned to me and we crawled into the big king-sized bed.

Jace rolled over on top of me and we made out again, this time slowly exploring each other's lips and tongues. He nibbled my earlobes and neck and rubbed my clit with his thumb. His lips worked his way lower to my breasts. Feasting on my soft mounds and all around my nipples, he slipped two fingers inside my pussy and fluttered the rough pads against my sweet spot, unleashing a literal flood of wetness.

He peered at me through the veil of his dark-blond mane. "Mmm. Does that feel good?"

"So good." I shut my eyes, feeling shy to look at him directly while his fingers were embedded so deep inside me.

Gone was my bravado. When I'd seduced Jace before we left, I had an excuse for my lack of skills. He seemed like the perfect guy to de-virginize me, then I'd be free to explore my sexuality all across Europe. What I hadn't known was that he'd ruin all other men for me. I'd barely made out with anyone since I'd left Seattle because they still couldn't compare. I was just as inexperienced now as I was the day that he left the note on my pillow. Suddenly, I worried that I would be a huge disappointment to my sexy drummer.

He didn't seem to notice my distress. Jace's face was rapturous when he pulled his fingers out of my opening and palmed my ass with both hands to lift me slightly. Stroking down the backs of my thighs, he splayed them under my hamstrings and opened my legs wide.

"Look at me, Alex," Jace ordered quietly but firmly.

I did. His lashes were so dark it looked like he wore permanent eyeliner. The contrast with his light-green eyes was hypnotic and mesmerizing.

"Don't ever be shy about what we do in bed," he said, piercing me with his gaze.

"I'm not?" My denial sounded like a question. He raised an eyebrow.

"Do you want me to lick your pussy?" He didn't break eye contact with me.

"Yes." I choked, squirming because I was so aroused at the thought of his talented tongue down there.

"Yes, what?" He encouraged.

"I want you to lick me," I whispered.

"Alex, I'm holding you wide open. Your pussy lips are puffy and glistening because you are so wet for me that you're dripping. Your gorgeous clit is so hard it's poking out at me. Beckoning me. I want to taste you so badly," Jace rasped. "But I won't do it until you ask."

Gazing through my legs I saw this magnificent Viking god, his granite-hard cock flush against his stomach. For me. His expression was ravenous, like he was literally starving to go down on me. I had a choice—act like a scared, shy little girl or embrace the sexy, erotic woman who this man had woken up months ago. I mean, he was naked in my bed right now. What was I waiting for?

"Please, Jace. Lick my pussy." I begged, and as the words spilled out my walls contracted strongly in a sudden shudder of release.

"God damn, I will." Jace sucked in air and buried his entire face in my folds, sucking and licking me through my orgasm, which seemed to keep rolling as he feasted on every inch of me.

"Oh my gawd!" I moaned, both hands clutching at his hair. He was unrelenting. I was unable to stop bucking and writhing with pleasure against his talented lips.

"I can't wait another minute." Jace raised up on his forearms, rolled on another condom, and slammed his cock into my soaking core, setting off a new round of tremors. With my legs firmly held wide by my palms, Jace drove into me relentlessly, riding my release until his entire face contorted into a beautiful grimace and then slackened when he came so hard he slumped on top of me, spent.

Caressing his soft hair with both hands, I brought his lips to mine. We languidly tasted and nibbled at each other until our breathing returned to normal. Still inside me, Jace attempted to roll off. The thing is, I loved his full weight on top of me. Feeling full of him. I gripped his firm bottom to keep him where he was.

"Alex, wait. I better take care of this." Jace braced himself on one hand and pulled out of me, circling the condom to keep it intact.

When he returned to bed, he tucked me against his chest and stroked my matted
hair.

"You here in Barcelona is such a trip." Jace kissed my head. "Thank you for
surprising me, I didn't expect this night to turn out so awesome."

"I'm glad it worked out." I traced the lines of his Viking tattoo.

"So . . . I'm assuming that there have been a few stinky hostel guys since you wanted me to use a condom?" Jace asked, not accusingly, mostly curious.

Propping myself up on my elbow, I gazed at him knowing that I'd never lie. "Nope, not so far. A few have auditioned, but none could have met a standard that would have compared to our night. So, I thought, 'what's the point?'"

"Alex—" Jace seemed surprised. He gulped and closed his eyes, as if regretful that he couldn't claim the same thing.

"Dude! It's okay, I know you're living the rock star life." I shrugged. "It doesn't bother me, we're friends. Really sexy friends."

"We never . . . Let's just say I thought you'd have broken hearts across Europe by now." Jace snuggled me back down to him.

"I didn't say I haven't." I laughed. "Turns out, that for me it's not easy to be easy."

"So, why did we need a condom?" Jace wrinkled his brow. "I loved being bareback

with you in Seattle, it's the only time I've ever done it."

"Well, playboy, I wasn't sure where your dick has been. Plus, I just finished a round of antibiotics for a sinus infection, so I didn't want to have any surprises." I booped his nose with my finger.

"Yeah, fair enough. I'm glad you're being safe." He booped me back. "The world doesn't need any little Jace's right now."

"Well, at least not from me." I hugged him close.

"Oh, I don't know. Maybe in ten years." Jace looked toward the ceiling, pretending to consider the possibility.

"Not this girl." I used my thumbs to point at myself. "I don't want kid babies, only animal babies."

"Really?" His eyes went wide. "All my sisters do is talk about having babies, it drives me nuts."

"Zoey used to be the same," I agreed. "I just don't have that maternal instinct."

"Huh. I've never given it much thought." Jace's eyes glazed over.

"So . . . are you able to hang out tomorrow?" I decided to change the subject, it was a little weird for me to talk about children with the sexy drummer.

"Yep, I have the whole day and night to myself."

"Excellent, then we can be tourists." I clapped my hands. "But it's nearly 4 a.m., should we get some sleep?"

We woke wrapped around each other at noon, went at each other like rabbits, showered, and found ourselves hand-in-hand exploring the stone buildings of the Gothic quarter by mid-afternoon. I wore cutoffs, a white tank, and my Frye boots. Jace borrowed a pair of my boy short underwear since he didn't have a change of clothes, which made me giggle to myself just thinking about it. They were so tight, they couldn't have been comfortable. He bought a Barcelona T-shirt, board shorts, and ball cap from one of the tourist shops, and no one recognized us as we caught up on the past ten months while we admired street art, strolled through the shops and stopped for tapas.

It was the most fun I'd had since being in Europe.

"To a fun day!" Jace clinked his glass of cava with mine.

We were sitting in a little alleyway just off of Las Ramblas, the main tourist street in Barcelona, strings of lights crisscrossed above us from building to building. Leaning back in his chair on the patio, Jace grinned at me. He looked gorgeous and also silly in his tourist gear, but it had done the trick. No one was the wiser that the drummer of the most up-and-coming band in the world was in their midst.

"A really fun day," I agreed and took a sip of the sparkling wine as the waiter brought our tapas.

"How long will you work at the horse rescue?" Jace chewed on a delicate slice of Iberian ham. "God, this is delicious!"

"Probably until New York," I mumbled through a mouthful of scrumptious crusty bread topped with spicy tomato spread.

"Will you be home for Christmas?"

"Yeah. I'm going to spend time with mom because next year I'm thinking that I'll go to Australia, maybe even travel throughout Asia." I explained. "You?"

"Doesn't look likely." Jace's face crumpled a bit. "I mean, I hope so, but our schedule seems to expand every time I get an update. We're booked through next June right now, and management wants us to release new music ASAP, so there's added pressure."

I grabbed his hand and squeezed, settling into the fact that we were really and truly good friends now. This gorgeous, seemingly unattainable sex god was someone whom I cared about, I got him. It felt good that he could talk to me about everything.

"Jace picked up a piece of bread and fixed his gaze on me. "What are you smiling about?"

"I was such a babbling idiot around you last year." I rolled my eyes. "I was just thinking that I'm so glad that we're such good friends. Today has been awesome."

"Oh, jeez. Are you friend-zoning me now?"

"Yes, but I'm sexy-friend-zoning you, remember?"

Jace's eyes were hooded and he looked down at his plate. We were silent for a minute until he looked back up again.

"I didn't realize how much I needed a day like today," he confessed.

I was stunned. "What do you mean? You've been traveling the world with your band. I'm just happy that I knew you before you were so famous."

"It's actually a pretty solitary life. All of those trite songs bands write about being on the road are true." He leaned back in his chair. "Zane and I have been partying. But Connor is with Jen, and Ty has been a reclusive, sad clown."

"Are you complaining, rock star?" I cocked an eyebrow, not exactly feeling sorry for him.

Jace sucked his lips in and then pushed them out. "No, no. It's really fun. I'm just saying there are a lot of people around us, more now than ever. Everyone wants something from us, but aside from the guys and our crew, no one really *cares* about us."

"Apparently, lots of pretty girls care."

Jace furrowed his brow. "Do you want me to apologize, Alex? Is there something we need to discuss?"

Weirdly, the way he said it felt a little like he stabbed me, which was confusing. It wasn't like I wouldn't have hooked up with a guy. Jace and I didn't have any type of commitment. I was picky, maybe I was hoping Jace would be picky too.

"I'm not shaming you, Jace. You are free to do whatever you want and whoever you want." I sat back in my chair and hoped I sounded sincere. "Just like I am."

"God, am I defensive much?" Jace's face turned red. "I'm sorry."

"No need."

"You will."

I rested my chin in my hand. "Will what?"

"Meet someone." He looked down at the table, and I could have sworn that he gulped.

"Probably."

"So . . ." He looked back at me again and threw me an apologetic grin.

"Tonight, we're hanging out together." I gripped his hand from across the table. "There's nowhere *I'd* rather be, so can we just chill for a few more hours until you have to go back to the rock star thing?"

"I'd like nothing more."

We both stood and looked at each other from under our hair. For me, I just wanted to reset the evening. I strode over to him and hip-checked him. In an instant, all was right between us again.

We walked for miles all day into the wee hours of the morning exploring the streets of Barcelona and taking goofy pictures of ourselves for our respective socials. We hit the major tourist spots, including, *Sagrada Familia, Arc de Triomf, Casa Batlló, La Catedral de la Santa Creu*, and the Port Olímpic. Along the way we did whiskey shots at an Irish pub, danced at a nightclub, and stopped for ice cream and made out in a downpour. I was having the time of my life. I'd never laughed so hard with someone other than Zoey. We made fun of ourselves and filmed each other's increasingly crazy antics as the night wore on. When the sun was coming up, we found ourselves walking along the marina back to my hotel.

"We raged all night!" I did a little dance when the first light hit the sky.

"Welcome to my world." Jace threw his arms wide and swirled around.

I wrapped my arms around myself, the whiskey coat had worn off and I was chilly from being damp. "It's not a bad world."

"You're cold." Jace wrapped himself around me. "Look at the size of those goose bumps."

"I guess I am." I had a full-body shiver. "And my feet are killing me."

"Mine too. Let's go back to your hotel. We can call a cab." He kept me close and took out his phone.

I asked, already preparing to miss him, "What time do you go back?"

"Not until late afternoon." Jace fired up a taxi app and plugged in our location. "Plenty of time to warm up under the covers. Among other things."

I didn't even notice the short cab ride back to the hotel, we were wrapped around each other with our tongues down each other's throats the entire trip. By the time we reached my room, I wanted to climb him like a tree. Spilling through the door, we tore at each other's clothes. Jace backed up to the roller chair and plunked down. Kicking off my shorts and boots, I yanked off my tank top and got to work pulling his board shorts down to his ankles. Eagerly, I reached inside the underwear he had borrowed from me and freed his hard length.

"Grab a condom from my wallet, Poppy. I want you to sit on my cock." Jace gripped the armrests on the chair, his dick pointing to the ceiling proudly.

"Oooh, very bossy!" I teased, retrieving a foil packet and handing it to him.

He kept his hands where they were and challenged me. "No, you put it on."

Carefully, I tore open the wrapper and when I looked perplexed, Jace did me a solid and helped me roll the latex over his steely erection. Straddling him, I sat on his thighs with my hands on his shoulders and he pulled me flush against his torso. Gripping himself, he flicked the tip of his dick back and forth against my clit before feeding it inside me while clasping the small of my back to keep me still. Using the leverage of the floor with my toes, I rocked against him, pressing my breasts against his chest and leaning my head on his shoulder.

We stayed rocking against each other in the chair, and the pressure he kept at the base of my spine created the friction I never knew I needed against my clit. We weren't moving at a fast or furious pace, but it felt magnificent. I was nearly caught off guard when I came hard, squeezing his cock tight with my contracting muscles. The intensity of the pleasure made me push from his shoulders, arch my back, and moan.

"You're so incredible." Jace moved me against him through my release, watching me almost studiously while remaining lodged deep inside me.

My body felt filled to capacity, and I never wanted to be empty again. "Ohhhhh," I panted.

"Your body is insane, my God." His fingers caressed my sides and moved up to cup my breasts, his thumbs strumming my nipples.

"I'm so full of you." I sighed, circling my hips around him, my arms now braced back against his knees.

"I like filling you." Jace watched himself thrust up into me, his hands now gripping my ass to keep me stationary so he could continue his movement.

My eyes closed in euphoria. Jace bore most of my weight when he rapidly moved me up and down on his cock. All I wanted to do was live in the moment with him, but it felt like I was floating above myself as his groans and the intense pleasure lulled me into a nearly dreamlike state. Vaguely, through my cries of release, I heard him shout when he came. At some point, I slumped over his shoulder after our bodies stopped moving.

"Alex . . . Alex . . ." I heard Jace's voice as if from a distance. "Mmmm." I couldn't form words.

"Oh, Poppy, you're exhausted. Let's get into bed." Jace must have had superhuman strength because even though I was only a couple inches shorter than him, he picked me up and held me like a toddler against his chest and walked the ten steps to the bed where we flopped down.

My sexy drummer rolled me under the covers and crawled in beside me to spoon. We slept for a few hours until sunlight streamed into the room. Then he made me come over and over again with his lips, fingers, and cock well past the time he was supposed to leave. Eventually, after his phone blew up from the guys and various managers, the hourglass ran out. We promised to keep in touch and to get together in New York. Jace said goodbye, took a car back to LTZ, and I slept for twelve hours straight before I flew back to Ibiza

LIMITLESS

JACE

CHAPTER 9

Leaving Alex was surprisingly hard for me, and I wasn't sure how I felt about it. She seemed really into me and I was really into her, but there was no real future for us. Because of her, the night exploring Barcelona ranked as the best night of my life. Unfortunately, no amount of texting would put us in the same city at the same time again. It seemed best to just let her go.

Plus, when we got to Paris the next day, the band went through the first of a series of rough events.

Agonized about how to relay the information Alex shared with me about Carter and Zoey to Ty, I called a band meeting. In the nearly four years LTZ had been together, none of us had ever requested a formal meeting, so the rest of the guys were on edge. I hadn't wanted to ruin that night's show, so it was late because I waited until we finished the VIP event before we congregated in our dressing room.

"Guys, I've learned something that has affected us, especially Ty, and I can't keep it to myself." I began and proceeded to provide all the details that Alex had shared about what Carter said to Zoey.

When I finished the short but shocking truth, Ty's face remained eerily passive. Connor and Zane, however, lost their minds.

"That is a bald-faced lie, Jace," Zane raged. "Carter would never do that."

"It seems pretty unlikely." Connor was calmer, but he was still pissed. "I mean, what would be the point?"

I hated being the bearer of such crazy and bad news. "Look, I'm just relaying what I was told. I don't want to start anything, but Ty, you haven't been yourself since your thing with Zoey. It's affected all of us and still does. If I was in Ty's position, I'd want to know."

"Where did you get this information?" Zane angrily pointed a finger at me.

"I can't say."

"Fuck you, Jace," Zane yelled.

Connor crossed his muscled arms and narrowed his eyes at me. "Dude, you've got to tell us."

Ty remained silent, his head down, hands clasped together. All of us sat in silence for a few minutes, and he looked up directly at me, his long, brown hair nearly covering his face. His eyes brimmed with tears, which made me feel like shit on a shoe. I wondered whether I had done the right thing. With a heavy sigh, he sniffed in deeply to compose himself.

"Alex." Was all he said before he stood and walked out.

"Are you fucking serious?" Zane spat at me when he ran past to follow his best friend.

"Is it true?" Connor took a big-brother tone with me.

"Yes." I sat back in my chair and sighed. "Alex was in Barcelona, Zoey confided in her, but Alex felt like we needed—Ty needed—to know."

"He must've had his reasons." Connor considered the situation pensively. "Carter loves Ty like a son."

"Yeah, but the fallout has been a shit-show, Connor. We need to talk to both of them." I scrubbed my hands through my hair. "I thought the right thing to do was to keep it between the four of us at first."

"So, do you have something going on with Alex?"

"Not really. But for transparency's sake, we've hooked up a couple of times. Once in Seattle. Barcelona—" I smiled. "I don't want a relationship and she's so young, she needs to go out and spread her wings."

"Ah, so that's who you were with when you kept us waiting in Barcelona." Connor smirked. "It was so unlike you to be the fuck-up."

"Yep." I couldn't feel bad, even when we partied, I was always the responsible one. I deserved a little decadence. My smile must have split my cheeks because Connor just stared at me.

"That good?"

"Yep." I wasn't about to give details; I didn't work that way. Even for Connor.

He gave me a quick nod before sighing loudly. We hadn't spent much time just the two of us in Europe, mainly because I was buried in my laptop most of the time. A myriad of expressions crossed his face from confused to thoughtful to sad. He hung his head.

"So, uh. Um. Jen's been avoiding my calls for the past week."

"What? I'm sorry to hear that. Should I call her?"

Connor seemed reticent. "Don't even try, Jace. Even for me and your sister, it's impossible to keep a relationship going on a schedule like we have. I know I'm losing her, and the funny thing is? I don't blame her."

"You're not going to quit, are you?" I was alarmed.

"No." Connor looked me in the eye. "I'm where I belong."

And so it continued. We made it through Budapest, Serbia, Denmark, Belgium, and Portugal and were going to close out our tour with the Reading and Boomtown festivals in the UK, a week off in London, six weeks of club dates across Europe again followed by Oktoberfest in Munich. Since I had to be in New York for the *Vanity Fair* shoot, we added a show at Radio City Music Hall and a few dates to bring us back to Seattle for a secret Mission show.

Management took mercy on us and was letting us have a few days off at Christmas before we jetted off for five months in Australia, New Zealand, and Asia after New Year's.

I couldn't wait for a break. Touring for so many months had gotten old. It wasn't fun anymore, we were bickering, exhausted, and cranky. Ty refused to do any press or VIP activities. Zane barely let him out of his sight, only engaging in a few random hookups. Nearly every other day, Connor and Jen had heated FaceTime fights in the close quarters of the tour bus.

Because I rarely let my emotions get the best of me, being surrounded by so much drama and tension made me feel annoyed. After Barcelona, I simply buried myself in social, determined to make up for the weird energy in the band with some cool posts of us in the cities we were visiting. It worked; our reach grew by hundreds of thousands of followers each week.

Still, my excitement at getting to New York was unexpected, and it hit me that it was because I had a huge crush on Alex, the likes of which I'd never experienced before. Certainly not with Cassie or any other hookup over the years. I hadn't looked at another woman let alone hooked up with one since Barcelona. I had no interest. No one compared to Poppy, the feisty, funny adventuress.

We texted several times a week. She seemed to be loving her time in Ibiza, she sent dozens of photos of herself with the various horses she was rehabilitating. I'd never been a horse guy, but the vision of her sitting astride a shiny, black steed in a green field, her head thrown back in utter glee, honey locks caught in the wind, was breathtaking. It was like catching a glimpse of the true Alex deep down to her soul.

My communications with Alex were the highlight of my day and were also a welcome respite from our internal band drama. As we approached our final show, my heart felt so heavy and disappointed when she couldn't make it to the UK for our week off. She texted me from some event where she'd been paid to make an appearance. I ended up on a three-day pub crawl with Connor to drown my sorrows. It took me two days to recover.

For our final gig, Limelight was on the bill at Reading, and they were going on stage right after our set. All of us in LTZ were bracing for the inevitable confrontation between Ty and Carter, which couldn't be avoided anymore. By the time we rolled onto the grounds of the festival, I was sick from the stress of it all, and the only thing keeping me sane was the promise of seeing Alex in New York for the photo shoot.

Despite all the bullshit, we killed the live show. I mean *killed*. It was game- changing. Ty was the best I'd ever seen him, but so were the rest of us. Most of the Limelight guys were standing at the side of the stage cheering us on, clearly proud of how we'd evolved, but completely unaware of the storm clouds afoot. The second we finished our set, Ty stormed off the stage like thunder past Carter toward the dressing room without any acknowledgment.

Connor and I stopped for a minute to speak to other guys in the band, after all, they had supported us for years. Carter crumpled into a ball on a massive speaker while the set change went on all around us, his head buried in his hands. Zane sat next to him, talking to him softly.

None of us except Zane watched Limelight play that night, we all sat silently in the dressing room through their entire set. It sucked. When the last notes of their encore ended, the energy became super-charged because we were waiting for Zane to bring Carter to us. Ty sat slouched back on a couch, his arms crossed over his vintage Alice in Chains T-shirt, eyes closed, his mouth set in a grim line. It was almost like he was meditating.

Footsteps approached, we watched as Zane unlocked the door and Carter followed him in, drenched in sweat. Carter pulled up a folding chair and sat down in front of Ty, but Ty refused to make eye contact.

Carter looked around at the rest of us. "Guys, could you give us a minute?"

"No," Ty said definitively, with his eyes still shut. "They stay."

"Okay." Carter sighed with resignation.

We all sat in another uncomfortable silence for what seemed like a million years.

Finally, Ty spoke. "I haven't had a reason to trust many people in my life. I trusted you. That was a mistake."

"Ty . . . I'm so sorry but . . ." Carter reached for Ty.

"Don't touch me," Ty said coldly, as though ice had invaded his veins.

Carter's voice was haunted. "Can I try to explain?"

"No. You scared away the only person that I ever loved. You hurt the woman that I'd have given this all up for, and now she won't talk to me. In fact, she will probably never talk to me again. I can never forgive you for that."

"Ty, please. You are my son as much as Zane is." Carter pleaded. "I was trying to —"

"Shut the fuck up. I am not your son. My mom is an abusive junkie whore. I have

no idea who my dad is. That is the truth of who I am, I might as well face facts." Ty stood and looked at us all. "I don't talk about my life much, but you are all my family and have put up with me this past year when I didn't deserve it. Zane, you will always be my brother. But, Carter? From now on? Stay the fuck away from me."

"Don't quit the band, Ty," Carter whispered.

Ty literally roared. "Don't you *dare*, Carter. I would *die* for my band. They're all I have. You made sure of that, and I will *never* let them down."

Ty headed for the door. Before he thundered off, he turned back to address the room. "I'm going to pour everything I have into our music. I'm done moping around over a chick who didn't care enough about me to—You know what, I'm just fucking done."

Carter sat with his face in his hands after the door slammed. I got up to follow Ty, who gave me a run for my money.

"Dude, hold up." I chased him.

"Jace, I want to be alone," Ty bellowed.

"No fucking way." I caught up to him and we strode with determination to our bus. We grabbed our toiletry bags and towels and made our way to the facilities to shower. Ty wouldn't speak, and I didn't push him. Once we were back on the bus, Ty reclined in our lounge area, shirtless in a pair of sweats. I sat next to him and put my hand on his shoulder. Ty's sad look caused a lump to form in my throat.

Despite the past couple of months of squabbling, the four of us had gotten so close, our bond felt unbreakable.

Ty sobbed silently, big tears streaming down his face. I kept my hand firmly pressed on his shoulder in support.

"How do I get over her?" He choked out sadly.

"You loved her." A flash of Alex unexpectedly crossed my mind, and for the first time, I had a glimmer of understanding of how he felt.

"No, Jace. I *love* her. I fucking love her. Still. She was it." He wiped his eyes with his thumbs. "I'll never love anyone like that again. I'll never let myself."

"When we get home, maybe you could go talk to her folks. See if you can get back in touch now that you know what happened." I offered.

"Is that what Alex said to do?" Ty looked up at me, his eyes wet with fresh tears.

"No, we made a deal not to talk about you or Zoey that way. We're friends, that's
all." I leaned back. "But, if it's any consolation, the one thing she told me—"

"Stop." Ty sighed. "Don't betray Alex's trust. I actually don't want to hear about Zoey second or thirdhand. It's too hard."

"Okay."

"I just need to make a change; I'm exhausted from always being so sad." Ty knitted his brows. "What kind of man cries himself to sleep for over a year?"

"You. You're a good man. The best front man in the business. I'll— We all will be here, whatever you need." I stood. "Do you want some time for yourself?"

"Yeah, thanks." Ty rose from his seat and jumped up into his top bunk. "Oh, and Jace?"

"Yep."

"You don't have to hide your feelings for Alex from me." Ty smiled slightly. "Um," I stuttered.

"You were with her in Barcelona, right?" He flopped back on his pillow. "Um . . ." I hung my head.

"Like I said." He flung the curtain to his bunk closed.

"Okay." I smiled to myself and went into the bathroom to get ready for bed, feeling touched that we had such a profound bonding moment.

In the weeks that followed, as an unspoken rule, no one brought up Carter when Ty was around. When the first big publishing royalty checks arrived, all of us were stunned to learn that we were millionaires. While Ty wrote most of the lyrics, all of us contributed to the music so we shared our songwriting credits equally. Somehow financial freedom lightened everyone's mood. Our hard work had paid off. We were truly a success, our bank accounts showed it.

We ended up scheduling a few more dates in Europe, and during our travel days Ty, Connor, and I all browsed real estate sites for properties in Seattle. Connor and I wanted to pay off our family's mortgages, and I bought a condo in a new downtown high-rise, sight unseen. Ty wanted to purchase his own place outright, so he'd never be homeless again, and he lined up a realtor to help him. Zane was less enthused about becoming a landowner and wanted to wait until he got home to make any decisions.

Just when things seemed to be getting happier, my sister dropped a bombshell when she showed up in Munich for Oktoberfest. Connor had been ecstatic for Jen's visit; he hadn't seen her in person for months. Many of their fights were because Jen hadn't made the effort to visit him on the road. Their relationship was strained, but he seemed hopeful that reconnecting would put them back on track.

They left right after the show for the hotel. Ty, Zane, and I, on the other hand, went out and got obliterated on giant mugs of Augustiner beer with some of the other bands. There may or may not have been lederhosen involved. When I finally stumbled into my hotel suite near dawn, I was shocked to find my sister curled up and asleep on the pull-out couch.

"Jen? What the fuck?" I slurred.

"Sorry, baby bro, do you mind if I sleep here?" She sat up, pulling the blankets around her.

"Of course not. Where's Connor?" I plopped down next to her.

"I had to break it off, J-bird," Jen said, puffing a bit of air out between her lips. "It's been coming for a long time, and I couldn't keep going anymore."

I just stared at her, shocked.

"I cheated on him." Jen looked down.

"What? Why?" I felt immediately defensive for Connor.

"Because I fell in love with someone else." Jen reached out and clasped my wrist. "I'm in love with Becca, Jace."

"Oh. Wow." I was instantly sober.

"I've known for a long time." She sighed. "It was just hard for me to admit it to myself."

"Oh, Jen." Her revelation was surprisingly unsurprising now that it was out. "If that's how you feel, I'm so glad that you did. You should always be true to yourself; Connor will understand that."

"He's sad and confused, he's going to need you and the guys." She started to cry. "I love him so much, but I—"

"You can't love him that way because you're gay." I pulled her to me and squeezed her tight.

"Yes." She sobbed. "I didn't want to hurt him, I never wanted to hurt him."

"It will be okay." I held my sister tight. "He'll be okay."

"He deserves to have someone who can love him the way he deserves. He's the best man I know." Jen snuggled into me. "Well, besides you."

"I love you." I looked at her with compassion, I really did love my sister. All of my sisters.

"I love you more." Jen elbowed me.

"Nah." I gave her a soft noogie. She might be older than me, but I was bigger.

Connor actually took the news as well as could be expected. In many ways, it was like a weight was lifted off him. He had remained staunchly faithful to her despite their rocky relationship and the hordes of groupies that vied four our attention each night. For the first time in the band's history, all of us were single.

After we finished the final shows and had a few days off while the crew got our equipment sorted out and shipped to New York, the four of us went to a resort in the country. We hadn't hung out together with no schedule and no work obligations for nearly two years, and it was a welcome break. For three days we slept, ate good food, and did nothing except jam through some of the songs we all had been writing.

The material was explosive, raw, and explored the gamut of emotions we were all feeling. Ty's attempt to get over Zoey. Connor's reflection on the demise of his long-term relationship with my sister. My developing feelings for Alex. Zane's underlying anger at his father.

Anguish. Hope. Anger. Resolution.

We captured each of these emotions in the new material. All in all, it was magic.

After we heard the final masters, I'd like to say that the four of us looked at one another and knew that our lives were about to change even more than they already had.

Once the world heard our new music, however, no one could have prepared us for the type of fishbowl fame waiting for us just around the corner.

ALEX

CHAPTER 10

My face looked completely different after the hair and makeup people were through with me. I'd never worn so much foundation or eyeshadow in my life. I never planned to do it again. As if I weren't already nervous enough to see Jace, I wondered if he'd even recognize me. We hadn't been in touch in a few days, which was weird, but I figured I'd see him on set.

Dragging the long, unwieldy skirt attachment to the flesh-colored romper they dressed me in, I was led to an empty studio where I was posed on a square, white box against a green backdrop. After ten minutes of photos that I assumed were testers, I finally raised my hand to get the photographer's attention.

"Um, excuse me, but where are the others?" I gestured around me, genuinely confused.

"What others?" Photo-dude looked at me strangely.

"The others for the photo, one of my friends is supposed to be here."

"Um, no, we take shots of you individually, and then I'll splice everyone together during editing." He shot me a snobby look like I was an idiot. "You're my last subject."

My heart dropped to my knees. I'd been looking forward to New York for months. It had been so disappointing when I couldn't meet Jace in London. Trying to be professional, I followed directions and finished the shoot, but broke down in tears when I got back to the dressing area. A full, blubbering meltdown. Grateful that no one was around to see me like this, I composed myself after a few minutes and found my phone.

Alex: Ru in NYC?

Jace: ... Jace: ... Jace: ... Jace: No

Alex: Where u at? Jace: Seattle Alex: Damn

Jace: Ru ok?

Alex: Y just sad ur not here

Jace: sorry

Alex: See u in Seattle?

Jace: leaving tomorrow

Alex: oh

Jace: sorry

Alex: me too

I hated myself for doing it, but I Googled LTZ to find out where he would be, and it looked like they had dates all across Asia for the next two months, starting with Hong Kong for New Years. A part of me wanted to drive right to JFK and jump on a flight to intercept him, but something deep inside me started putting up a wall. Jace hadn't promised me anything, and we certainly were not a couple. It was time for me to get over my girlish crush on a man who had the world at his feet.

Freedom from chasing Jace around gave me an opportunity to have some downtime with my mom. The two of us had an extended visit from Thanksgiving through New Year's Day. It wasn't relaxing, we made about a zillion holiday pies to fulfill her orders. Working side-by-side with my mom was strangely satisfying. It was surprising when my dad was actually complimentary about my success, as were my brother, Allen, and sister, Ariana. It felt good not to be the baby-didn't-go-to-college-fuckup anymore, I had more money in my bank account than any of them at this point. Somehow that gave me credibility. And freedom.

Sadly, Zoey didn't come home for the holidays, her folks met her in Texas and took her to Florida for Christmas. She barely texted me anymore, claiming that she was too busy trying to get through undergrad quickly to go to law school. Truthfully, I thought she was hurt when I'd confessed about my hookup with Jace. And angry that I told the band about Carter. We'd never gone through a stretch like this during our entire friendship. I felt very abandoned and alone.

By January, I was ready to get back to work again and decided that Sydney, Australia, would be my next destination. For one thing, it was summer there, and why not chase an endless summer? For another, I'd lined up a few high-paying gigs and a six- month volunteer stint at a horse rescue north of Sydney in a rural town that looked absolutely stunning.

I told myself that I had already planned on going this direction before I'd learned that LTZ would be in the same part of the world. Telling myself this little white lie over and over made it seem quite true.

Regardless of why I went to Sydney, the experience was life-changing for me, in more ways than one. Once the *Vanity Fair* article hit in February, my social presence increased to nearly ten million followers, which put me in an entirely new influencer category. My mind was blown by the level of success and opportunities that were coming my way.

Being a public persona was weird, so I really wanted to choose what I did wisely. Agents, managers, and lawyers were circling my wagon, but I decided to manage myself. Mainly because I knew what mattered to me. The money I made gave me the power to raise awareness of animal rights issues throughout the world. When I volunteered at an organization and set up a fundraiser, my following gave them access to more money than they had ever dreamed possible.

It was a big responsibility. An endorsement from @ alexlerouxseattle meant exposure. The exposure led to scrutiny. Before I'd commit to a non-profit, I had to research it meticulously. I'd even created applications. A lot of my time was spent vetting these places to make sure that any money raised under my name would be used for the right things.

Australia was such an incredible country that placed such a high value on conservation. They also had so many species that needed help. My plan was to spend six months, one month each at rescues for racehorses, dingo-hybrids, kangaroos, emus, and two months at the Great Barrier Reef to delve into all of the sea life conservation efforts. Each of these organizations received over a million Australian dollars from my followers, which was record-breaking fundraising in the animal rights community. The best part about all this was now I was more famous for my animal charitable work than my single- girl travel tips.

Television, radio, and podcast hosts began to book me, literary agents contacted me to write books, producers wanted me to be on television shows. One company wanted to create an entire docu-reality show around my adventures, it was crazy. Despite all these opportunities, I found that I didn't crave the spotlight. I preferred to work behind the scenes.

The other big change for me was my Australian boyfriend, Sam. We met at the Great Barrier Reef and hit it off immediately. He was gorgeous. His sandy-brown hair was longish and wavy, his chocolate-brown eyes were kind, and his body was surfer- licious. His heart was in the right place too, including our shared passion for animal rights. We were still in that googly relationship stage where we couldn't keep our hands off each other.

Until Sam, it had been a nearly eight-month sex drought after Barcelona. I was desperate to recreate the immense pleasure I'd discovered with Jace.

There was only one small problem.

Yeah.

Sam was on his "gap" year, which many Aussies took during college, so he didn't have any responsibilities. We could spend all of our time together, and he traveled with me for work and fundraising activities. I'd never dated anyone so proud to call me his girlfriend. I'd met all of his friends, learned how to surf, and spent a lot of time at his parents' house in the suburbs of Sydney. Everything was perfect on paper, and it was awesome to have companionship after being on my own for so long.

Plus, I loved Australia. My only problem was the visa. I was on my second ninety- day visitor's visa, and once it ran out, I'd have to leave. During my first stint, I'd popped over to New Zealand for a couple of weeks for a vacation and came back to Oz. With my social media presence through the roof, I didn't want to risk getting kicked out on a technicality.

According to the Australian government, I wasn't legitimately working. The "influencer" career was such a new "profession" that there were no rules to follow about how I was paid or where to pay taxes. My dad helped me get a business manager to help with all of that, but I couldn't help but wonder if the shit would hit the fan.

Toward the end of my second visa, Sam and I were having dinner at his folks and Sam got down on his knee and asked me to marry him. Shocked, I didn't know what to do. I loved him, but I certainly wasn't sure about forever with him.

His whole family got excited and all of a sudden there was talk about fiancé visas and me moving to Australia permanently. Aside from my mom, it was the first time in forever that I felt enveloped with acceptance. Zoey and I hadn't spoken in months. Jace and I had basically lost touch too, only checking in with each other occasionally.

Suddenly, becoming Sam's fiancée felt like the best idea in the world. In fact, I convinced myself that it was the answer to more than just my travel issues. He gave me his grandmother's ring, a simple band with a small diamond and two emeralds. When we called my mom to tell her the news, I couldn't help but think of Jace when the sparkling green of the precious stone flashed in light. Pushing the thoughts away, I threw myself fully into the engagement.

Sam's folks didn't waste any time setting us up with a solicitor to begin processing my fiancé visa. Once I didn't have to worry about getting kicked out of the country, time went by super-fast. I was caught off-guard when a calendar reminder popped up on my phone about LTZ's Sydney show.

It hadn't seemed relevant to tell Sam about my not-quite romance with Jace because, in all honesty, there wasn't much to tell. When every media outlet began advertising the concert, I stupidly let it slip that I knew the band. And that my best friend had dated the lead singer. Sam lost his mind and begged me to try and get us into the show.

Even though I could find my way into any event in the world, something compelled me to reach out to Jace for passes.

He enthusiastically said yes.

Hand-in-hand, Sam and I picked up our tickets at will-call. Jace left us all-access laminates, which we hung around our necks and entered the stadium. It should have been a fun night, but my stomach churned with anxiety at the situation I'd put myself in.

All I could think about was seeing Jace and launching myself into his arms.

So inappropriate.

A bigger part of me was dreading seeing the sexy drummer. I hadn't told him about Sam, let alone that we were engaged. I was a professional withholder of information.

Gawd.

My fiancé was so damn excited to meet the band, I didn't have the heart to say no. Did I mention how much the word "fiancé" bugged the crap out of me?

Fee-yawn-say. Ugh.

With all of my random thoughts, I did realize that it would be weird not to go, and at least say hi. After all, I did get the passes. Sucking it up, I pinged him.

Alex: Yo - I'm here.

Jace: Cool where ru, I'll have security come get you.

Alex: I'm with a date.

Jace: Oh, ok.

Alex: Is it?

Jace: Of course.

Alex: I'm stage right.

Jace: ok sending someone

A big, burly, tribal-tattooed aborigine dude approached the security gate and motioned me over. Clutching Sam's hand tightly, I followed him through the backstage area down a dark hallway into LTZ's dressing room. The minute I was through the door, Jace, Connor, and Zane surrounded me and gave me full-body hugs.

"Hi, guys! This is my boyfriend, Sam." I motioned to my guy, who looked shellshocked to be in the same room as his favorite band.

"Fiancé," Sam said politely as he shook their hands. "We just got engaged." Ugh.

I couldn't meet Jace's eye for some reason, but Zane reached down and grabbed my hand to look at the ring.

"Nice one, Alex." Zane threw his arms around me again. "It's good to meet you, Sam, welcome to the family."

Looking up from under my fisherman's hat, I caught Jace's eye. He was delicious. His cheekbones were more pronounced than usual. His green eyes were the same color as my ring. The front part of his dirty-blond hair was pulled back into a braid. All he had on were tight black bicycle shorts, an LTZ T-shirt, and sneakers. Keeping his expression blank, he subtly swept his eyes up and down my body.

"Congratulations." He looked like he swallowed a watermelon, but he still held out his hand to Sam. "Nice to meet you, Sam. You better take good care of her."

"Surely, I will mate!" Sam said too loudly in his distinct Aussie brogue. Which suddenly sounded cartoonish.

"Dude, we gotta get warmed up for the show." Connor broke up the reunion up by herding the guys.

"Feel free to hang out here, you can go wherever you want." Jace motioned to the spread before ripping off his shirt and tossing it onto the couch. His eyes never left mine.

I knew what he was doing.

"If you want to watch from the side stage, it's pretty cool. The sound's not as good, though." Zane offered helpfully.

"Does Ty know I'm here?"

"Yeah. I told him. He's warming up in his dressing room." Jace grabbed a bandana and tied it around his hair, his pecs and biceps flexing with the effort. "I doubt he'll make an appearance, don't take it the wrong way."

"Okay. Well, we'll head out and stay out of your way." I took Sam's hand and headed for the door. "Great to see you all."

"Come back after the show, Alex!" Zane called after me.

Rather than watching from the side of the stage, Sam and I stood right in front of the security gate. Out of some sort of loyalty to Sam, I positioned myself purposefully so that I didn't have a good visual of Jace.

Even though he was the only member of LTZ I wanted to ogle.

The only band member I *would* ogle.

Which still wasn't appropriate.

So it just seemed easier to resist temptation.

Shirtless Jace in the dressing room stirred up the most intense sexual longing I'd ever experienced. My life choices suddenly seemed stupid and meaningless. I felt like I was going to throw up. Sam was rocking out and oblivious to my distress, thank God.

The part of the show I managed to pay attention to was incredible.

Ty was absolutely hypnotizing. Zane and Connor rocked. Jace probably did too. But, again, I couldn't see him.

I was miserable. I had to get out of there.

Sam was disappointed when I pleaded with him to leave early after claiming that I was getting a migraine. In reality, just seeing Jace made me want to stowaway on their tour bus. I knew that if I wanted to give Sam half a chance, I had to immediately get away from LTZ and my past.

I also knew, without a shadow of doubt, that if Jace and I were to find ourselves alone somewhere backstage or at an afterparty, I wouldn't be able to stop myself from kissing him. Or sucking on his. . .

I was a monster.

Hours later back at our flat, Sam was sleeping soundly. I was wide awake. Careful not to disturb him, I snuck outside to sit and think on the veranda. My mind raced. I wondered what the hell I was going to do. I needed my BFF.

Alex: Z are you there? Zoey: ...

Zoey: ... Zoey: Hey!

Alex: I miss you.

Zoey: I miss you too.

Alex: I'm engaged to Sam the Aussie. Zoey: What????

Alex: Long story, I'm living in Oz.

Zoey: WTF! R you going to get married?

Alex: Dunno, for fucks sake, I'm only 21.

Zoey: Huh. Well, I'm going to law school.

Alex: Will you come to Australia and be in my wedding if I go through with it? Zoey: Something tells me that I won't need to worry about it.

Alex: Full disclosure - I saw LTZ tonight in Sydney.

Zoey: ...

Zoey: ...

Zoey: I can't talk about Ty. Sorry.

Alex: I know, I'm sorry, but I didn't want to lie to you.

Zoey: It's ok.

Alex: Please don't disappear again, I need you.

Zoey: It's hard when you're with them, I'm jealous and sad.

Alex: You could talk to Ty.

Zoey: ...

Zoey: ...

Zoey: Gotta go, love you don't get married without me.

Alex: love u2, I won't.

I despaired as I wrapped myself snugly in a blanket, and I was not the despairing type.

How did I end up engaged? Why did I bring Sam to the show? Did I want to throw it in Jace's face? Did I want to be with Jace? Even though I only saw him for a few minutes, his mere presence brought up a groundswell of feelings. Feelings that had no basis in reality. Jace had never given me any indication that he wanted us to be a couple. So why was I so conflicted?

My phone buzzed interrupting my thoughts.

Jace: Where did you go?

Alex: headache

Jace: huh

Jace: You looked beautiful, are you happy?

Alex: I don't know how to answer that.

Jace: huh

Jace: Sam seems nice.

Alex: He is.

Jace: Do you love him?

Alex: Yes . . .

Jace: But?

Alex: I'm barely 21, WTF am I doing.

Jace: You said you'd meet someone.

Alex: I know.

Jace: I can admit that I was hoping tonight would go a different way.

Alex: huh

Jace: We head back to Seattle tomorrow.

Alex: Say hi to Seattle, I'm missing home.

Jace: So, do you live here?

Alex: Y for now

Jace: I want the best 4u.

Alex: I know, I want the same 4u.

Jace: I should get going.

Alex: Ok.

Jace: jealous, u know

Alex: Have u been celibate for a year?

Jace: What if I told you I was?

Alex: ???

Jace: No, I can't lie.

Alex: Then u can't be jealous, it doesn't work that way.

Jace: I know.

Alex: ok Jace: ok

Alex: keep in touch

Jace: Maybe, it's best I let you off the hook on that.

Alex: we're friends

Jace: sexy friends

Alex: right

Jace: Take care, Poppy.

Alex: You too.

Tears streamed down my face and I curled up into a ball and wept, trying hard to sort out the mess I was in. Sam was awesome and I loved being with him, but after seeing Jace, I realized that I didn't love him the way I should. I was pretty sure I loved Jace.

But, did I know what love was?

Jace was unavailable. It wasn't like if I broke up with Sam that my sexy drummer would call me his girlfriend or propose marriage. For nearly three years, outside of our two days in Barcelona, I'd been alone. I'd met a lot of friends, but they were transients like me. Sam was truly awesome, and now that I had someone who really wanted to be with me, how could I leave him behind?

Then again, how could I stay?

CHAPTER 11

TWO YEARS LATER

Ordinarily, we didn't have to be at the venue on a load-in day, but since it was the beginning of the Z tour in Europe our new publicists hired a crew to shoot a bunch of behind-the-scenes footage and we wanted to do a run-through of the live show. Now that we had truly hit the big-time, our schedules were more packed than ever before. Even with an actual staff to handle a lot of the mundane things we used to do, it felt like we had even less time for ourselves.

Strolling through the bowels of the SSE Arena in Belfast, I watched the flurry of activity related to our new stage, which was in the final stages of being set up. The crew was scurrying around troubleshooting the lighting, rigging, and PA systems, and the arena staff was equally as busy making sure catering was perfect and the dressing rooms followed our riders.

My favorite part of production was watching the safety checks on the special effects we had incorporated into our live show. The LTZ experience now involved lasers, pyrotechnics, and a couple of aerial tricks which, when you were in the middle of playing, were hard to fully appreciate. I wanted to take photos for the social media feeds from the audience's perspective.

Afterward, I headed to the dressing room. Connor and Zane were already there getting ready for our photo shoot. With my uniform of a T-shirt and khaki shorts, I was ready. I still hated the bullshit man-primping our "advisors" kept encouraging. My one act of rebellion.

No one knew where Ty was, so I went to look for him. Sure enough, he was in the stairwell getting a blowjob from some random chick. I could see her tousled black hair bobbing back and forth on his dick. His new normal. When he caught my gaze, his blue eyes were hollow. His face didn't really register any sense of enjoyment.

"Dude, finish up." I rolled my eyes.

"That's enough." Ty pulled the chick off his cock by her cheeks and stood up, tucked himself back into his threadbare jeans, and followed me back to the dressing room without giving her a second look.

"Ty—" I really didn't know what the fuck he was doing anymore.

"Don't say a fucking word." Ty glowered at me.

"I'm not going to tell you what to do." I clapped his back. "But, fucking Zoey out of your system isn't working."

"I sing these songs about her night after night." His deep voice was strained. He leaned over and shook out his hair. "I thought it would be cathartic. But it's not. It's still killing me. Slowly. Each day."

"Well, that's pretty dramatic." I cocked my head. "She's probably heard the record, maybe they're killing her."

"You'd know more than me."

My heart constricted a bit, but mostly, I tried not to think about the willowy stunner. "I haven't talked to Alex in a long time, my brother."

"The truth is, I wish I could hate her." Ty fixed his eyes on me. "But, I don't. I could never hate her."

"What bullshit are you trying to prove by fucking all of these randoms?" I squinted at him.

Ty shook out his arms and hooked his thumbs in his jeans. "I'm just trying to have some fun."

"Well, is it working?"

"Sometimes?" Ty scrubbed the dark stubble on his face with his hand.

I could relate, though I couldn't tell Ty that. When I'd learned that Alex was engaged to the Aussie, I'd gone straight back into fuck 'em and leave 'em mode. Consequently, she and I lost touch after our show in Sydney.

With the exception of her angry demands that I protect Zoey after Z was released, which I did, the airwaves had been radio silent between us. Occasionally I trolled her 'Gram, which nowadays only had pictures of her doing charitable things for various animals.

It sucked. Losing touch with the people who knew you before you were famous was one side-effect of becoming well-known. We were away from our families and friends for years at a time, and life went on without us. When we'd get back home, there was an adjustment period to assimilate back into some semblance of a regular routine. Which was virtually impossible because you missed so much day-to-day stuff.

I was still fairly close with Jen, but I hadn't seen my parents and other sisters in almost a year. My family's thrill at my fame waned when fame became "normal."

But being recognized everywhere didn't allow us to live like normal people.

Another side-effect (or perk, depending on how you looked at it) was the sheer abundance of yes-men/women who surrounded us. People would do anything to spend time with a famous musician. And because they read about you in the press and saw your photos posted all over social, they really thought they *knew* you.

Sure, the first couple of years it was cool to be recognized. Mostly because I appreciated the fans so much. It got tougher and tougher because more information was available about us. Not much was accurate. The truth of the matter was no one really knew us. Not really. Everyone just thought they did.

The sex, drugs, and rock and roll lifestyle was hard to resist. Women and men propositioned us relentlessly all day long. We had world-class travel and entertainment at the snap of our fingers. Access to anyone or anything at pretty much anytime, whether it was good or bad for you, was expected. The crew and management staff took care of all of our needs, including grocery shopping and laundry. This was a necessary evil because it became a real pain in the ass to try to do any of this ourselves.

A simple trip to the supermarket for a pint of ice cream could, if you let it, turn into a two-hour autograph and selfie marathon in the best of times. Or, a mob-mentality security nightmare in the worst.

I'd often reminisce about that wonderful day in Barcelona with Alex when I was able to roam the streets without being recognized. I couldn't think of too many days since where I was able to be fully incognito.

We were making our way back to the dressing room when my thoughts were interrupted by our publicists, Sienna and Andrew, who handed me a laundry list of tasks for us to complete over the next two days. We were also presented with invites to a number of parties all over Belfast tonight and again tomorrow after the show. We'd never been to Ireland, and the red carpet had been rolled out.

A big part of me missed being fully in charge of our marketing, but my day-to-day obligations as a member of LTZ had made it too hard to manage both. For the most part, I still kept up our social. But the new team was professional and had long relationships with the media. We had more press coverage than ever. Was it good coverage? I wasn't so sure. Everything felt contrived.

In my opinion, their strategy was in direct contrast to our core values as a band and as authentic Seattleites.

My biggest concern, at the moment, was that our manager Katherine was on the verge of staging an intervention with Ty. Sienna, in particular, encouraged him to drink and party because he did stupid things that generated press. In my opinion, our singer's self-destruction had bigger ramifications than how many views LTZ got on YouTube.

But it wasn't my call on the marketing anymore.

What I could control was steering things with Ty in a more positive direction. Since the Carter debacle, Zane and Ty hadn't been as close. Zane had also given up trying to stop Ty from partying.

I planned to try to break through. After the photo shoot, we rode to the hotel together and I resumed our earlier conversation.

"I've been thinking. I'm going to quit drinking on this next leg of the tour and start working out instead. Do you want to join me?" I knew that if Ty didn't clean up his act soon, Katherine would likely send him to rehab.

Ty wrinkled his nose. "I don't know, Jace."

"No pressure."

"Look, I know that my emotions have been all over the map for years. I think I've finally run out of gas on the anger thing."

I didn't say anything, I just looked at him.

"Tell me this—Why is everyone so freaked out about me finally getting drunk and laid? Isn't that what everyone expected me to do when we started this thing? Carter sure did."

"Forget Carter." I leaned back against the smooth leather of the town car. "In answer to your question, you just aren't yourself. I mean, are you doing what you want to do? Or what Andrew and Sienna want you to do?"

Ty shot me an arrogant smile. "Fuck if I know. It sucked ass being a sober recluse emo-guy. I'm trying on party slut aggro-guy for size."

"Dude." I didn't know what to say.

Ty fixed his gaze past me out the window, a faraway look in his eyes. "The thing is, when I'm onstage it all goes away. There's nothing like it, right?"

"Yeah."

"But after? I'm so fucking lonely. I just want that feeling of peace that I had with Zoey. I'm chasing it, and I don't want to stop until I find it again." Ty crossed his arms protectively around himself. "I know you think I just want to fuck her out of my system, and maybe you're right. But, nothing else has worked."

"It's not working though, is it?"

"Not even a little bit."

I was just as guilty. But fucking wasn't the root of the problem. The party favors were.

Zane and Connor had substance abuse in their family history. Even though they had their own proclivities, both were surprisingly regimented when it came to drugs and alcohol. I'd always been able to take it or leave it. On the other hand, Ty, who at one time had been the most diligent to avoid repeating his mother's descent into self-destruction, was on the brink of disaster.

Zane was so sick with worry that he couldn't bear to be around him. He's already lived through his father's addiction.

Although Connor and Ty didn't have the type of relationship where they confided in each other, our burly bassist often protected him when he was inebriated.

On the other hand, hours of my time had been spent dealing with the fallout on social media.

We rode in silence for a while.

"Fuck. I think I need to talk to someone." Ty's admission surprised me, although it shouldn't have, his self-awareness had always been astute when he actually focused on it.

"Who? Like a counselor?"

"Maybe? Look, I know I'm acting out. I don't want to be like my mom, and just listening to myself—Fuck, that's exactly who I'm becoming." Ty's voice was barely audible, but I heard him loud and clear.

I had hoped for a breakthrough and now that it was happening, didn't want to interrupt.

"It's exactly who I'm becoming," Ty repeated. His blue eyes were haunted as we pulled up to the hotel.

"My brother, you just need to be yourself. You can turn this around." I clamped my hand on his shoulder. "I'm always here if you need to talk. We all are."

"Yeah." Ty squinted at me. "Thanks."

"When you're ready. Love you, man." I patted his back. Ty's puzzled expression took me by surprise.

"I do love you. You're my brother. And an amazingly strong man.

You've endured a shitty childhood with grace. Your ability to craft a song from your life experience is masterful. Your voice is what makes us a band. You're a great friend, loyal and kind. I'm lucky that you're in my life." Words poured out of me, which was so unusual because I wasn't ordinarily a sentimental type. "I'm here for you, always."

His eyes welled but, in an instant, he sniffed the tears away and let out a heavy breath to compose himself.

"I'm going to do my best to live up to that, Jace." Ty's deep voice was strong and firm. Then he shot me a wry smile before fixing his expression into his stage persona when he got out of the car.

Before I could get out, he popped his head back through the door and winked. "But, not tonight."

All I could do was shake my head and vow to mind my own business going forward.

That night we put on one hell of a show. Years of touring in so many different types of venues had given us mad performance chops. Every one of us was in sync. With all of the new production bells and whistles, Belfast was officially phenomenal.

Which meant that I was on a super-high after burning off what felt like 10,000 calories beating on my drums.

The tour's next stop was in Edinburgh, which meant the crew had to break down and pack up the stage right after the show. The entire next day would be a travel day for them followed by a day of load-in.

LTZ had two entire blessed days off in Northern Ireland before we had to catch a hopper flight to Scotland. There was discussion about a private *Game of Thrones* tour which we had all finally caught up on, but that night we all had an appearance at the Titanic Experience, which was closed for an LTZ exclusive afterparty.

With nine interactive galleries over multiple floors, the tourist attraction was really impressive. For logistics' sake, it wasn't often that we had an after-show event at such a cool location. Despite the late hour, the four of us were in great spirits. As guests of honor, we received a private tour and enjoyed all the special effects and the meticulous full-scale reconstructions of the fated ship.

Because we were in Ireland, my own pledge from earlier in the day to not drink went out the window. The Guinness and whiskey were flowing like water, and the party was like nothing I'd ever been to.

Fuck it, why not celebrate?

A few hours later, we had finished all the glad-handing and were sufficiently drunk. A traditional Irish band was playing lively songs, the partygoer's inhibitions were beginning to loosen, and everyone was having a fantastic time.

Ty was on a bench outside one of the exhibits, sloppily making out with a redhead who was sitting on his knee. His hand was shoved into her top gripping her tits.

Connor was missing.

Zane was up onstage with the trad Irish band rocking out to the delight of the VIP fans who were lucky enough to be there.

Gripping a new perfectly poured Guinness, I was enjoying my buzz watching the music when I felt someone watching me. A few feet away, a girl with long, straight black hair and unusual violet eyes swayed to the music while trying to catch my eye. It worked, I nodded to her and she smiled back at me. Shoving my hands in my hoodie pockets, I leaned back on the pillar closest to me and waited to see if she'd come over.

They usually did.

She laughed. She actually threw back her head and laughed, which was absolutely delightful. I was playing games, and she was calling me on it. Shaking my head, I approached her making sure my dimples were on full display. She was beautiful and exotic. Her eyes were heavily lined in black. She wore an off-the-shoulder, long white shirt over black leggings with—black Frye boots.

By the time my inebriated mind caught up with what I was seeing, I was standing right in front of her. My eyes snapped up and locked with hers.

Alex held her arms open. I rushed to her, squeezing her close like a boa constrictor before picking her up off the ground to swing her in a full circle. Carefully setting her back down, I gripped her face with both hands and pressed my lips to her forehead.

"Ohmygod, I'm so happy to see you!" My heart exploded with joy. "Please tell me you didn't dye your hair black!"

"Nope, I'm in disguise!" Alex posed before bursting into giggles and shaking her dark hair out.

"Were you at the show?"

"Of course! You guys were so great." Alex's eyes shined with sincerity. "I hadn't seen a show since, well, I left the last show early. The second I found out you'd be in Belfast, I made plans to be here."

"Wait, so you came to Belfast to see us?"

"No, I live here," Alex grabbed my hand excitedly. "At least for the moment, Ireland is awesome."

"Didn't you get married?" I looked around. "Where's the guy?"

"No, it didn't work out."

"I'm sorry." I hoped my voice sounded somewhat sincere.

I wasn't sorry.

"Eh. It's fine." Alex seemed pretty indifferent, but it was clear she didn't want to talk about it. "What's your schedule? I'd love for us to catch up."

"We're off for two days, then heading to Scotland." I looked around for the guys. "We could start now, I'm done here."

Alex caught my gaze, her intention crystal clear. "Do you want to come back to my place?"

"I'd love to." My voice nearly broke with anticipation.

"Jace, I've missed you."

"I've missed you too, Poppy." I wrapped my arms around her tightly. "But, seriously. Why the costume?"

"Because it's fun. Barcelona was fun. Being undercover keeps you on your toes." She winked. "Plus, Ty."

I laughed, really laughed for the first time in ages.

Alex and I wound through the crowd toward the exit. I made sure to thank the promoters and a couple of the Belfast VIPs on the way. When we passed Ty, who still had his tongue down the ginger girl's throat, Alex made a gagging gesture with her finger. Zane and Connor were nowhere to be found, but I texted them that I'd be in touch the next day.

Then we were free.

Sinking back into the leather seats of the limo they provided, Alex and I faced each other. Neither of us could stop smiling.

She pressed her long legs outside of mine, our knees touching. A fire raged through my system. I wanted her. I couldn't believe it had been almost two years. She was the most stunning woman I'd ever seen. With almost no trace of the innocent schoolgirl I'd met at The Mission.

"You get more handsome every time I see you." She leaned back, looking at me confidently.

"And you get more beautiful," I countered, keeping her gaze.

It was on. It was so on.

Alex's studio flat was located on a tree-lined street. Small, but modern, the entire layout consisted of a queen bed, a small desk, a utilitarian bathroom, and a kitchenette. Watching her gracefully navigate around her space, something clicked into place.

Game of Thrones tour be damned, I didn't plan on leaving Alex until I had to catch my flight to Scotland.

Or maybe ever.

"Beer?" Alex reached down and opened a small fridge. "Why not?" I accepted it and plopped down on the bed.

Leaning against the wall with a beer in hand, her long legs crossed in front of her, Alex regarded me.

"I'm actually feeling a little nervous," she admitted.

I took a long pull from my beer. "Why?"

She cast her eyes down. "Last time I saw you, it was weird for me." I remained silent, waiting for her to continue.

"Even though I should have done it right after your show, I finally called the engagement off last year. I was too young." Alex's voice was measured. "Sam was awesome, but he wasn't my forever."

"Well," I didn't even try to hide my elation at the turn of events, "I was taken by surprise when you brought him."

"Yeah." She kicked the toe of her boot in the ground. "So, no fiancés in Ireland?"

"Not yet."

"Boyfriends?"

"Not yet." She laughed. "You?"

"Me?" I feigned surprise.

"Seems like all of you guys are hooking up with the most famous women in the world." Alex used finger quotes when she said the word famous.

"Hmmm." I crossed my arms, considering. "I can't deny that. It's meaningless."

She walked over to the bed and sat next to me. "How are you handling being so famous now?"

"It's weird. Our lives aren't really our own anymore. I think we're all trying to adjust in our own way." I finished my beer and leaned back on my elbows. "We're never home anymore, even when we're there it's hard to leave the house."

"Yeah. I get that." She turned to her side and leaned back on her elbow, resting her head in her hand. "Thank you for protecting Zoey. You didn't have to do that, but it was the right thing for her."

"Ty—none of us—had any idea all of this would happen. The songs, this music? They've taken on a life of their own." I turned on my side facing Alex, mirroring her pose.

"I won't lie, Zoey hasn't ever recovered, and this has taken a toll." Alex reached out and stroked my hair. "She's gone back into reclusive study mode; she'll graduate from law school in a few months."

"We owe her some royalties." I leaned into Alex's hand.

"You sure do." Her nails raked my scalp gently. "In all seriousness, in time I hope they'll both come out the other side."

"It's already been a long fucking time," I guffawed before moving my face closer to
 hers.

"Okay, well, enough about them," Alex murmured before pressing her lips softly to
 mine.

My heart was beating like crazy; I'd thought of her so often over the years, believing we'd never have this again. Tasting her, smelling her oceany, tropical scent, feeling her body flush with mine, I wound my arm around her and cupped her head to deepen our kiss and realized she still had the stupid wig on. As sexy as her costume was, I wanted Alex. Not the imposter.

"Can I take this off?" I backed off slightly and gripped a handful of the dark wig, holding it out to the side.

Alex reached up, took a few pins out, and pulled it off, shaking out her honey- blonde hair, which fell in soft waves around her face.

"Done." She rested her cheek on her hand looking up at me, her blue eyes popping with the dark eyeliner.

"There you are." I traced her lips with my finger, unable to stop looking at her.

We watched each other silently as I caressed her face then moved to her neck and then down to her cut shoulder, which was exposed. Her eyes were half-mast, as were mine. Our lips met again. Tenderly, we kissed, barely touching our mouths together over and over again. Almost like we were in awe to be here in this moment. Together. My dick was harder than it had been in years and twitched in my jeans, aching to be reunited with this woman.

"I'm clean," I whispered in between kisses. "I haven't been with anyone in a few months, you're still the only one."

"Good." She stroked my hair and leaned in to suckle my earlobe and kiss along my jawline. "I've been careful too."

"Not my innocent girl anymore?" I cupped her ass to drag her against my swollen dick. She hooked her leg over mine to grind her core against me.

"What can I say? Sex is awesome." She fused her mouth to mine. We made out like teenagers and dry humped almost desperately.

Needing her naked, I pulled off her shirt. Braless! Her dark nipples were puckered into delectable tight nubs.

Alex kicked off her boots, peeled off her leggings, threw them to the floor, and lay back watching me. Moaning softly when I kneaded her breasts, I couldn't stop suckling their taut peaks one after the other. The aromatic smell of her arousal filled the room, and when I reached down to her slick, wet clit she was already rubbing it.

Sitting up, I quickly slipped out of my shoes and pulled off my hoodie. My dick was getting harder by the minute just from watching her pleasure herself. Alex lay back on the bed and shamelessly looked me in the eye, opening her knees wide to fuck herself with her fingers.

That was it. Ridding myself of my jeans and socks in less than a second, I fisted my thick shaft and pumped it in cadence with her rhythm. Never losing eye contact, Alex removed her fingers and sucked them, spreading her legs even wider to show me her exquisitely bare, drenched pink pussy. I lost all control. I had to be inside her.

In one motion I covered her body with mine and impaled her, grabbing her fingers and suckling the rest of her delicious essence from them. Never had anything tasted so good or felt so incredible. Her tight, velvet warmth enveloped my cock in the most heavenly way. Pushing her thighs up and apart, I held her open so my hips could roll over and over into her core. Alex's slender hands gripped my biceps. Her eyes squeezed shut in pleasure from the merger of our bodies.

A deep, burning possessiveness overtook me. Suddenly, it was imperative for me to infiltrate her soul. Nothing was going to stop me from making her come so hard she'd forget that any other guy would ever exist now or in the future.

I rolled over so she could ride me. Stroking my fingers through her wet pussy lips, I strummed and circled her extended clit. While she arched backward, she braced herself on my thighs. Alex puffed out little breaths and circled her hips, grinding against me. Her hair and perfect breasts bounced while she sought her release. Then she found it. The exact right angle. Her entire body shuddered; and her euphoria made her look like the sexiest angel. I was mesmerized. Smitten.

My angel's head lolled back, and she emitted a guttural, devilish yowl. Her inner walls tightened around me like a vise.

Rolling us back over, I knelt between her legs and drove back inside her roughly. I couldn't get deep enough, fast enough. Gripping her ankles, I rested her legs on my shoulders and held her thighs to my chest so I could piston my hips into her. Alex fisted the sheets to her sides, her head thrashing back and forth while I feverishly drove my cock into her tight pussy. The tingle at the base of my spine consumed me like wildfire. Shouting her name, I came so hard that my vision blacked out from the pleasure of it.

When I regained some measure of composure, I was still pulsing inside her. Alex's keening moans filled the room. Both of us were gasping for air. Gingerly, I pulled my cock out of her, releasing a flood of our combined juices onto the bedspread. Not caring one iota about the mess, I flopped over and cradled her tightly until our breathing finally regulated.

When our lips met again, we sipped deliciously from each other's mouths in the aftermath of our explosive reunion.

"Jesus," I said when I could finally speak. "God," Alex sighed.

"Come to my hotel." I smoothed her hair and kissed her temple. "We can hole up for a couple of days and stay naked for days."

"Okay," Alex agreed without any argument whatsoever.

"Then hurry up and pack some things, woman." I sprung up and pulled her with me, indulging in a saucy spank on her bare ass.

In record time I'd clothed myself and admired the view of Alex's spectacular naked, tight, body scurrying around the room, gathering clothes and toiletries. She was such a turn on, I loved how she had no inhibitions about being completely nude in front of me. When she attempted to move past me to grab her clothes, I pulled her down on my lap instead.

Her long legs splayed over mine, she rested her head on my shoulder and I stroked her silky inner thigh. Holding my face in her hands, she caressed the day's stubble and closed her eyes before she drew me to her lips. Our kisses were sweet, but her eyes popped open when I inserted three fingers into her pussy, which was still very lubricated from our recent activities. When I found her G-spot I rubbed it and lazily circled her clit with my thumb. My other arm supported her upper body, giving me just enough room to tweak and pinch her nipple with my fingers.

"Jace!" Alex chanted every time I hit the mark. She thrust her hips up and clenched my fingers tightly in her channel through another spectacular orgasm.

"If the only thing I did all day was watch your beautiful face when you come, I'd be a happy man," I growled in her ear, suckling at her earlobe while her spasms subsided.

"I'd be on board with that." Alex panted; her blue eyes locked with mine. "And I'm down for seeing more of your O-Face, Jace."

The funny thing is, although I'd blurted the sentiment without thinking, I knew what I said was inherently true. Something had immediately shifted inside me when I saw her again at the party. This wasn't just fun and games. It wasn't just sex. I wanted her to be mine. I needed her to be mine. I'd never had such intense emotions.

How can I make this happen?

CHAPTER 12

We didn't leave Jace's luxurious hotel suite in Belfast for forty-eight hours. True to his promise, we stayed gloriously naked the entire time and Jace took me in every position he could think of in every location. We were starved for each other. Muscles I didn't know existed ached deliciously in every way possible, I was in a constant state of arousal just thinking about his muscled body, his cleft chin, dimples, piercing green eyes, and gloriously and perpetually erect cock. When he wasn't inside me, I felt like a piece of me was missing, and so we'd start all over again.

It was clear that something had changed between us. We weren't fucking, we were making love. Jace had always been caring and sweet, but both of us always remained a bit distant.

Now, the way he looked at me seemed different. Loving. Reverential. Possessive.

Content.

Gawd, I knew it because I looked at him the same way.

On the morning he had to fly to Scotland, I felt a little blue but tried to hide it. We lay in the big bed wrapped in each other's arms, savoring our last hours together. Jace was kissing my head and face. I was raking my fingers through his thick, blond hair, staring into the distance. I wanted to live in the moment forever. Instead, a stupid timer was in my head ticking away the minutes until he left.

"Hey, are you with me, Poppy?" Jace used his finger to tip my chin up to look at him and, dammit, my eyes filled with tears.

Mortified, I tried to cover it up because I did *not* cry.

"I hope it's not another two years until I see you again." I managed to choke out.

"No, that's not going to happen." Jace teased my nipple with his finger, smiling as it puckered.

"It could." I hated how my voice sounded so needy. "The thing is, Alex—I don't want that."

Wait. What?

"What do you mean?" I studied him, confused but also hopeful.

"Come with me." Jace's green eyes flickered as though he'd solved a difficult puzzle. "Yes! Come on tour with us."

"Jace—" I knew I couldn't tour with the band. I had my own plans. Zoey and I were back in each other's lives and—well—girl code and everything. Unless Jace and I had something real, how could I risk wrecking that?

I wouldn't. Not if we were just regular hook-ups.

"Oh shit, this will be great," Jace's was more animated than I'd ever seen him. "The guys think you're awesome, I'm sure they'd totally be cool with it."

"Um. No. I can't do that." I booped his nose.

"Oh." Jace visibly deflated. "Why?"

I gestured between us. "Do any of the guys even know about me? About this?"

"Not exactly." He averted his eyes.

"So, you see? It's not a good idea." I shook my head sadly. "Besides, after the album, Zoey wouldn't understand."

Jace squinted with determination as he often did when noodling over some LTZ issue. "Maybe you could meet me sometimes?" We can look at my schedule and see when I have more than one day off, you could just fly in."

"I don't know . . ." I wasn't sure that I liked the direction this was headed. It felt a little groupie-ish.

"Poppy, we have five more months in Europe. I want to see you as much as possible." He had a look in his eyes that I'd never seen before. Like I was a special prize. No one had ever looked at me like that and I'd been engaged. "I mean. Well, I'd really like to see where this thing between us goes."

"Us as in 'us?'" I was visibly shocked but in such a good way.

He looked hurt that I'd not considered it.

"Is that so weird?"

"A little? I never thought you felt that way about me. I never thought you would think of us as an 'us.'" I used air quotes.

"Well, you're wrong. I've thought about it for years." Jace's confession shocked me to my core.

It's finally happening.

"But how do we make this work? You live on the road, so do I." My mind was a whirlwind, I wanted to do it, but it seemed so impossible. "We both have a lot going on."

Jace lay back and punched the pillow lightly. "Yeah. I know it probably won't be easy. We'd both need to figure it out."

"I wouldn't want there to be anyone else, Jace." I propped my head on his chest, feeling the hard planes of his abs. "I wouldn't want to share you."

"Well, if it means anything, there's never been anyone that I've cared about since I met you. Maybe ever." He wrinkled his brow as if he were surprised to hear himself say it. "But, okay. I get it and can say the words. No one else. We'd be exclusive."

"And we shouldn't tell anyone yet." I poked him in the chest. "Why not?"

"Let's be stealth. Just until you and I figure out what's going on here."

"Oh-kay. How in the hell will you come with me to the shows then?" He trailed his hand from my shoulder blade down to my breast. He was obsessed with my boobs. Not that I minded.

"I'll just have to get a few disguises together to keep you on your toes." My mind began to whirl with the possibilities.

"Hmmmm." Jace hauled me on top of him and guided the bulbous tip of his cock into me." Just thinking of you in costume makes me want to be inside you."

"You're insatiable." I canted my hips and squeezed.

"So are you." He thrust up. "I can't help that I love watching you ride me."

Too soon it was time for him to leave and time for me to go back to my flat. Armed with a calendar of our chosen destinations, I scheduled some appearances and booked some of my flights. We would see each other for one or two days about every week/week and a half. I couldn't believe it, after all this time, Jace and I were kind of a couple.

I just wished we didn't have to be a secret couple. But, circumstances necessitated it. At least for now.

My first stop was in London, where LTZ played two shows at Wembley Stadium. Jace left a key to his suite for me at the Savoy Hotel. In return, I greeted him naked in the giant bathtub when he got done with his show. We made love until dawn.

Replicating our Barcelona experience, I dashed out in the morning and bought us both British flag T-shirts and ball-caps, and we were able to ride around on the hop-on, hop-off bus unnoticed. That night, with my VIP All-Access pass, I watched the second show from the soundboard. Best-laid plans. My Twiggy-inspired wig and shift dress was a tad too conspicuous and I nearly got caught by Zane backstage.

My disguise did inspire some *Austin Powers* moments at the hotel. Jace told me that Ty and Connor, who were in the neighboring suites, had teased him for weeks by calling out, "Yeah, baby!" every time he walked by.

The band had four days off in Paris after they played to a sold-out crowd at *Stade de Paris.* We took full advantage because they never had much time off. The reason for the break was so Carter and Zane could take Ty to a wellness resort outside the city.

A few days prior, Jace showed Ty a picture of Zoey with her law school boyfriend on Instagram. By the next morning, Ty woke up in bed with some woman after blacking out from drinking. Not remembering it was the very last straw. The tortured singer finally wanted to get some help.

Having now witnessed his antics firsthand in Ireland and London, I was glad Ty was dealing with his issues. I truly wanted him to get back on his feet.

In even better news, Connor made plans with a mystery woman in

Provence. For the first time in forever, Jace had no one to take care of and we were both free from any responsibilities.

But the best news was the Paris dates happened to coincide with my twenty-third birthday. Jace pulled some strings and arranged for us to have a private tasting dinner at *L'Ambroisie*, a fancy three-Michelin star restaurant. Before dinner, he took me shopping for a birthday outfit and I chose a peach-nude Chanel dress and gorgeous Dior sandals. He outfitted himself in a dark-brown Dolce & Gabbana suit with some funky wing-tipped dress shoes. We dined on the most decadent food I'd ever tasted, and I felt truly grown- up for the first time in my life.

Afterward, we walked hand-in-hand through the romantic Paris streets. Jace's hair was pulled back in a ponytail, emphasizing his gorgeous green eyes and chiseled jaw. When the heavens opened up and we found ourselves in another downpour, he still looked more relaxed than I'd ever seen him.

Spreading his arms out wide, he shook out his hair and laughed. We were soaked and my new dress was ruined, but nothing mattered in that moment. On a quaint bridge overlooking the Seine, I launched myself at him and our mouths crashed together.

It was in that moment that I knew, without any shadow of a doubt, that I loved him.

I loved Jace Deveraux with all my heart.

When we arrived back to our opulent suite at Hôtel Barrière, we made love all night. In the morning, sitting on our veranda overlooking the *Arc de Triomphe*, the look in Jace's eyes told me all I needed to know, he was feeling it too.

"Poppy," he whispered and clasped my hand, bringing it to his lips and kissing it.

My breath caught. "Yes?"

"You're so incredibly beautiful, and funny. And sexy." He gulped almost nervously. "You have to know that I have feelings for you."

"I fell for you a long time ago, Jace." I kissed his palm.

Jace leaned over and kissed me. "I'm pretty sure that I love you."

"I'm pretty sure that I love you too," I murmured against his lips. Suffice it to say, it was a perfect visit.

But it wasn't a perfect time.

Jace's challenge was that LTZ's fan base increased dramatically every day. He was basically living two lives with two full-time jobs. His public life consisted of the same crazy schedule of travel to shows, the shows themselves, interviews, fan events, press, and appearances. He and all the guys had full-time bodyguards. They were in high demand, and Jace was rarely alone.

His private life amounted to herding all of the LTZ cats to keep the PR momentum going.

So it became harder to find a stretch where he had more than one day off. My plans to join him in Amsterdam, Stockholm, and Frankfurt were thwarted by his schedule changes.

We managed super-quick overnights in Prague, Dubrovnik, Vienna, and Athens where I arrived during their evening show and he had to leave by mid-morning. Aside from our physical gratification, which was always epic, these hurried visits left me feeling emotionally empty because he had to leave so quickly after we reconnected.

Trying to keep a positive attitude, because none of the scheduling was Jace's fault, I popped over to Milan to meet him after a show. I was excitedly waiting for him in his hotel suite when I his text came in.

Jace: Just got done, I'm sorry but management is here, they're making me go to a party.
Alex: Ok but I'm already at the hotel. Jace: I know, I'll try to

hurry.

Alex: xo

Jace: xo

Usually, he raced back to me as soon as humanly possible so we could have the whole night together. This time he didn't. I must have fallen asleep because when I heard the door click open, daylight was already peeping through the blackout curtains. Jace tiptoed into the room and through the slits in my eyes I saw him undressing before crawling into bed with me.

"Are you awake?" Jace cuddled me close, his erection poking into the back of my thigh.

"Now I am." I wiggled my ass back against his cock.

"I don't have long. The bus leaves in three hours." Jace kissed my neck, lifted my thigh over his, nudged his dick in between my legs, and then entered me from behind. "God, you feel good."

A lump formed in my throat when he gripped my hips and pumped into me. No foreplay. No sweet nothings. We weren't even looking at each other. This sex felt rushed and utilitarian. This was not what I signed up for.

The love bubble that I'd been living in was bursting.

When Jace reached around to pluck my nipple and then rub my clit, my body wasn't reacting. I just wasn't feeling it. I deserved to be more than a quick lay to him.

"Poppy, are you okay?" Jace stilled inside me, I could feel his breath at the back of my neck.

"I'm fine," I whispered into the pillow, even though I wasn't fine at all.

Jace pulled out and reached across my body to turn on the lamp. My eyes winced at the light and I put my hand up to shield the glare.

He tenderly stroked my cheek. "Something's wrong."

Tears pooled in my eyes. "I don't want to be a vessel, Jace."

"What do you mean?" He looked genuinely confused.

"It's not cool for me to wait for hours in a hotel room when you're at some stupid, goddamn party. Sex like this makes me feel like it's just a release for you." I sniffed through my emotions. "I mean, I could be anyone right now."

Jace looked horrified. "No. Fuck no. Alex, you mean everything to me. I love you. You're what I look forward to, you're what keeps me going."

"If you really love me so much, where were you all night?" My voice was small which made me mad at myself.

"I told you, I had to go to this stupid sponsor party, you've been at them with me before." Jace cupped my face with his hands and kissed me. "There's no one else. I wouldn't do that to you. I just couldn't fucking leave."

Kissing me senseless wasn't good enough, and I had to draw a line. "There's this thing called texting. And manners. And consideration."

We stared at each other. For too long. I was about ready to get up and get the hell out of there when all pretense of his defensiveness evaporated. "I'm sorry. You're right. I was wrong."

It was a start and he seemed genuinely sorry. "It's just, I mean, I have a life too and I rearrange a lot so I can meet you. I do it because I love you. I want to be here with you. Just show me a little respect for my time too, rock star."

"I won't let it happen again, Poppy." Jace touched his lips to mine and this time I was able to enjoy it. After all, the splendor of my naked drummer wasn't something I planned to miss.

Our tongues danced and my tears dried, and once again being here with Jace was everything I wanted. He kissed down my neck and stroked my breasts, tracing my nipples with his thumbs and laving them tenderly one after the other. Moving down, he trailed his tongue across the muscles of my stomach and nibbled at my belly ring. Nuzzling my inner thighs, Jace pushed my legs open and lapped at my pussy and pressed his fingers inside. Sucking my clit in between his lips, he pulsed and licked and fucked me with his tongue until I came hard.

Kissing his way back up my body, my sexy drummer slid inside me more gently this time and we sipped from each other's mouths languidly. Jace's elbows bridged my head and his hands spanned my head, allowing his hips to roll his cock into me over and over again. I ran my hands up and down his back, clasping him close to me as I shuddered through another orgasm.

Piercing me with his gorgeous emerald eyes, his soft hair fell in a curtain around our faces when Jace cried out and released a flood inside me.

He withdrew and cuddled me so that I lay against his chest basking in our afterglow. I felt better at that moment, but I was a realist. A night like tonight could easily happen again given the current state of affairs. It was partly my fault. Jace had been more than willing to make our relationship public. It was my insistence at keeping it secret that cost us precious time together and forced us to sneak around.

Jace's voice jarred me out of my thoughts. "What's going on in that head of yours?"

"This is such a mess." I stroked his chest and traced his tattoos on his arms. "A mess
  that I've created."

170

"I'm sorry this is hard for you."

I yawned, struggling to keep my eyes open. "Maybe we should just tell everyone . . . "Yeah—" Jace's voice was barely audible. His breathing slowed, and I knew he was sound asleep.

When I woke up at noon, Jace was long gone, but like always when he left before I got up, a sweet note was waiting for me. This time, when I checked my phone, he had also sent me a video. When I clicked play, his gorgeous yet scruffy face filled my screen.

"Poppy, I'm on my way to Madrid. I miss you already. I'll FaceTime you when we land. Oh, and I love you!"

Of course, my heart swooned. While I loved the message, the practical protect-your- heart side of me had already kicked in. With only three weeks left on their European leg, I had to start facing facts. After shooting a television special in Seattle, LTZ would be leaving on another long stint throughout South America.

Love or not, our time together was coming to an end.

It was time to prepare myself for heartbreak.

Back in Ireland, after I cleared out my flat in Belfast, I returned to Ibiza to spend some time at a rescue I'd volunteered at when I first started.

I met up with Jace for awesome overnights in Lisbon and Cardiff with plans for a longer visit in Italy. Despite how much fun we had, I still felt myself mentally pulling away. By the time I boarded my plane to Rome, where LTZ would play their closing European festival, in my mind, the hourglass had run out.

I pushed the thoughts out of my head, though. We had a full week before Jace flew back to Seattle, and he'd arranged for a private villa in Lake Como, just the two of us. I was equally looking forward to it and dreading it. My mind was everywhere.

Using my All-Access pass, I went through the band entrance to the show. No disguises, I just laid low. Everything about the performance was incredible. Clearly, Ty was feeling better. He looked and sounded like his head was back in the game. The Italian crowd went bananas. Watching them, it was hard to reconcile this band with the version of LTZ I'd seen so many years ago at the Mission. I found myself dancing and singing along to the entire set. They had come so far.

Jace didn't get done until well after two in the morning, mainly because of the over- the-top closing party. It was second nature to work the room, but I'd come to the realization that this lifestyle was something I'd outgrown. I was ready to move on to something more meaningful.

When we were drinking the last beer of the night, I eavesdropped on a conversation between Sienna and Andrew, the band's new publicists who were talking about the band's schedule for the next year or so. I learned that after the television show and the Latin America shows LTZ were recording an album in Los Angeles. There were a couple of award show appearances and a New Year's' Eve headlining gig in New York. After New York, they were traveling to Asia and Australia for another four-month tour. By the time they got back, after a few weeks off, the new album would be released, and the entire cycle would begin again.

In other words, Jace's schedule was already booked up for approximately two to three years.

As much as I wanted to be with him, I just wasn't the type of girl who would give up everything I was doing to be at his beck and call.

It didn't surprise me when Jace dozed off in the private plane he'd chartered for the short trip from Rome to Lake Como. When we landed, a town car was waiting to drive us to the villa. It was still dark when we pulled up the private drive. Lights illuminated the path to the ornate front door. Although it was nearly dawn, a small staff in full uniforms scurried out and ushered us inside.

Exhausted, we staggered like zombies into the big master suite. The room smelled amazing, of flowers and citrus. The giant four-poster bed with a fluffy comforter was turned down, and the black-out curtains were drawn. Tumbling into bed, we wrapped around each other and promptly fell asleep, not waking up until nearly 3 p.m. the next day.

I woke first and lay still against Jace's chest, listening to his heartbeat while he slept for God knows how long. I was thinking about how hard it must have been for Zoey to leave Ty all those years ago. In those quiet moments, I finally understood my BFF's sacrifice. And heartbreak.

Things were just not going to work out for Jace and me. It was time for me to move on. I didn't know how I was going to tell him.

I *did* know it wouldn't be a note on the nightstand.

"Hey." I heard him say, his voice gravelly with sleep. "Hey."

"I feel like I could sleep for a week." He stretched his body out like a cat.

I yawned and moved off of him. "Well, we can do that."

He looked at me strangely as if he knew something was off. Neither one of us could nor would acknowledge it. Instead, we just got up and got ready for the day like we were a real couple. I threw on some cutoffs and a T-shirt over my black bikini, Jace wore black and white board shorts and an LTZ T-shirt.

In the light of day, I noticed that we were extremely isolated in the gorgeous, lush villa with a panoramic view of the lake. The house itself was magnificent, crafted from Italian marble and the finest finishes. Modern yet comfortable, the luxurious surroundings helped my mood improve significantly.

I vowed to enjoy my time with Jace, it would be a wonderful place to spend our last few days together.

We made our way to an exquisitely detailed tiled patio, filled with ceramic pots of flowering trees and bushes. Shielded by foliage, no prying paparazzi lenses would have a vantage point to spy on us. The cooks had prepared a wonderful spread of tapenade, crusty bread, fruit, and charcuterie. We devoured most of it while sipping crisp white wine on cushioned lawn chairs next to the clear, aqua infinity pool.

Satiated from our meal, Jace leaned back in his chair. His lips curled in a slight smile. Gahd. I was going to miss those dimples.

I got up, pulled off my T-shirt and shorts, dove into the crystal-blue water, and floated on my back, soaking up the sun's warm rays on my face. I heard a splash and felt a spray of water shower over me. My eyes popped open to the vision of Jace—in all of his Viking God glory—swimming over to me. Towing him through the water to me, I could feel the hard planes of his abs against my flat stomach and his hard cock against my pussy.

"This place is amazing." I threw my arms around his shoulders, linking them around his neck. "Thank you for setting this up."

"I wanted us to be somewhere special for a few days." Jace nuzzled my ear and soon we were hungrily devouring each other's lips.

Swimming us to the side of the pool, Jace caged me against the rail. When he shifted his hips against my core, my legs hooked around the small of his back. I could now feel the full girth of his erection through his board shorts. Reaching down between us, I slipped my hand under his waistband and stroked him as we made out. His little groans coincided with each pass of my hand. Dipping under his arm, I guided him to turn around and change positions with me and then gestured for him to sit on the side of the pool.

He hoisted himself up and I pulled his swim trunks down and off his legs, then tossed them behind him on the patio. Gloriously naked, his muscled stomach flexed as he braced himself back on both arms, his feet dangling in the water on either side of my body. I stroked my palms up his granite thighs encouraging Jace to recline even farther. By the time he was leaning back on his elbows, his thick cock jutted proudly toward the sun.

"I'm going to suck on it."

"Jesus." Jace squeezed his eyes shut when, smacking my lips, I cupped his balls lightly and sucked the head of his cock into my mouth. His strong fingers threaded through my hair as I sucked and licked him thoroughly. Along his shaft, down along his sac, and along his perineum.

"Holy hell, that feels incredible. Jesus. Shit, Poppy. I'm gonna come so hard." Jace rasped, his hips bucking against my lips.

I doubled down, running my tongue along his slit while my hand gripped him at the base. Laving him with my entire mouth, I wanted this to be the best blowjob of his life, something to remember me by. Jace tapped my head, gyrating wildly and pumping against my lips. Shaking my head, I hummed against his pulsing shaft and watched when he bit his lip, grimacing before he released a flood into my mouth with a shout. I swallowed every drop and tenderly licked him clean.

Jace flopped back, unable to speak, his arms thrown above his head. I rested my head on my hands, which were clutching the ledge in between his legs. My body remained submerged in the cool water, which was a relief against the hot temperature. After a while, he reached down and stroked my hair before he plunged into the pool next to me.

Like a shark, Jace sluiced through the water, only his eyes and the top of his head were visible. Giggling, I tried to push him away by his forehead, but he wrapped his arms around me and untied my bikini top and threw it up on the patio. His hands moved along my sides and down my hips and he untied my bottoms and they floated to the top of the pool.

When we were both naked, Jace dove under and swam in between my legs so that I was now back to his front. Wrapping his arms around me, his strong hands cupped my breasts, teasing my nipples with his thumbs.

"It's your turn." Jace bit my earlobe. His nipple teases turned to pinches, sending an ache of desire straight to my core.

Already, his cock had recuperated and was stiff against my ass. I tried to wiggle against him, but Jace held me firm, banding one arm across my stomach and swimming us over to the ladder at the side of the shallow end of the pool. Nuzzling my neck, he turned me around, so my back was against the steps.

He growled in my ear, "Grab the rail."

I did.

Jace urged me backward up the steps until my pussy was level with his face and he licked me all along my seam. When he saw that I had a good grip, Jace cupped my ass so that both legs floated up and over his shoulders. Holy fucking Mary and Jesus, Jace used my weightlessness to move me against his lips and he devoured me like he was starving, feasting on my pussy from every angle and sucking and nipping at my clit in between.

The sensation of the sun beating on my body and the stimulation to my sex was completely otherworldly. I could barely keep my grip while he moved me back and forth against his mouth. My screams of unabashed pleasure filled the air when I came all over his face.

I was barely coherent when Jace flipped me over, so my arms were crossed but still gripping the ladder. Moving behind me, he held on to my calves and stepped on the bottom rung in between my legs. The crown of his cock pressed against my opening and he pushed all the way into me until I was completely full. Using the leverage of my legs, he balanced on the step and rocked me back and forth on his hard length. My nipples were diamond hard and crazily sensitive because of the movement against the rippling water.

Jace moaned my name and picked up the pace, changing angles until his cock dragged deliciously and repeatedly against the jackpot of nerves inside me. I whined when my inner walls convulsed against his shaft. He let go of my calves, gripped my hips, and slammed into me until I couldn't tell my parts from his. I couldn't stop coming, it was hard for me to tell if it was one long orgasm or multiples, but sex with him had never felt so intense.

Our cries of passion and pleasure were so loud, there was no possible way the staff and all the neighbors within a two-mile vicinity couldn't have heard.

I didn't even think about that until later.

Eventually, we came to Earth. Jace pulled out and cupped my exposed breasts until we found our footing on the floor of the pool. I turned in his arms and our lips met. He drew me flush to him by my waist. My arms encircled his neck as we kissed.

Jace looked down at me, his hair dripping down his face, his green eyes sparkling in the sunlight. "I really do love you."

"I really do love you." I nestled into his neck. I meant it, but I was unable to look him in the eye.

By then the sun had fallen behind the trees surrounding the villa.

The pool felt more chilly than refreshing, and goosebumps broke out on my arms. Ever the gentleman, Jace jumped out of the water and grabbed the oversized beach towel that he wrapped around me when I climbed up our sex ladder. Fastening a towel around his waist, we walked back to our bedroom arm in arm.

After our loud pool activities, Jace sent away the staff—but not before ensuring that our fridge and cupboards were stocked with basic supplies. This left us truly alone. Our chemistry was like wildfire, we had sex whenever the mood struck. Considering we were always naked, the mood struck often. We joked that we were living in a sex bubble because we never once left the villa grounds the entire week of our stay.

It was the first time Jace and I had a long stretch of time together alone with no other distractions. While I felt I knew him well, I learned small bits of information about his future plans and life outside of the band.

He mentioned settling in Seattle and wanting to start a family someday. I shared my own plans of buying acreage somewhere remote and opening my own horse rescue.

Oh, how I wished things were different.

As much as I adored Jace, those moments together were bittersweet because we just didn't have the same idea of what the future held.

CHAPTER 13

My thoughts were on a continuous loop about how much I wanted Alex in my future.

Permanently.

Several times when we were at the villa, I nearly put all my cards on the table. Something held me back. Mainly, I sensed—or maybe worried—that she didn't feel the same way. Or maybe, she wasn't quite ready. It didn't matter. My own uncertainty kept me from expressing my true feelings.

My friends-with-benefits relationship history and more than five years on the road failed to provide me with any clue how to successfully ask for what I wanted.

I knew I was falling into old habits by keeping my true feelings inside. Our attraction to each other was off the charts, and I didn't want to do anything to ruin it. We literally could not stop having sex.

I couldn't keep my hands off her.

She couldn't keep her hands off me.

I wasn't about to do or say anything that would spoil our long-awaited time together. Enjoying the hell out of her banging body in every room and in every position, was so much better than dealing with stupid feelings.

By our last night in the villa, I knew I wanted her—no, I needed her—to know how I felt.

We were out by the pool under heat lamps, naked in the moonlight. My golden girl was sprawled in front of me, wrapped in my arms in the cushy lawn chair. "I don't want this to end, Alex."

"I don't either, but—" Her blue eyes seemed even bluer when illuminated by the water.

"No buts."

"Jace, it's not realistic." Alex tried to squiggle away, but I kept her flush against me. "You're already tied up for the next two years!"

"You can come with me." I pleaded. "Let's out ourselves."

"I *can't* just come with you." Alex blew out a frustrated breath. "You *know* this. Don't ask for something that isn't even possible."

"Let me talk to management, at some point I need to be able to have a life." I was frustrated too. Did being a successful dude in a rock band really mean I couldn't be with the woman I loved?

"I don't want to be in a relationship when we are away from each other more than we are together," Alex said as if reading my mind. "We'd end up hating each other. I don't ever want to hate you."

"I could be different now." I insisted. "LTZ is at the top of the charts, I have more leverage to get a better life balance."

"C'mon, Jace. I know you've been very successful with *Z*, but your next album is crucial. It will determine LTZ's staying power." Alex spoke quietly.

My heart started thumping. She was totally right.

We lay in silence cuddled together for a long while. To someone observing us, we probably looked calm. Peaceful even. Not the case. The rollercoaster of fear and resolution in my head was anything but.

There was no way on Earth I'd leave my band. We were just finally making life- changing money. I couldn't ask Alex to give up on what she had built either.

The entire situation was fucked.

"Jace, it's okay," Alex whispered, entwining her fingers with mine.

"Would you at least come back to Seattle with me?" I was desperate to hold on to her, which was unlike anything I'd ever felt before. For anyone.

"It will just postpone the inevitable."

"So what?" I said petulantly. "It gives us another month."

"You'll be busy the whole time!" Alex sounded exasperated and annoyed with me. "It won't matter if I'm there."

"It will matter because I want you there. Please," I begged, abhorring how weak I sounded.

Alex kissed the stubble under my chin. "Jace, I don't ever want this to be over."

"You don't?" I gripped her tightly, wondering how Ty managed to ever get through

five years of this heartbreak shit.

"I'll come home for a visit. I gave up my flat in Belfast, and I need to see my folks anyway. But we can't go on like this." She was firm. "I have my own life, my own stuff. I can't put my own work on the back-burner like I have for the past few months, or my momentum will change."

"I'm sorry you made such a sacrifice to hang out with me." I snarked.

Was it really such a fucking hardship?

"C'mon, don't pick a fight tonight. I didn't say that," Alex soothed me. I realized that somehow our roles had reversed. "I'm just saying, don't be the type of guy that expects his girl to drop everything she's worked for."

"I'm not that guy! I never expected that."

"Let's please just live in our awesome sex bubble for one more night?" Alex pleaded. She snuggled into my side and stroked my cock slowly. "We can hash through this in Seattle."

"Fine. Okay," I conceded as my dick grew under her touch.

And so we were able to compartmentalize our geography situation for the rest of the night and focus on each other. I memorized the details of her beautiful, lithe body with my fingers, hands, and lips. Every dimple, every freckle, every erogenous zone, every moan, every breath.

I wouldn't allow any thought that we would break up enter into my mind. Not when every part of her body was touching every part of mine. Not when I was inside her and I didn't know where she began, and I ended.

By the time we left the villa, I felt more confident that we'd figure it out.

I wasn't prepared for it to all come crashing down around me.

Alex stayed behind for a couple of appearances and didn't arrive in Seattle until I'd already been home for ten days. Our television production schedule was insane, and my promise of the endless hours we'd spend together in our hometown had been broken.

We were like ships in the night. I could feel the connection we had in Europe slipping away each minute. My body ached for her. My heart yearned to hold her and kiss her. To fuck her so she'd never forget me.

But our time was up.

Alex filled up her schedule and pulled away from me even more.

Which crushed my soul because I tried so hard to make time to see her. To find stolen moments. To bring her to the set. To have her stay over and at least eat breakfast together.

Instead, we were settling for a few nights of frantic sex, which wasn't enough for me. I could tell it wasn't enough for her either.

I was irritated. She deflated.

Our stupid secret love affair meant I had no one to talk to about my frustration. The rest of the guys, even Ty, were having a ball filming and were psyched to get back out on the road in South America.

For me, after having some time off in Italy, I wanted to stay home. It was exhausting thinking about the fact that we wouldn't be back home for at least another year. Maybe more. The only thing I could do to free up my time was to finally turn over social media to Andrew and Sienna.

So I did.

As my departure date neared, Alex became even more distant. Almost like she was waiting for me to leave so we could just get the breakup over with and go our separate ways. I, in turn, became more clingy. It was like I couldn't help myself calling and texting her all day.

Frantic to reassure her we could keep our relationship going, I decided to try one last grand gesture.

Alex was visiting her dad on Bainbridge Island overnight, and I had the entire day to kill before her ferry arrived that evening. I called in a favor with my tattoo artist friend at Slave to the Needle and spent the day in Wallingford to incorporate a new design on my arm. Hours later, I was really pleased with the results.

I made a few stops before it was time to pick her up and get on with my plans.

When her ferry pulled to the dock, I was waiting with a giant bouquet of flowers I'd picked up at Pike Place Market. In homage to our time in Barcelona and London, and an attempt to be incognito in my hometown, I wore a Seattle Supersonics T-shirt, a Seattle Mariners baseball cap, and aviator sunglasses.

From my parking spot under the Alaskan Way Viaduct across from the dock, I saw Alex stride out of the terminal wearing her trademark T-shirt, jeans, and Frye boots. I stuck my head out the window to wave her over.

"Ohmygod." Alex laughed when she saw my getup. "You are fucking adorable."

"I'm a Seattle tourist!" I bowed deep and handed her the flowers.

Embracing me with her whole body, Alex breathed me in. "I never get sick of how good you smell."

Not content with a hug, I cupped her head and threaded my fingers through her soft hair and pulled her toward me. Her lips parted and our tongues touched tentatively, then she opened for me and we had a proper kiss that turned into groping on my part. I couldn't help but get carried away around her.

"Jace, wait. I have to tell you something," Alex's expression shuttered, and she stepped back from me.

"Nooooooo." I shook my head and put my fingers in my ears. Her face scrunched up. She seemed very stressed. "I'm serious."

"Poppy, what is it?" Now I was worried.

Alex took a deep breath and gestured for me to get into the truck. She walked around and sat in the passenger seat, clasping her hands in her lap, looking forlorn.

"No, don't break up with me," I whispered.

"I'm late." She puffed out air, ignoring my plea, but it was clear that she was trying to stop herself from crying.

"For what?"

She looked up at me like I was an idiot.

Oh. Shit.

Realization dawned on me. "Wow."

"Yeah." Tears pooled in her beautiful blue eyes. For the first time since I'd known her, she made no attempt to hide them.

"It will be okay." I hadn't considered having kids this early and the thought terrified me, but I would never let Alex know that in a time like this.

"I really don't want kids, Jace." Alex clenched her eyes shut. "And I don't want to have a kid with a guy who doesn't even live in the same country as me."

Her words were like a punch to my gut. My heart hit the top of my throat. I didn't know what to say. Did she think I wasn't good enough to be a father? My dad was a great father. I had a great family.

What the fuck was her problem with me?

Then I realized she was scared. She was only twenty-three. So young. Alex was the age I had been when we met. It would be up to me to be the strong one.

"Poppy, I've got you. Let's go get a test." I took her hand and rubbed her knuckles with my thumb. "There's no point in getting so stressed when we don't know anything for sure."

"I'm *never* late, Jace." Alex burst into tears.

"Well—It will be okay. We'll figure this out." I brought her hand to my lips and kissed it. "There is a Bartell Drugs a block away from my condo, we can just go there first and then head back to my place."

By the time I parked in my underground garage, Alex's tears had subsided. She leaned over and stroked my cheek, giving me a small smile. I wrapped my arm around her and held her head to my chest.

"You'd be a great father, Jace," Alex mumbled into my chest. "I'm sorry if I hurt you, it came out wrong."

"It's okay, we're both scared."

"Let me run over and get the tests, I don't want to risk you getting recognized."

"I should be with you for all of this, we are in this together." The last thing I'd ever do was abandon her, no fucking way.

"Don't be stupid, if someone takes your picture buying a pregnancy test it will be a disaster for both of us. You know this." Alex opened the car door. "I'll be back in a second, I'll see you up at your place."

Alex returned ten minutes later with four different tests. She wouldn't let me in when she had to pee on each stick, but we put them on paper towels on my kitchen counter and sat on the bar stools waiting for the timer to go off. When the stove dinged, hand in hand we went to examine the tests. I put on my reading glasses and looked at the sticks with her.

Negative

Negative

Negative

Negative

"Oh, thank God." Alex buried her face in her hands and sobbed like I'd never heard her sob before.

My heart fucking hurt. Unexpectedly.

I realized that I was hoping the test would be positive. I wasn't sure why she was so goddamn relieved. Was it because a baby would bind her to me? I couldn't really process my thoughts because I wasn't even sure if I was ready to raise a child with Alex. My mind was reeling.

"You're happy then," I stated, not asked.

"Yes, I really, *really* don't want kids." Alex was so visibly relieved. "I've been thinking about getting my tubes tied so I don't ever have to worry about it."

"That seems a bit extreme." I was shocked that she'd be so drastic about it. "For you maybe, because you want kids."

"Sure, I'd like kids. But it's not a deal breaker, Alex," I answered honestly. "Why do you feel so strongly?"

"I don't know. It just isn't for me." She shrugged unapologetically. "I love animals. When I'm around kids, I like them. But I don't have motherly instincts."

"That's because you're only twenty-three." I furrowed my brow.

"You don't get to tell me what I want, Jace." Alex was angry now. "I've been stressed about this for two weeks, and you haven't been around long enough for—"

Two fucking weeks?

"Alex, I've done everything I could to free up time to spend with you. You're the one who went over to Bainbridge on the one day I had off." I was pissed. "Why didn't you tell me before today?"

"Because at first, I wasn't sure I *was* going to tell you." Alex couldn't meet my eye.

"What the *fuck*?"

"I couldn't do that to you," she whispered. "I couldn't ever hurt you the way Zoey hurt Ty."

I sat there in shock.

"Talk to me." Alex grabbed my hand.

"Just promise me you won't do anything permanent in case you change your mind later." I let her keep hold of my hand, but now I couldn't look at her.

"Jace, I'm young. Too young to be a mother."

"Well, crisis averted then," I spat out bitterly.

"Wait, so did you want it to be positive?" Alex looked at me incredulously. "Well, I didn't *not* want it to be positive."

"So, it *is* a deal breaker!" She pointed at me.

"Alex, all I meant was that if the test was positive, I'd absolutely want *our* kid." My anger was rising with each minute, and trying to hold it in was proving very, very difficult.

It was all I could do to stop myself from blowing up.

"Oh Jace," Alex moved over to the couch and slumped into the cushions.

Looking at Alex crumpled against the pillows, knees pulled up to her chin, her face agonized over the pregnancy scare, I realized at that moment that it was over.

She *was* young. She hadn't figured out her life yet. And neither had I.

I crossed the room and sat next to her on the couch, put my arm around her and tucked her into my side. She buried her face in my neck, and I kissed the top of her head about a thousand times in a row.

"When are you going back to Europe?"

"Day after tomorrow," she muttered into my shirt, her hand absentmindedly traced my tattoo on my shoulder and arm.

"Okay." I was resigned, I just needed to soak in whatever I could in the time we had left. So, I hugged her tightly.

"Did you hurt yourself?" She had discovered the outline of my new bandage.

"No. I had a surprise for you."

"What is it?" She sat up and pulled the sleeve of my T-shirt up over my biceps revealing the clear protective layer over my new art.

"I'll just show you." I peeled off the bandage revealing the addition to my Viking compass and dragon. An intricate, abstract, vibrant red poppy woven into the knotted design, with slashes of black and white.

"Oh, Jace." Alex's delicate, slender finger hovered over the design. "It's absolutely beautiful."

She turned her face to mine, her blue eyes shone with tears again. A single drop rolled down her face into her flowing hair. She climbed into my lap and flung her arms around my neck. Knowing that we would soon say our goodbyes, probably for good this time, I choked back a sob.

It escaped anyway.

Clutching her to me tightly, I cried into her blond tresses while she raked her fingers through mine. The wetness of her tears spilled down my neck.

I took her face in my hands to look at her in the eyes. "Let's not be Ty and Zoey. Stay with me tonight, but don't fucking ghost me tomorrow."

Alex let out a guffaw and smiled. "Never."

"I need to be inside you." I touched my forehead to hers.

Alex cupped my face and stroked my cheeks with her thumbs, wiping away my tears. I'd never cried in front of a woman, no one had ever had the power over me to make me feel this devastated.

I was pretty sure that no other woman ever would.

Our lips met tentatively with barely any pressure, just softness. Intimacy. My arms snaked around Alex's back so I could cup her head and increase the intensity of our kiss.

When my erection grew stiff against her thigh, Alex straddled me, and I could feel the penetrating heat of her core against me. Gripping her ass, I stood and pulled her flush against me. She wrapped her legs and arms around me while I strode across the room and carried her to my bedroom.

In quick succession, I plopped her down on my bed, divested her of her boots, jeans, and T-shirt, and tore her tiny blue bikini panties off her. She scooted up the bed to rest her head back against the pillow while I shed my clothes and tossed them in a heap on top of hers on the floor.

Taking a moment to appreciate the perfection of her beautiful, sleek body, I devoured the sight of her honey-gold hair, gorgeous blue eyes, and smooth, silky complexion down to her pointed brown nipples and glistening pink, hairless pussy. The white outline of her bikini against her tanned bare skin was from our time in Italy. My already granite-hard dick lengthened at the memory.

I crawled up the bed and hovered over her. Moving my weight to one arm, I placed her hand on my thick cock, intertwining our fingers so we could stroke it together. My eyes rolled back into my head at the pleasure. When I placed both hands back on the mattress and lowered my head and captured her mouth with mine, she kept up the pace on her own.

"Ohh—Mmm," Alex breathed, her hand tightening on my cock when I sucked her bottom lip into my mouth, swiped my tongue into her mouth, and devoured her. My hips thrust into her as we kissed, my dick driving into her fist, which held me tight like a glove. When she spread her legs and shifted, her pelvis tilted so that she could slide her wet pussy along my thigh.

Knowing that this could very well be our last time together, I really wanted to take things slow. To make the moment last forever. I wanted to savor her. What I wanted was in direct opposition to what I needed. I was a dude in a barrel going over the waterfall.

A sexy whimper escaped her lips when she ground against my leg. I kissed and suckled all along her jaw and down her neck and feasted on her perky breasts, laving her nipples with my tongue as I lined my cock up against her opening.

With my arms taut on either side of her head, I slid into her inch by inch, until my entire cock was buried inside her. Alex pressed her palms onto my chest and dug her heels into the mattress, her slick pussy thrusting up to meet me.

Sinking back to my knees without losing our connection, I pressed my palms against the backs of her thighs so I could deepen my penetration. Watching myself disappear over and over inside her made me lose my mind. I gripped her hips to pull her to me, and then used my thumb to furiously rub her clit exactly how she loved it.

Rhythmic tremors overcame her, and she came apart immediately, which catapulted me into the abyss of my own release. Jackhammering my cock into her with desperate thrusts, I couldn't stop until Alex screamed out her pleasure, and I shouted when I emptied myself inside her.

Collapsing, but being careful not to crush her, I wanted to prolong the time that our bodies remained melded as one.

As we lay intertwined, my cock twitched deep inside her. I wondered if it was normal to feel like I was physically addicted to

Alex. My body felt like it was born to be interlocked with hers like this. We were two parts of a puzzle and I didn't want our time together to ever end.

When Alex's breathing regulated as she drifted off to sleep, I lay awake all night wondering how it would be possible to love someone so much that you could let them go.

It turned out that Alex and I were very civilized about it. After sleeping in until noon and making gentle love when we woke up, we took a shower together, got dressed, and I drove her over to her mom's. We sat in the front seat of my old beater pickup truck for a long time until finally Alex clutched my hand and looked up at me.

"I'll always love you." She peered up at me from under her eyelashes.

"I'll always love you."

"You don't need to be exclusive with me anymore, Jace." She looked down at her lap.

"You don't either." I gulped, nearly choking on the words. "But I probably will have to kill whoever you end up with."

"Are we having a Whitney Houston moment?" Alex looked up at me with a small smile.

I guffawed. Leave it to my Poppy to make me laugh during the saddest moment of my life.

Alex laughed sharply. "I should go."

"Okay." The lump in my throat was unbearable.

Alex leaned over and pressed her lips to mine. Our tongues tangled desperately for a minute before she pulled away.

"I'm going to need some time." She sighed, not looking at me.

Tipping her chin up with my finger so she couldn't avoid my gaze, I nodded. "I know. Me too."

Nodding, Alex opened the car door and her long legs strode across the walkway, up the steps, and to the front door. Turning, she lifted her hand and wiggled her fingers at me, then blew me a kiss and went inside without another glance.

A few days later, I trolled her to make sure she arrived in Germany safely and saw her post from a horse rescue outside of Munich. With her long, blonde hair blowing in the breeze in front of a pasture full of horses, she looked happy. And free. I smiled. Then I unfollowed her because I couldn't bear it.

For the next forty-eight hours before we left for South America, I isolated myself under the guise of resting up before the tour. I couldn't talk to anyone, and my heart hurt.

Unfortunately, my only coping mechanism was to get literally black-out drunk for two solid days. It blocked out the pain, but I was too old and had too many responsibilities with my band, so I felt even worse when I boarded the plane.

It struck me that for the first time since LTZ became famous, I wasn't happy to be starting a new tour.

CHAPTER 14

ALMOST TWO YEARS LATER

Zoey stacked the last of the boxes against the wall in my childhood bedroom. Seeing my life packed up into piles and ready to either donate or move to my new apartment felt cathartic. Now that I'd permanently moved back to Seattle, I was looking forward to setting up my own place.

After looking for a couple of months, I purchased a new, modern condo in Belltown a few blocks away from where Jace lived.

Or used to live. I had no idea.

We hadn't kept in touch at all after we parted ways. He'd unfollowed my social media. And although I couldn't bear to unfollow him back, I'd made no effort to see him. It was hard, but as the months dragged on, I'd come to terms that it was truly over between us.

"When do you leave for Paris?" Zoey snapped me out of my reverie.

"Not for another week, I'll only be gone a few days." I stretched my arms and legs in preparation to move the boxes. "I'm so excited to be home. To *have* a home."

Home base. After so many years in a suitcase, I was ready.

Zoey threw her arms around me, and I hugged her tightly back. So much had happened over the past six years, but it was like time had stood still between us. Sure, we had kept a few secrets from each other. Sure, we had lost touch after high school for a few months.

The reality was, loving our LTZ boys had really taken a toll on both of our hearts.

I didn't know why I couldn't bear to tell Zoey—or anyone really—about Jace and how far things had gotten between us. Simply put, I just couldn't talk about it. Plus, I didn't want to hurt her. She rarely mentioned Ty anymore, but I saw the pain flash in her eyes when we'd see a new story or blog post of him with yet another model or actress.

It seemed to be happening more and more with all of them, the media couldn't get enough of the guys of LTZ.

Truthfully, my heart exploded every time I saw Jace with the latest of his own conquests. He still kept himself out of the press, for the most part, so his exploits were not as public as the others. Considering I'd chased after him for years, part of me regretted running away the moment he was ready to make a commitment to me. Seeing him with other women—beautiful, talented, perfect women—made me want to poke my eyes out.

After I left him and made it to Germany, my plan was to go back to my old, carefree life. Let loose and date as much as possible to get him out of my system. Reality was different. I couldn't bear the thought of anyone but Jace touching me. Especially after my pregnancy scare and our breakup. I ended up taking all of this time to "just do me."

196

Needless to say, I'd been celibate for almost two years.

In Munich, I soul searched about why I was so opposed to having kids. I knew that it was the reason Jace backed off from our relationship, so it was important for me to get clear. Partly, it stemmed from my teenage angsty self. My parents' divorce sucked, and I didn't ever want my own kids to go through that.

After a year, my perspective was broader. I still wasn't sure that having a baby was for me, but the thought of a tiny Jace made me smile. Not that it was a possibility anymore. My reaction to the potential baby we could have had hurt him irreparably.

He was through with me.

Zoey and I made a fine pair. She didn't date much. Well, at all. Her excuse was the long hours she worked, which had replaced the long hours she buried herself in college and law school studies. I didn't bother making my own excuses.

"God, I'd sure love to travel with you sometime." Zoey looked at me wistfully. "I'm heading toward thirty and losing out on the best years of my life."

"You're barely twenty-five, you geek. Hardly thirty. Why don't you take a year off?" I encouraged. "We could see the world together!"

"I so want to take you up on that." Zoey pulled her wild mane of hair into a messy knot on top of her head. "Maybe someday."

Not wanting to pressure her, I let it go. Each of us grabbed a box and brought it out to her car. It took about five trips and all I owned was ready to move. We jumped into her Toyota, and soon, we pulled into my parking space under the new condo building. We grabbed a flatbed dolly and in one trip brought the boxes up the elevator to my coveted corner unit.

"I can't believe this view!" Zoey ran to the floor-to-ceiling windows that overlooked the Olympic Mountains and Puget Sound. Two ferries crossed as they made their way to Bainbridge Island and Seattle, respectively. If you craned your head, it was possible to see a glimpse of Mt. Rainier to the left.

"Yeah, the place is small, but the view is to die for." I was going to love having a gorgeous view of the water, so peaceful.

"Can we order pizza and watch some TV?" Zoey flipped on the big-screen TV that came with the condo. "I never do that anymore."

"I haven't watched TV in years." I laughed, plopping down next to her. "Why not?"

After ordering a large Pagliacci AGOG pizza, we settled into the oversize double chairs and started flipping channels. We struggled to find something to watch and laughed at the fact that I had over 600 channels, but "nothing" was on.

Finally, we settled on an entertainment show that was featuring Emmy nominees. As they were reporting on the best actress category, Ty's gorgeous face filled the screen and the shot panned back to reveal a full shot of him wearing a black-and-green-plaid suit, his hair flowing wild around his shoulders. He was holding the delicate hand of the beautiful actress Ronni Miller, who gazed up at him lovingly through a cascade of chestnut curls.

"Tyson Rainier, the sexy singer of LTZ and Ronni Miller, who is nominated for an Emmy this weekend make a gorgeous couple. Hearts are breaking all over the world now that Ty has finally coupled up. Does this mean he is finally over the mysterious Z? She's no doubt crying in her pillow tonight . . ."

Zooming in on Ronni's gorgeous green eyes, even I had to admit that she was stunning. Peaches-and-cream skin, full, pouty lips, and a smile that would make the saddest person happy. Her toned body was the perfect canvas for the understated black Versace dress. Black Louboutin pumps made her legs look like they were miles long.

As the cameras on the red carpet flashed, Ty and Ronni looked at each other with huge smiles on their faces, almost like they shared a secret.

I shut off the TV quickly and looked over at Zoey. Her face was, at first, impassive.

Then she looked at me and tears pooled in her eyes and then spilled.

"I can't handle it," she could barely get the words out. "Even now. I'll never get over him, Alex."

"I don't know what to say." I leaned over to her and rested my head on her shoulder. "I actually didn't mind as much when he was a slutty whore-man. Those girls didn't

mean anything." She buried her face in her hands and wept.

I let her get it all out for a few minutes.

Zoey's voice was raw, anguished. "Now he's settling down with someone. It could have been me, but I threw him away. How pathetic am I that I'm still in love with a guy who doesn't even give me a second thought."

"That's not true." I stared out the window and tried to give her some of the insight I had without overstepping the boundaries she'd always set. "He wrote an entire album about you."

"A hate album." She cried harder.

"It's also a love letter to the only woman I think he'll ever love. Focus on the positive." I gripped her hand. "Sometimes I wish we had never gone to that show."

"I don't. I don't regret any of my time with Ty." Zoey looked up at me and absently touched the butterfly necklace she never took off.

199

"I know it seems that way, and I know that I'm a fucking mess. I'll probably end up a crazy cat lady. I do know what we had was real. How I felt was real. I'm glad that I knew, at least once, what true love really is."

"I am too." I squeezed her hand.

"I mean, you knew love like that with Sam, right?" Zoey squeezed back.

"Sure," I assured her, annoyed at myself that I was not able to tell her that I *did*

know that kind of love, but it was with Jace.

"I really hope that one day we will meet our forever guys and all of us will hang out together." Zoey sniffed. "I missed you, I've been a bad friend."

"You're my best friend." The type of friendship we shared was unconditional. "You've never been a bad friend."

"Even when I disappeared?" Zoey sounded unsure, almost insecure.

"So did I."

"I feel more grown-up than I should at my age." Zoey shifted her position to look at me. She reached out and held a big clump of her hair out. 'I'm pretty sure I'm going gray."

Mock-scoffing, I got up and put the pizza box on the counter. "I'm just glad we're back in the same city. We can live in a retirement community together with three dogs and ten cats since we clearly are never going to be able to get over these stupid boys."

"Fuck Ty and fuck Sam!" Zoey thrust her fist in the air.

"Yeah!" I put my fist in the air, figuring there was no need to correct the name. "And I'm not watching the fucking Emmys." Zoey flipped the channel and joined me in the kitchen to get dessert snacks.

Or, in other words, M&M's, brownie bites, and Sour Patch worms.

"Me either!" I helped her gather the treats.

Giggling, we sat back down and decided that the safer viewing decision would be the latest season of *Ozark*. No chance of LTZ landmines with that show.

Until, of course, one of their goddamn songs played in the background.

Glancing over at my best friend when it started, she caught my eye immediately. We both laughed until tears streamed out of our eyes. Sure, our emotions might be all over the place, but we had each other.

The funny thing about having someone like Zoey in your life, it didn't matter how many minutes, hours, days, or years went by without seeing each other, we'd always have each other's backs.

We'd always be the first one in each other's corner.

For that, we were lucky.

CHAPTER 15

Scrubbing the sleep out of my eyes after the alarm went off at 6 a.m., I jumped up, threw open the curtains, and surveyed the view of the Hollywood Hills from my hotel suite. Yawning, I put on my gym clothes, had a piss, and brushed my teeth.

Ty and I had both stopped drinking in South America a couple of years ago and had replaced our late-night partying with early-morning workouts. It was awesome to feel healthy and physically fit, it helped our stamina onstage and off.

Not that I needed it off stage much anymore.

Reluctantly, I'd gone along with Sienna and Andrew's ridiculous plan for Ty to pretend that he had a serious relationship with Ronni Miller. The embarrassing pictures and videos of Ty fucked-up beyond repair, making out with random chicks, and acting like an asshole was all behind us. We'd finally followed through on the plan I'd first hatched in Belfast.

Clean living. Sober living. And for Ty, therapy.

When I heard him knock on the door to my hotel suite, I was ready to burn some calories.

"My dude." I nodded and let him in.

Ty grinned at me; his long hair was tied up in a top knot. "Weights today?"

"Why not?" I socked him in the arm.

After a grueling two-hour workout, we returned to my suite and ordered healthy egg-white omelets and bacon, because—bacon. He popped back over to his room for a shower and I did the same. Ten minutes later, he returned with his Breedlove acoustic guitar right before breakfast arrived. After we finished eating, we sat down to write.

"How were the Emmys?" I asked. We were in LA to record, which enabled Ty to make another red-carpet appearance with Ronni.

"Meh." Ty wrinkled his lips. "At least the Grammys have performances. The Emmys are really boring. I felt like a dick, people knew me, but I had no idea—"

"How's Ronni?" I waggled my eyebrows, hoping that Ty was really moving on.

 Maybe if he did, then I could.

"She's cool." He shrugged indifferently. "We're becoming good friends, but as you know we aren't really together. It's just for show."

"Why not just get with her?" I asked. "I mean, she's easy on the eyes. Plus, it gets people off your case for a while."

"I'm really not into lying. But she needs to dirty up her image as much as Andrew and Sienna think that I need to clean up mine, so—"

"I get it." I pulled out my reading glasses and the small keyboard

I used when I wanted to write music, something I'd been doing a lot more of. Since Alex.

"Do you ever get sick of the travel?" Ty sat back on the cream sofa and crossed his arms. "It's really wearing on me."

"Yeah. I've spent a grand total of two weeks in Seattle this entire year." I had been having similar thoughts since Alex and I broke up. "Yet, I'm not quite ready for the ride to end."

"Me either." Ty looked off into space and muttered, "I'm not sure if I could handle living in Seattle again."

"I get that." I did. Living in Seattle meant possibly running into Alex. I certainly wasn't sure if I could handle that.

"I'm buying a place here in LA." Ty sat forward, his elbows resting on his knees. "I put an offer in a couple of days ago."

"Wow," I exclaimed. "You're going to be a land mogul. You've come a long way, grasshopper."

"I have." Ty beamed. "I still have a long way to go."

Bonding time over, we began jamming and writing lyrics. Ideas for songs were flowing. A knock on the door interrupted our rhythm when Zane and Connor came in to join us. Together we worked through the rest of one song and came up with the beginnings of another as a group. Aside from Connor, who had a bug up his ass, the chemistry was incredible. It felt like old times.

"My dudes." Zane put his arm around Ty and Connor. "I wanted to run something past you."

"Shoot," I said pointing a finger gun at him.

"Dude! Not very PC," Zane chastised and then continued. "Fiona's in a real bind. The owner of the Mission's building is threatening to sell it."

"I thought her dad owned it." Ty scrunched his eyebrows together.

"I did too, but no." Zane shrugged. "When Gus passed away, she inherited a real mess. Dad has tried to help, but Seattle's changing so much. Anyway, it's part of history. I don't want to lose it as a venue. Would any of you want to go in on it and buy the building?"

"I'd do it, but I just put an offer on a house here in LA." Ty frowned. "Sorry."

"What the fuck?" Connor shot him a dirty look. "Why would you move down here? Oh, right. Ronni."

"Not the reason, dude. You know that. It's just that we're here all the time. Did you see the band's hotel bill last year?" Ty was decisive and firm. "It's bad financial decision making."

"Uh-huh." Connor didn't seem convinced. He sounded pissed. At Ty.

"Is everything cool, Connor?" I nudged him.

"Fucking great," he muttered.

"Uh, guys?" Zane glared at all of us with his arms crossed. "Can we stay on track?"

"Connor, did I do something to piss you off?" Ty was pained, he hated when any of

us were mad at each other.

"Of course not, Saint Ty," Connor said in a mocking voice.

Ty's face scrunched up with hurt. Clearly, he had no idea what was going on. I gripped his shoulder and squeezed my support and shot Connor a stern look. He narrowed his eyes and looked away.

It made me sad that Connor and I had drifted apart year by year after he and Jen broke up. We were still tight as bandmates and the rhythm section, but our lifestyles were just different. He ended to either keep to himself or go out doing God knows what with Zane. Zane rarely drank because he was such a natural extrovert, but Connor

206

needed liquid courage to be social.

Over the years the crew whispered a lot about their weird dynamic of picking up and sharing chicks. I'd not seen any evidence of it myself, but I'd gotten off the merry- go-round.

"Connor, stop being so pissy." Zane elbowed him. "The focus right now is on the Mission."

"I'll chip in," I said. "My condo's paid off and so is the house I bought my parents."

"Fuck it," Connor growled. "I'll chip in something."

"Great!" Zane fist-bumped the two of us. "Carter's in too. He's figuring out what needs to be done, I'll let you know."

"I'm outta here." Connor got up and gave Ty a pointed look and stalked out.

"My dudes, we'll see ya in a few hours." Zane followed him.

"What the fuck did I do to Connor? He's being so weird." Ty looked at me, confused.

"You're right, he totally seems mad at you." I didn't know what was going on either, it was unlike Connor to be so overt with his feelings.

"I can't figure it out." Ty shrugged. "I'll talk to him later about it."

We got back to work on the song. Ty was working out a beautiful melody on his acoustic. Grabbing my phone, I began filming him playing. Although there were no lyrics, Ty's head was bouncing to the melody, his eyes squeezed shut as he hummed out a vocal line. After a while, he sighed and put down his guitar. Slowly opening his eyes, he looked like he was far away.

"Do you still miss her?" I knew without a shadow of a doubt the song was not about Ronni.

"Zoey?" Ty smiled when he said her name.

"Yeah." I looked at him directly. "That's who you were thinking about in that song, right?"

"Every day." Ty looked down at the worn leather bracelet he wore and rubbed it with his fingers. "Every day."

"Time doesn't make it better?"

"Do you want me to say yes?" He cocked his head.

"I want you to tell me the truth." I leaned back and crossed my arms behind my head.

"Why do you want to know?" Ty stared me down, a challenge to tell him what was really on my mind.

"No reason."

"Tell *me* the truth."

"I miss Alex." I couldn't stop myself. "We only had a few good weeks together. I wanted it to be more. She didn't. Now I can't stop thinking about her."

"Hmm. Sounds familiar." Ty looked pensive. "Are you in love with her?"

"Um."

"Well—" Ty shook his head. "I guess you just have to have hope."

"Hope for what?"

"Hope that the timing will be right someday." Ty sat back and considered his own words. Then nodded to himself as if acquiescing to that possibility.

"Do you still hope that?" I was shocked. That ship had sailed long ago. "Every day." Ty clapped me on the back. "Every day."

CHAPTER 16

A few weeks after I moved, I was on my way to Palm Desert. Gratefully, I took the small bottle of water the flight attendant offered me when I plopped down in my seat. I'd only been to Coachella once before, it wasn't really my scene.

Especially now.

Under normal circumstances, I wouldn't have gone, but the money was too big to pass up. In addition to my condo, I'd saved up enough to buy property on the Olympic Peninsula outright. Now I was socking away the funds so when I found the right location, I could finally start a horse rescue and run it for many years without other donations.

In another year or so, my influencer lifestyle would be a thing of my past. My future was saving horses.

Until then, a high-end shopping platform aimed at millennials was paying me six figures to exclusively endorse some featured jewelry. It wasn't so bad. The pieces were cool. And, I got to keep them.

Around my neck, I wore a stunning sterling silver necklace of moons, stars, and planets encrusted with tiny diamonds. Angling my phone like a pro, I took several shots and then uploaded the best one to Instagram, tagging the designer and adding in a fun description and some hashtags.

One down, fifty more posts to go.

When the plane began its descent, my nerves began to fire. LTZ was headlining the third night of the festival. I was expected to be backstage and at all of the parties to post pictures of the jewelry and make sure that celebrities would see the pieces. It meant I'd likely run into Jace, and it had been nearly two years since we'd had any contact.

Sadly, I was on my own for the entire lonely weekend.

A car service picked me up and took me to the JW Marriott, an enormous luxury resort in the desert where talent who weren't put up in private mansions often stayed. My room was basic but had a nice view of the pool and their resort's flamingo pond. With a couple of hours to spare, I decided to get some Vitamin D. After donning my American flag bikini, a white, gauzy cover-up, a floppy hat, and sunglasses, I was ready and headed for the pool.

Luckily, I found a great spot right at the edge of the adult area, sprayed myself down with sunscreen, and lay back to soak up the sun. The winters and spring in Seattle were not warm, so feeling the rays permeate my body with heat and Vitamin D was relaxing.

I dozed off.

Vaguely, I heard someone get settled in the chair to my right, but I was enjoying my peaceful afternoon, so I didn't even open my eyes. Soon, I began to drift off again.

"Alex." I heard my name spoken softly; the familiar raspy voice made all the hairs on my arm stand up.

Sitting up suddenly caused my boob to pop out of my bikini top. Quickly, I adjusted myself and looked over.

"Jace." My heart began beating a million miles a minute.

"I like how you say hello." Jace sat upright on the lounge chair in all his shirtless glory, wearing the same black-and-white board shorts he wore in Italy. His dark-blond hair was shorter—almost a long bob, which accentuated his cleft chin.

The man was ridiculous.

He lowered his mirrored aviator shades, and his piercing green eyes assessed my cleavage. His grin spread across his face, causing his goddamn lickable dimples to sink into irresistible craters.

"Well, it's nothing you haven't seen before." I shrugged, trying to act nonchalant while adjusting my top to make sure that things were where they were supposed to be.

"Alex, you are fucking stunning." Jace leaned back on his muscled arms, regarding me. I couldn't help but stare at the striking poppy art on his shoulder, the bright reds seemed to burst from the Viking compass winding around his biceps and shoulder. My heart raced. Somehow, I'd forgotten all about the tattoo. Blocked it from my mind, more likely.

"You surprised me; I didn't know the band would be staying here." I tried to keep my voice even, unaffected. He seemed so confident ogling me when I was completely discombobulated. "I figured you'd be put up in a mansion."

"Nope. After Coachella we're heading to Europe to do some shows on the festival circuit before we're back in the States for a couple of iHeart Radio events. We're actually all staying and rehearsing at Ty's house in LA," Jace rambled, now it seemed almost like he was

211

nervous. "The guys are driving in tomorrow for the show. Since I planned to catch some music this weekend, I booked into the hotel to make a weekend of it."

Jace gulped and then shifted his position so he was lying down in the lawn chair next to me after his word vomit.

"Okay." I relaxed back into my lounger, but I was still indecisive about whether I should stay or make an excuse to head up to my room.

"Um." Jace looked at me sideways behind the mirrored lenses. "It's really good to see you. For the record, I don't like that we've lost touch."

"Hmm." I remained non-committal. I didn't like it either, but I also didn't know how we even could start this conversation. Almost two years was a long time to go without speaking.

Although, we'd done it before.

"I've missed you." His voice was barely audible. "I kept thinking you would show up somewhere."

"No. That wasn't going to happen." I shook my head. "I'm not that girl, anymore."

"Oh. Right." He looked dejected. "So, are you here with someone?"

"No. I'm just here to work."

We sat in silence for a few minutes.

"Um. Did you not show up again because of what, um, happened?" He looked down at a loose piece of the rattan on the lawn chair and began fiddling with it.

"It wasn't the only reason, but it made things very clear," I said truthfully. "That you didn't want to be with me?" His voice caught.

I crossed my arms over my body, almost protectively. "I did want to be with you. I did not want to chase after you like a groupie and give up my own goals."

Jace sighed and lay silent for a long time. After ten minutes, I thought he might have fallen asleep and was listening for his breath to even out so I could sneak away and go back up to my room. I hadn't been prepared to see him, let alone in this sneak-attack situation. Gawd. I wasn't over him, not by any stretch of the imagination.

I hadn't cried in two years and now after seeing Jace, all I wanted to do was escape to have a good cry. By myself.

I was so fucked up.

"Poppy, that's not how it would have been." Jace's voice was still barely a whisper. "I would have done anything to keep you. I let you go because I figured you needed time to catch up to me."

"What does that even mean?"

"You're so much younger." Jace mansplained. "You just weren't ready to be with me. After what happened I knew that I had to let you go and have your own experiences to—"

"Wow. That's some bullshit." I spat.

"It's true."

"Stop, Jace." I gave him the hand and reached for my cover-up. "I can't even."

"What? I don't understand." He sat up and faced me. "I thought I was doing what

you wanted."

"God, you guys are all so dense." I was so fucking perturbed. "You know, between you, Carter, and the guys, you kind of made that decision for Zoey too. How did that turn out?"

"That wasn't me." Jace protested.

"Right. Back when you still called me 'Beanie,' you told me you thought Zoey was too young for Ty." I muttered.

"Alex—" Jace pleaded.

"Jay-son. You're not that much older, dude." I wagged my finger at him and, after realizing I looked like my mom, I put it away. "God, the mansplaining is infuriating. Have I ever been someone that doesn't know my own mind?"

"No." Jace looked down, flustered. "Never."

"So, please just shut up then." I was so pissed; I'd never spoken out like this to him.

I wasn't going to hide who I was anymore.

"How was I supposed to know, Alex?" Jace leaned his elbows on his knees, speaking in a hushed tone. "Sure, you'd show up to see me. But you also *always* were the one who had plans to bail."

I stared at him.

"Even your first time, you wanted me to—" Jace cut himself off. "And then, after Barcelona, do you know how much it sucked when you got engaged to that Australian guy?"

"This is so stupid. We can't keep doing this, and we *really* can't do this here." I managed to keep my voice quiet to avoid any more attention. I was desperate to get away from having this conversation.

"Poppy, just tell it to me straight. Have you moved on?" Jace took both my hands in his and rubbed the tops with his thumbs. And dammit, watching him caress me with his strong fingers provided a sense of comfort I'd been missing since I last saw him.

I didn't answer, I just intertwined my fingers with his. We sat there silently for what seemed like hours, but it was probably no longer than a few seconds. Zaps of energy buzzed between our fingers. Without thinking, my head tilted up and my lips gravitated toward his, and he met me halfway. Our mouths parted to taste each other for the first time in so many months. Jace's grip on my hands tightened and he used the leverage to drag me toward him to deepen our kiss.

Conscientious that we were in full public view of hundreds of rooms, I broke our connection completely and grabbed my cover-up in one motion. I pulled it over my bikini, toed on my flip-flops, and picked up my bag. Without saying a word, I strode purposefully away from him, winding through the lawn chairs and around the kiosk where the towels were handed out. Jace followed close behind all the way through the big glass doors and into the corridor leading to the guest elevators. I didn't stop until I pressed the "up" button.

"Alex, wait." Jace gently caressed my elbow.

"I really can't deal with this weird thing we have going anymore." I steeled my emotions. "It's too difficult."

"Do you know what isn't difficult? I still *want* to be with you." Jace's voice broke. "Now more than ever."

"Your words and actions are different." I gulped down the lump lodged in the back of my throat that formed when I realized it was him sitting next to me.

"Let's go to your room and talk." Jace regained his composure. "Or, you can come to mine."

"All we'll do is end up naked, Jace." I shook my elbow loose from his caresses. "And once we're naked, well? We'll start up again."

"What's wrong with starting up again?" Jace was so goddamn gorgeous. And earnest. I knew my resistance would be non-existent if I didn't get away soon.

"Because, I couldn't even tell you *what* we'd start up again." I practically flung myself into the elevator once it opened.

"We'd start seeing each other again." Jace sauntered in after me. "It doesn't have to be complicated."

"So, being separated by continents for months at a time isn't complicated?"

"Unlike most people, we don't have to be separated." Jace pulled his sunglasses off and leveled his green eyes at me.

"Right, as long as I get a copy of your schedule and you let me know which dates work for you?" I crossed my arms over my chest.

"It doesn't have to be that way."

"Why didn't you ever reach out if I meant so much to you? You just let me go." I slumped against the wall. "You never even texted me."

Jace shrugged his shoulders. "I thought you must have needed a break from me pressuring you."

"Two years." I stared at him. "That's a long fucking break. Especially—"

"You didn't make any effort either, Poppy." Jace raised a dark-blond eyebrow, the dimples in his cheeks popped when he smirked.

"This isn't funny, Jace. I've made all of the effort with you. First, I basically begged you to take my virginity. Then I chased you across the world. Our relationship consisted

 of six months of flying into cities so I could fuck you in a hotel room." I seethed. "It began to get humiliating."

"I never knew you felt that way. It wasn't until Italy that I realized you had serious doubts. I thought we were having the best time together." Jace furrowed his brow and slumped against the side of the elevator too. "Then when we got home, you—"

"Ran away back to Europe." I finished. "Which was what you wanted me to do."

"That's not fucking true, Alex."

Ignoring him, I marched down the hall to my room when the elevator door opened on my floor. Jace followed close behind. I swiped my card key and pushed inside. Jace followed me in and locked and deadbolted the door before wrapping his arms around me and pulling me against his chest.

"That's not true," Jace whispered in my ear. "You wanted to leave. I loved you enough to let you go."

"Maybe I wanted *you* to follow *me* for once."

"Poppy, guys are dense. You should have just said that." Jace tightened his arms. "How would I have known that?"

I melted back into his arms. "Well, it doesn't matter now. I moved back to Seattle a year ago."

"I know." Jace rested his chin on my neck. "Jen has been staying at my place with her girlfriend. She's seen you around."

"Oh." All the fight went out of me. "Wait, she knows about me?"

"Of course. She knows about the most important people in my life." He kissed along the back of my neck causing my entire body to ignite.

"Jace—"

"Oh, Alex." Jace tightened his arms and buried his face in my nape like he was breathing me in. "You're all I think about."

"You're all I think about too." I conceded. "You know me better than anyone in the world."

"Except Zoey." Jace nibbled my ear.

"Better than Zoey, unlike her you have tasted every part of my body." I turned to face him and clasped my arms around his neck.

Jace bent his lips to mine and kissed me softly over and over again. Cupping my head and weaving his strong fingers through my hair, he positioned my head so he could control the pace of our kisses.

Only Jace kissed me like this and dammit, his kisses were the only ones I ever wanted.

217

Dreamily, he sipped from the corner of my mouth, traced my lower lip with his tongue and then in one motion gripped my ass and hauled me up against him. Hooking my legs around his waist, I gyrated my molten core against his hard length. Our kisses turned sloppy and frantic.

"Please. I need—" I begged.

"Shh. Let me take care of you." Jace's erection pulsed against me, and he walked me to the bed to lay me down on my back.

In one fluid motion, he pulled my bikini briefs off, flung them to the floor, palmed under my knees, and pressed my legs apart. He devoured me like he hadn't eaten in years.

My entire core was like a live electric wire, and each swipe of Jace's tongue and nibble of his lips set off firecrackers. Madly grinding my pussy against his mouth while Jace suckled and moaned against me, I spread my legs as wide as they would go. He inserted two fingers to press against my G-spot and suctioned my clit in his mouth while dragging his tongue through my folds. I detonated like an atom bomb, screaming his name, bucking and gushing against his face.

"God, I missed you." Jace murmured into my pussy, suckling my folds as I came down from the type of earthshattering orgasm I hadn't experienced since the last time we were together.

I couldn't speak. He kissed up my body and gave me a taste of my own release. "I don't want anyone but you, Alex."

"I don't want anyone but you," I echoed, pulling him down, needing to feel the weight of his body on mine.

Jace wrapped his arms around my upper body. His dick twitched against my stomach through his thin board shorts. We lay cuddled like that for a few minutes until he braced himself on his elbows on either side of my head and looked at me intently.

"Are you ready for me now?" Jace's husky voice was tinged with passion. He touched his forehead to mine.

"Yes." I tenderly stroked his messy hair, smoothing it back as it flopped over his brow.

"No." Jace's arms caged my upper body and his emerald eyes pierced my soul. "I don't mean sex."

My heart was beating so hard that I couldn't tell if I was panicked, thrilled, relieved, or all three. All I knew was that I never wanted another man to touch me for as long as I lived.

So, scared. Scared was what I felt. It made me squirmy.

"I'm scared." Shockingly, I somehow managed to express exactly how I was feeling.

Jace rolled off me and scooted up on the bed against the pillows, taking me with him and tucking me into his side. One arm encircled my body, holding me snugly to his side. With his other hand, he stroked my temples and cheek with his knuckles like a whisper.

"Well, I'm terrified too right now," Jace said into the air. "Why?"

"Because I told you how I felt in Italy. That I loved you. That I wanted to be with you—" He scrubbed his strong hand over his chin, his long, sun-streaked hair wild about his face. "I'd never said that to anyone before. I'll never say it to anyone else."

"I never allowed myself to believe it." The truth of my words stung. I sagged against his chest.

"But you said you loved me too." Jace blew out a frustrated breath. "I *believed*

you."

"Well, I meant it." I deflated even further. I didn't consider myself an insecure person. It stung being confronted with the reality that my subconscious self-doubt might have pushed away this gorgeous man. "I guess I didn't trust that you did."

Jace pondered what I said for a minute. "Christ! I asked you to go on tour with me.

You have the most flexible fucking job in the world. I don't even know what to say."

"Jace. You know why. You can't put this all on me."

"Hey. Hey—Poppy. Geez. I'm really not trying to make you feel bad." Jace's voice softened. "Let me get this off my chest. Because we need to be honest with each other."

"Okay." I blinked back my escalating emotions. Inhaled and exhaled. I willed the lump in my throat to go away.

"When I asked you to come back to Seattle with me, it was so obvious to me that you didn't want to be there. With me." Jace's mouth was set in a firm line, his hands clenched together. "I know that I had obligations, but you were not mentally there. I *felt* it."

I didn't say anything, just nodded at him to finish.

"When we had that, um, scare." He puffed out air. "I think why I was so, um— Disappointed, in the results, I guess. Was, well. I *knew* it would have been the only thing that would have kept us together at that point."

"I was disappointed too," I admitted, probably for the first time even to myself.

"I don't think you were then," Jace said quietly, his face squinched with pain. "Your reaction. God. It was so, *definitive.* You wouldn't even consider ever raising a kid with me. You said you were getting your *tubes tied.* It broke my heart."

"Jace—" I reached for him.

He shook his head, and I moved my hand back, stung.

"I was out getting this poppy tattoo, planning a future with you.

You'd already booked your ticket to get away from me." Jace looked at me sadly and stroked the red flower on his arm. "Even before you took the tests. It was already booked. I was so pissed. Hurt. You even contemplated not telling me. Even if you'd been pregnant, you might've have left. That's when I knew you didn't want me."

I covered my mouth with my hand.

Jace took a deep breath. "I can't believe it's been almost two years."

"You unfollowed me, and I never heard from you." I shook my head. "I thought you were relieved for it to be over."

"No, I just didn't want to see—I couldn't see you with anyone else." Jace lay back down next to me. "I wanted to give you space. I really thought you'd show up somewhere. I never stopped hoping."

"Part of me has always thought that I was chasing you and you were just humoring the kid who had such an obvious crush on you." I couldn't stop a tear from escaping. "It's been our dynamic."

Jace wiped my tear with his finger before it rolled down my cheek. "Fuck, Poppy. That's what you think our dynamic is? You've had me completely wrapped around your finger all of these years, and you don't even know it."

"Since that first time we had sex, I've never wanted anyone the way I want you, Jace." My heart was overwhelmed with his confession. "But I've always had my own goals and dreams that were just as important to me. I've settled back down in Seattle now. I'm going to start my own horse rescue soon. I don't want to go on the road anymore."

"And I'm about to go back out on tour." He took my hand, brought it to his lips, and kissed it.

An endless cycle of heartbreak.

JACE

CHAPTER 17

There was nowhere I'd rather be than quietly cuddling on the bed after such cathartic and long-overdue confessions. While we wound down from the emotional afternoon, I tried to process what this unexpected reunion meant.

Earlier, after I'd checked in and stepped out onto my hotel balcony to take in the view of the pool, my eyes had been drawn to and fixed on Alex immediately. My heart had stopped. Even from a distance, I'd know her anywhere.

Anytime.

Anyplace.

My first instinct was to ignore her. To try to forget I'd seen her supple, tan curves, sexy hipbones jutting just above her bikini bottom. Her toned long legs. Her succulent tits straining against the tiny scraps of fabric. I'd paced my room. Went and got a beer at the lobby bar.

Went back to my room and closed the curtains. Peeked out of the curtains to gawk at her flawless body, hard dick in my hand, stroking one out like a creepy stalker.

Nothing worked.

The next thing I knew I was sitting in the chair next to her.

"Jace?" Alex snapped her fingers in front of my eyes, taking me back to the present.

"You said that I know you better than anyone. I don't think that's true. But I want to. I really want to know all of you."

"I don't get what you mean." She blinked up at me, obviously not following what I was trying to say.

"I'd like to go backward in time and start over."

"Well, I don't want to play games." Alex buried her face back into my chest.

Stroking her hair, I really wanted to turn things around for us. "Me either. Maybe all we have done is play games."

"You're right. You're *so* right."

"So, let's be together." I kissed her head.

"Just like that."

"Yep."

She rubbed my stomach, tracing my still-rock-hard abs. All the working out Ty and I had done over the past couple of years had changed my six-pack into an eight-pack.

We lay staring at each other for what seemed like forever.

"So, just like before, you want me to stop what I'm doing to go on tour with you?" Alex didn't seem all that thrilled at the prospect.

I couldn't blame her. It didn't make sense when she had so much going on. It was time for me to make a few changes.

"No. My time is so packed when we are on the road. It will be even worse this time because we are compressing the tour. We're going hard for four to six weeks then taking at least a week, maybe two, off. Repeat."

Alex looked at me incredulously. "Well, then I'm not sure what you mean about us being together."

"I'll come home to you."

"Huh?"

I ran my hand up and down her arm and squeezed her to me. "I mean, I'll come to Seattle on my breaks. Unless you're gonna be somewhere else, and then I'll go there."

Alex's eyes bugged out like a cartoon character. "You'll come to me?"

"Sure. Wherever you are." I couldn't stop smiling at the thought. "Or we could go away for a vacation. Whatever we want."

Alex looked around the room, her expression confused. "Am I being punked? Do you mean it?"

I settled even deeper into the bed pillows and wrapped my arms around Alex, compelling her to relax against me again. "I do mean it. All of us are trying to find a better balance after seven solid years of working. This is sort of a test year to see if this is a pace we can live with."

She snuggled under my arm and let out a long breath. "When I woke up this morning, I can honestly say that I didn't expect this in a million years."

"Me either." I laughed. "Maybe it's fate."

"I'd like to try it to see how things go." Alex tipped her head up for a kiss.

Our lips touched tentatively for just a millisecond until she opened for me, and our tongues danced and our lips explored. Her long, elegant fingers wove through my mop of hair and lured me in closer. The truth was, I needed to be as close to her as I knew how to get.

"Poppy, I don't mean to be crass, but I need to be balls-deep inside you." My voice was a rasp. "Right fucking now."

Grasping her soft hair at her neck, I pulled it tight into a ponytail with my fist and angled her face to mine. Hungrily, I devoured her lips, moving her head at the angle that allowed me the most access. Wrapping my other arm around her waist, I guided her on top of me so her bare pussy covered my erection. Alex immediately reached inside my board shorts and began deftly stroking my cock just the way I liked it, a little flair over my engorged tip.

"I don't want to ever leave this room." She murmured in between kisses.

Growling, I lifted her cover-up over her head and with both hands pulled the cups of her bikini to the sides, exposing her perfect, perky breasts. Rubbing my thumbs over her nipples, I loved how they beaded and darkened with my strokes. My dick was now painfully hard and throbbing with the necessity of being inside my girl. My girl. Alex was my girl.

I wasn't going to fuck it up this time.

Glancing down at her fingers stroking me, I groaned when her thumb smeared precum over my crown. My cock twitched appreciatively. Her smile was deceptively sweet.

"Two can play at that game, Poppy." I pinched her nipple and watched it pucker tightly before suckling it hard into my mouth and swirling the bud all around with my tongue and repeating on the other side. Alex's breathing became shallower and shallower as she continued pumping my cock. Not wanting to wait another minute, in one motion I maneuvered on top of her and knelt in between her legs.

"This is a good game." Alex grasped my shaft and pointed it to her opening.

Nothing turned me on more than seeing Alex spread and ready for me, her long, tan legs spanning the bed. Her flat stomach quivered in anticipation, the blue jewel in her belly ring shimmered in the sunlight peeking through the curtains. Replacing her hand with mine, I rubbed the tip of my cock against the erect nub of her clit and swiped my dick through her creamy juices. When my crown was glistening with her moisture, I fed my hard length inside her inch by inch until she was completely full of me.

"Ohhhh." Alex's head was thrown back in ecstasy. She dug her heels into the bed behind my ass.

My hands spanned and caressed her stomach, her ribcage, and her breasts. I watched myself thrust slowly and deeply inside her. All I wanted was to worship her gorgeous body, to celebrate our reunion. Reaching under her hips, I clutched the firm globes of her ass and guided her upright to sit on my thighs. Alex wrapped her arms around my neck and her legs around my waist. I cupped her butt and hips to rock her onto my cock. Deeper. Deeper.

Our eyes met and we clung more tightly to each other, trying to get as close as physically possible.

Burying my head into her hair, her tropical oceany scent filled my lungs. I could hear her bangle bracelets jingle as she writhed against me to find her nirvana. She cried out and clutched me even harder. In that moment I decided, without any further question, that this was it. I would never let anyone touch my precious Poppy ever again, she was mine and mine alone.

I placed opened-mouth kisses along her ear and neck, trying to taste every inch of her. Reverentially, I bathed her with my tongue. My cock grew harder inside her. Alex tenderly explored the planes of my shoulders and down my spine, settling at my lower back where she pressed me into her faster and faster. Using her grip on my shoulders as leverage, she leaned back, causing her diamond-pointed nipples to thrust up delectably. I caught them in my mouth, one after the other, and suctioned hard.

"Jace!" Alex shrieked. Her thighs gripped my waist like a vise. "I'm so close, it's sooo close."

That was it, my hands bridged her hips and I moved her against me like a wild man, driving up and into her, never releasing the suction on her nipple. Alex's entire body went stiff and she threw her head back, convulsing against me uncontrollably. Squeezing me. Wailing. Letting go like I'd never seen before. I couldn't hold back; tingles ran down my spine through my cock and I exploded inside her with a loud shout.

We embraced each other tightly through our aftershocks. I traced my finger across her eyebrows, her eyes, down her cheek. Amazed that she was here. Feeling content. Whole, maybe.

I just knew that things were different, not just for me but for her too.

I sank onto the bed and Alex flopped against me, lying back in the crook of my arm. The emotional and physical exertion of the past couple of hours had exhausted me, but I was finally satiated. Happy. Alex was back where she belonged, her eyes half-mast, watching me while absentmindedly stroking my hair.

"I'm so glad I saw you by the pool." I kissed her forehead. "Who are you working for down here?"

"I'm promoting this awesome jewelry line." Alex held up her slender arm and shook her wrist. The silver bangle bracelets she wore jingled, tiny stars, moons, and planets sparkled with diamond chips.

"These are cool." I reached up and touched the bracelets.

Alex laced her fingers with mine. "You've never asked me about anything I've ever promoted."

"Maybe it was me that needed to grow up. My head has been buried up my ass long enough."

Alex giggled.

"Hey, you aren't meant to agree!" I tickled her, causing her to squeal.

Alex turned on her side and circled my nipple with our fingers, causing it to pucker.

I brought our clasped hands to my heart.

"Is this real?" Alex whispered against my chest. "You better fucking believe it."

The next three days were a real whirlwind.

After a night and morning of passion, we moved Alex's things into my bigger room and christened it everywhere. We spent the next day at Coachella decidedly together, holding hands and taking in a few bands using my All-Access pass to watch from the side stage. Alex looked stunning in a white, crochet halter top and long, flowy skirt with her ever-present black Frye boots, a floppy hat, and long, colorful scarf protecting her from the dusty terrain. She also wore dozens of her client's dainty astrological chains around her neck and wrists.

After she got her posts done on the second day, we decided to skip Beyoncé, who was headlining. Instead, we spent the next twelve hours reconnecting and revisiting every position we could think of in my hotel suite.

On the final night, since we were headlining, I had to duck out early in the morning to do a soundcheck before the gates opened.

While I was gone Alex planned on posting the final shots she needed for her client. Needless to say, we got caught up and I was late for my drum check.

Two years ago, headlining Coachella would have been the most important thing in my life.

This year . . . Well, every year from now on, it was Alex.

Whistling, I strolled backstage where everyone was waiting for me. I took my place on the drum riser without saying a word.

"Nice of you to show up, J." Ty boomed into the mic, looking over his shoulder at

me.

"Must have been a pretty good night," Connor replied into his on mic.

Ignoring the peanut gallery, I grabbed a pair of drumsticks from my bag and began warming up without feeling any need to explain. After we finished our quick soundcheck, we headed to our dressing room before we began the first round of press.

"Jace, where have you been? You haven't blown a gasket, so I guess you haven't heard the news." Zane said quietly as we made our way through the maze of production to the band area.

"Stop making it such a big deal." Ty caught up to us.

"What happened?" I was confused and still pretty giddy from my Alex reunion. "Ty and Ronni broke up," Connor said gruffly. "It was quite a spectacle."

"We staged the whole relationship, she's in love with someone else," Ty protested. "We were both sick of the lies."

I grabbed my reading glasses and pulled up the gossip sites and LTZ's Instagram after being blessedly free of social media for the past day. "Jesus, I'll leave you alone for a minute."

Immediately I was inundated with reports and images of Ronni and Ty screaming at each other outside of Mr. Chow in Beverly Hills. Booze and sex paparazzi pictures of Ty from a few years before had also made a comeback. Article after article about their breakup cast Ty in the asshole role. Sure enough, Ty had blown his good-guy image up again.

"For fuck's sake." I leveled a glare at him. "You're determined to ruin your own
 life."

"No, I'm trying to take control back. I'm not a liar." Ty stared me down. "It was
 wrong of you and the PR team to make me have a fake girlfriend."

"Well, you certainly managed to get yourself in the press again." I showed him a gnarly picture of him passed out somewhere with his cock getting sucked by some random groupie. "Nice work."

"God damn it!" Ty handed my phone back to me and stalked toward the dressing room. "I'm not going to the press room."

I yelled after him, "You sure as fuck are."

Sighing, I flipped through the coverage. Headline after headline of what a fuck-up Ty was and how he broke the pure-and-innocent Ronni's heart inundated my feed. Ty had become so famous that this breakup had pushed all the other headlines of the day into the background.

After placing a quick call to Sienna and Andrew, I began feverishly scrubbing the stories and pulling down the old pictures again in between interviews before the show.

Of course, the "breakup" was all the press wanted to talk about with us, so we probably seemed lame when we kept repeating, "no comment." Needless to say, we were all a little testy by the time our set rolled around.

I texted Alex to give her the heads-up about the situation and the mood backstage. She decided to watch from the crowd and meet me back at my room after the show.

Years of being on the road and suffering through bad press had made us consummate professionals, and our show was the best we had played in months. When we finished our last encore, all I wanted to do was shower and get back to the hotel and Alex.

"Dude, I'm sorry." Ty was waiting for me in the lounge area of the dressing room.

I sat down next to him; he deserved a break. "Don't sweat it."

"I just couldn't do it anymore, I'm so sick of feeling like a fuck-up." He sighed, leaned back into the couch, and stared at the ceiling.

"I've got a team taking down all of the photos."

Ty peered over at me. "You don't need to do that."

"I do."

"It won't matter." Ty laughed bitterly. "I did all of those things; I might as well own

it."

"Owning it is one thing, being stupid is another." I raised an eyebrow at him. "I'm

not a believer in all press is good press."

Ty sounded exhausted, over all of the bullshit. "No one cares, Jace."

"I care. You care." I reminded him. "You don't want those out there for the world to

see."

"And by the world you mean—" Ty rubbed his temples. "It's

humiliating looking

like a whore, but I guess if the shoe fits."

"You're too hard on yourself. All of us have been there." I reassured him. "Being on the road nonstop for seven years is lonely."

Ty squeezed his eyes shut and puffed out a few breaths. "There's only been one brief time in my life when I wasn't lonely. I'm resigned at this point."

"Jesus. You're still not over Zoey?" I squinted at him.

"Ding ding ding," he said listlessly.

"Well—" I started.

"I don't want to hear anything." Ty sat up and pointed at me. "Seriously, I don't want to hear anything you've found out from Alex."

"They are best friends, I could—"

Ty shook his head conclusively. "No. I don't want anyone interfering in my personal life anymore. I mean it. You have to promise me."

"Dude, okay." I shook my head. "But you should at least know that she's back in Seattle."

"Fuck." Ty buried his face in his hands.

"I haven't seen her." I clasped his shoulder. "But maybe you should."

"No." Ty shook his head. "I need some time and space to just figure out who I am and what I want. No interference from you guys. Carter. Ronni. Groupies. Management. No bullshit. I'm going to finish the next months of the tour celibate, clean, and sober and focused on just me and what I want to do."

"That's probably a healthy thing for you." I conceded.

"I never thought we'd be this successful. Or famous. But I have to believe that I can do more now that I have this platform." Ty crossed his arms and studied me. "You know? I've wasted too many years."

"Yep, I know. More than you think."

"Hopefully, your situation will turn out better than mine." Ty's phone pinged and he got up, grabbed his bag, and headed for the door. "The helicopter is here, I'm heading back to LA, see you in the studio in a few days."

"Later." I waved.

Ty had grown up before my eyes. He wasn't the insecure nerd-turned-rock-god anymore. He was a man, taking responsibility for himself and refusing to do anything that made him feel uncomfortable or fraudulent. I respected him for it. I was also relieved because without consciously realizing it, I had taken on the role of his protector for years. I was ready to focus on myself too.

My thoughts were interrupted when my phone pinged. Thinking it was Alex, I stared into the camera to unlock my phone.

C: Jace, I really need to see you.

Fucking Cassie. I knew it had been a mistake to hook up with her six months ago in LA. I hadn't seen or heard from her in years after she and her sister had moved out of Seattle. Thinking it would be fun to see them both again, I'd met them for drinks after a long studio session.

Wrong.

Stretched, botoxed, and filled beyond recognition with giant watermelon tits, the sisters both looked like deformed plastic versions of their former selves. After fifteen minutes of insipid conversation about all the celebrities they'd hooked up with, I was determined to finish my drink and go.

To my surprise, the next thing I remembered was waking up the next morning in Cassie's bed. Both of us naked. I felt like shit. The hangover was like nothing I'd ever experienced, and my recollection about the previous night's activity was fuzzy at best. It was clear that we'd had sex, even though I didn't remember a thing.

When I couldn't find the used condom, I got the hell out of there and went straight to the nearest clinic to get tested. My results returned clean, but to be safe I got tested a couple of weeks later and then again, a couple of weeks ago. Each time the results were clean. Thanking God for small favors, I never bothered confronting her about it.

It didn't mean I wasn't pissed. I simply tried to push it out of my mind and vow that she was permanently out of my life.

Angry with myself for not doing it back then, I deleted her text and blocked the number. Nothing and no one was going to interfere with Alex and me ever again.

Least of all Cassie.

CHAPTER 18

THREE MONTHS LATER

Rushing out of the elevator on the way to my condo, I dropped all my packages to let myself in. Jace was going to be there shortly, and I wanted to look amazing for our date. Once inside, I corralled my purchases into the bedroom and rifled through to find what I was looking for. After I laid out my clothes, I grabbed a small overnight bag and shoved jeans, my Frye boots, and a sweater inside.

Next, I jumped into the shower to clean up, shave all my body parts, slathered my body with my tropical ocean lotion, and quickly dried my hair. With little time for makeup, I settled on some lengthening mascara and nude lipstick. Shimmying into a tight, black halter that pushed my boobs up, I pulled on some black-leather shorts and toed on my indulgent pair of Prada wedge espadrilles. My doorbell rang as I pulled on a few bangle bracelets for good measure.

"Holy hotness." Jace yanked me in for a deep kiss. "This is the right way to greet a man."

He looked incredible in faded, gray moto jeans, a simple, black T-shirt, and black boots. Smiling down at me in between kisses, Jace pushed his Ray-Ban glasses back on his head. I couldn't help but grip his big biceps and lightly trace his poppy tattoo with my thumb.

"We're going to be late." I saucily pushed him away.

"I wish I knew where you were taking me." Jace didn't miss a beat and picked up my bag.

"Then it wouldn't be a surprise." I tucked myself under his strong arm. "But we need some alone time after three months apart."

"We have an entire week before I have any commitments." Jace stopped and held me tight against him. "I hope you didn't bring any clothes; you won't be needing them."

Laughing, we made our way downstairs to my garage. After we put our bags in the trunk of my new Range Rover, I drove the short distance to the ferry terminal and bought a ticket to Bainbridge Island. Once we were on the ferry, Jace tucked his hair under a skull cap and put on aviator glasses to avoid recognition. Then we made our way upstairs to the upper deck.

"It's warm for June." Jace wrapped his arms around me from behind. We stood at the rail and watched the Seattle skyline get smaller and smaller as we headed toward the island.

"Are we really talking about the weather?" I reached up from behind and stroked his cheek.

"I'm a little out of my element, Poppy." Jace grinned down at me. "We're actually out on a date."

"Get used to it." I leaned up and kissed his soft lips. "We're dating now."

"I like it. And, I intend to." He tightened his arms around me, and we snuggled through the rest of the ferry ride across Puget Sound with the fresh, salty wind caressing our skin.

Once we docked, I drove up through Bainbridge to Allen's Cove where we parked at my dad's house. Leave it to Allen LeRoux to buy a house in a neighborhood bearing his name. He loved to joke about how the house was located in "his" cove, and even I had to admit that his sarcastic sense of humor carried it off.

"Wow, this is some house." Jace looked in wonder at my dad's magnificent Cape Cod-style estate set on an acre of beautiful, professionally landscaped gardens with sweeping views of Puget Sound.

No one was home, so I used my key to let us in and showed him around. For someone who had been in many a celebrity mansion, he oohed and aahed over the huge pool, wine cellar, movie theater, and the custom finishes throughout the house.

"So, as breathtaking as this house is, did we come all this way to have a date with your dad?" Jace leaned on the kitchen counter, his eyebrow raised.

"No, he picked something up for me, and I need to get it before we can go to our final destination." I grabbed bottles of water for us out of their Sub-Zero fridge. "But we can say hi, I'm sure he'll be home soon."

"Ahh, mysterious woman." Jace crossed the room to the sliding doors and looked out at the gorgeous, sparkling blue water. In the late spring, even though it was early evening the sun was still high in the sky.

"Not that mysterious." I wrapped my arms around him from behind and cheekily cupped his package, stroking him through his jeans. "Maybe we can find some way to spend some time until he gets home."

Jace cupped his hand over mine and gently moved me away.

"The last thing I'm going to do is make a shitty impression on your dad by having you in a compromising position." Jace turned and clasped both my hands in his tightly. "I'll just make sure you keep your hands where they won't get me into trouble."

Not giving up, I touched my lips to his but did nothing more. His tongue traced the seam of my lips and, of course, I allowed him access. It still felt a little naughty making out at your parents' house. Even when you were a grown woman with a full bank account.

Not ten minutes later, we heard the garage door open and my dad swooped into the kitchen through the attached door. He always was so well put together. He wore a natty red sweater and skinny black slacks, his silver hair cut short, and his handsome face crinkled with happiness when he saw me.

"Alex!" Dad strode to me and enveloped me into a huge hug. "And you have a shaggy-haired friend."

"I'm Jace Deveraux, sir." Jace tried to contain his laughter and held out his hand to my dad. "Alex's boyfriend."

"Oh, so you have a boyfriend now." Dad winked at me conspiratorially, even though I'd told him about Jace. "Alex hasn't mentioned you."

"Um . . ." Jace looked at me in a panic. "Well . . ."

"Dad's just initiating you into his unique brand of hazing." I rolled my eyes.

"I'm Allen LeRoux." Dad reached for Jace's hand. "You're that band guy from the girls' graduation party."

"Yes." Jace looked relieved. "I'm him."

After making small talk for a few minutes and turning down my dad's offer for dinner, I retrieved my large Amazon package and big envelope from his home office. Finally, we were driving back toward town toward our final destination. My heart raced with excitement when we turned on Big Valley Road to the driveway leading to the ranch I had just purchased.

Grabbing the keys out of an envelope, I jumped out of the car into the quiet oasis that was going to be my new home. Jace got out of the car and looked around in wonder. Grabbing his strong hand, I led him up across the sprawling porch to the front door.

"This is all mine!" I clapped my hands and squealed. "It closed yesterday. My dad picked up the keys for me today!"

"Wow!" Jace looked awestruck. "Show me around."

My new home was five minutes from the town and was surrounded by forest, gardens, a big pond, a firepit, and a state-of-the-art horse barn. The house itself had a huge wraparound porch overlooking the grounds, three bedrooms, and a large, newly renovated master suite. A tiny but functional kitchen looked out onto the pasture and connected to a living room with a wood stove. The barn had three stalls with a tack room and hayloft, and outside there was an outdoor arena and two pastures enclosed by new fencing. To top it off, a small but modern cottage was nestled at the border of the property close to the pastures.

"Poppy, this is beautiful." Jace gazed out at the pastures in wonder. "You've accomplished your dream."

"I know, I can hardly believe it." I twirled around. "You're the first person who has seen it besides Dad."

"Not even Zoey?" Jace looked shocked. "Or your mom?"

"Not yet." I took his hand. "Are you surprised?"

"Yes." He clasped our fingers together tightly and brought our hands to his chest. "The bed in the master is new, I had it delivered this morning." I pointed to the package. "This is some bedding so we can stay tonight!"

Jace waggled his eyebrows. "So our date is that we're going to christen your house?"

"Complaints?"

"Nope!"

The sun had started to finally duck behind the trees, which made the night a bit chilly. After I showed him all around the property we went inside and made the bed. My plan was to get busy right away but when I made my big move, Jace's stomach growled so loud that we both burst out laughing.

"Let's run into town and grab something to eat and some provisions for tomorrow, then we can come back here and get naked."

"Your entire fridge is full of food." Jace opened the door. "It looks fresh."

"Dad must have stocked it for me." I peered inside beside him. "That's so weird, he never does stuff like that."

"Let's just make sandwiches." Jace pulled out bread, ham, mustard, and cheese. "The last thing I want to do is be in public and sign a bunch of autographs tonight. I just want to have an entire blissful evening with my girlfriend. Alone."

Swoon. Every time he called me his girlfriend.

After we wolfed down our sandwiches, Jace loaded our bags out of the car and up into the bedroom. We brushed our teeth side-by-side, giving each other smirky side glances in the mirror. Jace's green eyes twinkled, and he strode into the bedroom, stripping off his clothes. He turned to me completely naked, except for his skull cap and a smile. His magnificent erection saluted me when he posed with his arms akimbo.

"Come and get it, baby." Jace threw off his cap and opened his arms.

"Don't worry, I'm not waiting another minute!" Squealing with joy, I peeled off my clothes, kicked off my shoes, and launched myself at my man.

"God, I've missed you." Jace's strong hands ran up and down my back and gripped my ass, pulling me flush against him, his hard length pressing against my belly.

"I'm right here." I wove my hands through his hair and lifted my lips up to his. "Poppy, I'm not gonna last long the first time." He kissed me and then suckled his way down my neck.

Before I even knew what was happening, Jace backed me toward the newly made bed and ground his cock against me. Devouring my neck, collarbone, and all around my breasts, his lips had my entire body tingling. Which intensified when he nipped at my right nipple and sucked on it enthusiastically. My head lolled back because my entire body felt like it was bursting into flames. Moving down my body, Jace gripped my hips and kissed my stomach, swirling his tongue around my belly-button piercing.

Grabbing his biceps, I writhed against him, trying to press my body closer to his. Abruptly, he knelt down. so that his mouth was level with my pussy.

"You smell so sweet, Poppy." Jace nuzzled my nether parts. "I can't wait to hear every little sexy sound you make when you come."

My moans were visceral when his calloused fingertips caressed my hipbones and his warm lips softly kissed the concave beside my belly button. Jace pulled my pelvis into his face and his warm, wet tongue lapped up my juices voraciously. He laved my throbbing clit with long swoops of his tongue, like he was licking an ice-cream cone. Drawing it out, he teased and suckled, sending me into a frenzy until I propped my right thigh over his shoulder to thrust my pelvis against his lips. Looking down at him eating me out like a gourmet meal, I couldn't stop myself from bucking against his face like a dog in heat.

"I fucking love going down on you," Jace growled, his disheveled mane wild around his face as he wolfishly stared up at me.

On the very brink of release, I had no self-control. Gripping his long, blond hair while he moaned into my pussy, I pressed my pelvis into his face desperately. His hands cupped my ass to rhythmically control my thrusts with the hungry movements of his lips and tongue.

"Ohmygod," I breathed out as all of my parts began to clench forcefully from deep inside me. "Jace, I'm going to come so hard."

"Jesus, you taste so fucking good," Jace mumbled from between my legs as he slid two thick fingers deep inside me and curled them in a come-hither motion.

His relentless manipulation of my sweet inner spot was all it took for my body to release so forcefully that pleasure slammed into me like a freight train. My body twisted and shuddered as I struggled to maintain my balance. I kept clawing and gripping his hair to keep myself upright or to keep his mouth on me, I wasn't sure. Jace suckled and licked me gently through the aftershocks.

When I finally released my viselike hold on his head, Jace gently took my thigh off his shoulder and stood, licking his glistening lips. My clit was still vibrating when he embraced me. Melting into my drummer's arms yet still quaking with desire, I moaned when we aligned our bodies for the big show. His right hand pulled all of my hair into a ponytail, tight at my nape, to move me where he wanted. Gripping his cock with his other hand, he rubbed the crown against my pussy lips.

"Please. I want you inside me now," I begged.

"Alex, you are so fucking beautiful. You're my fantasy every day," he breathed, tortuously flicking the tip of his dick back and forth against my clit.

I couldn't comprehend, let alone respond. I was on the edge of my sanity with anticipation and could feel my arousal dripping down my inner thighs. Suddenly, Jace turned me around and leaned me over the duvet, pulling my ass against his shaft. His percussive fingers reached around my body to massage my clit rhythmically just when he thrust his cock inside me.

"Come for me again." Jace leaned over me, his lips right against my ear as he worked me into a frenzy. With his other hand, he pinched my nipple so hard that it sent jolts to my already-stimulated pussy and another orgasm ripped through my body, wrenching my insides like a towel being wrung out to dry.

"Ahhhhhhhhh." I heard myself keening. He'd brought me into a zone where I couldn't stop coming.

"Oh my God, you're so fucking hot, Poppy." His hard cock was so deep inside me from behind. Filling me. Jace's guttural moan of pure pleasure was enough to push me over the edge another time.

"Ohmygod, Jace!" I screamed again as my body clenched forcefully around his hardness.

Jace and I had been having sex for years, but I'd never been so orgasmic. And, I'd never come just from him simply entering me. I felt like I was turned inside out, but unable to process as the waves of pleasure gripped me and my body tightened, warped, and rippled around Jace.

His low, husky groans quickened, and his cock felt absolutely enormous each time he burrowed into me, his balls hitting my thighs with each thrust.

"You're perfect," he whispered into my ear, driving into me faster and faster while his hands groped every inch of my body.

"Ahhhhhhhhhhh," I screamed, unable to speak.

Cupping my breasts in his hands, Jace rammed into me more and more forcefully, as though he couldn't control himself. Overwhelmed with desire and losing control, I couldn't help but slam my hips back against him, grunting and riding his cock as hard as I could manage. Somehow his free hand found its way to my mouth and I couldn't help sucking ravenously on his fingers.

Jace emitted a strangled sound from deep in his throat and reached around to rub my clit furiously as he jerked his hips in short, fast bursts, spurting deep inside me. My pussy squeezed every drop out of him when I climaxed yet again. The only sounds in the room were our tortured, labored breaths. Jace collapsed over my back, his cock still twitching inside me.

After a few minutes, Jace pulled out and turned my limp, noodley body around to face him.

"You're mine." He cupped my face tenderly in between his palms.
"Yes." I breathed.

I traced the seam of his lips with my tongue and then kissed him as though my life depended on it. Our greedy mouths consumed each other; our sweaty bodies pressed together. Jace gestured for us to get under the covers then got up to turn off the light. When he crawled into bed and spooned me from behind, my body melted into his.

"It's perfect here."

"I know," I whispered.

"I can't wait to see what you do with this place."

"Ohmygod, you have no idea!" I listed all the projects that I had in mind and the horses I wanted to rescue.

Jace's arms were wrapped tightly around me and his finger stroked my belly button ring while I shared all my hopes and dreams for the place. He responded enthusiastically and supportively in all the right places until his arms went slack when he fell asleep holding me.

Turning toward him, I stared at his beautiful face, now peaceful in slumber. Stroking his hair, I kissed his forehead and sighed. Life was finally settling down for me, but I had no idea what he wanted for his future.

At some point, I must have fallen asleep in his strong arms. When I woke up, the sun was streaming through my window and Jace wasn't in bed. Wrapping the duvet around myself, I padded into the kitchen where he was standing in the window, looking out at my pastures wearing nothing but his jeans.

"Morning, sunshine." I moved to his side and slipped under his arm and ran my hand along the planes of his hard abs.

"Good morning." Jace draped his arm around me. "It really is blessedly quiet here."

"I know, it's what I always loved most about being away from the city." I nestled

against him. "Did you have trouble sleeping? You're probably used to road noise and chaos."

"Yeah." He took several long, deep breaths. "The air smells so clean."

"Yep. Another one of the things I loved about being out in the country at my rescues."

"There's this whole side to you that I never got to know." Jace sounded wistful. "I've never hidden anything from you." I looked up at him, locking into an intense gaze with his gorgeous green eyes.

"No, you never have." He kissed my head. "I totally get it now."

"Get what?"

"Why you couldn't get fully on board with us as a couple."

"Geez. Do we need to be dressed for this conversation?" I tried to lighten the mood. He took my hand and brought it to his lips. "I'm just so sorry, Poppy."

"For what?"

"Not making the effort to be in your world." Jace sighed heavily. "You were right all along. My context with you has always been about the band. About me. First, it was rehearsal and the studio, then you meeting up with me at gigs. I never made the effort to learn what made you tick."

"Do you want to know now?"

"Yes." Jace lovingly tucked a stray hair behind my ear. "There's nothing I want more."

JACE

CHAPTER 19

The next several months were a whirlwind, for the most part, I had the best of both worlds. With the exception of an extended tour of Asia over the holidays we had just finished, LTZ had settled into an easy routine of touring for a month and then taking two to three weeks off. The band had gotten smarter about our commitments while we were on the road and made sure to schedule plenty of time to rest and stay healthy.

My time off was usually spent at Alex's place on Bainbridge Island, where we worked on her house. Jen and Becca had come over several times during the summer and fall to help with repairs and improvements. As it turned out, Becca was a lifelong horse owner and lover. She helped Alex get the barn and pastures ready and was trying to talk my sister into moving into the guest quarters so she could take an active role in the rescue and be in charge when Alex traveled.

I'd never felt more at peace in my life than when Alex and I were together on her ranch. For the first time, we had a really long stretch together to firm things up in our relationship. Looking out across the choppy waters of Puget Sound as the ferry headed toward the dock, the familiar feeling of anticipation gurgled up in my belly.

I couldn't wait to surprise her.

Alex's car wasn't there when I pulled into the drive, which meant that I could carry out plan A. Letting myself into the house with my bag of goodies, I sprinkled pink rose petals from the door into the bedroom. Next, I set up a bottle of wine with two glasses. Finally, I pulled out my pièce de résistance, the Lady Gaga and Bruno Mars posters, which I tacked up on her wall. Not long after, I heard the crunch of tires on the gravel, so I quickly stripped off my clothes and jumped on the bed, reclining on the pillows.

Clomp, clomp, clomp. I heard boots heading toward the bedroom, and my dick lengthened into an iron rod against my belly.

"Oh, shit!" Becca winced when she peered in the door, turning away quickly. "I did not need to see that."

"Oh God, baby J!" Jen covered her eyes with her fists. Hastily I cupped my junk with both hands, mortified.

"Jace?" Alex peered over Becca's and Jen's shoulders. "Are you naked?"

"Yes." I huffed. "I'm naked. Enjoying the show, ladies?"

Standing, I moved my hands away, so my bits were swinging free and opened my arms wide. Jen and Becca squealed and ran off. Alex laughed, closed the door behind her, and stepped into the bedroom. She leaned against the door, her arms crossed over her perky breasts, long, blonde hair tousled about her face. My cock swelled again. I needed her.

"Oh, wow!" Alex finally took in the scene. "You recreated our first time!"

"Yeah." I could barely speak, overcome by desire.

I was so incredibly over-the-moon for my stunning girl. I'd been a carefree, sexual dude back when I was twenty-three and she was eighteen. I took her virginity because being around her all summer made me horny. It had been impossible to say no.

Somehow in those few hours, she'd gotten under my skin. I even fell in love with her. After we broke it off, I'd dreamed of her. Missed her. Knew that my own selfishness drove her away.

Now that I was thirty and she was twenty-five, I could admit that my love for her had deepened into something overwhelming. Scary. Necessary. I wasn't going to do anything to fuck it up this time.

Alex crossed the room and confidently took my hard length in hand.

Finally reunited after I'd been away for three months, all I wanted was to make love to her. To taste her. To lose myself in her body.

"Come to bed." I guided her to where I'd spread the petals over the duvet. She undressed quickly and lay back, her head reclining on the pillow with her hair fanned out. My breath stopped. The look on her face was nearly identical to the one she gave me so long ago before we first made love. No other woman had ever looked at me like that.

Ever.

Like I was the only man who'd ever mattered.

Caging her in by leaning down over her on my elbows, my hair cascaded around her face and she caught my mouth with hers, slipping her tongue between my lips. Cradling her head, I canted my hips to drive as deep inside her as possible. Claiming her.

Gazing into her eyes as our bodies became one, I nearly crumpled from the emotion we both shared. I was a man who prided myself on my ability to control my feelings. With Alex, this wasn't possible. And I didn't want to anyway.

I knew I was going to lock her down. I wanted to be with her forever.

"I *love* you, Poppy." I willed her to understand how much she meant to me.

Alex blinked and sought my mouth, kissing me deeply. Our bodies slowed. I clasped our hands together above her head. We watched each other. Savoring how incredible it felt to be joined.

Pleasure overtook us both at the same time and she shuddered underneath me. The only sound she made was a little squeal. So damn cute. Unable to hold back, I emptied inside her. Collapsing when my orgasm ripped through my entire being. Spent, neither of us could move.

When I was finally able to roll to the side and spoon her to me, she wrapped her arms around mine over her belly and intertwined our fingers.

"I *love* you too," she finally answered.

"Thank God." I squeezed her from behind. "You haven't said it in a long time."

"I know." She glanced back over her shoulder at me. "But I do."

"So—I need to tell you something. We came to a group decision after this long Asia leg." I rested my cheek against hers. "We're taking a year off."

"Really?" Alex turned to me. "A whole year?"

"Yeah, Ty wants to get his foundation started. He has a meeting about it in a few days." I sighed happily. "Well, we all have other things we want to do, so it makes sense."

"When will your break start?" She traced my lips with her finger.

"We still have a few things to finish up this fall and winter, so probably after the new year." I sucked the tip of her finger into my mouth. "But we have no more tours planned. We just need to record some songs for a movie and a few one-off shows here and there."

"Hmmm."

I figured I'd throw what I was hoping would happen out there. "You and I should come out of the closet, so to speak."

Alex animatedly rolled her eyes. "Um. The band already knows about us."

"They think hookup, if anything. They don't know that we're a real couple, Poppy." I regarded her seriously. "We promised no more games, and now that we are in a committed relationship hiding it is beginning to feel like a game."

"Yeah—"

"I don't want to hide anymore." I couldn't quite get a read on how she felt. "For anyone. For any reason."

"I know you're right." She sighed. "Zoey is doing great. You know she set up my rescue, right?"

"No, I didn't."

"She's at a big law firm specializing in setting up non-profits. Carter actually DM'd me to get her number." Alex wrinkled her nose. "They had coffee, and she is going to help him with some project he has going on."

"Huh." I looked up at the ceiling. I had little interest in talking about Ty and Zoey, it had impacted my own relationship with Alex for too many years.

"Well, anyway." Alex seemed to get it and waved her hand in front of my eyes. "About us going public—"

We lounged in bed talking for a few hours before emerging from her bedroom. Jen and Becca were making dinner. After much teasing, we managed to make it through dinner and settled into the living room to watch a movie on the most comfortable, cushy couch known to man. It wasn't long before both Alex and Becca were sound asleep.

"So, is she the one, Jace?" my sister asked quietly so we didn't wake our mates. I nodded and kissed the top of Alex's head, she stirred but didn't wake up.

"I need to ask you something," she whispered so softly I could barely hear her. "Did Cassie ever get ahold of you?"

"She texted me a while ago, I blocked her." I shot her a pointed look and brought my finger to my lips. I didn't want to talk about Cassie in front of Alex.

Easing Alex off of me, I motioned for Jen to get up and go into the kitchen. I figured it was far enough away from the living room to have this conversation privately.

"Yeah, I ran into her around Christmastime," Jen continued in a whisper. "She had a newborn *baby*."

My eyes must have widened. I know that suddenly I couldn't breathe. "Um. Uh. Um . . ." I stuttered.

"Relax. She told me to tell you it wasn't yours."

"She said that? Why would she assume you'd think it was mine?"

"There might have been some mention of the hook-up in LA." Jen's squeamish expression said it all.

"If you could call it that. I'm pretty sure she roofied me, Jen." I pinched the bridge of my nose. "It was over a year ago. I hung out with her and her sister. They came to a show, and I brought them backstage thinking enough time had passed that it would be nice to have old friends visit. Friends who knew me before I was famous. Alex and I still weren't even speaking at that point. Frankly, I was lonely. The next thing I remember was waking up naked in bed with her feeling really groggy."

"Jesus." Jen was horrified. "You could press charges."

"What? God no. Really?" I crossed my arms protectively around myself. "I got myself tested a dozen times because even though I'm sure that she fucked me, I wasn't sure if she used protection."

"Oh shit." Jen pulled me into a hug. "Have you spoken to anyone about it?"

"What do you mean?" I was confused.

"Jace, she violated you." Jen's sisterly protectiveness was fierce.

"Huh. I didn't think of it like that, I really just worried about getting some STD or that she was trying to get herself pregnant." Suddenly it felt like I couldn't swallow. "It's probably why I've ignored her calls and blocked her. She scared the shit out of me."

"Scared about what?" Alex padded into the kitchen behind me.

"Nothing." I fake-smiled, giving Jen a pointed look to STFU.

Alex crossed her arms looking disappointed in my response. "There is no need to keep secrets. I heard you talking."

Fuck.

"Well, then you overheard what happened. Which, by the way, was months before we got back together." I felt super defensive.

"I'm not mad at you for sleeping with someone else while we were apart, Jace." Alex moved toward me. I held up my hand, not wanting her touch right now.

"I wouldn't call it that." My head was spinning into a vortex.

"Little J, this is so fucked-up." I allowed Jen to give me a side hug, which didn't go unnoticed by Alex. "Are you okay?"

Cloaking myself in an invisible protective layer, I tamped down my panic and assumed my calm, in-control demeanor. "Sure, I blocked her number months ago."

"Jace . . ." Alex said empathetically. "That's not what she meant."

"I'm fine." I dismissed them both. "It's over, she's out of my life."

"You should make her do a paternity test," Jen crossed her arms, regarding me. "Nah. Why would I want to open that can of worms?"

"Because, if that child is yours you will want to be in their life," Alex said softly. "She already told Jen it wasn't mine," I spat. "Believe me, if there was a chance of it

being mine, she'd have been shaking me down months ago."

"Hey. Let's drop this for now." Alex went to the fridge and poured herself some orange juice. "There's no need for us to get upset over something that isn't in our control."

Relieved to postpone the inevitable discussion, I was grateful for the out. "I'm tired anyway, I haven't really had a good night's sleep in weeks."

"I'm tired too. Let's go to bed." Alex reached for my hand. "Jen, don't leave tomorrow before we have that talk about the caretaker job."

"I won't." Jen hugged her and I heard her whisper, "take care of him."

Alex nodded and led me into the bedroom. The air was ice cold between us when we undressed and got into bed. Thankfully, Alex didn't press me for more information or scold me for keeping information from her. She seemed to know what I needed. Which, for now, was for her to let me spoon her until we fell asleep.

Leave it to me to fuck up my first night back.

By morning I could sense my world was moments away from crashing down around me. I just knew it.

I kept it inside, but I was panicking at what this all meant. If Alex freaked out when she had her own pregnancy scare, our odds were screwed if this baby turned out to be my kid.

Something inside me knew. Regardless of what Cassie told Jen. I just felt it in my bones. That baby was mine.

Which meant that Alex and I were over before we had a chance to start.

CHAPTER 20

W e didn't talk about it. We had to talk about it, but Jace never brought it up. So, I didn't bring it up.

Instead, during the week since Jace had come back, we buried ourselves in projects. Our biggest task was creating an extension to the guest house. Luckily, Jen and Becca knew exactly what to do. Working together, we framed, wired, and sheetrocked two additional rooms.

At night, Jace and I made passionate love.

But there were no discussions.

I was sitting on my front porch sipping my coffee watching Jace chop wood when my phone rang. I was happy to see it was Zoey. I planned to let her know that Jace had been staying with me in the spirit of outing ourselves as a true couple.

"Hey!" I happily chirped into the phone and ducked into the house.

"Hey! You are never going to believe it, Alex." Zoey's voice was half-excited, half-emotional. "I saw Ty."

I knew from Jace that Ty went to great lengths not run into Zoey since she moved back to Seattle. Including spending most of his time in LA. "Where?"

"He hired my law firm to work on his new foundation, I'm his lawyer," she said with more enthusiasm than I'd heard in a long time.

Considering how happy I was with Jace, I was hopeful for her. It had been too long with too much unnecessary drama. They really needed to be back together. "Wow! How are you handling it?"

"We talked, but he wants to talk more. I've got to keep things professional because of ethical reasons. I mean, I'm his lawyer. Oh, Alex. he's so beautiful. And sweet." Zoey's sounded like my high school friend for the first time in eight years. "I'm in so much trouble. I can't let myself go there. But the energy between us. Wow."

"That's really cool, Z. I hear what you're saying, but I'm really hopeful for you two."

Jace walked into the room, shirtless, sweaty, and stunningly sexy. His hair was loose and unruly. The wood-chopping manly thing was so sexy. He kissed my neck before he got a bottle of cold water out of the fridge. Even though I was on the phone, I couldn't help but watch his Adam's apple glug as he drank the entire thing. He could be in any commercial, that's how good looking he was.

Quickly saying my goodbyes to Zoey, I moved back toward him. "Zoey and Ty—" I began.

"Yeah, Ty texted me." Jace sucked air in. "He's kind of freaking out."

"Jeez." I wrinkled my nose. "She is too."

"I really want to stay out of it, Poppy." Jace put the bottle in the recycling. "We've been dealing with the Zoey and Ty fallout for too many years. Let them figure it out. I don't want to jump back on the train."

"I agree. But, Jace?" I pointed at him. "You and I need to talk. We are building something together and we should clear the air about Cassie."

"I really don't want to talk about it, Alex." Jace crossed his arms and looked down. "I just want to go back to a few days ago."

"For someone who is so able to take care of everyone around him, you're not great at taking care of yourself." I stroked his back, eager to show him that I was there for him. "Are you going to leave me?" Jace looked at me tensely, a vulnerability shone in his eyes that I'd never seen before.

"Why would you think that?" I was completely taken aback by his question.

He leaned against the kitchen counter, staring at me for a few minutes before speaking. "Because knowing Cassie, she's going to drop a bomb on me."

I had time to think about it and while he didn't owe me an explanation into his love life during the time that we were apart, he needed to be able to open up to me if we were going to have a future. Especially about something like this. Especially if a child was involved. "Well, what happened to you is shocking, Jace."

"You know I don't need to have kids, Alex." Jace reached out and took my hand, avoiding my comment. "I want to make a life with you."

"I want that too, but you need to trust me." I squeezed his hand, hopefully reassuringly. "You can't be worried about doing or saying something that might break us up. If we're going to be all-in, we need to be all-in. Kids or no kids."

"I'm all-in." Jace gripped me tightly. "Alex, this is it. I'm not letting you go again.

 Promise me we are doing this."

"Of course we are doing this. It's decided. No matter what."

The conversation ended there, but I couldn't help but feel as if he didn't believe me. Truth be told, I didn't know if I believed it myself. I didn't know how to talk to him about what happened to him. Or how to help him. Or what to do if he was suddenly a dad.

So I dropped it because it was just easier.

Luckily over the next couple of months finalizing the renovations on the property took all of our focus, so we lived in a bit of a bubble. Now that Jen and Becca lived in the guesthouse permanently, I finally met Jace's folks, Jason Sr. and Grace along with his other sisters Jaylynn and Jordan.

Grace and I hit it off immediately, we were two birds of a feather. When she'd been in her early twenties, she had traveled extensively before settling down with Jace's dad. Jace was Jason Sr.'s doppelgänger in all ways other than age. I could see how Jace had obtained his demeanor. The layer of confidence and integrity, with no trace of arrogance.

They say you can learn a lot about a man by how he treats his mother. Well, damn. After watching Grace and Jace together? They were so in synch that it made sense that their names rhymed.

Suffice it to say, I was even more sold.

Plus, with no further contact from Cassie, Jace and I both fooled ourselves into believing the situation had resolved itself.

By the end of spring, I was ready to actively look for my first two rescues. Jace was in LA recording a few songs for a movie soundtrack. While he was gone, Becca and I road-tripped around the state figuring out criteria on how to select the horses. Turns out, choosing was the hardest part. For me, it was agony because taking one horse meant leaving another. My emotions were all over the place.

We ended up picking Gloria, a ten-year-old black mare who had been abused and left for dead and Bingo, a former racehorse who was scheduled to be euthanized. When they arrived at my barn, the feeling was unbelievable. I was so overwhelmingly happy that I set up a cot and slept by them for days to make them feel welcome and to make sure their every need was met.

The only thing missing was Jace, but he wouldn't be back for a couple of weeks. Just in time for the show at the Space Needle for Ty's foundation.

Jace hadn't filled me in on the details other than knowing that he wanted me to be there. I truthfully wasn't paying too much attention because my plate was full. One evening, when I'd been out in the barn all day tending to Gloria, I returned to the house ready to grab a peanut butter sandwich and take a bath before FaceTiming Jace at our designated time.

My BFF was waiting.

"Hey, stranger!" Zoey jumped up from her seat on the front porch, clutching a cider. "Dude!" I gleefully ran up the steps and crushed her with a hug. When she handed me my own cider, I gratefully accepted it.

"I missed you and was sick of texting, so I thought I'd come out and crash for a night." She clinked her bottle to mine.

"God, you're a sight for sore eyes." I sank into my chair. "But I'm loving my life right now, I'm so happy here with the horses."

"I was going to come out to the barn but didn't want to spook them. I know you're getting them settled in." Zoey always paid attention to my life, something I appreciated more the older I got.

"I'll bring you out in the morning with me," I assured her. "They're beautiful."

Relaxing on the porch with my best friend was just what the doctor ordered. We caught up on more of our life events before she let me know the real reason for her visit.

"So, I have an ulterior motive for being here. I got invited to Ty's party." Zoey showed me the gorgeous invite. "I wasn't sure if I was going, but he encouraged me to invite you as my plus one. Please say yes, otherwise I won't have the courage to go."

I scanned the invite. Internally, I groaned. If I didn't say something now, this would be just one more event where Jace and I weren't being honest with those closest to us.

"Sure, as long as Becca can stay out here with Gloria and Bingo." I squeezed her hand. As if I'd say no to my BFF.

"You can stay at my place in the city," Zoey offered.

"Okay. It will be fun." In Seattle's hot real estate market, I'd received an all-cash offer on my condo and sold it a few weeks prior, so I'd have more money for the rescue.

"Or you'll be at Jace's." She gave me a sly, knowing look. "Maybe." I mimicked zipping my lips.

"C'mon," she pleaded. "His sister and her girlfriend practically live here, don't tell me things aren't moving into relationship territory."

"He wishes," It came out before I could stop it. Hiding my wince. I knew I was digging myself into a hole.

"You're terrible at giving me Jace gossip," she chastised me. "I'll show you how it's done. Ty told me he wants to talk everything out after the show."

"Wow!" The news came as a shock, which meant Jace knew

nothing about this. "About the two of you?"

"Yeah." Zoey rubbed her temples. "I'm scared to even think about it, I hurt him so badly. I don't know where this is going to lead."

"I have a fair idea who he wants." I pointed at her. "You. You. You."

"Did Jace tell you that?"

"Look, Zoey." It was time for me to get off the childish rollercoaster and let my friend handle her own shit. "You and Ty are now grownups. I've seen him here and there over the years, and he's been miserable without you. He has always loved you. I don't have any idea whether you guys can work it out, but it is up to you two to do that. Whatever happens, you have my support."

"I know I do." Zoey squeezed my hand. "I just want him back so badly. We've already talked a bit and discussed how much we had loved each other. But, it was in the past tense. I still love him. I'm so scared that he's going to tell me he can't love me anymore. That's probably why I've been living in purgatory. The fear. It's like I'd rather not know and have hope than have him confirm my biggest worry."

"Zoey, he's never stopped hoping you'd be back together someday." That much was obvious to anyone who ever saw them together. "But you're right. You have to start communicating with him and tune out the rest of the world—including me. Put your big girl panties on and, hopefully, he'll take them off."

I was such a hypocrite.

She laughed nervously. "God, I hope so!"

At least our conversation gave me clarity. Something clicked, and I couldn't wait to see Jace in person and take my own advice. The Space Needle show couldn't come fast enough. The band wasn't coming back to Seattle until the morning of, so I wouldn't get to see Jace in person until that night.

Ty's event, which was a private radio show for Sirius announcing his foundation, was a very exclusive but casual affair. Jace was busy preparing, but not too busy to text me cute messages all day. I loved him so much, I couldn't wait to get into Seattle.

Just like old times, Zoey and I got ready together at her condo. I wore my usual uniform, a gray T-shirt, Levi's, and my Frye boots. Zoey did herself up a bit more, as was her custom. She was going to snag her man back and looked fantastic wearing minimal makeup and her hair in a long side braid. I'm pretty sure both of our hearts were beating a mile a minute in anticipation of seeing the delectable rockers when the elevator door opened, and we stepped into the intimate setting.

Jace caught my eye the minute I walked in, but he was in the middle of a group of people who were fluttering around him. I kept my distance even though every fiber of my being wanted to run and jump into his arms. He shot me a subtle air kiss when his publicist pulled them into preshow interviews. I texted him a heart emoji and patiently waited for him to take care of business.

We'd already arranged to meet back at his place after the show. He knew that my focus was getting Zoey through the night. Which is exactly what I did by marching Zoey to the back of the room and grabbing wine for both of us. We were sipping a delicious Viognier as the sun set over the Olympic Mountains. The energy was palpable when the guys took the stage.

Zoey clung to me but stared at Ty throughout the entire show. He sang his heart out as if no one were in the room but his butterfly. When he dedicated a new song and performed it for her, I thought my hand would fall off from how hard she was squeezing it. The love between them was so clear. I was happy for her.

Tonight would be their reunion, I just knew it.

Throughout the show, Jace kept watch over me. He was so hot; I couldn't get enough of his biceps flexing while he played the bongos. It wouldn't be long before we would have our own reunion. My entire body was aroused in anticipation of getting naked with my man.

Unfortunately, the press and fans crowded the band after they finished. Zoey and I had to wait outside on the observation deck to let them do their thing. When Ty shyly approached us, I waved him over and gave him an encouraging squeeze on the arm. Looking him in the eye and willing him to do the right thing, I passed him to Zoey with my blessing, which they didn't need but seemed to want. With a parting kiss on her head, as far as I was concerned, it was now up to them.

A few hours later, I was peppering Jace with kisses while he tried to unlock the door to his condo. When he managed to get it open, we stumbled, laughing, through the doorway in a tangle of limbs, but we managed to stay upright long enough for him to lock and bolt the door behind us.

Immediately, Jace spun me around and pinned me against the wall. Our mood turned even more heated in the privacy of his place. His eyes scanned my face, and he pushed his fingers through my hair to the back of my head, cupping me to pull my face toward his.

"That's the last event that you stay on the sidelines, Poppy," Jace rasped before our lips crashed together. The low moan that filled the room was from me when Jace pushed his tongue into my mouth. We made out like our first time when I was still a teenager. Gawd. The way he made me feel. I clutched his T-shirt tightly with both hands to keep him flush against me as our kisses grew deeper and more intense.

It was all I could do not to climb him like a tree, but Jace ran his hand down my lower back and pressed his palm to the curve right above my ass. I could feel every inch of his cock pulsing against the seam of my jeans. Arching toward him, I rolled my hips against his pelvis in my quest to get as close to him as possible. His other hand trailed down to my hip and with one motion, he lifted me up so I could wrap my legs around his waist.

"Jace—" I tried to speak, but his lips claimed mine again in a passionate kiss.

"Shh." He tightened his grip under my thighs. "I love when you're wrapped around
me."

My hands slid over his broad, muscular shoulders, and I combed my fingers through
his hair. Before I could process what was happening, Jace was marching us down the hall with me clinging to him like a monkey. Our lips still fused together, he kicked the door to his bedroom open and lowered me to my feet. When he took a small step back, my chest heaved in ragged breaths. My lips were swollen from our kisses.

"You're so handsome, Jace Deveraux," I moaned, looking him up and down. When my eyes caught his, they were full of hunger when he studied my face.

"You're incredible, Alexandria LeRoux." Jace grazed his knuckles over my nipples, which beaded even tighter at his touch. Moving downward, he splayed his hands across my ribs and stomach, trailing his index finger inside my jeans before he unfastened them and pushed them down my body.

We'd undressed like this together many times, but tonight felt more intense. Our energy had shifted in a way that was both scary and exciting at the same time. Toeing off my boots while Jace divested himself of his own boots and jeans, we were finally, blissfully naked.

Every time we reunited, knowing how much my Viking god wanted and desired me made my heart open just a little more.

Using his patented move, he rolled us over in one motion to his favorite position where I straddled him, and he impaled me all at once. Bracing my hands on his chest, I rode my cowboy, undulating in a figure eight. Everything else disappeared as our bodies merged. Groping, biting, nipping each other like animals, Jace canted his hips, driving himself deeper and deeper inside me. Scraping my nails on his shoulders, I wanted to leave marks. Everything about Jace consumed me. I wanted him completely, nothing mattered except us.

Jace rubbed my clit in tight circles and it took all of two seconds for me to fly apart with a strangled moan. His muscles strained, and he let out a guttural sound when his body spasmed and he ejaculated everything he had inside me. When we both came down to Earth, and were lying wrapped in each other's arms, I breathed in his delicious sandalwood scent mixed with our lust.

"Whenever we've been apart over the years, did you know how many times every day I thought about us together like this?" Jace kissed my temple. "It's enough to drive a person crazy."

"Well, then we're both crazy." I licked his neck.

Jace snuggled me tight into his side. My hand ran up and down the hard planes of his abs, I never got sick of feeling the ridges of his muscles there.

"Are you okay?"

"Now that you're back, I'm better than okay. I'm awesome." I leaned up to kiss him.

"You're shaking, Poppy." He sweetly smoothed my hair from my eyes. "Are you cold?"

"Honestly? I think it's adrenaline from seeing you again." I sank against him. "Probably a lot of emotion from the show. I guess I didn't realize how much energy I spent worrying about Zoey. Now I can hopefully let that go."

"Yeah." Jace seemed lost in thought.

"Are *you* okay?" I traced his lips with my finger.

"Yeah." Jace looked at me with his intense green eyes. "It feels so different knowing I can come home to you. Good different."

"That's because we're together for real now, Jace." I smiled at him. "Really and truly. No more running."

He wrapped his arms around me to pull me tightly against him. "Thank God."

"Through thick and thin," I assured him. "You're my guy."

"I love you so much, Alex." Jace was uncharacteristically choked up. "While I was in LA, Ty was so confident about Zoey. He kept saying, 'Everything happens for a reason.'"

I stared at the ceiling, reflecting on the past eight years. "You know what I've realized? We've had something they never had over all of these years."

"What?" Jace nuzzled my hair. "Sex across many continents?"

"No. Friendship." I kissed his full lips. "We've always been friends. Even during our breaks, we never got nasty, we've always genuinely liked each other through all of our ups and downs."

"That's because you're my absolute favorite person in the whole world, Poppy." Jace's voice broke again.

"I've never seen you so emotional, what's going on?" His demeanor was scaring me a bit. I wasn't used to seeing him so vulnerable. "I'm right here, I've always been right here. You're my favorite person too."

"You," he said simply. "That's what has changed, you're really

270

ready to be in this now. You're not just saying the words."

"I am ready." I closed my eyes against his chest, breathing him in again. "You're my home. I know that with every ounce of my being."

"I've been waiting to hear you say that for years, Poppy." Jace wrapped himself around me. "I can't wait to build our future together."

CHAPTER 21

Sunlight streamed into the bedroom, cars honked, and a siren squealed by. A group of children were screaming on the street. All the noise meant we were most certainly not waking up at Alex's oasis on Bainbridge Island. Scrubbing my eyes with my fists, I heard an annoying and relentless *ping ping ping* sound emanating from Alex's phone. I put on my readers, checked my phone for the time and it was past noon.

We were both early risers but going four rounds last night meant we didn't get much sleep.

"Whoever keeps texting, I'm going to kill them," I grumbled.

"Zoey." Alex was sitting up, typing into her phone. "They had a fight, Ty stormed out."

"Jesus fucking Christ." I slammed my head back down and pulled the covers over my eyes. "And I thought we'd finally cut them loose."

The strains of *Butterfly* streamed through her phone. Alex answered and mouthed, "Zoey" before answering.

"Duh!" I mouthed back and rolled my eyes. All the way back into my head.

Pounding at my front door startled me at the exact same moment. Punching my fist into my palm, I jumped out of bed, grabbed my jeans from the floor, hoisted them up, and padded out to the door.

Surprise, surprise, it was Ty. I gave him a quick pep talk and sent him on his way and was heading back to the bedroom when Alex emerged wearing only my T-shirt.

"So much for our best intentions." She put her hands on her hips.

"Pray for them." I reached for her. "They need it. For the record, I fucking hate this drama. At least we've kept our drama to ourselves."

"I want to be a good friend." She traced my poppy tattoo with her index finger. "Zoey knows something is up with us."

"Good. Ty also knows you're here." I cupped her head to my chest. "For the record, I like sleeping at your place better, fewer interruptions."

"You should move in with me," Alex murmured against my pecs.

"Really?" I took ahold of both her shoulders and moved her gently away so I could look her in the eye and gauge if she meant it.

"Yes. If you want." She looked up at me through her lashes, almost shyly.

"So, you're inviting me to move in with you? I want to make sure I'm hearing you correctly." There was nothing more that I wanted, but I couldn't help but raise an eyebrow.

"Jace! Shut up." Alex giggled.

"Alexandria LeRoux? I, Jace Deveraux, do hereby accept your

offer of cohabitation." I bowed low. "So long as you know that living together without marriage is a sin, and I ain't gonna be a sinner for too long."

"Are you serious?" Alex's mouth formed a little "o."

"Of course I am." I caressed both of her cheeks and kissed her tenderly. "I want to ask you the right way, though, so this is not a proposal yet. Just a 'please put me out of my misery if you're not on the same page' heads-up."

"I'm overwhelmed. And so happy!" Alex's smile was brighter than the sun. "I hoped this was where this was going, but I didn't want to assume."

"We *really* have to tell people, Poppy. Even though our families are on board, most of our friends don't know about us. It's weird. They are going to think me moving in with you is weird." I moved to the kitchen to get some water. "It's beyond time, I don't want our relationship to be another LTZ spectacle. Plus, when we got back together, we agreed not to play games."

"I totally agree." Alex followed me and sat at the counter crossing her long, tan legs, hooking one foot under her ankle. "It's not our thing."

The next few weeks the band was scattered around, living their own lives so Alex and I concentrated on moving me into her house. Because we decided to keep my condo as our place in the city, there wasn't much to move. After so many years on the road, I never got overly attached to material possessions other than my instruments. Plus, with all our endorsements and freebies, I had enough shoes, clothes, and personal products for both places.

Jen and Becca had finally finished their move into the guest house at Alex's property, so the four of us spent a lot of time together. My other sisters and folks came back out to visit and met Alex's dad.

When we were back in the city, we had dinner with Alex's mom and her brother and sister. Our parents and siblings were fully on board with our relationship, we just needed to pull the trigger and go public in front of my bandmates and Zoey. Which still felt like the hardest part, for some reason.

We weren't too worried about it though; Alex and I were blissfully happy to be entrenched in our own world.

I was surprised at how much I loved working with the horses. Alex taught me some of the basics, like mucking stalls, feeding them, putting them out to pasture, and my favorite—grooming. Bingo became my guy. When I methodically brushed out his coat every morning and combed his mane and tail, we bonded. He waited at the fence surrounding the pasture for me to give him carrots, and I swear he smiled when he saw me.

Gloria was in worse shape, but Alex was so patient and caring. She'd hired a wonderful veterinarian who had given her an exam and had measured her body chemistry to help manage her appetite. Alex taught me that when horses went for a long time without food, they had physical changes in their body that compromised their ability to digest nutrients, which made it difficult to recover.

It made me so angry that such a sweet horse had been mistreated and malnourished.

Alex had worked miracles, though. At first, she fed her small amounts of special food every hour, then every two hours, then three, and so on. Slowly and surely Gloria gained weight and was able to move to a more normal feed schedule. Meanwhile, Alex started her physical therapy routine slowly. First, by walking her gently through the pastures. As she built up strength, she let her trot and canter on a line. Not only was this good for her body, but it created such an amazing bond between my Poppy and her rescue.

We rejoiced and celebrated each step of her recovery, but the years of abuse took its toll. She had been frightened and defensive, but Alex was patiently working through all of it and a sweet and loving mare was emerging.

Witnessing how she was with the horses made me fall even more in love with Alex each day.

A part of me was secretly ashamed of myself. For as long as I'd known her, I'd been so engrossed in my band. I'd never taken the time to learn why she was so passionate about her rescues.

My eyes were now open. Experiencing just a fraction of what Alex had been doing all around the world made me a not-so-instant convert. Rather than focus on the years I hadn't paid enough attention, I planned to make it up to her. Nothing would keep me from helping her save as many horses as we could.

Sitting on the front porch with my iPad, I was searching for property in the area when Alex bounced over to me.

"There you are!" Alex bounded up the stairs. "Good Lord, you are so sexy in your reading glasses."

"I wasn't hard to find, I've been sitting here for an hour." I set my iPad down and pulled her into my lap.

"I thought we're taking the four o'clock ferry." Alex stroked my poppy tattoo. "Are you packed?"

"No." I sighed. "I'm thinking about bailing for a day or two, they don't really need me right away."

"Jace, didn't you say the movie people chartered a private jet for you guys? You have to go." She nudged me with her shoulder.

"Not when I'd rather be here with you." I cradled her head with my hands and drew her to me, kissing down her neck softly and nibbling on her earlobe. "Especially because Jen and Becca are in town and we have the place to ourselves."

"You are so bad." Alex giggled and then sucked in a breath when I suckled on the hollow of her throat. Cupping her shoulders, I stroked down her bare, toned arms and pulled off her tank top and threw it on the porch.

"Sometimes it's okay to be bad." I licked her ear and tweaked each of her nipples between my fingers, rolling them into hard points.

"Don't I know it." Alex shifted to straddle and undulate against my cock.

"Poppy, I've left you for the band so many times. I don't want to go," I murmured, peeling my shirt off and chucking it down on top of hers.

"Beth, I hear you callin', but I can't come home right now." Alex sang a line from the KISS song.

"How do you know the words to so many ancient rock songs?" I grazed her nipple lightly between my teeth.

"I'm a good student." Alex nodded and nuzzled my neck before scooting off me, pulling down her cutoffs and tiny panties and tossing them on our pile of clothes. Kneeling before me, she unzipped my jeans and pulled out my throbbing cock and stroked me lovingly. God, she was so, so beautiful.

Caressing my balls with one hand, Alex gripped the base and licked the underside of my hard length like an ice-cream cone, before sucking my tip, hard, into her mouth. Purring against me, she flattened her tongue and took me almost all the way down her throat before repeating the sequence several times, driving me to madness. My hips involuntarily thrusted at the sheer exquisite decadence of her deep-throating me.

"Jesus, Poppy." Sweat broke out on my brow.

"Mmmmm." She caught my eye and hummed against my cock.

"That feels—ahhhh." It was all over when she took me fully into her mouth and dipped her tongue into my tiny hole and swirled. An electric storm consumed my entire body and I flooded her mouth.

Lifting her gently to standing, I shimmied out of my jeans, stood, and led her through the house to her bedroom. Worshipping her tight, lithe body until she came apart became my mission, which I accomplished. She flopped into my arms like a noodle, staring at me through glassy, blue eyes. Her expression was dreamy. Open. Emotional.

She breathed out softly. "That was unbelievable."

We'd had moments like these over the years. Moments where I knew we were meant for each other. Since we'd moved in together, each time we made love bonded us even closer. I'd never felt so sure of anything in my life. We were solid. Definitive. I had full trust in who we were individually and as a couple.

Alex reached for me and nothing mattered but the elation I felt when I was with her. So intense. So exquisite.

When her breathing slowed and she fell asleep, I quietly slipped out of bed and went to the porch to retrieve my iPad. Grabbing my device and our pile of clothes, I went back to her and crawled back into bed. Loading the Alaska Airlines website, I checked flights in the morning. Finding one that left around 8 a.m., I quickly booked a first-class ticket to LA for the next day and texted the guys to let them know to go without me.

"When do you have to go?" Alex mumbled, half-asleep.

"Not until tomorrow." I lay back down and wrapped my arms

around my beautiful nymph. "I want to stay here with you."

"Can you do that?" Alex wriggled back against me.

"I just did."

CHAPTER 22

Once Jace returned from Los Angeles, we had every intention of inviting the band over, so they'd know we were serious. Unfortunately, Ty and Zoey went another round in the drama department and by the time they made up, the guys were once again spread out and doing their own thing.

So, it never quite worked out.

Then Zoey left her firm, moved in with Ty, and was in her own sex bubble. Rather than make it such an issue, we figured I'd just come with Jace to New York for the premiere of *Phantom Uprising*.

Easy peasy.

Plus, we had our own shit going on.

With the holidays and winter right around the corner, Jace, Becca, Jen, and I were busy from dawn to dusk getting the ranch ready for our first cold season. We built a dry hay-shed and had enough delivered to get us through any potential snow days. Luckily, we didn't get too many in the Pacific Northwest, but I didn't want to be caught off guard. I bought a large generator and put together some emergency supplies.

Becca and Jen gave all of our blankets a wash and the tack a good thorough cleaning and conditioning. We also bought some new bedding for the stalls, in case of bad weather when Gloria and Bingo had to stay inside.

Jace was surprisingly handy and installed a ton of new floodlights around the property. Next, he and Jen paved a wide pathway from the house to the barn out of flagstone. We all took a few days to check all the fences, mow the pasture one last time, have all the equipment serviced, and install an automatic waterer for the barn.

After a couple of weeks of intense labor, we were done. Becca cooked us an amazing dinner. Over a few bottles of wine, we made a list of all the things we planned to do next year, once we had more horses to take care of.

Life was perfect. The holidays were planned. Jace only had a few more band commitments, and then we'd have an entire year just to be together. With no other responsibilities other than the ranch.

Satisfied with my life, I was relaxing in the living room with a glass of wine and a book when my phone pinged.

Zoey: U there?

Alex: Y

Zoey: So, apparently, Ty is a gazillionaire.

Alex: ??

Zoey: He wants me to work for his foundation.

Alex: So, your dream job – awesome.

Zoey: Are my dreams coming true? I'm having a hard time believing all of this is happening.

Alex: It is, embrace it.

Zoey: I'm sorry I've been so busy. I do want us to get together.

Alex: I've been busy too, let's do it soon.

Zoey: Yes! Love you

Alex: Love you.

"Hey, I hate to interrupt." Jace stood in the doorway, buff arms above his head gripping the crown molding. His sweats hung low on his hips, and my mouth salivated at the happy trail that was visible from his taut abs to the waistband.

"I'm on board with a sexy interruption!" I motioned him over.

"I have the info for New York, get your mind out of the gutter." Jace came over and sat next to me.

"Oooh!" I squealed. "Let me see!"

Just as we began to go over his itinerary, Jen knocked on the front door and came in without waiting. Her face was crumpled with grief.

"Jen, what's wrong?" Jace bolted to her. "Is it Mom?"

"No." She erupted in tears. "I need to speak with you alone."

"Anything you say can be said in front of Alex, Jen." Jace scolded. "We don't have any secrets. Tell me what's going on."

"I just got off the phone with Jessica." Jen could barely talk.

"Jessica?" Jace seemed clueless.

"Cassie's sister."

Jace's face went white. "What did she want?"

"Cassie's dead." Jen's voice caught; tears streamed down her face.

"Wait. What? Shit." Jace plopped down next to me shellshocked. I gripped his knee, searching his face for a reaction.

"She was killed in a car crash a few days ago." Jen sat down opposite us. "She left behind the baby I saw her with. A girl named Helena."

"Oh." Jace's face was still blank.

"The funeral is on Saturday." Jen closed her eyes and sighed heavily.

"I can't go. I'll be in New York," Jace's voice was strangely robotic, completely devoid of emotion.

"The family wants to get some DNA from you, J-bird," Jen said softly. "As soon as possible."

"Why?" Jace asked, his voice distant. Detached.

"They think you're the baby's father," I interjected, trying to catch his eye.

My heart was beating out of my chest. How could this happen just when we found our perfect balance? Our lives were completely shattered with one phone call. Shaking the negative thoughts from my brain I decided it didn't matter.

I would be there for Jace, in any way he needed me to.

"Jen, let us have a few minutes," I said gently.

"Sure." Jen stood to leave. "I'm heading back out to our place. I left her number on the kitchen counter."

We sat silently for at least fifteen minutes. Jace's hands were clasped in a giant fist, his elbows resting on his knees. His head hung down; his hair was tousled around his face. I remained where I was, unsure of what to do or say. I was so scared about whatever was going to happen next, I almost relished the limbo we were in.

"Fuck." Jace finally broke the silence. "You should give her a call."

"I know, but I don't want to." Jace looked at me, fear permeated his gaze.

"This little girl could be a huge blessing to your life." I eeked out a smile, trying to be positive.

"I don't want to be a father to *her* child." Jace's voice caught. "I'm feeling like I'm having an out-of-body experience right now. How the fuck does this happen?"

"It's going to be okay, Jace. We will figure all of this out, I'm not going anywhere." I got up placed my hands over his.

"Yet," Jace spat and abruptly stood and walked into the kitchen.

I followed him but didn't react. This was intense. Fighting with him over a stupid comment wasn't going to help things.

He picked up the slip of paper Jen had left him and grabbed his mobile and punched in the number before I could stop him. My initial worry was that Cassie's family shouldn't have his direct, private phone number. But it hit me that if Helena was Jace's daughter and Jace and I were together, the infant child would become part of our lives. I involuntarily shivered and wondered if it was me that Jace was worried about.

In the middle of my own thoughts, I didn't pay close attention to his conversation. My brain fogged over. Mostly Jace grunted "nos", "I don't knows", "uh-huhs" and "okay." He asked why her family wanted him to take a paternity test when Cassie told Jen that Jace wasn't the father of her kid a few months ago.

Unfortunately, judging by his frustration when he hung up, he didn't seem to get any answers.

"So?" I said tentatively.

"They are demanding that I do a DNA test. Cassie apparently left a will naming me as the girl's father." Jace slumped down on the couch. "If I don't agree, they are threatening to go to the press and then to court."

"If they threatened you, maybe we should get a lawyer." I tried to be helpful and include myself so that he knew I'd stand behind him. "I could talk to Zoey when I'm at her house tomorrow."

"No!" Jace held up his finger. "No. No. *No.* I do not want Zoey or Ty or any of the guys to know about this. Not yet. Maybe not ever, if I can help it."

"Okay. Then we need to find a lawyer."

"Alex, let me just process. And think." Jace scrubbed his hands over his scruffy face and kept them over his eyes.

I marveled at how gorgeous he was even in a stressful situation. Physically, he did it for me like no one ever would. His hair was streaked a million different colors of blond, his body had developed a leaner, muscular physique from his work on the ranch, and his piercing green eyes—Gawd.

But watching him try to control his emotions in order to reason through this situation—I loved him. I loved every single part of him, and if Helena was part of him, I knew I'd love her too.

"Jace, babe. We should do whatever we need to do to find out if Helena is your baby." I sounded almost enthusiastic, I hoped he could tell that my intentions were good.

"Well, sure. You want to make sure this baby isn't mine," Jace said sharply, cutting me off.

"No. Yes. I mean—" I stammered before recovering. "What I meant was that either way we need to know."

"Alex. Please. Can you try to keep your thoughts to yourself right now? Is that too much to ask? It's a lot to take in, and I just want a few minutes to sit here and think." Jace brought his fists back up to his eyes.

"Okay." I felt hurt but supportive of his own process. So we sat in silence again for easily half an hour.

"I'm scared out of my mind right now," Jace finally said so quietly

I could barely hear him.

"I know. What can I do?"

"Make all of this go away?" he said sadly.

"I wish I could." I tried to empathize with him.

"Yeah, I know you probably do," he muttered and brought a shaky hand to his brow. In all the years I'd known him, I'd never seen Jace break down. My earlier assessment of his calm demeanor was wrong. He was *freaking* the fuck out. I held out my hand to him and he clasped it to his chest and pulled me over. Wrapping my arms around him, I hugged him as tight as I could.

"I'm not going to leave, Jace," I tried to assure him. "No matter what."

"Don't make that promise, Alex." Jace stroked my hair. "I might have a baby to take care of soon. Jesus."

"We will cross that bridge when we come to it." I looked up at him, but he was staring off into the distance.

"I should just go and see her," he said, almost to himself. "If I see her maybe I'll know whether I need to lawyer up."

"I disagree, before you see her you need to get a lawyer, Jace." I stroked his chin. "You have deep pockets. You need to protect yourself, or at least have some help with this process."

"Christ, Alex. Stop telling me what to do. *You* need to let *me* figure this out," Jace growled, breaking free from my embrace to stand.

"Oh, Gawd. I'm sorry, I don't mean to be bossy. Come to bed." I tried to make amends. "Things won't seem as bad tomorrow."

"Go ahead." Jace moved toward the kitchen. "There is zero chance I'm sleeping tonight."

"I get it. Okay, then we'll stay up."

"This isn't your problem to solve, Alex." Jace was exasperated and strode toward the bedroom. "I'm trying to be nice, but when I say I need some time alone, I need some time alone."

"Wait, you said you wanted space to think. Now you want some time alone? Are we not in this together?" I followed him. "I mean, if this is our first crisis, then we should be working on it together."

"Are you serious right now?"

"U-Um—" I stuttered, completely unsure of what to do or say. I just wanted him to know that I was all-in no matter what. But he was so upset my words kept getting jumbled.

"You know what? I'm going to catch a ferry back to my place." Jace stormed through the house on the way to our bedroom. "I need time to process this without distractions."

"We leave for New York on Friday." I kept pace with him, feeling panicked. "Why can't you just stay here and cool down? I can sleep in the barn or on the couch if you need to be away from me."

"You're not fucking sleeping in the barn, this is your house, Alex." Jace went to the closet, grabbed his backpack, and threw it on the bed.

"I have no idea what to say to you right now." I sat on the bed. "I don't think anything I say or do will be the right thing."

"Probably not," Jace muttered as he put some toiletries into his backpack.

I couldn't help it, my eyes sprung leaks. It was hard to comprehend how we had gone from blissfully happy to rock bottom in an instant. Wiping the tears from my eyes as they fell, I sat silently while he packed.

"I can't deal with you being upset on top of all of this shit, Alex." Jace looked at me coldly with his backpack hanging off one shoulder.

His words hurt. All I could see was my world exploding. At that moment, my feelings were shredded. I figured that he couldn't leave me if I left him first.

"Fine. Take all the time you need. No need for me to burden you with my presence in New York." I hiccupped through tears, not really meaning it, but unable to stop my lips from flapping.

"Are you serious? Fuck, Alex. That's not what I meant, but fine. Best I know where you stand now," Jace roared.

I stared at him through my tears.

"That took a lot less time than I expected."

"What do you mean?"

"You bailing on me." He stalked out the door so fast my reaction time was delayed. Wait? Wasn't he bailing on me? Arguments sucked so bad. I had thought we were on such solid ground, but with our track record, it began to feel more like quicksand.

When I finally came to my senses enough to run after him, he had already shut the door to his truck and started the engine. Stopping in front of the driver's side, I gestured for him to roll down the window, but he waved me off and began to back up to go down the drive.

Frantically I flailed my arms to get him to stop and talk to me, but he ignored me and peeled out into the night. Wracking sobs overtook my body. I wasn't sure what had happened.

Did we really just break up?

Running back into the house, I grabbed my phone off the charger and called him. No answer. I tried half a dozen times. He wouldn't answer. Part of me considered throwing my stuff in a bag and following him, but I'd just never been in the situation before. Plus, I had chores to do to take care of Gloria and Banjo. I stood there shivering in the cold, staring at the tire marks for God knows how long before I felt a soft hand on my shoulder.

"Hey." Jen gave me a side hug. "Hey," I said sadly.

"Did Jace leave?"

"Yes." I wiped my nose with my sweatshirt. "Let's go have a chat." She steered me inside.

Once inside, she put the tea kettle on. I wasn't much for tea, but it sounded comforting, so I gladly accepted a steaming cup. My crying had subsided, but the throb in my head and heart hadn't. All I could think about is how badly our lives had been fucked up by that one call.

Jen got right to the point. "Alex, do you love my brother?"

"Yes, with all of my heart." My voice caught; I was on the verge of tears again.

"Enough to stick with him if this is his kid?" Jen tapped her chin with her finger and

stared into my eyes with the same crazy green eyes that Jace had.

"We will cross that bridge—" I began.

"No." She shook her finger at me. "Nope. Not the right answer."

"Jen, he left me just now. He said he needs a break." My voice was so whiny, which made me angry at myself.

Jen sat back and blew on her tea and steered the conversation in a way I didn't expect. "I know about your pregnancy scare all those years ago."

"Oh." I looked down, unable to hold her gaze. "I hoped he hadn't told anyone about it."

"Well, you broke up the next day and his heart was smashed in bits for a long time afterward." Jen assessed me. "He was planning to commit to you. He was devastated when you left and gutted about your reaction to that test. You fled the scene, babe."

"There's more than one side to the story, you know," I protested. "What you probably aren't aware of was his idea of a commitment was me flying into cities where LTZ was playing on dates that were

290

convenient for his schedule. He didn't even ask about what I was up to."

"Well, I didn't say he wasn't a dumbass."

"His inability to place value on the work that I was doing is why I left, Jen." I tucked my legs under me and wrapped a soft throw around my body. "I don't blame him; when we first met, I was in high school, and he gave me ideas of how to build up an Instagram following to pay for travel. It morphed into so much more when I started raising money for animal rescues, all of the fluffier stuff I did was to save money for this ranch. We got back together when he finally realized how important my work was. It was only then that we were equals."

"I was surprised that you guys got back together, truth be told."

"Me too, but at the same time I'm not." I shut my eyes. "We belong to each other. I think we always have."

"I hope so." Jen reached over to stroke my shoulder. "Have you changed your stance on kids then?"

I sighed. It was a lot to process, and it wasn't really Jen's business. Until this situation with Cassie was brought to our attention, I hadn't really thought about kids at all. Horses had been all I ever wanted to focus on.

"I mean, well—" I stammered. "I mean, I don't feel as strongly as I once did."

"Dude, I love you. So does Becca. But Jace loves you more than anyone, and I'm guessing he's scared shitless that you're going to leave him over this. Can't you understand that?" Jen regarded me with a furrowed brow. "Can you imagine suddenly being a single father with a child that—"

"He doesn't remember making," I finished.

"He's been through a trauma." Jen blinked. "I'd give anything to protect my baby brother from that witch, God rest her soul. I can't believe I let her near Jace."

"I don't know what to do," I lamented. "He wanted just a bit of space, and now I've gone and uninvited myself from New York."

"How about you pack your things and go get him? Let Becca and I handle things here. He's probably at his condo. Show him you really will be there for him no matter what," Jen advised.

"Jen, for the record. If that little girl is a part of him, then I will welcome her into my life. Our life." When I said it out loud, it felt right. True.

"Good." Jen smiled. "I hope it's his child, if I'm honest. If she's not, who the hell knows what will happen to her."

"What do you mean?"

"Their whole family is fucked up." Jen sighed. "For years I felt bad for Cassie, so I let her hang around for far too long. She all but stalked Jace until LTZ was successful enough that he had security and buffers.

"Were they together long?" I was trying to place who she was. Vague memories of the red-haired girl from the club crossed my mind.

"Jace probably let it go too far, she was wild and sexual, he couldn't stay away when he was younger," Jen explained in too much detail for my taste. "Even after he still hooked up with other girls, she still had fantasies of him being her boyfriend. He managed to keep her as a friends-with-benefits thing up until right before he left on his first tour."

Until we slept together.

I felt a little nauseated.

"Did they still see each other after?" I tried to sound unaffected, but my insides were burning with rage and jealousy.

"Not until that time in LA." Jen looked off as though she were remembering. "I'm sure he figured that time had healed any wounds, and then—"

"That night," I finished.

"Yep. He was scared shitless about catching something." Jen scrubbed her fingers through her hair, a Deveraux trait. "Love him or hate him, thank God Carter really preached to those band boys the importance of wrapping it up."

"I need to go see him." I got up abruptly and moved toward the bedroom.

"You missed the last ferry, just go in the morning. Should give you both some time to cool down." Jen clutched my hand and squeezed. "I'm off to bed."

There was no way to sleep, so I packed my bag and sat in the kitchen watching YouTube videos until it was time to leave for the first ferry. After I arrived in Seattle, I headed straight to Jace's condo, parked out front, and used my key to let myself in. Although muted, I knew from the sounds emanating from his condo where he was, even at the early hour.

I crept up to the practice room door, trying to be silent. Not that it mattered, Jace couldn't have heard anything through the loud rhythmic thumping. The intricate and delicate beats juxtaposed with the heavy and hard thrashing made me stop to listen for a while.

I'd never taken the time to think about how much the intensity of Jace's drumming mirrored his own emotions. Percussion was such a part of him, and he hadn't touched his kit since he'd left the recording sessions in LA.

Sinking down on the wall next to the door, I was able to take a minute to look around Jace's condo while I listened to him play.

Most of the time we spent there was in his bedroom, it wasn't really somewhere we hung out. Now that I was paying attention, it said a lot about my sexy drummer. The room was sparsely furnished with a table and chairs, a couch, and an ottoman. Otherwise, it was filled with various drums, LTZ swag, and boxes of books, clothes, and household items that looked like they were packed to bring over to my place.

Quietly, I opened the door to the practice room, which was covered in high-tech soundproofing that allowed him to practice whenever the mood struck. Jace's back was to the door, he was shirtless wearing athletic shorts, his hair tied back in a blue bandana.

Headphones covered his ears. His entire body was moving, muscular legs pumping the pedals, head bopping to the beat in his mind, ripped, tattooed arms like a blur as he pounded away on the skins.

Almost like he sensed I was there, his head turned to the side and I could see his profile. His eyes were closed, his mouth set in a grimace, which contorted his handsome face into an expression of elemental grief. He finished out the song. Witnessing him thrash on his drums as if his life was in shambles made tears spring to my eyes.

I wondered if I'd pushed him too far. He was a famous musician; his entire life was built around his career. For the past month, I'd monopolized every spare moment of his time.

Had I forced him into a life with me at my rescue? Had I inadvertently given him an ultimatum that kept him from making music with the people he loved in order to be with me? Had I been so focused on building my own life on the ranch that I'd completely steamrolled over the life he loved?

And now, he might be a father. Of a baby he didn't remember fathering. Of course, he was freaking out, his entire life as he knew it was changing abruptly. It had to be overwhelming and scary. A sob slipped out and his drumming stopped abruptly. Jace wiped his brow and set his sticks into his stick-bag.

"I didn't realize you were here," he bellowed, and then took his headphones off. "Sorry, I didn't mean to yell."

"Don't stop playing because of me," I said, wiping my eyes.

"Why are you crying, Poppy?" Jace squeezed his eyes shut, his fist on his forehead.

"Your life is changing so fast, I'm just sorry—sorry for adding to your stress." I

struggled to express what I'm feeling. "You need this, Jace. I . . . I . . . want this for you. It's part of you."

"Yeah." Jace sighed deeply.

"I love watching you play the drums." I moved over to him and put my hands on his shoulders. "Play some more, Jace."

"Okay." He grabbed his sticks. "Can I stay?"

"Whatever you want."

Thump. Thump. Thump. His bass drum thudded. In moments, Jace's entire body was moving again as he got lost in the rhythm. He was so beautiful; I admired his flexing arms and back. Unable to keep my hands to myself, I reached out and traced the tattoo on his shoulder. My touch broke his concentration and he abruptly stopped playing and set his sticks down on the snare.

Spinning on his stool to face me, Jace gripped my hips and pulled me in between his legs and rested his forehead on my stomach, I clutched his shoulders. We stayed that way for a long time, until he looked up at me, his green eyes piercing with an expression I couldn't read.

"We need to take a break, Alex." He held my gaze. He was serious.

"What do you mean?" Pain stabbed me through my heart.

"I need some time to get through all of this. Figure my shit out."

"Okay, how long?" I mumbled, still in shock.

"As long as it takes." His hands moved from my hips to lace his fingers through mine. "I'm not going to put you through all of this, you don't have to worry."

"I came here to tell you that I'm going to be right at your side no matter what, Jace." I clenched his fingers. "Not to break up with you."

"Well, I appreciate that, but I guess it's me that needs some space right now." He pressed his lips together, his voice once again nearly devoid of emotion.

"Oh. Okay. Wow." I couldn't process it. "I still don't understand how we go from planning our future together twenty-four hours ago to breaking up."

"C'mon, Alex don't go down that path." Jace dropped my hands and raised an eyebrow at me.

"Why not?" I hissed.

"We both need to take some time, Alex. Life isn't the same today as it was yesterday." Jace moved around me to head out to the living room.

"It is for me." I crossed my arms and followed him. "You don't have to do this alone."

"Ah, but I do." Jace grabbed a bottle of water from the fridge and guzzled it. "Plus, it works out okay. I know you don't like to be at band events where I have a ton of stuff to do. For these gigs, I'm going to be dealing with all of this press stuff about Zoey, so we wouldn't even really see each other than at the premiere, so no harm no foul."

"So, you just get to make the decision?" I said disbelievingly.

"Yeah, I guess I have to be the one that does what is best for both of us." Jace leaned against the counter.

"Jace!" I sobbed as though my life was over because it felt like it was. "Don't do this."

"It's for the best, Alex." Jace patted my shoulder, almost like he couldn't bear to touch me again. "I need to get going."

Stunned, I grabbed my suitcase and backpack and rolled it out the door, which Jace closed behind me without even a wave goodbye. When I got to my Range Rover, I sat in the driver's seat and bawled and bawled and bawled. Not sure what to do, I stayed put because I was afraid to drive erratically.

About fifteen minutes later, Jace's truck emerged from the garage and sped off, he didn't even notice me. Although I was tempted to follow him, I was frozen. Uncertain why my life had disintegrated before my eyes.

JACE

CHAPTER 23

New York was going to suck without Alex, but fielding questions about why she was there with me would have been even worse. Especially with all that I had on my mind. Ordinarily, I loved flying private for a number of reasons, but my mood hadn't improved and now we were en-route to New York. Trying to show the guys all the metrics that tracked our media impact was getting on my last nerve. Ty couldn't keep his eyes and hands off Zoey, which was just one more reminder that Alex wasn't in her rightful place on the plane with us.

Snapping my fingers in front of Ty's face, I snarled, "Fuck, Ty. I'm doing this for her own good, you could at least fucking pay attention."

"Shit, Jace. I'm sorry, she's distracting." Ty shrugged; his expression was so joyous that it was hard to stay mad at him.

It was true that due to my own pending scandal, I was

disproportionately stressed about the press coverage about Ty and Zoey. She had always been terrible at social media, but now we were coming up with an entire strategy that involved her for the band's benefit, and for her own benefit too. Even though I knew that no matter what we did she'd probably be publicly shamed and ripped apart, it was important for me to try to stop it from happening.

To take my mind off things, I threw myself into implementing a social media plan to incorporate Zoey into the LTZ fold during the entire flight. She wasn't super receptive, which annoyed me further. Then I became really pissed when she kept challenging my ideas by spewing nonsense about her own brand identity. I couldn't tell if Zoey's obstinance stemmed from her true feelings about her media presence or if she had spoken to Alex and was pissed at me.

Truthfully, Zoey was a reminder of Alex and any thought about her made my heart feel like it had been stabbed. I knew that I'd fucked up, treating her the way I did. While it killed me to pull away, it was best for both of us if I let her go before things went too much further. I knew that I couldn't expect her to change her stance on having kids. If she had been conflicted about having my baby, there was no chance she'd stick around for a baby I'd fathered with a different woman.

I couldn't blame her.

My emotions were further on edge when, after we landed, I saw that I'd missed half a dozen texts. One was from Alex, simply asking if I was okay. The rest were from Jessica demanding that we set a date for the paternity test or else. Her threats were a complete distraction. Which meant that Alex's text got lost in the shuffle. It wasn't like I was going to answer in the affirmative. Because I was not okay.

Not by a long shot.

There was no time to deal with either of them anyway, when we arrived, we went directly to a PR meeting in our manager's office.

While trying to listen to our publicists' idiotic strategy for Zoey, I finally responded to Jessica and ended up in the middle of a text war. Distracted by two very different but intense situations, I decided to ignore my own problems. As Zoey got more and more upset, I was about to intervene when Ty jumped in and gave them a piece of his mind. This gave me an opening to back him up, take over and get the fuck out of there.

Once I shared my plan and Zoey and Ty were on board, we were able to leave. As we navigated the labyrinth of hallways to avoid the paparazzi, Zoey reached out and grabbed my arm. "You're amazing, Jace. Thank you."

I tried to play it off, but I was shocked that she was being nice to me. Which meant that Alex hadn't said anything to her. Relieved, I distracted myself for a few hours getting her new Instagram page set up. When I finally made it to my own room, my resolve to stay away from Alex nearly vanished. I missed her so much. Still, I convinced myself not to call or text.

The next morning, I reconsidered. Or, if I was honest, I finally caved and texted her right before we started our day of press.

Jace: Poppy u there?
Poppy: Y.
Jace: hi
Poppy: Hi – r u still mad at me?
Jace: I'm not mad at you I'm so fuckin sad.
Poppy: U don't have to be sad, I love you so much
Jace: I love you more than you know.
Poppy: I miss you so much. I hate being without you.
Jace: I'm not handling things well.

Poppy: Ur going thru a lot at once.

Jace: ...

Jace: ...

Poppy: How r things in NYC?

Jace: goin thru the motions

Poppy: Ok – BTW I'm rejecting the breakup.

Jace: What?

Poppy: We are not broken up.

Jace: ...

Jace: I love you.

Poppy: I love you too.

Jace: I'm sorry. Poppy: It's ok.

Jace: FT after the show? Poppy: Only if you're naked. Jace: (thumbs up emoji) Poppy (eggplant cherry emoji) Jace: You made me lol.

Poppy: good

Relieved that Alex would stick by me after my epic melt-down settled me down a bit and allowed me to focus. Unfortunately, Ty's indiscretion with Sienna gave me an entirely new situation to handle. Anger overtook me. I yelled at him. It was like I couldn't control my feelings at all.

I knew I was triggered and probably projecting my own Cassie situation on Ty, but it felt like there was no way to manage my rage and it scared me.

I focused on the fact that soon I'd be FaceTiming with Alex, and it calmed me down. I made it through the movie premiere and just needed to get through the performance and get back to the hotel.

From the time I tapped out the beat to *Rise* we put on a show to end all shows. Everyone was on fire. Playing live made everything we did worth it, there was no feeling like it. I actually had fun and forgot my problems for a couple of hours.

Wishing Alex was on the side stage with Zoey, I glanced at the petite dynamo and my hackles went up when I saw Sienna slink in next to her.

I knew shit was going down.

After irrationally lashing out at Ty and Zoey and being rightfully yelled at, I followed Ty into the VIP tent. When we arrived for the meet-and-greet, I took one look around and got the fuck out of there. I couldn't do it. With so much looming over me, I wanted Ty to finally step up and handle his own shit.

I already had too much on my plate.

Luckily, the car got me back to my hotel quickly. Immediately after closing my door to the suite, I crawled under the soft, fluffy comforter and called Alex. When she answered, we switched to FaceTime, and my heart thudded when her beautiful face filled my screen. In an instant, all my cares melted away.

Or so I thought.

"Hey," I said softly, and before I could stop it tears welled up in my eyes.

"Oh, Jace." Alex was in her bedroom, the lamp on the nightstand illuminating her golden, honey hair.

"Poppy." I could barely get her nickname out before I full out started crying. Hard.

"Jace! Jace!" I could hear Alex yelling. "Please pick up the phone, I need to see that you're okay."

"I'm a fucking mess," I blubbered, and I could see from the tiny picture on the screen that I looked slightly crazy. "Let me call you back after I pull myself together."

"No!" she admonished and then her voice turned soothing. "You don't need to hide anything from me. Especially your feelings."

"Everything is spinning out of control." My voice was a little more stable now. "I don't have it in me to deal with Ty and Zoey stuff anymore and there's a whole new issue."

"What happened?" She settled back against the light-yellow pillows that we had slept on together for the past few months.

By the time I'd filled her in on the day's events, I'd stopped bawling like a child. My breathing was normal, and I'd settled back into my own hotel bed. Just having her with me made such a difference, I didn't ever want to be without her. The thought of how close we came to breaking up made me nearly well up again. Then I remembered what we were facing with my paternity situation.

I was so fucked.

I knew my emotions were all over the map and I didn't want to play Alex like a yo-yo, but I felt completely unable to think clearly. "You must be crazy to want to be with me, Poppy. You're going to run screaming at some point if I don't get my shit together."

"You are in the middle of what might be the biggest personal crisis you've ever had, Jace." Alex's calm voice soothed me. "Wherever your emotions take you, it's all fine. I will be here for you, no matter what."

"I love you." I looked right at her through the screen. "I really, really love you."

Her entire expression softened, and she looked like she was about to cry.

"I love *you*." She brought the phone close up so her face filled the screen and puckered up her soft, pink lips.

I kissed her back through the screen. "I'll be back home tomorrow evening. Can you meet me at my condo?"

"Yes, because I can't wait to be skin-on-skin with you."

"You have no idea." I pointed to the coverlet, which had begun to tent when she gave me the screen kiss.

"Can I see?" She lifted her T-shirt and threw it on the ground, circling a tight, brown nipple with her finger.

My cock immediately became hard enough to cut diamonds. Slowly, I pulled the fluffy comforter down to reveal my shaft flush against my stomach. Looking down, I gripped myself and stroked from root to tip and began jacking myself so she could see me.

"Why haven't we ever done this before?" Alex was breathless as she slipped her scrap of underwear off.

"Don't think. Just touch yourself, Poppy. Let me see your pussy." I rubbed the precum all over my crown and began jacking faster.

I could hear a distinct buzz and Alex positioned her bullet vibrator against her clit. Her hips gyrated against the toy. Watching her pleasure herself put me over the top, electricity zapped along the base of my spine and, before I knew what was happening, I was spurting all over my hand, stomach, and comforter. Alex was moaning through her own orgasm, moisture glistening along her thighs as she came.

Alex purred as she pulled the covers up around her. "You're my Viking sex god."

"I can't wait to see you tomorrow." I got out of bed to grab a towel from the bathroom to wipe up with.

"Me either." Alex was falling asleep, even though it was later in NYC, she had been doing physical labor all day at the rescue.

"Good night. Love you." I kissed the phone.

"Love you too." She kissed back.

Unfortunately, the next morning all hell broke loose.

CHAPTER 124

I woke up early the next morning, feeling like my life was back on track. Definitely not perfect, but at least Jace had come to his senses. The thought of being without him had nearly spun me into a deep depression, and only the fact that I had so much work to do around the barn kept me somewhat sane. My heart melted when I checked my texts and found one from my gorgeous drummer.

Poppy – I miss you. I'm counting down the minutes until I get on the plane back to you. I love you so much.

I'd also been texting Zoey. She wasn't handling the salacious article well and wanted to talk to me about something that was going on, but I didn't have many details. All I had were short two-to three- word texts. What I gleaned was: 1. she thought someone had set her up; 2. Ronni Miller was in her hotel suite and she wasn't happy about it and 3. she was pissed at Ty but more pissed at his publicist. Then nothing.

Remembering that Jace and I were trying to distance ourselves from their drama, I didn't engage other than to tell her that they would work it out. Instead, for the next few hours, I finished all my chores. I also worked with Gloria and felt very proud when she allowed me to saddle her up. She wasn't ready to be ridden yet, but I was really building trust with my beautiful mare. Jen and Becca had gone into town to pick up some supplies and lunch, and as I was walking to the house from the barn, the work truck came barreling down the drive. Before Becca could put it in park, Jen jumped out and was running toward me with a look of utter panic. I stopped in my tracks.

Oh God, not again. Don't let it be Jace.

Jen skidded to a stop in front of me and clung to me. "I'm so, so sorry," she sobbed.

I was frozen because I had absolutely no idea what was going on. I must have looked spooked out of my mind because Becca calmly strode over and gently pried Jen off of me. "Jen, stop. Alex clearly hasn't heard the news."

"What the fuck is happening?" I shrieked, finding my voice. "What happened to Jace?"

"Sweetie, no. It's Zoey." Tears streamed down Jen's face. "It's all over the news."

Screaming, I ran into the house to find my tablet. Becca followed and pulled up *CNN* on TV. Bawling uncontrollably, I watched the footage of Zoey running out of the hotel like a crazy person, paparazzi chasing her into the street. A big dude pulled her out of the way before she was hit by a taxi, but she was clearly unconscious. Gasping for air, Ty pushed people out of the way to get to her, and then cradled her limp body. My heart shattered when you could hear him wailing like she was dead.

Then it really hit me. My best friend might be dead.

I couldn't reach Jace and it was maddening. I didn't have any of the guys' phone numbers, and I certainly didn't have any of their management contact information. Helplessly, I watched as the locust media descended upon my best friend. It got worse. Ty was screaming and threatening to kill anyone who got near. When the ambulance finally got through and they loaded her in, the last shot was Ty's face, which reflected total and utter devastation.

Oh my god, Zoey's parents.

Scrolling through my contacts, I found Olivia's cell phone and called. She didn't answer. I tried Jace. He didn't answer. Back and forth I tried both numbers, fruitlessly. I'd never felt so scared or powerless in my life.

Like zombies, Jen, Becca, and I watched the news coverage on an endless loop, hoping to get some word on Zoey's condition. Jen also kept trying to reach Jace, but his phone went right to voicemail. I scrolled through the hundreds of articles about what was happening. We were rewarded with sensational stories about Zoey and her "sordid" past, Ty and some mystery woman, speculation, rumor. All of it bullshit.

After a few hours, I was numb. I wished Jace would call, but I knew he was in the thick of it. Obviously, he wasn't coming home tonight. I felt so alone, so immobilized. Trying to stay productive, I trudged out to the barn to feed my horses and clean the stalls, but I had absolutely no energy. My emotions and the stress of not knowing were morphing into exhaustion. I was heading back to the house and was saying goodnight to Jen and Becca when my phone pinged.

Jace: Call me.

I immediately dialed, and he answered as soon as we made a connection. "God, Poppy. We have a disaster."

I tried but couldn't talk, I was sobbing and had lost the ability to breathe.

Jen took the phone from me and put Jace on speaker. After she let him know that he was on speaker, he filled us all in at once. When I found out that Zoey hadn't suffered any life-threatening injuries and Ty was flying her parents to New York, I was able to slightly relax. With everyone sufficiently updated, I grabbed the phone and took it off speaker before withdrawing to my bedroom.

Jace's voice was hoarse.

"It's okay." My voice was small, weak.

When Jace activated the FaceTime feature I started bawling even harder when I saw his exhausted face. "I'm so sorry I couldn't call earlier, and now I won't be home for a few days."

"I figured." I curled up in a ball on my bed. "Are you sure she's okay?"

"Ty said she's out of surgery and she's okay, but they won't let him in to see her. Her parents should be here any minute, but we are going to be doing damage control all night and probably for the next week." Jace was distracted, he was in what looked like a PR war room. I could see their manager, Katherine pacing in the background.

As much as I wanted to talk to him and dominate his time, he was needed where he was. I put on what I hoped was a brave smile and touched the screen. "I'll let you get back to it, call me whenever you have a minute. Don't worry about me."

"Okay, I—" Someone in the background was yelling his name and demanding that he read something.

"Just go." I air-kissed him. "Call me when you can."

The guy was still yelling and Jace's face disappeared from the screen, and he screamed at them to shut the fuck up before addressing me. "I'm sorry, I do have to go. Our own goddamn publicists are behind a lot of this. It's a mess. I'll call you when I can."

Then the phone went dead

CHAPTER 125

After two solid days of utter and total bullshit, Katherine and I managed to contain the shitstorm surrounding Zoey's accident and confiscate all copies of Ty's sex tape with Sienna. Ty had been holding vigil at the hospital. Zane had brought him some fresh clothes and checked up on him. We were all anxiously waiting for news because Zoey's parents had finally let Ty in to see her.

Ty showed up at the hotel where we were finalizing the text of the settlement and release agreement that we planned on forcing Sienna and Andrew to sign. He was strangely calm when he read it.

Then, he threw the paperwork on the coffee table. "Fuck this, I'm not signing shit until I see the video that bitch showed Zoey."

"Dude—" I had seen it, and it was something I wanted to unsee immediately. It was triggering, and I was barely holding it together as it was.

"Show me." It was a demand, not a question.

I pulled it up on my tablet and handed it to him.

His expression didn't change one iota while he watched. When it finished, he shut off the tablet and picked the settlement agreement back up. Pen in hand, he scribbled notes in the margins and handed it to Katherine. Meanwhile, I busied myself in drafting an "official statement" while Ty arranged a private charter to fly Zoey home with her parents after she was released from the hospital.

When I finally remembered to check the time, nearly thirty-six hours had gone by since I'd spoken to Alex. I hadn't noticed that Connor and Zane had joined us, they were reviewing the revised agreement and the statement. I could hear Katherine finalizing the details for the charter jet that would take all of us guys back home to Seattle in just over an hour. I stretched and decided to go to my hotel room to pack.

Ty's deep voice held me back. "Jace, hold up."

"I'm exhausted, it's nearly three in the morning, Ty."

Ty stood at the window, almost holding court in the room. "It will only be a couple of minutes; I need to apologize to all of you and to Katherine."

"You don't owe us anything, my brother." Zane always defended Ty. Always. Connor sat stoically.

Katherine slumped down in a side chair. "Ty, Jace, and I have been going for nearly two solid days with no sleep, if you want to say something, that's fine, but please make it quick."

"Fine. Okay. I know this shit has been going on for eight years." Ty shut his eyes and swallowed before regaining his composure. "So much of what happened in the last two days has been completely my fault—"

"Dude—" Zane interrupted, trying to intervene.

Ty held his hand up. "No, Zane. Connor. Jace. And, of course, Katherine. Hear me out. I'm not going to recap how we got here, I just want you to all know that I own my part in getting us here. For Zoey being hurt and in the hospital. For not taking accountability for myself and relying upon all of you to hold me up. For my addictions. I appreciate all you have done for me, but I'm ready and need to take it from here. Katherine, from this point forward anything having to do with me, Zoey, social media, and all of this horseshit with Sienna, I'm in charge."

"All of you are officially off the hook, I'll consult you when any decision involves the band. Bottom line, I'm mentally and physically capable of taking care of myself. It's time I start doing it. Even if Zoey and I never get back together. I owe it to all of you and to her."

Connor surprised us all by speaking. "How is she? No one has told me anything."

"She's got a lot of PT in her future, but she'll fully recover." Ty's lips formed the hint of a smile before turning back into a frown.

I couldn't help but ask, "Are you staying here with her?"

Ty visibly shrunk into himself just for a second before shaking it off and standing tall. "I'm flying her home with her parents in a few days. But, no. I'm flying back to Seattle tomorrow with you guys. When her parents finally let me in to see her, she told me that her life was ruined and that we weren't going to be together. I guess I'm going to finally take the hint."

"Jesus Christ," Connor snarled, folding his arms. "Here we go—"

Ty's gaze locked with our grumpy bassist. "Connor, I'm not sure what the fuck your problem with me is, but it ends here. While I'm sure you're rightfully annoyed by my latest scandal, rest assured it's the final one. Finito. And, for the record? I didn't fuck Ronni. Okay? I never fucked Ronni. She's become one of my best friends, so deal with it. And if you don't mind, I'm going to get Zoey home, I'm going to fuck up Sienna and Andrew so badly they'll never work as publicists again, and then I'm going to spend every single day doing the right thing to be deserving of the love that woman gave me. Even if I never get her back. No matter what happens, for the next year, I'm going to make sure as many kids as possible can play music."

Katherine, Zane, and I all stared at Ty with our mouths agape. He ignored us but addressed all of us in succession.

"Katherine? Are we good?" She nodded in the affirmative.

"Jace?"

"Yep?" I mumbled, exhausted.

Ty pointed at me. "Thank you for holding down the fort. Again. Your services with respect to me and Zoey are no longer required. I appreciate all that you have done, but I will take over from here. Go take care of *yourself.* I love you, man."

My eyes threatened to swell, but I tamped my emotions down and gave him a small salute.

"Zane?"

Zane got up and embraced Ty, holding his cheeks in his hands, looking him in the eye. "Yes, my brother?"

Ty embraced him and mumbled something I couldn't hear into his ear. They clapped each other's shoulders and Zane strode out.

Connor got up to follow Zane, but before he left turned to Ty. "I've been a dick; you haven't deserved it. Well, all of it. Take care of her, she's worth it."

Katherine and I followed the others out, hugging Ty before we left. Not more than a half-hour later, we piled into a couple of cars and managed to avoid detection of the media that were still camped outside the hotel. None of us spoke on the way to the private airstrip. All of us slept the entire way home. And there wasn't much to say when we landed. Everyone was still fried.

When I unlocked the door to my condo at just after 9 a.m., I knew she was there. I could smell her. Tiptoeing down the hall, I peered into my bedroom. Alex was curled up in a ball, knees almost to her chin. My comforter was half-covering her, half off. She clutched her phone, as though she was waiting to hear from me. I stood staring at her for what seemed like an hour before her eyelids fluttered open. She blinked a couple of times, almost like she didn't believe I was standing there, then she smiled.

And she held her hand out to me.

God help me, I reached out and took it.

LIMITLESS

ALEX

CHAPTER 26

With Zoey laid up and the guys scattered around the city, I was counting my blessings that Jace was still living with me. To say things were back on track would have been a lie. He was so in his own head; we barely had a conversation. Our sex life, on the other hand, was off the charts. I spent my days doing chores around the property. Jen and Jace built a covered garage for the work vehicles with an attached shed for extra storage.

At night, we vegged in front of our respective devices.

Jen begged him to get some counseling and to deal with Jessica once and for all, but he refused. Anytime I tried to bring up the paternity situation, he shut me down. He wasn't acting like the man I knew, the responsible guy who had such a sly sense of humor. But going through hard times was part of being in a relationship, as was giving him a certain amount of space. So I persevered.

One thing that niggled at the back of my mind was Jace had completely stopped bringing up going public with the band. Completely.

We also didn't spend Thanksgiving with either of our families. Claiming that we had the flu, we spent the holiday weekend together but with little fanfare. And no turkey. Or stuffing. Or fun.

Once a week, I'd go into the city to sit with Zoey and help her do her PT. She hadn't seen Ty, but she was also so drugged that she barely remembered anything we talked about at my visits. Afterward, I'd visit my mom. And while she'd give me some great perspective, I couldn't exactly tell her about Jace's situation. Because he'd sworn me to secrecy.

Basically, I was being forced to keep two very big secrets about my life from the people who were closest to me, and I was feeling really bad about it. Bad enough that I didn't want to go down to LA for the holiday show, even though Jace said he wanted me there.

Then the stars aligned and the angels sang from the heavens because Zoey was off the strong painkillers, and she and Ty finally were able to reunite. And move in together. I was so thrilled, that it gave me new energy with my own relationship with Jace.

I had just finished setting the table when he came in for the day. "Whoa! Are you actually cooking?" Jace banded his arms around me.

"Yes, dinner is served." My mom had given me a couple of really easy recipes that I'd always loved as a kid, so I'd made them both for Jace. Tomato-basil soup and a baguette cut into slices, slathered in butter mixed with mustard and dried onion, then baked with slices of Swiss cheese.

After we ate and settled on the couch, I grabbed his phone and put it on top of mine on the ottoman. "Are we okay?"

Jace sighed heavily. "Can we talk about all of this another day?"

"We are supposed to leave next week for LA, do you still want me to go?" I was scared to hear the answer.

"Of course."

"Christmas is coming up, are we spending it with our families?"

"Of course." Jace raised an eyebrow and reached for his phone.

I was getting really annoyed. "Do you want me to suck your cock?"

Jace smirked. "Of course."

With sarcasm, at least I got a little bit of my boyfriend back for a second.

"Zoey wants me to fly down with her and her parents. Are you okay with that?" I sprawled out on the couch and rested my head in his lap, reaching up to stroke his cheek.

Jace leaned into my hand. "Sure, it makes the most sense."

Staring into his clear, green eyes, I felt the telltale zap that always happened whenever we wanted each other. Without breaking eye contact, I lifted my shirt, exposing my breast. His cock immediately sprang to life, I could feel it through his sweats where my ear rested. He cupped my breast and flicked his thumb across my nipple. When I pulled the waistband away from his taut stomach, the tip of his dick bobbed against my lips. I took him into my mouth.

Three hours later, thoroughly sated, I was on the brink of falling to sleep when a thought popped into my head.

We might not be able to carry a conversation right now, but at least we have this.

CHAPTER 27

When we landed in LA for the holiday show, I went straight to the hotel with the guys and texted Alex that I needed to get a few hours of sleep. In reality, Ty had arranged for Zoey and Alex to have a private meeting with Christian Siriano, a famous designer to style their red-carpet looks, and she didn't know about it.

When I woke up from my nap, I was greeted by a picture of Alex by the pool with Zoey and her mom. They were all waiting for me and the guys to get there for a barbeque. I was a bit surprised that she hadn't mentioned the style session.

Our relationship had devolved into a really weird dynamic. I couldn't wait to see Alex because just being with her gave me solace. Our sex life was out of this world. The problem was, since I'd come back from New York, I couldn't talk to her. Fielding the barrage of texts that Jessica sent me each day drained me of any ability to have more conversation. I was putting off all things paternity because I was in denial. My sister hounded me. Alex tiptoed around me. So we walked on eggshells.

Until we were naked. Then, we fucked like we'd never fuck again.

I was living on borrowed time. Knowing my Poppy, she wouldn't put up with my bullshit for much longer. I knew this because I wanted her on my arm on the red carpet. Hence, why I'd pushed Ty to include Alex in Zoey's fashion surprise. She'd agreed to accompany me and go public. To me, she didn't seem very enthusiastic. Or excited.

Because she's figuring out when she can leave you.

So I was constantly on edge. The edge of a breakdown. Waiting for the shoe to drop.

I was in the car on the way to Ty's house when I got another text from Alex.

Poppy: Heads up - Zoey's been grilling me about us all day, and I told her that I don't know where I stand.

Jace: WTF! You know where I stand. We agreed to let everyone know we're together, why would you tell her that?

Poppy: GAWD! Jace, we don't talk about what is happening with you, and you won't tell the guys. I don't know what to do.

Jace: I'm ready to tell them the truth.

Poppy: ugh

Jace: Ugh? Is it that hard? Is this what I'm walking into.

Poppy: It's kind of hard to tell them this truth when you won't tell them the entire truth. When you get here, I'll duck out and go into the guest room, find me, we'll talk, don't be mad at me.

Jace: Well, I am mad.

Poppy: No!!! I didn't want to add to the stress for the band since no one, but Zoey and Ty, know anything about us.

Jace: Jesus, Alex, everyone knows about us, goddamn, we're the ones making it weird.

Poppy: I don't know what to say.

Jace: Who do you think arranged for you to get styled? It's so we can go public.

Poppy: ...

Jace: What did you say to Zoey, tell me exactly.

Poppy: That I'm hoping we'll work out and that we are both tired of hiding, but also that I'm not sure where we stand.

Jace: Wow. Fuck.

Poppy: Well, it's kind of true, if you're all about the truth.

Jace: Why would you say that to her? She's going to tell Ty that, you've just created a shitstorm of drama!

Poppy: I'm the one being honest, Jace. But I promised to keep your secret, and you get so weird about me when it comes to talking about you possibly being a father.

Jace: Well if u didn't want to add to the drama u did a shitty job.

Poppy: ...

I couldn't respond. My blood pressure shot up and it felt like my head was going to explode. My heart felt like it was shattering. All my insecurities flooded and filled my head. Goddamn it. I was drowning. Alex *was* pulling away. I was driving her away. But what could I do?

A million thoughts went through my head, all ending in rage. Why couldn't we get on the same page and fucking stay there? The next thing I knew, the car had already pulled up to Ty's house and I was walking down the path to his front door.

ALEX

CHAPTER 28

I hated lying to Zoey. I needed desperately to confide in my best friend because I was flying blind with how to handle the situation. Telling her half-truths made me feel like gagging. Internally cringing because I knew Jace wouldn't want me talking to her at all didn't help, I just couldn't stop myself. Now Jace was upset. We were teetering on the head of a pin, and I could tell from the tone of his texts that he was about to fall off.

Then I saw my gorgeous, shirtless Jace standing in the patio doorway wearing his mirrored Ray-bans, board shorts, and flip-flops, his hair blowing in the slight breeze. My heart stopped. I loved him desperately. I knew he was looking at me even though I couldn't see his eyes. I chose to wear a bikini from Italy, hoping to get us back on track.

But Italy hadn't ended well, so I was now worried about bringing bad juju into an already volatile situation.

Hoping he'd follow me like I asked, I headed to the guest cottage, eager to at least get some one-on-one time. He didn't follow me. Eventually, I changed into a T-shirt and cutoffs and went inside to test the waters in the group. He said a polite hi but didn't make any move to talk to me the entire evening, instead, he got engrossed in a conversation with Zane and Connor.

So much for coming out to our friends.

While Ty cooked, I joined in a conversation with Zoey and Ronni Miller, the actress, who seemed to now be on the safe list. She was delightful, and we were all laughing and having a good time hearing about her and Ty's fake romance. Even though I was enjoying hanging out with the girls, I could feel Jace watching me. Every second.

Finally, when I looked over, his eyes locked with mine and then he very deliberately looked away, his jaw set.

The party was breaking up anyway. Ty and Zoey had to get up early to do an interview in the morning, so everyone began making moves to leave so they could get some sleep. Jace stood by the door with his arms crossed, waiting for Connor and Zane. Deliberately avoiding eye contact with me. I hung back, not knowing what to do. I was supposed to go to the hotel with him. All of this sneaky shit was so goddamn stupid.

I felt like such an asshole. We were surrounded by some of the most important people in our lives, yet somehow, I felt like it was my fault that Jace was questioning my commitment to him. I decided to make a move. To explain and get things back on track. Strolling closer to where he was sitting, I stopped when I was beside him and gave him a nudge and a smile. He didn't smile back.

"Can we talk for a second?" I said super quietly, no one really noticed because of all the goodbye conversations going on at once.

"I'm good." Jace didn't look at me.

"No, you don't. Can I meet you at the London?" I whispered, hoping he still wanted me to stay with him. And also hating myself for chasing after him. Games. Emotions. It was hard to tell what was really going on with us.

"Whatever."

"You've got it so wrong," I implored, my voice raised above a whisper. "Let's talk."

"Shhh. You don't want anyone here to know we were together, so you should keep

   your voice down." Jace rolled his eyes all the way back into his head.

"Were?" I gaped at him, shocked.

"You tell me," he said through clenched teeth.

"We're together."

"Doesn't really seem that way, Alex." He sighed and rubbed his eyes. "Look, I get it. None of this is your fault."

"I'll be there, give me an hour," I said under my breath and headed down to the pool house.

Exactly an hour later, my Lyft pulled into the drive of the London hotel in West Hollywood. I walked through the marble lobby, and Jace was sitting on a powder-blue velvet couch with white, fluffy feather pillows waiting for me. He looked tired and stressed, but slightly relieved to see me.

"I'm an asshole." I sat on his lap and kissed his full lips. "I'm sorry."

"Things are so fucked up, Poppy." Jace helped me stand, took my hand, and moved us toward the elevator. "Let's get up to my room, there's a lot of fans milling around now that they know we're staying here. I've already had to sign a bunch of autographs and pose for selfies. I'm not in the mood."

"Okay."

Jace swiped his card in the elevator, which was lined with gray velvet and we headed to his penthouse suite, which was huge and opulent with powder-blue furniture and gold embellishments. His room was darkened, and the turndown service had already been there so the curtains were drawn. Only the lamp by his bed illuminated the room. Soft, ambient music was playing through the television. The minute the door clicked, I reached for him and he let me hold him.

"I *do* want everyone to know, Jace." I reached up and smoothed his dirty-blond locks away from his cheeks. "I heard the words spilling out of my mouth, and they felt so wrong. But I can't keep half-lying."

"Maybe tonight was for the best, Poppy." Jace kissed my forehead. "At least until I find out."

"Why do we make this so complicated?" I traced his lips with my finger. "I love you so much."

"I love you too." Jace finally smiled at me, but it didn't reach his eyes. "But, to be honest, I feel like I have a boulder on my chest right now."

It was the first real thing he'd said to me since New York.

Guiding me toward the low-profile couch in the living area, Jace flopped down on his back. I lay next to him, snuggled in the crook of his arm. His hand lazily stroked my stomach, and he kissed my temple. I reached for his other hand and linked our fingers together. We lay wrapped together for a long time.

"I can never stay away from you," Jace murmured. "It's like you've cast a spell on me."

"Do you really *want* to stay away?"

"No, but I also don't want to keep going back and forth like this. It is so unsettling."

"Don't you think once you tell everyone what you're going through it will be easier?"

"Of course, but I've backed myself in a corner. We've kept things secret for too long. Now I'm not telling them another huge, life-changing event." Jace pinched his nose like he had a headache. "I feel like I'm under so much pressure, I'm not sure what to do. I'm going to lose my bandmates' trust."

"They will always be there for you. You know that deep down."

Jace just stared.

"I will too."

"I don't know." Jace rubbed his eyes. "Truthfully? I don't want to hurt you, I don't think you will if she's mine, Alex."

My suspicions were confirmed. It didn't make it hurt any less.

"You've always been very clear that you don't want kids. If I have a kid, you won't stay. Or you'll try, but it won't be for you and you'll leave after she becomes attached to you. I've read all about this."

My adamancy about motherhood had affected him more than I realized. To me, I was making a passing comment in the moment. Jace and I hadn't made promises to each other back then. "I felt that way years ago! Do you really think that I'd leave you?"

"Well, she's a baby. Her mother's dead." Jace regarded me. "Are you telling me that you've changed your mind? That you are willing to be a mother to a child that isn't yours when you didn't even want to have your own baby?"

My breath caught at his bluntness. I was speechless.

His green eyes bored into mine. He didn't say anything either.

"Wow." I rotated my body so we were face-to-face. "I thought we were past our trust issues, but I guess we aren't."

"Alex, you were traumatized when you thought you were pregnant." Jace's arms tightened around me. "I don't think you realize how much you freaked out about having a baby. You were adamant that you didn't *ever* want children. With me. You didn't want my child if I'd be on the road. How could I ever expect you to change your mind? For a baby that isn't yours?"

"I'm not going to lie. The thought is terrifying." I put my finger on his lips when he tried to interrupt. "But, I'm sure that you are just as terrified, if not more."

"I am."

"And I want to be with you, whatever that means."

Jace stared at me for a while, then he bent down to slowly explore my lips with his. Our tongues touched, and we made out lazily. Our legs tangled together, and our hands stroked all over each other's bodies. Soon enough, I could feel my studly man's erection against my thigh, and I reached down to stroke him over his board shorts. Sex was our outlet.

"I want to make love to you, Poppy," Jace breathed, his forehead touching mine.

I wasted no time shimmying off the couch and removing my clothes in record time. "Yes."

Standing naked before him, as always, I never got enough of the way Jace looked at me with utter adoration. Reaching back over his shoulder, he grabbed his T-shirt and it was off and on the ground in one motion.

Placing his hands on my hips, Jace moved me to stand in between his knees and kissed my stomach, laving my belly button ring with his tongue. Moving lower, he covered my hipbones and mound with soft flickers of kisses until I was thrusting my hips against his mouth. His hands stroked up and down my outer and then inner thighs until I spread my legs wider. Using his thumbs, he spread my pussy lips and nuzzled and suckled my folds until my breath was ragged. When I was close, he sucked my clit in between his lips and flicked his tongue back and forth until I detonated.

Jace kissed my stomach before standing and leading us into the bedroom. "Let's go to bed."

Crawling under the covers, I reached for Jace's hard cock. Jace tipped my chin up with his finger and gave me a slow, soulful kiss, which was so scorching hot, I wrapped my arms around him to make sure our bodies were as close as they could possibly be. Positioning himself in between my legs, Jace gripped his shaft and flicked the tip against my opening before plunging inside of me.

Cradling my head between his strong forearms, Jace covered my body with his and thrust his cock inside me. Our foreheads touched again. I reached up to grip his biceps as our bodies moved together. Taking my hands in his, he brought our arms above our heads and we stared into each other's eyes. Jace's hips rolled against mine, his cock filled me over and over again. Hooking my legs around his, I locked my ankles around his lower back while we chased our release.

Jace pushed up on his forearms and drove harder and more deeply into me. My legs fell to the sides of him, and he pressed his body to mine. My hips jutted up to meet him, and with each pass, his shaft rubbed against my G-spot, and I clamped my inner walls around him. His head snapped back. His face contorted with rapture. My own orgasm spread through me like wildfire, and I gripped his ass to hold him against me when I came apart.

"I. Fucking. Love. You," Jace shouted with each thrust. Then he exploded his release and collapsed in a heap on top of me.

"I. Fucking. Love. You. Too." I kissed each word on his temple.

We lay together, kissing in the afterglow until Jace softened and slipped out of me. He rolled off me, flopped back against the pillows, and shut his eyes. He still looked exhausted, but he was satiated.

"Let me get a towel to clean us up." I kissed his chest.

Slinking out of his embrace, I quickly went into the bathroom, ran a towel under some warm water, and returned to bed to clean us up. Jace regarded me as I gently wiped his cock, balls, and inner thighs. Tossing it on the ground, I climbed back in bed. In all the years we'd been making love, he always cleaned me up. Tonight was my first time cleaning him.

I kissed his chest and urged him to turn over. "Let me spoon you."

When he was situated, I reached around and clasped myself tightly into his back. Kissing his shoulder blades while my hands stroked the rigid planes of his abs, I breathed in his manly, sandalwood scent. I squeezed him and pressed every part of my body to his. After making love with such intensity, I felt much calmer. It seemed like everything would be okay.

That's what I'd been telling myself for weeks.

Jace's body grew more and more relaxed until I could tell he'd fallen asleep. My own eyes began to get heavier and heavier and before I knew it, the room was full of light and Jace wasn't next to me anymore. A little disoriented, I called for him but there was no answer. Looking over at the nightstand, I saw he'd left me a note just like old times, although the sentiment wasn't quite as sweet and my heart sank.

Poppy – had to go rehearse. I'm not doing the red carpet. See you at the show.

Cold. So cold.

Dressing quickly, I called a Lyft to head back to Ty's. When I arrived, I slipped into the pool house without detection, showered and changed, and then headed up to the main house to check in with Zoey. I found her and Ronni in the kitchen getting their nails done.

"Hey!" Zoey called to me. "Where have you been? Maybe at the London?"

I went to the fridge to grab a bottle of cider. It counted as juice. Today. "Maybe."

"Are you going to glam squad with us?" Ronni batted her eyes dramatically. "I saw your dress, it's killer!"

"I'm not going to do the red carpet, after all." I sat down at the counter with my juice-cider. "Zoey, I need to talk to you when you get a minute."

"Hey, don't worry about me, I've got to make a few calls." Ronni jumped up. "I'll head out to the pool for a bit."

Both of us watched the beautiful, chestnut-haired beauty leave, and then we looked at each other.

"Is this really happening two days in a row?" I shook my head in awe. "You're actually becoming friends with a famous actress who dated Ty?"

"She was only a fake girlfriend." Zoey laughed. "Fair enough." I laughed with her. For a second.

"I think it's time you stop hiding your relationship with Jace, Alex." Zoey looked at me pointedly, but her expression was kind.

"It's been a crazy ride." I slumped over on the counter, took a few deep breaths, and decided. She was right, I wanted to come clean. So I proceeded to fill her in on the truth of our relationship over the past eight years, including losing my virginity to him before they went on their first tour. The only thing I left out was the paternity issue, mainly because that was Jace's secret to tell when and if he was ready.

"Wow." Zoey was blown away. "I'm sorry you felt like you needed to keep such an important part of your life from me."

"It wasn't your fault, we never had more than a couple of months where things were stable until this year. And in the beginning, there was no way to tell you and Ty without it being super painful. When we didn't know what was going on, why would we hurt you guys?"

Zoey twirled gleefully. "Why aren't you shouting it from the rooftops! I mean, we bagged our rock stars! It only took eight years, but—"

"Because I think we are broken up right now. We were together last night, but he has something personal going on that he needs to handle. It's a shit-show. I'm not sure where we stand."

"Is he okay?" Zoey stroked my back comfortingly. "Should I have Ty talk to him—"

"No." I cut her off. "Telling you would betray Jace's confidence. I can tell you that he is fine. He will be fine. It has nothing to do with the band. It has nothing to do with his health."

"O-kay." Zoey looked puzzled.

"Give us—him—a couple of weeks." I shook my head. "He just needs to sort a situation out."

"Are you sure he doesn't need help?"

"I don't know. I'm trying to help him, but he's stressed. We planned for me to go to New York so we could tell everyone we're together, but the night before we had a stupid fight and I stayed home." I confessed. "We made up then fought then made up again last night, and I figured we'd tell everyone today. Then he left before I woke up, and I don't even know why."

"Wow." Zoey nodded empathetically. "You're on your own rollercoaster."

"Yeah. Let's just say that he's afraid I'm not going to stay with him. I'm afraid he won't let me."

"Is that why you aren't doing the red carpet?" Zoey retrieved another cider for me and one for her.

"We were going to walk together; he arranged the style session with Ty yesterday. When I woke up this morning, he left me a note saying he's not going to do it." We clinked our ciders in solidarity. "I don't care about a stupid red carpet; I've done them before."

"You're not asking, but I'm going to give you the same advice that helped me a few months ago." Zoey took my hand and squeezed. "Don't let him get away. And, some extra advice. Stop sneaking around."

"I know. He wanted to go public years ago." I closed my eyes, remembering all the times I came up with excuses. "But then I thought I was pregnant. I wasn't, but I freaked out and told him I never wanted kids."

"Alex, ohmygod." Zoey looked stricken. "I'm so sorry that I wasn't there for you."

"It's okay, it was between me and Jace." I tucked her hair behind her ears. "As it

should have been. But he was leaving on tour, and the real reason we split up was that he just didn't understand what I was doing with the rescues. He didn't take time to learn my passions."

"Has that changed?"

"So much! He's basically moved in with me, and most of his stuff is at my house. He's learning about the horses, working on the ranch." I smiled thinking about our summer and fall together. "Everything was on track until a couple of weeks ago."

"Until this situation that you won't tell me about?" Zoey poked me.

"Yes." I wanted to tell her so badly, but I couldn't betray Jace when things were so tenuous.

"Don't give up on him, Alex." Zoey squeezed me. "He's worth it. You have no idea how much he's helped Ty over the years."

"He's really grown to think of Ty as a brother."

"The feeling's mutual." Ty's low voice interrupted us. "Sorry to interrupt, but Z, we need to leave in an hour and you're not ready."

"Shit! Alex—we need a follow-up." Zoey shot up, kissed Ty, and made a beeline into the house.

"You and Jace going public yet?" Ty crossed his arms, his beautiful brown hair cascaded around his face.

"Gawd. Everyone already knows, don't they? I've just filled Zoey in on the details, so you can get them from her if Jace hasn't already told you." I leaned back on the stool. "Changing subjects, I'm glad you finally found your way back to Zoey."

"Me too." Ty sat next to me. "But, Alex, I need to ask you something. Is there something going on with Jace that we need to know about?"

I wasn't sure if Jace had said anything to Ty. Or if this was a test. "Why do you ask?"

"He's not been himself for a while." Ty squinted. "He's always the stable one of our crazy group and he's acting super aggro."

I studied Ty, trying to gauge his intentions. "You're putting me in a hard position. I'm going to tell you that, yes, he has a situation he's dealing with, and he'll tell you when he's ready."

"Fair enough." Ty gave me a pat on the shoulder. "I've got to go get ready, my girl's making her debut tonight."

"I'm really happy you found your way back to each other." I hugged him.

I hope Jace will find his way back to me.

CHAPTER 29

Just when I felt like Alex and I took some steps forward, something pulled us back again. The emotional rollercoaster of the past week was relentless and exhausting. It was more like multiple rollercoasters which had merged into one giant ball of stress and emotion.

I couldn't remember any other time in my charmed life where everything was so complicated. My family had always been solid, my band was successful, I'd lived an amazing life on the road, now I had love with the most beautiful girl in the world.

At the same time, I had no idea how to process being a father to a little girl whose mother might have drugged me. It sure wasn't the baby's fault. If she was mine, I'd live up to my responsibility and probably love everything about her.

Who could I even talk to about this? I'd done a search online, and the resources for men who had been roofied were practically nonexistent. The resources that did exist were for gay men. In my case, could I have even performed if she drugged me?

To add to my confusion, I couldn't figure out if what happened was actually rape. As hard as I tried to piece together what happened, after the first drink I couldn't remember a thing. Did we even have sex? If we did, I'd always had great chemistry with Cassie—maybe I'd even initiated it. If she drugged me, then wow. Just fucking wow. The memory thing was fucking with my head in a big way.

And now that Cassie was dead, I'd never have any answers.

Her sister wanted some. My time for avoiding the inevitable had run out. Beginning early in the morning, Jessica had sent me about twenty threatening texts about going public to get me to "do the right thing." Whatever that was. She was so insistent on me getting tested that I was beginning to believe that Helena was my daughter. Why else would Jessica be so determined?

Needless to say, I was overwhelmed.

All my plans to proudly show Alex off on the red carpet were off the table. Under no circumstances would I allow Jessica and her family to learn about her from the tabloid and press coverage of the event. It was better to let Ty and Zoey have their moment and for me to fade into the background as much as possible.

Like I always had done.

Alex had texted me too, but I was too stressed out to respond for most of the day. We had a long rehearsal because of the special light effects, and I just hung out in the dressing room while everyone else got ready and walked the red carpet.

Back home in Seattle, my dad had helped me find a family lawyer to make sure that the situation was handled legally, and we had a plan in place an hour before the show was supposed to start.

> *Poppy: Is it ok to come to the dressing room?*
> *Jace: yes*
> *Poppy: I'm with Zoey's M&D.*
> *Jace: ok*
> *Poppy: How are you holding up?*
> *Jace: I got a lawyer, my dad helped me.*
> *Poppy: good*
> *Poppy: Feel better?*
> *Jace…*

All of the guys and Zoey were hanging out in our dressing room waiting for the show. Waiting for Alex to arrive, I leaned on the edge of the sofa, shut my eyes, and tried to fend off the headache that was threatening to overcome me. When Sergey opened the door to the dressing room and Zoey's mom and dad walked in followed by Alex.

She looked so beautiful. Forbidden.

When she started toward me, I could only shake my head "no" to ward her off.

Alex looked crushed, but to my surprise she ignored me. Placing her hand on my shoulder, she claimed me in front of the entire room. She sealed the deal when she reverentially brushed my hair away from my face.

"You are the most amazing man I know," she whispered into my ear before going over to Zoey.

I managed a small smile before Ty interrupted my thoughts. His offer to help was heartfelt, but I wasn't ready to share what was happening with him or any of the other guys in the band. Luckily, our tour manager gave us the sign and within minutes we were getting ready to go onstage in front of 20,000 people.

Opening with *Rise*, our show was fantastic. Wailing on my drums was always therapeutic for me, especially when I had stuff on my mind. Lost in our set, every now and then I caught glimpses of Alex dancing at the side of the stage with Zoey and Ronni. It occurred to me that she was actually here at my show to support me, and I was surprised at how comforting it was.

By the time we played our special version of *Butterfly* for Zoey, complete with a butterfly light extravaganza, I felt lighter somehow.

When Ty brought Zoey out onstage at the end of the show, the audience embraced and cheered for her. Knowing that LTZ wouldn't be onstage together for a long time, none of us wanted the show to end so we played rock classics for over an hour. The girls were dancing their asses off, our crew was having a blast. Best of all, I was feeling good for the first time in a week.

All of us stayed at the afterparty until dawn. Connor and I played pool for hours with a couple of actors from the movie. Ronni and Alex worked the room together, charming everyone in their wake. Zane had a guitar circle going. Zoey and Ty were holding court in a corner looking cozy and happy. Her parents were dancing like they were twenty years younger. After a couple of beers, I realized my mind was completely free and clear of all responsibility and worry, and it felt amazing.

When the party began winding down, Zane and I were the last men standing. Alex was half-asleep, resting her cheek on her hand against the back of a VIP booth. Her honey hair was wrapped up in a messy bun fastened by a rubber band. Sliding in next to her, I traced her lips with my thumb, and she surprised me by sucking it into her warm mouth.

"Let's get you to the hotel, sleepyhead." I wiggled my thumb.

"We didn't even hang out together tonight." She released my thumb with a pop and promptly yawned. "Do you think I'm that easy?"

"You were flirting with Idris Elba." I raised an eyebrow. "Don't think I didn't see."

"He's on my list." She looked defiantly into my eyes.

I mimed ripping up a piece of paper. "Consider your list ripped up."

"It was such a fun night."

"Agreed." I stood and pulled her up with me. "And now it's time to get some sleep." Arm in arm we made our way to the front of the club. Texting my driver, I looked around for the security guard who had been assigned to me but couldn't find him. Figuring it would be safe enough at the ass-crack of dawn, when I got confirmation from my driver we stepped outside to get into the car. Right into a flood of paparazzi. It was just getting light out, but the flashes blinded us.

Shielding Alex, I tucked her head into my chest and wrapped my arm around her while I tried to locate my car. For a minute, it was really scary navigating a hoard of media who held out phones and microphones shouting my name and asking for pictures. Luckily, Alex had some level of awareness and kept her face pressed into my chest, trusting me to get us to safety. Finally, I spotted the car and ensured Alex got inside before turning to address the masses.

"Great to see all of you, thank you for supporting LTZ." I smiled broadly and waved.

"Who is the girl, Jace?"
"Is that your girlfriend?"
"What's her name?"
"Did the band break up?"
"How much do you hate Zoey?"

"Where's Ty?"

Ignoring all the questions being shouted at me, I waved and ducked into the car and shut the door. Alex was leaning back with an amused look on her face.

"Well, they know about us now," I deadpanned, although fear permeated my body.

"They won't recognize me." Alex laughed. "I'm more known in the animal community than the influencer community now."

I scrubbed my hands through my hair, thoughts of what happened to Zoey permeating my mind. "I'm so rarely accosted, it gets a little squirrely, but it can also turn really bad."

"You definitely know the ins and outs of getting coverage and staying out of it." Alex held her hands out to me. "But now I'd like you to cover me with kisses, please."

Taking both of her hands in mine, I tugged her into my lap and placed soft kisses all over her beautiful face. Alex draped her arms around my neck and nestled against my chest. Not wanting her to move, I stroked her soft hair all the way to the hotel. The driver called ahead so we could drive into the private entrance and avoid the paparazzi that was no doubt waiting for us. We managed to make it up to my room without further interruption.

Our sex, as usual, was mind-blowing.

It wasn't until early afternoon before I woke up with a start to find Alex sitting in the living room watching TV in my T-shirt.

"Good morning, sleepyhead." She held her hand out to me. "Or should I say afternoon?"

I yawned and stretched, my morning wood bobbing against my stomach. "Wow, I haven't slept that good in weeks."

"Your phone is going nuts; you should probably have a look." Alex pointed at where it was charging on the desk.

Picking it up, I saw there were about two hundred messages and a ton contained links to news articles. Figuring it was coverage of Zoey's grand debut, I clicked on a few of the stories to discover that one very clear picture of Alex and I had been posted everywhere. My hair was a bit matted from being at the party all night, but Alex looked beautiful. Almost like a supermodel.

"Jace Deveraux dating Influencer Alex LeRoux."

"Zoey who? It's all LeRoux."

"Another one Bites the Dust: Influencer Alex LeRoux snags LTZ Drummer."

All the press would have been fine, but the series of texts from Jessica stopped me cold. Escalating from demands to call, to accusations of avoiding her to downright threats if I didn't get the paternity test done by the next day, it was the last one that stopped me cold.

Jessica: I've tried getting a hold of you all fucking day. I know you don't take your daughter seriously, but if you don't take care of this shit then I'm going to the press to tell them the REAL story. You dated my sister, cheated on her with that whore influencer, led her on for years until you slipped her a roofie, and got her pregnant, only to ignore your baby until she got drunk and got killed. I have the story ready to go Jace so fucking call me within the hour, or I'm going to go public.

Jessica: one more thing, if you are out with that bitch again, all bets are off. It's time to honor my sister's legacy. You did her wrong, and now it's time to pay.

My heart stopped cold. Ice prickled down my hairline. I had to get help, find a way to stop this from turning into a bigger nightmare than it already was. Knowing that a story like that—even a lie—would end my career and destroy the band, I had to be strategic. But I didn't even know what that meant. Wildly looking around the room, I focused on Alex, who was staring at me quizzically.

"Jace, what's going on?" Alex was calm. "You look like you saw a ghost."

"Alex, you have to go home," I implored.

"No, I don't."

"Yes. Please." I stared her down.

"Oh hell no. I'm not going through this fucking thing again, Jace." Alex crossed her arms. "I'm not leaving you. Don't buy into any drama, you hate it."

"I don't want you here," I said pinching my nose at the lie.

Alex stayed put on the sofa. Staring at me. Like she was trying to figure out what was going on. "I don't believe you."

"I need to sort this kid shit out, Alex." I took a deep breath. "I'm sorry for the mixed messages, but it's for the best."

"Stop, Jace." She stood and gripped my forearms. "Just talk to me."

I pressed my lips together to tamp down any emotion. "I can't."

"I love you." Alex shook her head sadly. "You're it for me, don't push me away." I turned away, I had to. "I'm not it for you. I'm a fucking mess."

"Shh… We will get through all of this." She tried to comfort me by rubbing my back, which made me keenly aware that I was still naked.

"Alex, trust me when I say this." I strode toward the bathroom. "I don't want to fuck with you, it's not fair. That little girl is mine; I know it. All of the plans we made are in the gutter, and I'm fucking

348

devastated about that. But it's not her fault, and I have to do the right thing for her."

Alex's eyes filled with tears. "And I'm not the right thing?"

"I don't know." I shrugged. "Right now, I just don't have the bandwidth to think about it. Or factor your feelings or to worry about whether you'll stay or go in. I have no choice. I've got to take care of this situation on my own."

"You've never pushed me away, Jace," Alex's face crumpled. "Not like the past couple of months."

I squeezed my eyes shut. I didn't want to hurt her, but I also didn't want to get hurt either. "It's for your own good, Poppy. I don't want to make you any more promises I can't keep."

"Fine. I'll go then." Alex stripped off my T-shirt and put on her clothes from the night before. Like an asshole, I watched her, knowing it might be the last time I saw her gorgeous naked body.

She moved toward where I was standing, stopping next to me. Looking me directly in the eye, a tear slipped down her beautiful face. Then she did something I didn't deserve. Pressing her soft lips to my scruffy cheek she kissed me and gave me the sweetest smile before she slipped out and shut the door.

CHAPTER 30

After I left Jace, not bothering to collect anything from Ty's house, I took a Lyft to the airport and caught the first plane home. Stoically, I thought about the past couple of weeks and Jace's up-and-down moods and erratic behavior. When I arrived home, no one was there so I immediately went into the barn to see my horses.

Nothing made me feel calmer and more peaceful than grooming a horse. Grabbing a brush and curry comb, I spent an hour on Gloria and another hour on Banjo. My head cleared, sadness dissipated, and I knew what I had to do. Give Jace some space and hope he came to his senses. Me foisting myself on him and making it about me wouldn't help anything.

As I was putting things away, Jen and Becca arrived, and we all went up to the house where I filled them in on the past week and my revelation.

"Alex, I think that's very mature of you." Becca hugged me. "The Devereaux's are very cerebral."

"Hey!" Jen poked Becca but deadpanned, "It's true."

"Jen, in all seriousness, I think Jace needs some help with this situation." I took her hands. "For some reason, he doesn't feel like I'm the one to help him, and I can understand that considering how adamant I've always been about children. But he won't talk to his bandmates either."

Jen squeezed my hands reassuringly. "I spoke to him earlier, Alex. My dad is helping him out. He has a lawyer and a plan to find out if the baby is his."

"I love him, you guys. I hope he realizes how much someday."

"He loves you too, his mind is a mess though." Jen sighed; her face was etched with concern. "My baby brother has never been great at long-term relationships; he has a hard time letting someone all of the way in."

Not wanting the conversation about her brother to go any further, I headed in the direction of my room. "I'm just going to get through the holidays, and I hope that once he knows one way or the other, then we will have some path forward together. I'm exhausted, I think I'll go to bed."

For the next few days, I didn't hear a peep from Jace, and I didn't call or text him either. As the hours and minutes ticked by, my peacefulness started to wane. Luckily, Jen fed me little tidbits of information so that I didn't go crazy. I knew that he'd taken the test and that there was a lot of contentiousness between Helena's family and Jace. He'd had to get a restraining order to keep them from releasing any of the allegations to the press.

As tempted as I was to show him my support, I persevered and kept my distance. Zoey had invited me over when Ty and the band were in some meetings, so I headed to Seattle to bake Christmas cookies. Not knowing whether Jace and I had a future, I'd started contemplating doing a little traveling in the new year as my backup plan.

When Zoey told me about her and Ty's plans to travel for the next year, I thought it might be fun for us to be in some of the same places if schedules worked out. When she asked about Jace, I had to set her straight and tell her that it probably wasn't going to work out with us. As much as I wanted to confide in her, I couldn't bear to spill Jace's secrets.

And as much as I was nervous to see him at Christmas dinner at Ty and Zoey's house, a big part of me couldn't wait. Since they were having nearly twenty people over, I arrived early in the morning to help out. Zoey's parents were helping Ty prep the dinner while Zoey set the table.

Once we had everything ready, she and I took a few minutes to put on a hydrating face mask before the madness began.

"I really cannot believe that Ty and I are together and hosting Christmas." Zoey's happiness was evident. "A year ago today, I'd never have believed this would be possible."

"I'm so happy for you guys." I hugged my best friend. "We've come a long way since that night at the Mission."

When I released our embrace, Zoey's face contorted with uneasiness. "Will you please tell me what's going on, Alex? I've never seen you so restless. So unsettled."

Fuck it. I had to tell someone, or I'd burst. It might as well be Zoey. I spoke the words that I swore I'd never say out loud. "If I tell you something, will you promise to keep it to yourself?"

"I can't keep secrets from Ty," Zoey said solemnly. "We've made a promise because our secrets destroyed us, and we won't do that to each other again."

Squinting at her, I finally nodded my assent. "I can respect that, and maybe it's for the best. Maybe Ty can help him."

"God, what is happening?" Zoey looked scared.

"His ex-girlfriend had a baby, and then she was killed in a car crash. Her family made him take a paternity test." I unloaded the secret. "What's worse, is that he doesn't remember even having sex with her."

I almost had to use a finger to close Zoey's mouth, which was open as wide as it would go. "How is this even possible?"

"He thinks she drugged him, he doesn't remember anything and woke up naked in bed with her." I shut my eyes, feeling really awful for saying anything but also a bit lighter for sharing something that was slowly killing me inside.

"Jesus. Ty drank himself into oblivion and that's how he ended up in bed with Sienna. And it happened to Jace too?" Zoey shuddered visibly. "The lengths these bitches will go is disgusting." In my haze of all that had happened over the past few weeks, I never connected Jace's experience to Ty's. "For Jace, it happened nearly two years ago. The little girl is a little over one year old. At least Ty didn't have to worry about that."

"Yeah, all he had to worry about was a video of her sucking his cock being played in a billion homes."

Mentally, I thunked myself in the head. Yuck. And what a shitty friend, I forgot that the video was why Zoey had been injured.

I was about to apologize when Zoey spoke again. "Knowing Jace, he's analyzing every part of this and leaving you out."

Relieved that she wasn't mad at me, I continued, "Yeah. And one big part of why he's leaving me out is because he doesn't think I want kids, or could raise one, or whatever."

"When will he know?"

My voice broke and I burst out in a flood of tears. "I'm guessing he knows since I haven't spoken to him since LA."

"Wow." Zoey pulled me to her. "I'm so sorry you're going through something so intense."

I gave her a pointed look. "Well, it doesn't hold a candle—"

"Stop." Zoey smothered me with a big hug. "It's different but still intense, don't diminish what you're going through."

She was such a great friend. "He broke it off after the show in LA. He told me he had to think of his daughter. I wouldn't ever abandon him, but he left me anyway."

"For someone who preaches against drama, he certainly is being a bit dramatic." Zoey looked at me pensively.

"Right?" I nearly yelled. "I'm going through the stages of grief, and I'm kind moving toward pissed right now."

"Try to talk to him tonight," Zoey encouraged. "I bet when you see each other, it will all fall into place."

"I miss him so much," I cried. "I love him so much."

"I know." Zoey clung to me. "I totally know."

"Zoey, the band doesn't know, so could you please make sure that when you tell Ty, you let him know that he can't tell Jace he knows," I begged. "Please, I don't want him to know I've betrayed him, he made me promise not to tell you."

"I'll tell him," Zoey promised.

On Christmas day, my mom and I went to Ty and Zoey's together. We helped Ty set up some extra lights and decorations after Ty pulled me aside to tell me that he was going to ask Zoey to marry him. Genuine happiness filled my body. I decided that, no matter how Jace acted, tonight would be a fun night. I wanted to celebrate my best friend and her long-lost love finding each other again. Which we did in spades when Zoey gleefully accepted his proposal.

After getting caught up in their happiness I hoped that Jace would feel the same way. When my overtures were rejected, I was devastated. When he stormed out the door, it felt like it was the final nail in the coffin.

JACE

CHAPTER 31

When the door slammed behind me, I crumpled on the front steps of Ty and Zoey's house. I'd never created a scene in my life. The past weeks had been so stressful, I knew I was falling apart. I wasn't accustomed to being out of control and I hated it. Leaning against the stone wall, I burrowed under my warm coat and pulled out the envelope I was too scared to open.

I heard the click of the door and looked up to see Zoey approaching tentatively. Wrapped in a big puffy coat, she sat beside me.

"Hey," she said, looking at me, trying to catch my eye.

"I'm sorry about my behavior in there, Zoey." I pinched my nose. "I didn't mean to ruin your engagement."

"You couldn't ever ruin it, Jace." She nudged me with her shoulder. "I've only been waiting for nearly nine years; nothing could bring me down today."

"Ah, well." I tried to conjure up a smile. "I'm still sorry."

"Jace, you've always been a good friend to Ty. And to me." She crossed her arms around her knees. "So, I'm going to be a good friend to you. Alex loves you. Really loves you. Like, she's all-in. Whether you're a dad or not, you're it for her."

"But—" I tried to stop her.

"No buts. Pull your head out of your ass and take a lesson from me and Ty, don't waste precious time. Love doesn't come around often and when it does, don't throw it away." Zoey smiled and gave me a side hug.

"It's complicated."

Zoey cocked her eyebrow. "About as complicated as the poppy tattoo on your shoulder?"

"Well—I didn't say that I didn't love Alex." I leveled my gaze at her. "We're just never on the same page at any given time."

"If you guys work on things together, you'll be fine," Zoey assured me. We sat side by side in the cold for a few minutes.

"These are the results." I showed her the envelope. "I'm petrified to open it."

"Jace, come back inside and go to Alex." Zoey stood and held her hand out to me.

"I'm so embarrassed, I really fucked up."

Zoey kept her hand held out, she wiggled it at me. "One more piece of unsolicited advice. You have saved every one of those guys from some of the most embarrassing situations imaginable. You are not perfect, and no one expects you to be perfect. Grow up and figure your shit out."

"You're bossy." I laughed ruefully, but still took her hand.

She yanked me up.

"That's why I'm a good lawyer," Zoey patted my shoulder. "C'mon."

Tentatively, I followed Zoey back inside where everyone was seated around the table except for Alex. I gave a little wave as I went in the direction that Zoey pointed to where Alex was. Heading down the hall, I quietly opened the door to a guest bedroom. Alex had her back to the door and seemed to be stuffing some things into a duffle bag.

"Poppy," I said quietly.

Alex swung around, her were eyes red with tears. My heart clenched.

I walked over to her. "I keep saying it, but I'm sorry."

"Don't do this again, Jace." Alex openly cried. "My heart is already broken. And bleeding."

"Shhh." I pulled her to me and banded my arms around her. "I'm a mess, but I don't want to live another day without you."

"What?" Alex looked at me with surprise.

"I have the results." I showed her the envelope. "I haven't been able to look at them, and my nerves are on edge. The only person I want to be with when I find out is you."

"Okay." Alex seemed wary.

"If she's my daughter, my life is going to change," I said seriously. "Are you really ready for that?"

"Yes," she said simply.

"I'm not."

"Well, I guess we'll need to grow up a bit." Alex stared at me.

"Me, you mean."

"Jace, the past few weeks have been really awful. I've been trying to give you space, but there are a lot of things we have to talk about and you freezing me out isn't going to work for me."

"Jessica has been threatening me, Poppy." I reached up and traced her hair by her temple. "She saw all of the pictures from the premiere and threatened to release all sorts of stuff about Helena and how she was conceived to the press. Lies. My lawyer thinks her family is going to try and milk this situation forever."

"What?" Alex was shocked, and I felt like a douche for not telling her sooner. "What a total bitch! Why wouldn't you just tell me that?"

"She knew about you from the paparazzi shots, and I didn't want you to get caught up in all of this until it was sorted. My dad helped me get a restraining order, and we negotiated the terms of the paternity test," I tried to explain. "She was texting me earlier, trying to get me to come over for Christmas, so I'm pretty sure of what's in the envelope."

Alex didn't seem super impressed with my explanation. "And keeping this information from me helped how?"

"Um—" I was at a loss to explain something that seemed so obvious to me.

Alex sat on the bed and patted the spot next to her. I sat. Turning to me, she combed her fingers through my hair with both hands, massaging my temples with each pass. Gently, she pulled my head to her shoulder and draped her arms around me, still stroking my hair. My hands rested on her thigh. We sat that way for a few minutes and before I knew it, I released a massive breath and sank against her, the tension in my body releasing.

"I love you, Jace," Alex whispered against my head. "Let's forget about today and the past few weeks. I know how hard this has been on you for so many reasons. From now on, and from this point forward keeping things from each other has got to be a dealbreaker. We are going to get through this and move forward with everything together. If you are on board with that, everything will be okay."

"Done," I agreed. "I mean it."

Wrapping my arms around her waist, I squeezed her and then sat back up.

"Okay." I grabbed the envelope. "Let's find out."

I ripped open the edge and pulled out the report. Alex looked over my shoulder and we read the results. After it sank in, I enfolded her in my arms, and she clung to me.

After a bit, she looked up at me. "Are you okay?"

"I am." I kissed her forehead. "I will be."

"Let's go to see your folks." Alex stood. "They'll want to know."

"Should we say anything to the guys first?"

She headed toward the door. "That's up to you."

Hand-in-hand we went back out to where everyone was sitting having dinner. When Ty saw us, he stopped what he was saying mid-sentence, and all at once everyone turned to look at us. Standing in front of my bandmates and Alex's dad, I turned and kissed her fully on the lips and turned to address everyone.

"Everyone, I know that I've been acting weird lately, and I'm sorry. Ty and Zoey, I'm sorry for yelling and causing a stupid scene at your engagement party, that was a dick move and please know that I'm very happy that you guys have found each other again." I took a deep breath and held up our joined hands. "I'm sure it comes as no surprise that Alex and I are in love, we've done a terrible job of trying to keep it secret. But you may be surprised to know that we have been living together at her house in Bainbridge Island since summer."

"You sly fox!" Zane clapped his hands. "Awesome!"

Alex squeezed my hand and nodded to me. "We have some other news."

"We had a long break where we didn't see each other a couple of years ago, and when we were recording in LA, I went out one night with Cassie and Jessica. Whom I hadn't seen in years." I swallowed. "Cassie thought I wanted to rekindle our old relationship, but I turned her down. The next morning I woke up in bed with her, but I didn't remember a thing."

Alex's mom shot daggers at me, and I didn't blame her.

"Jay-sus," Connor bellowed.

I puffed out a long breath. "So, anyway. Cassie was killed in a car accident a couple of months ago and left behind a baby girl."

"She's not Jace's daughter," Alex jumped in. "We just read the paternity results."

"Her sister and family have been trying to force the issue for a few weeks, I got a restraining order against them, but now that the results are in—" I shrugged.

"Holy shit, Jace." Carter got up and embraced him. "Why didn't you say anything?"

"He's too busy taking care of all of you," Alex interjected. "Now I'm going to go take care of him."

"Good." Ty and the rest of the guys had surrounded us. "Jace probably needs a break more than any of us."

"Guys, I'm fine." I felt uncomfortable with so much attention directed at me. "I know everyone means well, but if you don't mind, we're going to head over to my folks' house now."

"I'll leave with you." Connor got up and stood from the table.

After we said our goodbyes, Alex and I were about to get into her Range Rover when a sudden urge overtook me. I swept her into my arms and whirled her around. She giggled and clung to my neck. Setting her down gently, I softly pressed my lips to hers. Her mouth opened for me, and we touched tongues and deepened our kiss.

"I love you, Jace." Alex smiled as she got into the driver's seat.

"You have no idea, Poppy." I took her free hand. "You're never getting rid of me now."

ALEX

EPILOGUE
FIVE MONTHS LATER

Rushing out of the barn, I sprinted across the gravel pathway up the porch steps, stripping my dirty clothes off along the way. With only a half-hour until our visitor arrived, I had to shower and get appropriately dressed. When the water warmed up, I quickly soaped up and washed my hair, hoping I would be able to pull myself together in time. Just as I was rinsing out the last of my shampoo, the shower door opened.

"I couldn't resist." Jace grinned through a few days of scruff, his shaft bobbing against his eight-pack abs. Ranch life had kept my sexy drummer more cut than ever.

"I'm going to be so late." I laughed as he cupped my boobs and leaned in for a kiss.

"We can be quick." He licked my neck and hitched my leg over his arm, grabbing my ass with his other hand to keep me stable.

I braced myself on his shoulders. Jace backed me against the tiled wall of our walk- in shower, canted his hips and impaled me with one thrust.

Jace breathed into my ear as he surged inside me. "Rub your clit, Poppy."

Furiously, I flicked over my nub as we chased a quick release. Jace cupped my ass and lifted me up holding me against the wall, rolling his hips. I clawed at his neck to keep myself stable. Our foreheads touched; rivulets of water ran down our faces as the rain shower fell around us. Using his strong, muscled arms and shoulders, Jace rocked me onto his hard cock, shifting to find the right angle, and when he hit the mark I screamed in ecstasy.

"That's it, there it is." Jace sucked my earlobe, which sent jolts right to my pussy and I convulsed all around him.

"Jesus!" I cried.

"No, Jace!" He laughed and then groaned, his head lolling back as he climaxed inside me.

We were drying off when the distinct crunch of gravel on the driveway let us know a car had arrived.

"Shit! They're here!" I started panicking.

"It's fine, I'll go out first." Jace shook out his hair and pulled on his jeans, commando. He grabbed a T-shirt from the closet, toed on some flip-flops, and headed out to greet our guests.

Quickly, I dried my hair and put on a long-sleeved, blue T-shirt and black leggings, my new black Frye boots, and headed into the living room to the most heartwarming sight in the world.

Jace held Helena tenderly in his arms, her big blue eyes staring into his intense green ones. She tugged at his wet hair, and he blew a raspberry on her cheek. Lost in the little girl's sweet face, Jace cupped her head and held it against his chest as he turned to watch me cross the room.

I held out my arms. "Give me the baby."

Jace held her out to me, and I settled her on my hip. Helena's honey-blond hair curled slightly around her collar. Her black-and-white striped T-shirt had a mouse decal embroidered by the collar, and she wore tiny black Frye boots over black leggings.

She pointed to the bananas in the kitchen. "Ba-ba?"

"I'll cut one up for her." Jace headed for the kitchen.

"So, this will be the last weekend before the hearing," Janice, the social worker said. "I don't see any reason why the adoption won't go through within the month."

"Awesome," I said, kissing my daughter's head.

After we learned that Jace wasn't Helena's biological father, Ty insisted that Jace attend a few special counseling sessions with him. Ty was still working through some of his abandonment issues with his mother, and Jace was still feeling really conflicted about the Cassie situation. Years before, Ty had worked with a therapist in Los Angeles who specialized in counseling just for musicians. It had done him wonders.

Lisa Kinkaid was smart and gorgeous with a punk-rock sensibility, her raven-haired, waist-length hair had pink and violet streaks throughout. I should have hated her because she was so trendy and cool, but she was also unwaveringly professional. She had insisted that Zoey and I sit in on a group session and afterward, both of us were sold.

Neither of us really comprehended the physical and mental demands of being on the road and how much it took a toll on our men's physical and mental well-being. Both expressed feelings of extreme loneliness and depression while they were touring, and we learned how closely it was tied to their cortisol levels. During a live performance, they would be on a high, almost like skydiving, only to be let down once the show was over. These extreme feelings became more pronounced as their success increased, rather than the other way around.

Combined with lack of sleep, bad food, no set routine, and being away from family, it was no wonder so many musicians struggled with substance abuse and infidelity—they were conditioned to chase an artificial high.

Lisa's work with Ty had been instrumental in how they changed up their routine on their last tour. Once Jace began participating in sessions, he was so blown away that he planned on having group therapy with all of LTZ before they went out on the road again.

Another thing that helped Jace was our horses. When I had thought about it objectively, volunteer work at rescues had been very therapeutic and changed me. Not just because I wanted to save as many horses as possible. Taking care of them healed my own soul and made me a calmer, better person. After doing a little research, I found out that horse therapy was actually a thing. My own plan was to eventually become certified.

In the meantime, Jace and I wanted to keep things simple. Enjoy our own horses.

Reap all of the soul-healing rewards. Adopt Helena.

Which is why we added Beanie, a gorgeous chestnut pony, to our stable. It seemed like the right thing to do when we decided to pursue custody of Helena. Jace took lead on her rehab and was doing an amazing job.

Our decision to adopt originated out of one of Jace's sessions with Lisa and Ty. Jace hadn't known the depth of how awful Ty's childhood was and how living with a mother who couldn't—and wouldn't—take care of him negatively affected his life. My Viking drummer had a wonderful, supportive, and loving family and so did I. We wanted to share that love.

It was incomprehensible the great lengths Cassie's family had tried to manipulate Jace. Once the relief that he wasn't Helena's father wore off, we both began to worry about what would become of her without Jace in her life. Jace hired a private investigator to check on her well-being, and when we got the report back, there was no question of what we hoped to do.

Jace offered to take full custody of Helena and put his name on her birth certificate, as long as Jessica and her family gave up their rights. Not surprisingly, they jumped at the offer, especially because it came with a big check. Zoey's old law firm handled all of the legal paperwork, and the uncontested process only took a few months. Soon, Jace and I would officially be her parents, and Lena, as we nicknamed her, wouldn't know any other life.

"Here you go, miss Lena." Jace gave her a piece of banana, which she promptly smashed on my cheek.

"In your mouth, not my face." I laughed and kissed her sweet head.

Jace wrapped his arms around us both and smiled. "God, I love my girls."

Devotion resonated deeply in his green eyes. It made my heart swoon even harder than it had back at the Mission all those years ago.

He was mine and I was his, and we were hers.

"Let's go out to the barn so Lena can meet Beanie!" I made a move outside. "Lena, let's go meet your horse brother and sisters."

My family, I thought to myself as we walked down the gravel pathway surrounded by pink, blooming cherry trees, tall evergreens, daffodils, and tulips dotting the perimeter of the pasture. Lena walked between us holding both our hands.

All it took was nine long years to have everything I ever wanted, and so much more.

Every step of the way had been worth it.

THE END

If you loved LIMITLESS – I want to give you a FREE gift of RESTLESS,

the FREE Prequel Novella to the LESS THAN ZERO Rockstar Romance series NOW

If you have a couple of minutes, PLEASE leave an honest review! It really helps self-published authors like me to spread the word!

Keep Reading for an excerpt of FEARLESS (Connor & Ronni's story)

BEHIND THE SCENES
LIMITLESS EDITION

Limitless was such a joy to write, mostly because I love to travel, and it was so fun to see Alex and Jace enjoying some of my favorite places in the world.

Alex and Jace's story couldn't be more different than Ty and Zoey's tale, but I wanted to give readers an entirely different perspective—and another epic love story in the same time frame.

When you first met Jace in *Endless*, he is always the one taking care of business. Did you notice, he's great at making everyone the center of attention, but he's content to be in the background.

Alex is my spirit kindred spirit. She's everything I wanted to be in my twenties—bold, decisive, caring, and knows her worth. She sets her sights on Jace and gets him, only to realize that he needs to hold her in equal esteem for them to have a chance. And she doesn't back down.

I hope you were surprised at their HEA—because I was! Sometimes things just write themselves, and their happy ever after was destined.

Next up is broody Connor and bubbly Ronni—I'm already loving everything about them.

As a new fiction author, I can't express how much it means to me that you've read this book. I would LOVE and APPRECIATE any feedback you have about the Less than Zero world—you can write to me at kaylenewinterauthor@gmail.com,

visit my website Rocker Romance: www.rockerromance.com

or join my Facebook Readers Group! www.facebook.com/groups/rockromance/

I can't tell you how super important it is for authors to receive as many reviews as possible. If you have time, here's a link to my author page on Amazon amazon.com/author/kaylenewinter.

Please leave a review about Endless and follow me (and the band) on social media so you will be the first to know when the other books in the series are released!

So grateful to all of you,
Kaylene Winter

ABOUT THE AUTHOR

When she was only 15, Kaylene Winter wrote her first rocker romance novel starring a fictionalized version of herself, her friends, and their gorgeous rocker boyfriends. After living her own rock star life as a band manager, music promoter, and mover and shaker in Seattle during the early 1990s, Kaylene became a digital media legal strategist helping bring movies, television, and music online. Throughout her busy career, Kaylene lost herself in romance novels across all genres inspiring her to realize her life-long dream to be a published author. She lives in Seattle with her amazing husband and dog. She loves to travel, throw lavish dinner parties, and support charitable causes supporting arts and animals. The Less Than Zero Seattle Rocks Series is her debut in the world of Rock star romances. Kaylene hopes you'll love the gorgeous, sexy, flawed rockers and the strong, beautiful women who capture their hearts.

CONNECT WITH KAYLENE

Email: kaylenewinterauthor@gmail.com
Website: www.rockerromance.com
Kaylene: https://www.instagram.com/kaylenewinterauthor/
Reader Groups: https://www.facebook.com/groups/rockromance/
Bookbub: https://www.bookbub.com/profile/2883976651
Goodreads:
https://www.goodreads.com/author/show/20367389.Kaylene_Winter
TikTok: @kaylenewinter
Twitter: @kayleneromance

ACKNOWLDGEMENTS

This book was an absolute labor of love, and I couldn't have done it without the help and support of the following awesome rock stars:

Kaylene's Executive Assistant: Krisha Maslyk

Cover/Graphic Designer/Finder of hotties: Regina Wamba https://www.reginawamba.com/

Editor: Grace Bradley—https://gracebradleyediting.com/

Proofreading: Letitia Delan

Formatting: Cat at TRC Designs

Photo Crew: Debbie Murphy, Elena Chavez

PR: Next Step PR (Kiki, Anna, Colleen and team!!) - https://thenextsteppr.org/ (LINK)

Website Maven: Sublime Creations https://www.sublimecreations.com/ (link)

Jace: Garret McCall - Instagram: @mr.mcmodel
Alex: Carson Hunstad - Instagram @carsonhunstad

My VIPs/Readers/Alpha and Beta Readers Sheila, Kris, Anna, Beth

Thank you to all of my Beta readers, Street Team, and ARC readers—you are all awesome.

SPECIAL THANKS to Beth & Anna who have been such great new friends and supporters.

And last, but not least, thank you thank you thank you to all of the bloggers, reviewers, and readers who have helped to spread the word— it's a new journey for me, and I'm overwhelmed by your love, support, kindness, etc. Thank you for making my dream come true!

DEDICATION

To my BFF Sheila, my inspiration for Alex. We've been friends since I was three and you were four. When we met you punched me, and we've never been apart since. It doesn't matter where we are, what we're doing, or how our lives are shaping up—you are always my person. G—you're taking this ride with me, and it's a blast! I love you, thank you for all of your support.

OTHER TITLES BY KAYLENE WINTER

ENDLESS – LESS THAN ZERO Book 1 (Ty & Zoey)
"An absolute Rockstar Masterpiece!" – Anna's Bookshelf

LIMITLESS – LESS THAN ZERO Book 2 (Jace & Alex)
"#Utterperfection!" – The Power of Three Readers

FEARLESS – LESS THAN ZERO Book 3 (Connor & Ronni) http://
mybook.to/FEARLESS
"I gave this book five stars which is something I only do when the story
is perfect." - Maday Dearmus (BookBub - 5 Stars)

TIMELESS – LESS THAN ZERO Book 4 (Zane and Fiona) –
COMING
FALL 2021

RESTLESS – LESS THAN ZERO PREQUEL NOVELLA (Carter &
Lianne)
"Rockstar Story, Rockstar Writer!" – Karen C

ABOU THIS BOOK

LIMITLESS
"She snuck up on me and stole my heart..."

Friends with benefits, that's always been my relationship speed.
My band Less Than Zero is set to conquer the world.
Nothing and one is going to tie me down.
Except ethereal animal lover, Alexandria LeRoux, made me an offer
I couldn't refuse.
Our secret, spontaneous global hookups are decadent, erotic,
extraordinary.
For the first time in my life, I picture my future with her.
Until one fateful night threatens to destroy my chance forever...

"I'll travel the world for him..."

I set out that summer with only one goal in mind.
Conquer sexy Viking drummer Jace Deveraux before he left on tour.
Our first time was so sublime, it ruined me for anyone else
What's a girl to do? Enjoy him in as many countries as possible,
that's what.
Now, he says he wants a future.
But I'm tired of putting my own dreams on hold for the band.
Unless we can find a compromise, things aren't looking hopeful.

Our lives orbit on different courses.

But gravity always seems to pull us back together...

Will Alex leave Jace when a blast from his past threatens all they have built?
Or will Jace take matters into his own hands?

LIMITLESS is a steamy, whirlwind, playful, rollercoaster, round-the-world romance...with horses, drums and a bit of social media thrown in for good measure.

EXCERPT FROM FEARLESS

CONNOR & RONNI

LTZ BOOK THREE

A *LESS THAN ZERO* ROCKSTAR ROMANCE

FEARLESS

KAYLENE WINTER

PROLOGUE
PRESENT DAY

"Fuck my life!" Byron Angel, the pampered second-bit actor screeched just before shoving his chips over to me. Yanking his fancy mirrored-lens sunglasses off, he tossed them on the poker table, unable to mask his disdain at losing 50k to a lowly bass player in a rock band. His words, not mine.

Not bothered in the slightest, I carefully stacked my bounty of chips and assessed the situation without saying a word. I'd learned over the years that being stealthy allowed you to fly under the radar. It also came in handy to observe and learn things about the people around you. Stuff that was often quite useful.

Like winning big hands in an invitation-only poker game.

"Angel, you're out. So it's time to get the fuck out." The A-list director of *Phantom Rising* pointed to the door.

"Maybe I'll stay and just hang out for a bit?" Byron's desperate pandering was *not* endearing. It was pathetic, truth be told.

Glancing up at the other players' bemused expressions, I knew without a shadow of doubt that his failure to read the room was fatal. It had cost him a significant amount of money. Worse, it cost him respect.

Respect was always better than money. Always.

The director sniffed sharply. Probably to clear the last of the coke from his sinuses. Barely even giving Byron a second glance, he waved him off with a "shoo" gesture. "Nah. Jermaine will see you out."

And just like that, the eejit Byron Angel was booted the fuck out.

Good riddance.

The director's exclusive games were always a veritable male celebrity cock-fest. Filled with actors, directors, producers, and other industry big-wigs who felt the need to throw their power around. All it really meant was a bunch of yammering on and on about their looks, their women, and their stupid cars. Oh how I loved to slag these boyos. To their face. My slight second-generation Irish accent made my insults harder to understand if I turned up the brogue. Easier to swallow.

Tonight wasn't my first go-round. A few months ago, I'd been in LA with my band, Less Than Zero, recording the soundtrack to *Phantom Rising*. The director found out I liked poker and invited me to his regular underground game hosted in his Hollywood mansion. Tonight, my band was in New York City for the movie premiere and to play a private concert afterward. He'd practically dragged me out of the VIP party to attend his relocated poker game, which happened to be here in his Manhattan penthouse.

In other words, an underground game that wasn't *actually* underground. This one was thirty-six stories up.

After a few hours, I'd all but forgotten about the dim-witted actor. I had a huge pile of chips. It was turning out to be a good night. Especially when I mentally calculated my winnings. Factoring in the implied odds, I was on target to strip these losers of a couple hundred thousand dollars. Give or take a few grand after subtracting the buy-in.

Not that I'd keep any of this ill-begotten money for myself.

I just liked winning. Especially against arseholes.

Jermaine's booming voice snapped me out of my thoughts. "Need a beer, McGloughlin?"

"Nah, I'm grand." Studying my cards with a covert glance at the table, I estimated I was about one hand away from shutting the director out.

"I'm all in." The director pushed his chips to the center of the table.

Boom.

"Call." I barely looked up.

The director blanched, only for a second. Had to maintain the appearance of dignity. Or whatever. Just as the dealer was about to lay down the river card, the door burst open. Byron Angel was back, tugging a divine, auburn-haired woman behind him. I was surprised to see her, but steeled my expression to keep it neutral. Waiting to see WTF was going on. The mystery was solved when the actor produced a stack of hundred-dollar bills.

"Well, well, well." The director tapped a couple of chips roughly on the table and visibly ogled the woman's ample breasts. "I haven't seen you in a while. I think you've been avoiding me."

She ignored him completely. She pointedly ignored everyone, actually.

"I want back in, my girl is staking me." The desperate actor's slick, veneered grin made me want to punch a hole in his face just for existing.

Without being obvious, I kept an eye on her. For a split second her soulful green eyes locked with mine, but she quickly looked away to study something fascinating on the floor. It gave me a prime opportunity to more openly admire her. Delicious tits straining against a snug, plain black blouse that bared her shoulders. Lightly sculpted muscles. Curvy waist. Long, slim legs clad in tight jeans.

Luscious.

Licking his lips, the director leered at her while addressing me, "You in, McGloughlin?"

"Nah." My eyes snapped back to my cards and I knocked the table with my knuckle to encourage the dealer to keep it moving.

Byron whined at me, "C'mon. Stay for one more hand. A hundred grand buy-in."

The director leaned back in his chair and stared me down. I held his gaze without moving a muscle. Mentally calculating my odds. God, this guy was a tosser. So what if his movies made hundreds of millions of dollars. The way he threw his clout around was obscene. Probably to make up for a deformed, tiny dick.

Allegedly.

His entitled, disgusting ogling of the beautiful interloper? Confirmed he was a complete knob when it came to women.

Again, allegedly.

It made me want to intimidate him a bit, so I lowered my head and fixed him with my most intimidating gaze from under my curtain of long hair. The director looked away, of course.

Because *no one* fucked with me.

I knew that real power wasn't Hollywood power by any stretch. It came from within. I'd learned this the hard way at a very young age. Even now that I was rich, famous even, I never forgot where I came from. I'd worked hard to improve my station in life. To be proud of who I was. To never take anything for granted.

True power meant putting your family first.

At all costs.

This lowlife director would never, ever come between me and mine.

"Fine. One more hand. Then I'm out. I'm knackered." I fixed my gaze on my cards again but pointed to the hand lying on the table. "First we finish this."

I knew he was drawing dead and wasn't surprised when he simply threw his cards on the table. Then gestured for me to take the pot. Seemingly obsessed by the gorgeous woman in the room, the man wasn't paying attention to me anymore. He motioned her over. "Hey, beautiful. Come sit down, we need to catch up. I have a role that is perfect for you."

A shadow passed over her face. Defiantly narrowing her eyes at him, the stunner pasted on a perfect pageant smile and gracefully eased into a cushioned chair far away from the poker table. She crossed her legs and tucked them up underneath her. I was fascinated with the dynamic and couldn't stop staring. She caught me looking. A flicker of heat flashed in her eyes.

Uh-huh. Now we're talking.

"Nah, I'm all good." Crossing her arms over her chest, she looked away. Essentially dismissing him.

Undeterred, the director licked his lips. His smooth, syrupy voice nearly made me ill. "Baby. Don't *tease* me, I really want to collaborate with you."

"How wonderful. If you're actually serious we can talk about it Monday with my agent." She looked down at her dark-pink fingernails and examined her perfect manicure. One eye twitched slightly. Huh. She was nervous.

"Why do you always have to be such a bitch—" The director's tone changed. He pointed at her menacingly.

"Are we gonna do this thing or what?" I motioned to the director and Byron. Distracting him. Regretting my decision to play another hand, now I just wanted get the feck out.

With the hottie, of course. No way would I leave her with this melter.

Byron took a seat and each of us put our ante in the middle of the table. Once our hands were dealt, we engaged in requisite bravado as the dealer turned over each card. Then it was time for me to put them out of their misery.

Mr. Angel couldn't contain his toothy smile. "Three of a kind."

The director spread out his cards. "Full house."

Byron's smile was erased. He slumped down into his chair, his hands covered his eyes.

"Thank you, gentlemen." I laid out my four Jacks.

"Fuck!" The director narrowed his eyes at me.

"Call it the luck of the Irish." I pulled the chips toward my big pile. "Cash me out. I gotta go."

I made sure my winnings were wired to the right account while keeping an eye on the director, who'd sauntered over to the woman. She pierced him with a vicious glare. She moved to get up, but the director placed his hands on the arms of the chair, effectively caging her in. "Hey, baby, so glad you finally decided to join our after-party."

Jermaine dutifully stood guard to the side.

Assessing the situation, I hustled over. The director wasn't going to get anywhere near this beauty. Especially with his reputation. Not on my watch.

"Let's get more comfortable, sweetheart." He had the audacity to untuck his shirt.

She bared her teeth and spat, "Get out of my personal space. Now. And you don't *ever* get to call me sweetheart."

Her rebuke gave me the perfect opportunity to pull him back and shove him away. "Not in this lifetime. Keep your dick in your pants and your motherfucking hands off her," I growled.

"McGloughlin, take it easy. Stay for a change. This is when the night gets interesting." The director held his hands up in surrender. "Everything's cool."

Um, no. It wasn't.

The beautiful woman's shellshocked eyes caught mine. She was shivering with fear but trying to hide it. I held my hand out to her. She didn't take it. In an instant, just like a warrior princess, she transformed her energy and deftly shifted into badass bitch-mode. This was a woman who didn't want to be rescued. Probably didn't need rescuing. Her glare directed at me was an attempt to warn me off.

As if.

You could hear a pin drop in the room. The clock on the wall ticked like a metronome. Those who remained were frozen in place, equally horrified and intrigued at what was going down. In my book? All of them disgusting excuses for men. They were just going to stand by and let something happen to her. Not on my feckin' watch.

I moved toward her.

The director held up his hand to me and motioned to Jermaine with the other. "Now, Connor. If you're not in, you're out."

I felt Jermaine's big palm on my shoulder.

Bollocks.

Tucking a thick strand of hair behind her ear, the beauty fixed her big, green-eyed gaze on me then flicked her eyes to the door, which I took as a silent plea for me to leave. The tough-girl act was good. Almost good enough to work on most people. I guess that could be expected for an actress of her caliber.

I saw through it all.

And I'd seen enough.

Shaking Jermaine off me, I scooped her up and strode purposefully toward the door. Quickly side-stepping the big bodyguard.

"Who the fuck do you think you are?" The director motioned for the rest of his security goons to stop us.

"She's coming with me." I deftly evaded his crew. I shot the director my most evil don't-fuck-with-me glare. "And you best not follow."

The man was visibly shocked at my insubordination. But he smartly didn't make a move. I knew he wouldn't. He fancied himself a wise guy when he was really a scared rabbit. Besides, over the past few months, I'd planted some seeds. He had no idea I wasn't in the Seattle Irish mob. Or that there wasn't actually an Irish Mob. His hesitance gave me an opening, and I took it.

With precious cargo safely cradled in my arms.

Thank Christ she didn't acknowledge she knew who I was. Resigned, she wound her arms around my neck and kept quiet. Once we were outside the suite, I crushed her to me. Breathing in her delectable, fresh lemony scent, I strode to the penthouse elevator. Once the door closed behind us, I gently set her down and held her quivering body to my chest with one arm. I texted my driver with my free hand.

Still, neither of us said a word.

Through the floor-to-ceiling glass windows of the lobby, I was relieved to see the Town Car waiting for us outside the building. Only when we were settled into the buttery, black leather seats did I allow myself to look at Veronica Mae Miller's tear-streaked face.

She devastated me. Every. Single. Time.

"You have no idea what you've just done, Connor." Ronni nestled into my chest, her need for comfort outweighing her words.

"Of course I do," I growled. "If I hadn't been there—"

"I had it handled." She shoved off me rebelliously.

We stared at each other. A buffalo stance. Until she looked down at her shaking hands clasped in her lap. I got no pleasure in winning this staring contest. Not with her. Gently, I tipped Ronni's chin with my thumb and forefinger so she'd be forced to look into my eyes. "*No*. You. Didn't. This shite ends for good now. It's long past time."

A traitorous tear rolled down her cheek. "After everything I keep putting you through, why do you even care?"

"Because, my love. I take care of my own."

"But…"

"But nothing. Get it through that thick skull of yours. I'm your *husband* and it's high time you start acting like my wife."

TO READ MORE—GET FEARLESS
AVAILABLE NOW!